Praise for beloved romance author Betty Neels

"Neels is especially good at painting her scenes with
choice words, and this adds to the charm of the story."
—*USATODAY.com's Happy Ever After* blog
on *Tulips for Augusta*

"Betty Neels surpasses herself with an excellent
storyline, a hearty conflict and pleasing characters."
—*RT Book Reviews* on *The Right Kind of Girl*

"Once again Betty Neels delights readers with a sweet
tale in which love conquers all."
—*RT Book Reviews* on *Fate Takes a Hand*

"One of the first Harlequin authors I remember
reading. I was completely enthralled by the exotic
locales… Her books will always be some of my
favorites to re-read."
—*Goodreads* on *A Valentine for Daisy*

"I just love Betty Neels!… If you like a good
old-fashioned romance…you can't go wrong with this
author."
—*Goodreads* on *Caroline's Waterloo*

Romance readers around the world were sad to note the passing of **Betty Neels** in June 2001. Her career spanned thirty years, and she continued to write into her ninetieth year. To her millions of fans, Betty epitomized the romance writer, and yet she began writing almost by accident. She had retired from nursing, but her inquiring mind still sought stimulation. Her new career was born when she heard a lady in her local library bemoaning the lack of good romance novels. Betty's first book, *Sister Peters in Amsterdam*, was published in 1969, and she eventually completed 134 books. Her novels offer a reassuring warmth that was very much a part of her own personality. She was a wonderful writer, and she is greatly missed. Her spirit and genuine talent live on in all her stories.

BETTY NEELS

*Dearest Mary Jane &
Stars Through the Mist*

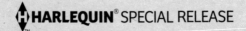

HARLEQUIN® SPECIAL RELEASE

ISBN-13: 978-1-335-04510-2

Dearest Mary Jane & Stars Through the Mist

Copyright © 2019 by Harlequin Books S.A.

The publisher acknowledges the copyright holder of the individual works as follows:

Dearest Mary Jane
Copyright © 1994 by Betty Neels

Stars Through the Mist
Copyright © 1973 by Betty Neels

Recycling programs for this product may not exist in your area.

Printed in U.S.A.

CONTENTS

DEAREST MARY JANE

Chapter 1

It was five o'clock and the warm hazy sunshine of a September afternoon was dwindling into the evening's coolness. The Misses Potter, sitting at a table in the window of the tea-shop, put down their teacups reluctantly and prepared to leave. Miss Emily, the elder of the two ladies, rammed her sensible hat more firmly on her head and addressed the girl sitting behind the tiny counter at the back of the room.

'If we might have our bill, Mary Jane?'

The girl came to the table and the two ladies looked at her, wondering, as they frequently did, how whoever had chosen the girl's name could have guessed how aptly it fitted. She looked like a Mary Jane, not tall, a little too thin, with an unremarkable face and light brown hair, straight and long and pinned in an untidy swirl on top of her head. Only when she looked at you the violet eyes, fringed with long curling lashes, made one forget her prosaic person.

She said now in her quiet voice, 'I hope you enjoyed your tea. In another week or two I'll start making teacakes.'

Her customers nodded in unison. 'We shall look forward to that.' Miss Emily opened her purse. 'We mustn't keep you, it's closing time.' She put money on the table and Mary Jane opened the door and waited until they were across the village street before closing it.

She cleared the table, carried everything into the small kitchen behind the tea-room and went to turn the notice to 'Closed' on the door just as a car drew up outside. The door was thrust open before she had time to turn the key and a man came in. He was massively built and tall, so that the small room became even smaller.

'Good,' he said briskly. 'You're not closed. My companion would like tea...'

'But I am closed,' said Mary Jane in a reasonable voice. 'I'm just locking the door, only you pushed it open. You are not very far from Stow-on-the-Wold—there are several hotels there, you'll get tea quite easily.'

The man spoke evenly, rather as though he were addressing a child or someone hard of hearing. 'My companion doesn't wish to wait any longer. A pot of tea is all I am asking for; surely that isn't too much?'

He sounded like a man who liked his own way and got it, but Mary Jane had a lot to do before she could go to her bed; besides, she disliked being browbeaten. 'I'm sorry...'

She was interrupted by the girl who swept into the tea-room. No, not a girl, decided Mary Jane, a woman in her thirties and beautiful, although her looks were marred by her frown and tight mouth.

'Where's my tea?' she demanded. 'Good lord, Thomas, all I want is a cup of tea. Is that too much to ask for? What is this dump, anyway?' She flung herself gracefully into one of the little cane chairs. 'I suppose it will be undrinkable tea-bags, but if there's nothing else…'

Mary Jane gave the man an icy violet stare. 'I do have drinkable tea-bags,' she told him, 'but perhaps the lady would prefer Earl Grey or Orange Pekoe?'

'Earl Grey,' snapped the woman, 'and I hope I shan't have to wait too long.'

'Just while the kettle boils,' said Mary Jane in a dangerously gentle voice.

She went into the kitchen and laid a tray and made the tea and carried it to the table and was very surprised when the man got up and took the tray from her.

In the kitchen she started clearing up. There would be a batch of scones to make after she had had her supper and the sugar bowls to fill and the jam dishes to see to as well as the pastry to make ready for the sausage rolls she served during the lunch-hour. She was putting the last of the crockery away when the man came to the doorway. 'The bill?' he asked.

She went behind the counter and made it out and handed it silently to him, and the woman called across, 'I imagine there is no ladies' room here?'

Mary Jane paused in counting change. 'No.' She added deliberately, 'The public lavatories are on the other side of the village square on the road to Moreton.'

The man bit off a laugh and then said with cool politeness, 'Thank you for giving us tea.' He ushered his companion out of the door, turning as he did so to turn the notice to 'Closed'.

Mary Jane watched him drive away. It was a nice car—a dark blue Rolls-Royce. There was a lonely stretch of road before they reached Stow-on-the-Wold, and she hoped they would run out of petrol. It was unlikely, though, he didn't strike her as that kind of man.

She locked the door, tidied the small room with its four tables and went through to the kitchen, where she washed the last of the tea things, put her supper in the oven and went up the narrow staircase tucked away behind a door by the dresser. Upstairs, she went first to her bedroom, a low-ceilinged room with a latticed window overlooking the back garden and furnished rather sparsely. The curtains were pretty, however, as was the bedspread and there were flowers in a bowl on the old-fashioned dressing-table. She tidied herself without wasting too much time about it, and crossed the tiny landing to the living-room at the front of the cottage. Quite a large room since it was over the tea-room, and furnished as sparsely as the bedroom. There were flowers here too, and a small gas fire in the tiled grate, which she lighted before switching on a reading lamp by the small armchair, so that the room looked welcoming. That done, she went downstairs again to open the kitchen door to allow Brimble, her cat, to come in—a handsome tabby who, despite his cat-flap, preferred to come in and out like anyone else. He wreathed himself round her legs now, wanting his supper and, when she had fed him, went upstairs to lie before the gas fire.

Mary Jane took the shepherd's pie out of the oven, laid the table under the kitchen window and sat down to eat her supper, listening with half an ear to the last of the six o'clock news while she planned her baking for the next day. The bus went into Stow-on-the-Wold on Fridays, returning around four o'clock, and those passengers who lived on the outskirts of the village frequently came in for a pot of tea before they set off for home.

She finished the pie and ate an apple, cleared the table and got out her pastry board and rolling pin. Scones were easy to make and were always popular. She did two batches and then saw to the sausage rolls before going into the tea-room to count the day's takings. Hardly a fortune; she just about paid her way but there was nothing over for holidays or new clothes, though the cottage was hers...

Uncle Matthew had left it to her when he had died two years previously. He had been her guardian ever since her own parents had been killed in their car. She and Felicity, who was older than she was, had been schoolgirls and their uncle and aunt had given them a home and educated them. Felicity, with more than her fair share of good looks, had taken herself off to London as soon as she had left school and had become a successful model, while Mary Jane had stayed at home to run the house for an ailing aunt and an uncle who, although kind, didn't bother with her overmuch. When her aunt had died she had stayed on, looking after him and the house, trying not to think about the future and the years flying by. She had been almost twenty-three when her uncle died and, to her astonished delight, left her the cottage he had owned in the village and five hundred pounds. She had moved into it from his large house at the other end of the village as soon as she could, for Uncle Matthew's heir had disliked her on sight and so had his wife...

She had spent some of the money on second-hand furniture and then, since she had no skills other than that of a good cook, she had opened the tea-room. She was known and liked in the village, which was a help, and after a few uncertain months she was making just enough to live on and pay the bills. Felicity had been to see her, amused at the whole set-up but offering no help. 'You always were the domestic type,' she had observed laughingly. 'I'd die if I had to spend my days here, you know. I'm going to the Caribbean to do some modelling next week—don't you wish you were me?'

Mary Jane had considered the question. 'No, not really,' she said finally. 'I do hope you have a lovely time.'

'I intend to, though the moment I set eyes on a handsome rich man I shall marry him.' She gave Mary Jane a friendly pat on the shoulder. 'Not much hope of that happening to you, darling.'

Mary Jane had agreed pleasantly, reflecting that just to set eyes on a man who hadn't lived all his life in the village and was either married or about to be married would be nice.

She remembered that now as she took the last lot of sausage rolls out of the oven. She had certainly met a man that very afternoon and, unless he had borrowed that car, he was at least comfortably off and handsome to boot. A pity that they hadn't fallen in love with each other at first sight, the way characters did in books. Rather the reverse: he had shown no desire to meet her again and she hadn't liked him. She cleared up once more and went upstairs to sit with Brimble by the fire and presently she went to bed.

It was exactly a week later when Miss Emily Potter came into the shop at the unusual hour—for her—of eleven o'clock in the morning.

Beyond an elderly couple and a young man on a motorbike in a great hurry, Mary Jane had had no customers, which was a good thing, for Miss Emily was extremely agitated.

'I did not know which way to turn,' she began breathlessly, 'and then I thought of you, Mary Jane. Mrs Stokes is away, you know, and Miss Kemble over at the rectory has the young mothers' and toddlers' coffee-morning. The taxi is due in a short time and dear Mabel is quite overwrought.'

Mary Jane saw that she would have to get to the heart of the matter quickly before Miss Emily became distraught as well. 'Why?'

Miss Potter gave her a startled look. 'She has to see this specialist—her hip, you know. Dr Fellows made the appointment but now she is most unwilling to go. So unfortunate, for this specialist comes very rarely to Cheltenham and the appointment is for two o'clock and I cannot possibly go with her, Didums is poorly and cannot be left...'

'You would like me to have Didums?' asked Mary Jane and sighed inwardly. Didums was a particularly awkward pug dog with a will of her own; Brimble wouldn't like her at all.

'No, no—dear Didums would never go with anyone but myself or my sister. If you would go with Mabel?' Miss Potter gazed rather wildly around the tea-room. 'There's no one here; you could close for an hour or two.'

Mary Jane forbore from pointing out that although

there was no one there at the moment, any minute now the place might be filled with people demanding coffee and biscuits. It wasn't likely but there was always a chance. 'When would we get back?' she asked cautiously.

'Well, if the appointment is for two o'clock I don't suppose she will be very long, do you? I'm sure you should be back by four o'clock…'

Miss Potter wrung her hands. 'Oh, dear, I have no idea what to do.'

The taxi would take something over half an hour to get to the hospital. Mary Jane supposed that they would need to get there with half an hour to spare.

'I believe that there is a very good place in the hospital where you can get coffee—dear Mabel will need refreshment.'

Mary Jane thought that after a ride in the taxi with the overwrought Miss Mabel Potter she might be in need of refreshment herself. She said in her calm way, 'I'll be over in half an hour or so, Miss Potter. There's still plenty of time.'

A tearfully grateful Miss Potter went on her way. Mary Jane closed the tea-room, changed into a blouse and skirt and a cardigan, drank a cup of coffee and ate a scone, made sure that Brimble was cosily asleep on the end of her bed and walked across the village square and along the narrow country lane which led to the Misses Potter's cottage. It was called a cottage but, in fact, it was a rather nice house built of Cotswold stone and much too large for them. They had been born there and intended to live out their lives there, even though they were forced to do so as economically as possible. Mary Jane went up the garden path, rang the bell and was admitted by Miss Emily and led to the drawing-room, where Miss Mabel sat surrounded by furniture which had been there before she was born and which neither she nor her sister would dream of changing.

Mary Jane sat down on a nice little Victorian button-back chair and embarked on a cheerful conversation. It was rather like talking to someone condemned to the guillotine; Miss Mabel bore the appearance of someone whose last moment had come. It was a relief when the taxi arrived and the cheerful conversation was scrapped for urgent persuasions to get in.

They were half an hour too early for their appointment, which was a mistake, for the orthopaedic clinic, although it had started punctually, was already running late. It was going on for three o'clock by the time the severe-looking sister called Miss Potter's name and by then she was in such a nervous state that Mary Jane had a job getting her on to her feet and into the consulting-room.

The consultant sitting behind the desk got up and shook Miss Potter's nerveless hand—the man who had demanded tea for his tiresome companion. Mary Jane, never one to think before she spoke, said chattily, 'Oh, hello—it's you—fancy seeing you here.'

She received a look from icy blue eyes in which there was no hint of recollection, although his 'Good afternoon' was uttered with detached civility and she blushed, something she did far too easily however much she tried not to. The stern-faced sister took no notice. She said briskly, 'You had better stay with Miss Potter, she seems nervous.'

Mary Jane sat herself down in a corner of the room where Miss Potter could see her and watched the man wheedle that lady's complaints and symptoms out of her. He did it very kindly and without any sign of impatience, even when Miss Potter sidetracked to explain about the marmalade which hadn't jelled because she had felt poorly and hadn't given it her full attention. A nasty, arrogant man, Mary Jane decided, but he had his good points. She had thought about him once or twice of course, and with a touch of wistfulness, for handsome giants who drove Rolls-Royce motor cars weren't exactly thick on the ground in her part of the world, but she hadn't expected to see him again. She wondered about his beautiful companion and was roused from her thoughts by Sister leading Miss Mabel away to a curtained-off corner to be examined.

The man took no notice of Mary Jane but wrote steadily and very fast until Sister came to tell him that his patient was ready.

He disappeared behind the curtain and Mary Jane, bored with sitting still and sure that he would be at least ten minutes, got up and went over to the desk and peered down at the notes he had been writing. She wasn't surprised that she could hardly make head or tail of it, for he had been writing fast, but presently she began to make sense of it. There were some rough diagrams too, with arrows pointing in all directions and what looked like Latin. It was a pity that no one had seen to it that he wrote a legible hand when he was a schoolboy.

His voice, gently enquiring as to whether she was interested in orthopaedics, sent her whirling round to bump into his waistcoat.

'Yes—no, that is…' She had gone scarlet again. 'Your writing is quite unreadable,' she finished.

'Yes? But as long as I can read it…you're a nosy young woman.'

'The patients' charter,' said Mary Jane, never at a loss for a word. He gave rather a nasty laugh.

'And a busybody as well,' he observed.

He sat down at his desk again and started to write once more and she went back to her chair and watched him. About thirty-five, she supposed, with brown hair already grizzled at the sides, and the kind of commanding nose he could look down. A firm mouth and a strong chin. She supposed that he could be quite nice when he smiled. He was dressed with understated elegance, the kind which cost a great deal of money, and she wondered what his name was. Not that it mattered, she reminded herself, as Miss Mabel came from behind the curtain, fully dressed even to her hat and gloves.

He got up as she came towards him and Mary Jane liked him for that, and for the manner in which he broke the news to his patient that an operation on her hip would relieve her of pain and disability.

He turned to Mary Jane. 'You are a relation of Miss Potter?' His tone was politely impersonal.

'Me? No. Just someone in the village. Miss Potter's sister couldn't come because of Didums…' His raised eyebrows forced her to explain. 'Their dog—she's not very well, the vet said…' She stopped. It was obvious that he didn't want to know what the vet had said.

'Perhaps you could ask Miss Potter's sister to ring the hospital and she will be told what arrangements will be made to admit her sister.'

He addressed himself to Miss Mabel once more, got to his feet to bid her goodbye, nodding at Mary Jane and Sister ushered them out into the waiting-room again.

'What is his name?' asked Mary Jane.

Sister had her hand on the next case sheets. She gave Mary Jane a frosty look. 'If you mean the consultant you have just seen, his name is Sir Thomas Latimer. Miss Potter is extremely lucky that he will take her as a patient.' She added impressively, 'He is famous in his field.'

'Oh, good.' Mary Jane gave Sister a sunny smile and guided Miss Mabel out of the hospital and into the forecourt, where the taxi was parked.

The return journey was entirely taken up with Miss Mabel's rather muddled version of her examination, the driver's rather lurid account of his wife's varicose veins and their treatment and Mary Jane doing her best to guide the conversation into neutral topics.

It took some time to explain everything once they had reached the cottage. Mary Jane's sensible account interlarded with Miss Mabel's flights of fancy, but presently she was able to wish them goodbye and go home. Brimble was waiting for her, wanting his tea and company. She fed him, made a pot of tea for herself and, since it was almost five o'clock by now, she made no attempt to open the tea-room. She locked up and went upstairs and sat down by the gas fire with Brimble on her lap, thinking of Sir Thomas Latimer.

Nothing happened for several days; the fine weather held and Mary Jane reaped a better harvest than usual from motorists making the best of the last of summer. She had seen nothing of the Misses Potter but she hadn't expected to; they came once a week, as regular as clockwork, on a Thursday to draw their pensions and indulge themselves with tea and scones, so she looked up in surprise when they came into the tea-room at eleven o'clock in the morning, two days early.

'We have had a letter,' observed Miss Emily, 'which we should like you to read, Mary Jane, since it concerns you. And since we are here, I think that we might indulge ourselves with a cup of your excellent coffee.'

Mary Jane poured the coffee and took the letter she was offered. It was very clearly worded: Miss Mabel was to present herself at the hospital in four days' time so that the operation found necessary by Sir Thomas Latimer might be carried out. Mary Jane skimmed over the bit about bringing a nightgown and toiletries and slowed at the next paragraph. It was considered advisable, in view of Miss Mabel's nervous disposition, that the young lady who had accompanied her on her previous visit should do so again so that Miss Potter might be reassured by her company.

'Well, I never,' said Mary Jane and gave the letter back.

'You will do this?' asked Miss Emily in a voice which expected Mary Jane to say yes. 'Most fortunately, you have few customers at this time of year, and an hour or so away will do you no great harm.'

Mary Jane forbore from pointing out that with the fine weather she could reasonably expect enough coffee and tea drinkers, not to mention scone eaters, to make it well worth her while to stay open from nine o'clock until five o'clock. The good weather wouldn't last and business was slack during the winter months. However, she liked the Misses Potter.

'Three o'clock,' she said. 'That means leaving here some time after two o'clock, doesn't it? Yes, of course I'll go and see Miss Mabel safely settled in.'

The ladies looked so relieved that she refilled their cups and didn't charge them for it. 'I hope,' commented Miss Emily, 'that Didums will be well enough for me to leave her so that I may visit Mabel. I do not know how long she will be in the hospital.'

'I'll try and find out for you.' The tea-room door opened and four people came in and she left them to their coffee while she attended to her new customers: two elderly couples who ate a gratifying number of scones and ordered a pot of coffee. Mary Jane took it as a sign that obliging the Misses Potter when she really hadn't wanted to would be rewarded by more customers than usual and more money in the till.

Indeed, it seemed that that was the case; she was kept nicely busy for the next few days so that she turned the 'Open' notice to 'Closed' with reluctance. It was another lovely day, and more people than usual had come in for coffee and if today was anything like yesterday she could have filled the little tea-room for most of the afternoon...

Miss Mabel wore an air of stunned resignation, getting into the taxi without needing to be coaxed, and Mary Jane's warm heart was wrung by the unhappiness on her companion's face. She strove to find cheerful topics of conversation, chattering away in a manner most unusual for her so that by the time they reached the hospital her tongue was cleaving to the roof of her mouth. At least there was no delay; they were taken at once to the ward and Miss Potter was invited to undress and get into bed while Mary Jane recited necessary information to the ward clerk, a jolly, friendly woman who gave her a leaflet about visiting and telephoning and information as to where the canteen was.

'Sister will be coming along in a minute; you might like a word with her.'

Mary Jane went back to Miss Potter's cubicle and found that lady was lying in bed, looking pale, although she mustered a smile.

'Sister's coming to see you in a minute,' said Mary Jane. 'I'll take your clothes back with me, shall I, and bring them again when you're getting up?' She cocked an ear at the sound of feet coming down the ward. 'Here's Sister.'

It was Sir Thomas Latimer as well, in a long white coat, his hands in his trouser pockets. He wished Miss Potter a cheerful good afternoon, gave Mary Jane a cool stare and addressed himself to his patient.

He had a lovely bedside manner, Mary Jane reflected, soothing and friendly and yet conveying the firm impression that whatever he said or did would be right. Mary Jane watched Miss Potter relax, even smile a little, and edged towards the curtains; if he was going to examine his patient he wouldn't want her there.

'Stay,' he told her without turning his head.

She very much wanted to say 'I shan't,' but Miss Potter's precarious calm must not be disturbed. She gave the back of his head a look to pierce his skull and stayed where she was.

She had had a busy day and she was a little tired. She eased herself from one foot to the other and wished she could be like Sister, standing on the other side of the bed. A handsome woman, still young and obviously highly efficient. She and Sir Thomas exchanged brief remarks from time to time, none of which made sense to her, not that they were meant to. She stifled a yawn, smiled at Miss Potter and eased a foot out of a shoe.

Sister might be efficient, she was kind too; Miss Potter was getting more and more cheerful by the minute, and when Sir Thomas finally finished and sat down on her side of the bed she smiled, properly this time, and took the hand he offered her, listening to his reassuring voice. It was when he said, 'Now I think we might let Miss…?' that he turned to look at Mary Jane.

'Seymour,' she told him frostily, cramming her foot back into its shoe.

His eyes went from her face to her feet, his face expressionless.

'Miss Potter may be visited the day after tomorrow. Her sister is free to telephone whenever she wishes to. I shall operate tomorrow morning at eight o'clock. Miss Potter should be back in her bed well before noon.' He added, 'You are on the telephone?'

'Me? No. We use the post office and Miss Kemble at the rectory will take a message. Everyone knows the Misses Potter. I've given the ward clerk several numbers she can ring. But someone will phone at noon tomorrow.'

He nodded, smiled very kindly at his patient and went away with Sister as a young nurse took their place. The promise of a cup of tea made Mary Jane's departure easier. She kissed the elderly cheek. 'We'll all be in to see you,' she promised, and took herself off to find the taxi and its patient driver.

By the time they were back in the village and she had explained everything to Miss Emily it was far too late to open the tea-room. She made herself a pot of tea, fed Brimble, and padded around in her stockinged feet getting everything ready for the batch of scones she still had to make ready for the next day. While she did it she thought about Sir Thomas.

The operation was a success; the entire village knew about it and, since they foregathered in Mary Jane's tea-room to discuss it, she was kept busy with pots of tea and coffee. Miss Kemble, being the rector's sister, offered to drive to the hospital on the following day. 'The car will take four—you will come of course, Miss Emily, and Mrs Stokes, how fortunate that she is back—and of course my brother.'

Miss Emily put down her cup. 'It would be nice if Mary Jane could come too…'

'Another day,' said Miss Kemble bossily. 'Besides, who is to look after Didums? You know she is good with Mary Jane.'

So it was agreed and the next day, encouraged by Sister's report that Miss Mabel had had a good night, they set off. Mary Jane watched them go holding a peevish Didums under one arm. She took the dog up to the sitting-room presently and closed the door, thankful that Brimble was taking a nap on her bed and hadn't noticed anything. She would have liked to have visited Miss Mabel and now she would have to wait until she could find someone who would give her a lift into Cheltenham.

As it turned out, she didn't have to wait long; Mrs Fellowes popped in for a cup of tea and wanted to know why Mary Jane hadn't gone with the others. 'That's too bad,' she declared, 'but not to worry. I'm driving the doctor to Cheltenham on Sunday—about three o'clock, we'll give you a lift in, only we shan't be coming back. Do you suppose you can get back here? There's a bus leaves Cheltenham for Stratford-upon-Avon, so you could get to Broadway…' She frowned. 'It's a long way round, but I'm sure there's an evening bus to Stow-on-the-Wold from there.'

Mary Jane said recklessly, 'Thank you very much, I'd like a lift. I'm sure I can get a bus home. I'll have a look at the timetable in the post office.'

It was going to be an awkward, roundabout journey home and it would depend on her getting on to the bus in Cheltenham. She would have to keep a sharp eye on the time; the bus depot was some way from the hospital. All the same she would go. She wrote a postcard telling Miss Mabel that she would see her on Sunday afternoon and put it in the letterbox before she could have second, more prudent thoughts.

Miss Emily, coming to collect Didums, had a great deal to say. Her sister was doing well, Sister had said, and she was to get out of bed on the following day. 'Modern surgery,' observed Miss Potter with a shake of the head. 'In my youth we stayed in bed for weeks. That nice man—he operated; Sir someone—came to see her while I was there and told me that the operation had been most successful and that dear Mabel would greatly benefit from it. Nice manners, too.'

Mary Jane muttered under her breath and offered Miss Potter a cup of tea.

She was quite busy for the rest of that week, so that she felt justified on Sunday in taking enough money from the till to cover her journey back home. If the worst came to the worst she could have a taxi; it would mean going without new winter boots, but she liked Miss Mabel.

She usually stayed open for part of Sunday, for that was when motorists tended to stop for tea, but she locked up after lunch, made sure that Brimble was safely indoors and walked through the village to the doctor's house.

Miss Mabel was delighted to see her; she seemed to have taken on a new lease of life since her operation and she insisted on telling Mary Jane every single detail of the treatment. She had got to the momentous moment when she had been out of bed when there was a slight stir in the ward. Sir Thomas Latimer was coming towards them, indeed, he appeared to be about to pass them when he stopped at Miss Mabel's bed.

On his bi-weekly round he had seen Mary Jane's postcard on Miss Mabel's locker and, without quite knowing why, he had decided to be on the ward on Sunday afternoon. It had been easy enough to give a reason—he had operated the day before on an emergency case and what could be more normal than a visit from him to see how his patient progressed? His casual, 'Good afternoon,' was a masterpiece of surprise.

Mary Jane's polite response was quite drowned by Miss Mabel's voice. 'Is it not delightful?' she enquired of him. 'Mary Jane has come to visit me—Dr Fellowes gave her a lift here. She will have to return by bus, though. I'm not sure how she will manage that, it being a Sunday, but she tells me that she has everything arranged.' She beamed at Mary Jane, who wasn't looking. 'I have been telling her how excellent is the treatment here. I shall recommend it to my friends.'

Just as though it were an hotel, thought Mary Jane, carefully not looking at Sir Thomas.

He stayed only a few minutes, bidding them both goodbye with casual politeness, and Mary Jane settled down to hear the rest of Miss Mabel's experiences, until a glance at the clock told her that she would have to go at once if she were to catch the bus. Not easily done, however, for Miss Mabel suddenly thought of numerous messages for her sister so that Mary Jane fairly galloped out of the hospital to pause at the entrance to get her bearings. She wasn't quite sure where the bus depot was and Mrs Fellowes's kindly directions had been vague.

The Rolls-Royce whispered to a halt beside her and its door opened.

'Get in,' said Sir Thomas. 'I'm going through your village.'

'I'm catching a bus.'

'Very unlikely. The Sunday service leaves half an hour earlier—I have that from the head porter, who is never wrong about anything.' He added gently, 'Get in, Miss Seymour, before we are had up for loitering.'

'But I'm not...' she began, and caught his eye. 'All right.' She sounded ungracious. 'Thank you.'

She fastened the seatbelt and sat back in luxury and he drove off without saying anything. Indeed, he didn't speak at all for some time, and then only to observe that Miss Mabel would be returning home very shortly. Mary Jane replied suitably and lapsed into silence once more for the simple reason that she had no idea what to talk about, but as they neared the village she made an effort. 'Do you live near here?'

'No, in London. I have to live near my work.'

'Then why are you here?'

'I visit various hospitals whenever it is found necessary.'

A most unsatisfactory answer. She didn't say anything more until he drew up before the tea-room.

He got out before she could open her door and

opened it for her, took the old-fashioned key from her and opened the cottage door.

It was dusk now and he found the switch and turned on the lights before standing aside to let her pass him.

'Thank you very much,' said Mary Jane once again, and bent to pick up Brimble, who had rushed to meet her.

Sir Thomas leaned against the half-open door in no hurry to go. 'Your cat?'

'Yes, Brimble. He's—he's company.'

'You live alone?'

'Yes.' She peered up at him. 'You'd better go, Sir Thomas, if you're going all the way to London.'

Sir Thomas agreed meekly. He had never, he reflected, been told to go by a girl. On the contrary, they made a point of asking him to stay. He wasn't a conceited man but now he was intrigued. He had wanted to meet her again, going deliberately to the hospital when he knew that she would be there, wanting to know more about her. The drive had hardly been successful. He bade her a pleasantly impersonal goodbye. They were unlikely to meet again. He dismissed her from his thoughts and drove back to London.

Chapter 2

September was almost over and the weather was changing. Fewer and fewer tourists stopped for coffee or tea although Mary Jane still did a steady trade with the village dwellers—just enough to keep the bills paid. Miss Mabel made steady progress and Mary Jane, graciously offered a lift in the rectory car, visited her again. Sir Thomas had been again, she was told, and Miss Mabel was to return home in a week's time and see him when he came to the hospital in six weeks' time. 'Such a nice man,' sighed Miss Mabel, 'a true gentleman, if you know what I mean.'

Mary Jane wasn't too sure about that but she murmured obligingly.

Miss Mabel's homecoming was something of an event in a village where one day was very like another. The ambulance brought her, deposited her gently in her home, drained Mary Jane's teapots and ate almost all the scones, and departed to be replaced by Miss Kemble, Mrs Stokes and after an interval Dr Fellowes, who tactfully sent them all away and made sure that the Misses Potter were allowed peace and quiet. Mary Jane, slipping through the village with a plate of tea-cakes as a welcome home gift, was prevailed upon to stay for a few minutes while Miss Mabel reiterated her experiences. 'I am to walk each day,' she said proudly, 'but lead a quiet life.' She laughed and Miss Emily laughed too. 'Not that we do anything else, do we, Mary Jane?'

Mary Jane smilingly agreed; that she had dreams of lovely clothes, candlelit dinners for two, dancing night after night and always with someone who adored her, was something she kept strictly to herself. Even Felicity, on the rare occasions when she saw her, took it for granted that she was content.

The mornings were frosty now and the evenings drawing in. The village, after the excitement of Miss Mabel's operation, did settle down. Mary Jane baked fewer scones and some days customers were so few it was hardly worth keeping the tea-room open.

She was preparing to close after an unprofitable Monday when the door was thrust open and a man came in. Mary Jane, wiping down the already clean tables, looked up hopefully, saw who it was and said in a neutral voice, 'Good evening, Oliver.'

Her cousin, Uncle Matthew's heir.

She had known him since her schooldays and had disliked him from the start, just as he had disliked her. She had been given short shrift when her uncle had died and for her part she hadn't been able to leave fast enough, for not only did Oliver dislike her, his wife, a cold woman, pushing her way up the social ladder, disliked her too. She stood, the cloth in her hand, waiting for him to speak.

'Business pretty bad?' he asked.

'It's a quiet time of the year. I'm making a living, thank you, Oliver.'

She was surprised to see that he was trying to be friendly, but not for long.

'Hope you'll do something for me,' he went on. 'Margaret has to go to London to see some specialist or other about her back. I have to go to America on business and someone will have to drive her up and stay with her.' He didn't quite meet her eyes. 'I wondered if you'd do that?' He laughed. 'Blood's thicker than water and all that…'

'I hadn't noticed,' said Mary Jane coldly. 'Margaret has family of her own, hasn't she? Surely there is someone with nothing better to do who could go with her?'

'We did ask around,' said Oliver airily, 'but you know how it is, they lead busy social lives, they simply can't spare the time.'

'And I can?' asked Mary Jane crisply.

'Well, you can't be making a fortune at this time of year. It won't cost you a penny. Margaret will have to stay the night in town—tests and so forth. She can't drive herself because of this wretched back, and besides she's very nervous.' He added, 'She is in pain, too.'

Mary Jane had a tender heart. Very much against her inclination she agreed, reluctantly, to go with Margaret. It would mean leaving Brimble alone for two days but Mrs Adams next door would feed him and make sure that he was safe. It would mean shutting the tearoom too and, although Oliver made light of the paucity of customers at that time of year, all the same she would be short of two days' takings, however sparse they might be.

Oliver, having got what he wanted, lost no time in going. 'Next Tuesday,' he told her. 'I'll drive Margaret here in the car and you can take over. I leave in the afternoon.'

If he felt gratitude, he didn't show it. Mary Jane watched him get into his car and pulled a face at his back as he drove away.

Oliver returned on the Tuesday morning and Mary Jane, having packed an overnight bag, got into her elderly tweed suit, consigned Brimble to Mrs Adams's kindly hands, and opened the door to him.

He didn't bother with a good morning, a nod seemed the best he could manage. 'Margaret's in the car. Drive carefully; you'll have to fill up with petrol, there's not enough to bring you back.'

Mary Jane gave him a limpid look. 'Margaret has the money for that? I haven't.'

'Good God, girl, surely a small matter of a few gallons of petrol…'

'Well, just as you like. I'm sure Jim at the garage will have a man who can drive Margaret—you pay by the mile I believe, and petrol extra.'

Oliver went a dangerous plum colour. 'No one would think that we were cousins…'

'Well, no, I don't think that they would, I quite often forget that too.' She smiled. 'If you go now you'll catch Jim—he'll be open by now.'

Oliver gave her a look to kill, with no effect whatsoever, and took out his wallet.

'I shall require a strict account of what you spend,'

he told her crossly, and handed her some notes. 'Now come along, Margaret is nervous enough already.'

Margaret was tall and what she described to herself as elegantly thin. She had good features, marred by a downturned mouth and a frown; moreover she had a complaining voice. She moaned now, 'Oh, dear, whatever has kept you? Can't you see how ill I am? All this waiting about…'

Mary Jane got into the car. She said, 'Good morning, Margaret.' She turned to look at her. 'Before we go I must make it quite clear to you that I have no money with me—perhaps Oliver told you already?'

Margaret looked faintly surprised. 'No, he didn't, he said…well, I've enough with me for both of us.' She added sourly, 'It will be a nice treat for you, a couple of days in town, all expenses paid.'

Mary Jane let this pass and, since Oliver did no more than raise a careless hand to his wife, drove away. Margaret was going to sulk, which left Mary Jane free to indulge her thoughts. She toyed with the idea of sending Oliver a bill for two days' average takings at the tea-rooms, plus the hourly wages she would earn as a waitress. He would probably choke himself to death on reading it but it was fun to think about.

'You're driving too fast,' complained Margaret.

Oliver had booked them in at a quiet hotel, near enough to Wigmore Street for them to be able to walk there for Margaret's appointment. He had thought of everything, thought Mary Jane, unpacking Margaret's bag for her since that lady declared herself to be exhausted; a hotel so quiet and respectable that there was nothing to do and no one under fifty staying there. Her room was on the floor above Margaret's, overlooking a blank wall, furnished with what she called Hotel Furniture. She unpacked her own bag and went back to escort Margaret to lunch.

The dining-room was solid Victorian, dimly lit, the tables laden with silverware and any number of wine glasses. She cheered up at the sight; breakfast had been a sketchy affair and she was hungry and the elaborate table settings augered well for a good meal.

Unfortunately, this didn't turn out to be the case; lunch was elaborately presented but not very filling: something fishy on a lettuce leaf, lamb chops with a small side-dish of vegetables and one potato, and trifle to follow. They drank water and Mary Jane defiantly ate two rolls.

'I cannot think,' grumbled Margaret picking at her chop, 'why Oliver booked us in at this place. When we come to town—the theatre, you know, or shopping—we always go to one of the best hotels.' She thought for a moment. 'Of course, I suppose he thought that, as you were coming with me, this would do.'

Mary Jane's eyes glowed with purple fire. 'Now, that was thoughtful of him. But you have no need to stay here, Margaret, you can get a room in any hotel, pay the bill here and I'll drive myself back this afternoon and get someone from Jim's garage to collect you tomorrow.'

'You wouldn't—how dare you suggest it? Oliver would never forgive you.'

'I don't suppose he would. I don't suppose he'd forgive you either for spending his money. I dare say it won't be so bad; you'll be home again tomorrow.'

'Oliver won't be back for at least a week.' Margaret paused. 'Why don't you come and stay with me until he is back? I shall need looking after— all the worry of this examination is really too much for me. I'm alone.'

'There's a housekeeper, isn't there? And two daily maids and the gardener?' She glanced at her watch. 'Since we have to walk to this place we had better go and get ready.'

'I feel quite ill at the very thought of being examined,' observed Margaret as they set out. She had felt well enough to make up her face very nicely and put on a fetching hat. She pushed past Mary Jane in a cloud of L'Air du Temps and told her sharply to hurry up.

Wigmore Street was quiet and dignified in the early afternoon sun and the specialist's rooms, according to the brass plate on the door, were in a tall red-brick house in the middle of a terrace of similar houses. Mary Jane rang the bell and they were ushered into a narrow hall.

'First floor,' the porter told them and went back to his cubbyhole, advising them that there was a lift if they preferred.

It was very quiet on the first-floor landing, doors on either side and one at the end. 'Ring the bell,' said Margaret and pointed to the door on the left.

It was as Mary Jane put her finger on it that she realised something. The little plate above it was inscribed Sir Thomas Latimer! She had seen it on the doorplate downstairs as well but it hadn't registered. She felt a little thrill of excitement at seeing him again. Not that she liked him in the least, she told herself, as the door was opened and Margaret swept past her, announcing her arrival in a condescending way which Mary Jane could see didn't go down well with the nurse.

They were a little early. The nurse offered chairs, made polite conversation for a few moments and went across to speak to the receptionist sitting at a desk in the corner of the room.

'I didn't expect to wait,' complained Margaret. 'I've come a long way and I'm in a good deal of pain.'

The nurse came back. 'Sir Thomas has many patients, Mrs Seymour, and some need more time than others.'

Five minutes later the door opened and an elderly lady, walking with sticks, came out accompanied by Sir Thomas, who shook her hand and handed her over to the nurse.

He went back into his consulting-room and closed the door and Mary Jane decided that he hadn't noticed her.

However, he had. He put the folder on his desk and went over to the window and looked out, surprised at the pleasure he had felt at the sight of her. He went back to his desk and opened the folder; this Mrs Seymour he was to see must be a sister-in-law—she and Mary Jane came from the same village.

He went and sat down and asked his nurse over the intercom to send in Mrs Seymour.

He could find nothing wrong with her at all; she described endless symptoms in a rather whining voice, none of which he could substantiate. Nevertheless, he sent her to the X-ray unit on the floor above and listened patiently to her renewed complaints when she returned.

'If you will return in the morning,' he told her, 'when the X-ray results will be ready, I hope that I will be able to reassure you. I can find nothing wrong with you, Mrs Seymour, but we can discuss that tomorrow. Shall we say ten o'clock?'

'He is no good,' declared Margaret as they walked back. 'I shall find another specialist...'

'You could at least wait and see what the X-rays show,' suggested Mary Jane sensibly. 'Why not have a rest in your room and an early night after dinner?'

First, though, they had tea in the hotel lounge and since it was, rather surprisingly, quite a substantial one, Mary Jane made the most of it, a little surprised at Margaret, despite her pain, eating a great many sandwiches and cream cakes. Left on her own, she poured a last cup of tea and thought about Sir Thomas. She hadn't expected him to recognise her and after all he had had but the barest glimpse as he had stood in the doorway. As he had ushered Margaret out of his consulting-room he hadn't looked in her direction. All the same, it was interesting to have seen him again in his own environment, as it were. Very remote and professional, thought Mary Jane, eating a last sandwich, not a bit like the man who had pushed his way into her tea-room, demanding tea for his friend. She sighed for no reason at all, picked up a magazine and sat reading, a girl not worth a second glance, until it was time to go up to Margaret's room and warn her that dinner would be in half an hour.

Getting Margaret there by ten o'clock was rather an effort but she managed it, to be told by the nurse that Sir Thomas had been at one of the hospitals since the early hours of the morning operating on an emergency case. He would be with them as soon as possible and in the meantime perhaps they would like coffee?

'Well, this is really too bad,' grumbled Margaret. 'I am a private patient...'

'This was an emergency, Mrs Seymour,' said the nurse smoothly and went to get the coffee.

Mary Jane sat, allowing Margaret's indignant whine to pass over her head. Like him or not, she felt sorry for

Sir Thomas, up half the night and then having to cope with someone like Margaret instead of having a nap. She hoped he wouldn't be too tired...

When he came presently he looked exactly like a man who had enjoyed a good night's sleep, with time to dress with his usual elegance and eat a good breakfast. Only, when she peeped at him while he was greeting Margaret, she saw that there were tired lines around his eyes. He caught her staring at him when he turned to bid her good morning and she blushed a little. He watched the pretty colour pinken her cheeks and smiled. It was a kind and friendly smile and she was taken by surprise by it.

'Your patient? Was the operation successful?' She went even pinker; perhaps she shouldn't have asked— it wasn't any of her business.

'Entirely, thank you—a good start to my day.' Thank heaven he hadn't sounded annoyed, thought Mary Jane.

The nurse led Margaret away then, and Mary Jane sat and looked at the glossy magazines scattered around her. The models in them looked as though they should still be at school and were so thin that she longed to feed them up on good wholesome food. Some of the clothes were lovely but since she was never likely to wear any of them she took care not to want them too much.

I'm the wrong shape, she told herself, unaware that despite her thinness she had a pretty, curvy figure and nice legs, concealed by the tweed suit.

The door opened and Sir Thomas showed Margaret back into the waiting-room, and it was quite obvious that Margaret was in a dreadful temper whereas he presented an imperturbable manner. He didn't look at Mary Jane but shook Margaret's reluctant hand, wished her goodbye with cool courtesy and went back into his consulting-room.

Margaret took no notice of the nurse's polite good-byes but flounced down to the street. 'I told you he was no good,' she hissed. 'The man's a fool, he says there is nothing wrong with me.' She gave a nasty little laugh. 'I'm to take more exercise, if you please—walk for an hour, mind you—each day, make beds, work in the garden, be active. I have suffered for years with my back, I'm quite unable to do anything strenuous; if you knew the hours I spend lying on the *chaise longue*…'

'Perhaps that's why your back hurts,' suggested Mary Jane matter-of-factly.

'Don't be stupid. You can drive me home and I shall tell Dr Fellowes exactly what I think of him and his specialist.'

'He must know what he's talking about,' observed Mary Jane rashly, 'otherwise he wouldn't be a consultant, would he?'

'What do you know about it, anyway?' asked Margaret rudely. They had reached the hotel. 'Get your bag and get someone to bring the car round. We're leaving now.'

It was a pleasant autumn day; the drive would have been agreeable too if only Margaret would have stopped talking. Luckily she didn't need any answers, so Mary Jane was able to think her own thoughts.

She wasn't invited in when they arrived at the house. Mary Jane, to whom it had been home for happy years, hadn't expected that anyway. 'You can drive the car round to the garage before you go,' said Margaret without so much as a thank-you.

'Oliver can do that whenever he comes back; if you

mind about it being parked outside you can drive it round yourself, Margaret; I'm going home.' She added rather naughtily, 'Don't forget that hour's walk each day.'

'Come back,' ordered Margaret. 'How can you be so cruel, leaving me like this?'

Mary Jane was already walking down the short drive. She called over her shoulder, 'But you're home, Margaret, and Sir Thomas said that there was nothing wrong with you...'

'I'll never speak to you again.'

'Oh, good.'

Mary Jane nipped smartly out of the open gate and down to the village. It was still mid-afternoon; she would open the tea-room in the hope that some passing motorist would fancy a pot of tea and scones. First she would have a meal; breakfast was hours ago and Margaret had refused to stop on the way. Beans on toast, she decided happily, opening her door.

Brimble was waiting for her. She picked him up and tucked him under an arm while she opened windows, turned the sign round to 'Open' and put the kettle on.

Brimble, content after a meal, sat beside her while she ate her own meal and then went upstairs to take a nap, leaving her to see that everything was ready for any customers who might come.

They came presently, much to her pleased surprise; a hiking couple, a family party in a car which looked as though it might fall apart at any moment and a married couple who quarrelled quietly all the while they ate their tea. Mary Jane locked the door with a feeling of satisfaction, got her supper and started on preparations for the next day. While she made a batch of tea-cakes she thought about Sir Thomas.

It was towards the end of October, on a chilly late afternoon, just as Mary Jane was thinking of closing since there was little likelihood of any customers, that Sir Thomas walked in. She had her back to the door, rearranging a shelf at the back of the tea-room and she had neither heard nor seen the Rolls come to a quiet halt outside.

'Too late for tea?' he asked and she spun round, clutching some plates.

'No—yes, I was just going to close.'

'Oh, good.' He turned the sign round. 'We can have a quiet talk without being disturbed.'

'Talk? Whatever about? Is something wrong with Miss Potter? I do hope not.'

'Miss Potter is making excellent progress…'

'Then it's Margaret—Mrs Seymour.'

'Ah, yes, the lady you escorted. As far as I know she is leading her normal life, and why not? There is nothing wrong with her. I came to talk about you.'

'Me. Why?'

'Put the kettle on and I'll tell you.'

Sir Thomas sat down at one of the little tables and ate one of the scones on a plate there, and, since it seemed that he intended to stay there until he had had his tea, Mary Jane put the plates down and went to put on the kettle.

By the time she came back with the teapot he had finished the scones and she fetched another plate, offering them wordlessly.

'You wanted to tell me something?' she prompted.

He sat back in the little cane chair so that it creaked alarmingly, his teacup in his hand. 'Yes…'

The thump on the door stopped him and when it was repeated he got up and unlocked it. The girl who came in flashed him a dazzling smile.

'Hello, Mary Jane. I'm on my way to Cheltenham and it seemed a good idea to look you up.' She pecked Mary Jane's cheek and looked across at Sir Thomas. 'Am I interrupting something?'

'No,' said Mary Jane rather more loudly than necessary. 'This is Sir Thomas Latimer, an orthopaedic surgeon, he—that is, Margaret went to see him about her back and he has a patient in the village.' She glanced at him, still standing by the door. 'This is my sister, Felicity.'

Felicity was looking quite beautiful, of course; she dressed in the height of fashion and somehow the clothes always looked right on her. She had tinted her hair, too, and her make-up was exquisite, making the most of her dark eyes and the perfect oval of her face. She smiled at Sir Thomas now as he came to shake her hand, smiling down at her, holding her hand just a little longer than he need, making some easy light-hearted remark which made Felicity laugh.

Of course, he's fallen for her, reflected Mary Jane; since Felicity had left home to join the glamorous world of fashion she had had a continuous flow of men at her beck and call and she couldn't blame Sir Thomas; her sister was quite lovely. She said, 'Felicity is a well-known model…'

'I can't imagine her being anything else,' observed Sir Thomas gravely. 'Are you staying here with Mary Jane?'

'Lord, no. There's only one bedroom and I'd be terribly in the way—she gets up at the crack of dawn to cook, don't you, darling?' She glanced around her. 'Still making a living? Good. No, I'm booked in at the Queens at Cheltenham, I'm doing a dress show there tomorrow.' She smiled at Sir Thomas. 'I suppose you wouldn't like to come? We could have dinner...?'

'How delightful that would have been, although the dress show hardly appeals, but dinner with you would be another matter.'

The fool, thought Mary Jane fiercely. She had seen Felicity capture a man's attention a dozen times and not really minded but now she did. Sir Thomas was like the rest of them but for some reason she had thought that he was different.

Felicity gave an exaggerated sigh. 'Surely you could manage dinner? I don't know anyone in Cheltenham.'

'I'm on my way back to London,' he told her. 'Then I'm off to a seminar in Holland.'

Felicity said with a hint of sharpness, 'A busy man—are you a very successful specialist or something, making your millions?'

'I am a busy man, yes.' He smiled charmingly and she turned away to say goodbye to Mary Jane.

'Perhaps I'll drop in as I go back,' she suggested.

He opened the door for her and then walked with her to her car. Mary Jane could hear her sister's laughter before she drove away. She began to clear away the tea tray, she still had to do some baking ready for the next day and Brimble was prowling round, grumbling for his supper.

'We didn't finish our tea,' observed Sir Thomas mildly. He looked at her with questioning eyebrows.

Well, he is not getting another pot, reflected Mary Jane, and told him so, only politely. 'I've a lot of baking to do and I expect you want to get back to London.'

Sir Thomas's eyes gleamed with amusement. 'Then I won't keep you.' He picked up the coat he had tossed over a chair. 'You have a very beautiful sister, Mary Jane.'

'Yes, we're not a bit alike, are we?'

'No, not in the least.' A remark which did nothing to improve her temper. 'And I haven't had the opportunity to talk to you…'

'I don't suppose it was of the least importance.' She spoke tartly. 'You can tell me if we meet again, which isn't very likely.'

He opened the door. 'You are mistaken about a great many things, Mary Jane,' he told her gravely. 'Goodnight.'

She closed the door and bolted it and went back to the kitchen, not wishing to see him go.

She washed the cups and saucers with a good deal of noise, fed Brimble and got out the pastry board, the rolling pin and the ingredients for the scones. Her mind not being wholly on her work, her dough suffered a good deal of rough treatment; notwithstanding, the scones came from the oven nicely risen and golden brown. She cleared away and went upstairs, having lost all appetite for her supper.

Felicity hadn't said when she would come again but she seldom did, dropping in from time to time when it suited her. When they had been younger she had always treated Mary Jane with a kind of tolerant affection, at the same time making no effort to take much interest in her. It had been inevitable that Mary Jane should stay at home with her aunt and uncle and, even when they had died and she had inherited the cottage, Felicity had made no effort to help in any way. She was earning big money by then but neither she nor, for that matter, Mary Jane had expected her to do anything to make life easier for her young sister. Mary Jane had accepted the fact that Felicity was a success in life, leading a glamorous existence, travelling, picking and choosing for whom she would work and, while she was glad that she had made such a success of her life, she had no wish to be a part of it and certainly she felt no envy. Common sense told her that a plain face and a tendency to stay in the background would never earn her a place in the world of fashion.

Not that she would have liked that, she was content with her tea-room and Brimble and her friends in the village, although it would have been nice to have had a little more money.

The Misses Potter came in for their usual tea on the following day.

Miss Mabel was walking with a stick now and was a changed woman. They had been to Cheltenham on the previous day, they told Mary Jane, and that nice Sir Thomas had said that she need not go to see him anymore, just go for a check-up to Dr Fellowes every few months.

'He's going away,' she explained to Mary Jane, 'to some conference or other, but we heard that he will be going to the Radcliffe Infirmary at Oxford when he gets back. Much sought-after,' said Miss Mabel with satisfaction.

Of course, the village knew all about him calling at the tea-room and, Mary Jane being Mary Jane, her ex-

planation that he had merely called for a cup of tea on
his way back to London was accepted without comment.
Felicity's visit had also been noticed with rather more interest. Very few people took *Vogue* or *Harpers & Queen*
but those who visited their dentist or doctor and read
the magazines in the waiting-room were well aware of
her fame.

She came a few days later during the morning, walking into the tea-room and giving the customers there
a pleasant surprise. She was wearing a suede outfit in
red with boots in black leather and a good deal of gold
jewellery. Not at all the kind of clothes the village was
used to; even the doctor's wife and Margaret, not to
mention the lady of the manor, wouldn't have risked
wearing such an outfit. She smiled around her, confident that she was creating an impression.

'Hello, Mary Jane,' she said smilingly, pleased with
the mild sensation she had caused. 'Can you spare me
a cup of coffee? I'm on my way back to town.'

She sat down at one of the tables and Mary Jane,
busy with serving, said, 'Hello, Felicity. Yes, of course,
but will you help yourself? I'm quite busy.'

The customers went presently, leaving the two sisters alone. Mary Jane collected up cups and saucers and
tidied the tables and Felicity said rather impatiently,
'Oh, do sit down for a minute, you can wash up after
I've gone.'

Mary Jane fetched a cup of coffee for herself, refilled Felicity's cup and sat. 'Did you have a successful show?' she asked.

'Marvellous. I'm off to the Bahamas next week—
Vogue and *Elle*. When I get back it will be time for the
dress show in Paris. Life's all go...'

'Would you like to change it?'

Felicity gave her a surprised stare. 'Change it? My dear girl, have you any idea of the money I earn?'

'Well no, I don't think that I have...' Mary Jane spoke without rancour. 'But it must be a great deal.'

'It is. I like money and I spend it. In a year or two I intend to find a wealthy husband and settle down. Sooner, if I meet someone I fancy.' She smiled across the little table. 'Like that man I met when I was here last week. Driving a Rolls and doing very nicely and just my type. I can't think how you met him, Mary Jane.'

'He operated on a friend of mine here and I met him at the hospital. He stopped for a cup of tea on his way back to London. I don't know anything about him except that he's a specialist in bones.'

'How revolting.' Felicity wrinkled her beautiful nose. 'But of course, he must have a social life. Is he married?'

'I've no idea. I should think it must be very likely, wouldn't you?'

'London, you say? I must find out. What's his name?'

Mary Jane told her but with reluctance. There was no reason why she should mind Felicity's interest in him, indeed she would make a splendid foil for his magnificent size and good looks and presumably he would be able to give Felicity all the luxury she demanded of life.

'He said he was going abroad—to Holland, I think,' she volunteered.

'Good. That gives me time to track him down. Once I know where he lives or works I can meet him again—accidentally of course.'

Well, thought Mary Jane in her sensible way, he's

old enough and wise enough to look after himself and there's that other woman who came here with him...

She didn't mention her to her sister.

Felicity didn't stay long. 'Ticking over nicely?' she asked carelessly. 'You always liked a quiet life, didn't you?'

What would Felicity have said if she had declared that she would very much like to wear lovely clothes, go dancing and be surrounded by young men? Mary Jane, loading a tray carefully, agreed placidly.

Since it seemed likely that the quiet life was to be her lot, there wasn't much point in saying anything else.

Chapter 3

October, sliding towards November, had turned wet and chilly and customers were sparse. Mary Jane turned out cupboards, washed and polished and cut down on the baking. There were still customers glad of a cup of tea, home from shopping expeditions—or motorists on their way to Cheltenham or Oxford stopped for coffee. More prosperous tea-rooms closed down during the winter months and their owners went to Barbados or California to spend their summer's profits, but Mary Jane's profits weren't large enough for that. Besides, since she lived over the tea-room she might just as well keep it open and get what custom there was.

On this particular morning, since it was raining hard and moreover was a Monday, she was pleased to hear the doorbell tinkle as she set the percolator on the stove. It wasn't a customer, though. Oliver stood there, just inside the door.

She wasn't particularly pleased to see him but she wished him a cheerful good morning.

'I'm just back from the States,' declared Oliver pompously. 'Margaret tells me that you have behaved most unkindly towards her. I should have thought that you could at least have stayed with her and made sure that she was quite comfortable.'

'But she is not ill—Sir Thomas Latimer said so. He said that she should take more exercise and not lie around.'

Oliver's eyes bulged with annoyance. 'I consider you to be a heartless girl, Mary Jane. I shall think twice before asking you to do any small favour...'

'You'd be wasting time,' said Mary Jane matter-of-factly, 'for you're quite able to find someone else if Margaret insists on feeling poorly all the time. I've my living to earn, you know.'

Oliver's eyes slid away from hers. 'As a matter of fact, I have to go away again very shortly...'

'Then you can arrange for someone to be with Margaret. Don't waste your time with me, Oliver.'

'You ungrateful...'

She came and stood before him. 'Tell me, what am I ungrateful for?' she invited.

Oliver still didn't meet her eyes. 'Well,' he began.

'Just so, go away, Oliver, before I bang you over the head with my rolling pin.'

'Don't be ridiculous,' he blustered. All the same he edged towards the door.

Which opened to admit the giant-like person of Sir Thomas, his elegant grey suit spattered with rain. He said nothing, only stood there, his eyebrows slightly raised, smiling a little.

Mary Jane had gone pink at the sight of him; blushing was a silly habit she had never quite conquered. She was pleased to see him. Oliver, after a first startled glance, had ignored him. 'You've not heard the last of this, Mary Jane—your own flesh and blood.'

'Ah,' said Sir Thomas, in the gentlest of voices. 'You are, I believe, Mrs Seymour's husband?'

Oliver goggled. 'Yes—yes, I am.' He puffed out his chest in readiness for a few well-chosen words but he was forestalled.

'Delighted to meet you,' said Sir Thomas with suave untruthfulness. 'It gives me the opportunity to tell you that there is nothing wrong with your wife. A change of lifestyle is all that she needs—rather more activity.'

Oliver looked from him to Mary Jane, who in her turn was studying the row of glass jars on the shelf on the further wall. 'Really, surely this is hardly the place,' he began.

'Oh, Miss Seymour was with your wife and of course already knows what I have told Mrs Seymour. I thought it might reassure you to mention it. You will, of course, get a report from your own doctor in due course.'

He opened the door invitingly, letting in a good deal of wind and rain, and Oliver, muttering that he was a busy man, hurried out to his car without a word more than a cursory good morning.

Sir Thomas brushed a few drops of rain off his sleeve and Mary Jane said, 'You're wet.'

He glanced at her. 'I was passing in the car and saw you talking to your—cousin? You looked as though you were going to hit him and it seemed a good idea to—er—join you.'

'I threatened him with a rolling pin,' said Mary Jane in a satisfied voice.

'Admirable. A very handy weapon. Do you often use it?' He added gravely, 'As a weapon?'

'Well, of course not. He was annoying me. Do you want coffee?'

'I was hoping that you would ask me. And are there any scones?'

She set a plate on the table and a dish of butter and he spread a scone and bit into it.

'Are you hungry?' asked Mary Jane pointedly.

'Famished. I've been at the Radcliffe all night…'

She poured coffee for them both and sat down opposite him. 'But you're going the wrong way home.'

'Ah, yes. I thought I'd take a day off. I've a clinic at six o'clock this evening. It crossed my mind that it would be pleasant if we were to spend it together. Lunch perhaps? A drive through the countryside?'

'Oughtn't you to go to bed?'

'If you were to offer me a boiled egg or even a rasher or two of bacon I'll doze for ten minutes or so while you do whatever it is you do before you go out for the day.'

'The tea-room…'

'Just for once?' He contrived to look hungry and lonely, although she suspected that he was neither.

'Bacon and eggs,' she told him before she could change her mind. 'And I'll need half an hour.'

'Excellent. I'll come and watch you cook.'

He sat on the kitchen table, Brimble on his knee, while she got out the frying pan and, while the bacon sizzled, sliced bread and made more coffee.

'Two eggs?' She looked up and found him staring at

her. It was a thoughtful look and she wondered about it until he spoke.

'Yes, please. Where is your beautiful sister, Mary Jane?'

She cracked the eggs neatly. For some reason his question had made her unhappy although she had no intention of letting it show. 'Well, she went to Barbados but she should be back by now—I think it's the Paris dress shows next week. She lives in London, though. Would you like to have her address?'

'Yes, please, I feel I owe her a dinner. If you remember?'

'Yes, of course.' She wrote on the back of the pad, tore off the page and gave it to him. 'That's her phone number, too.'

She didn't look at him but dished up his breakfast and fetched the coffee-pot.

'I'll go and change while you eat,' she told him. 'Brimble likes the bacon rinds.'

Upstairs she inspected her wardrobe. It would have to be the jersey dress, kept for unlikely occasions such as this one, and the Marks & Spencer mac. Somewhere or other there was a rainproof hat—if only she had the sort of curly hair which looked enchanting when it got wet...

She went downstairs presently and found Sir Thomas, his chair balanced precariously against the wall, his large feet on the table, asleep. He had tidied his breakfast plate away into the sink and Brimble, licking the last of the bacon rinds from his whiskers, was perched on his knees.

Mary Jane stood irresolute. It would be cruel to wake him up; on the other hand he looked very uncomfortable.

'A splendid breakfast,' said Sir Thomas, his eyes still closed. 'I feel like a new man.'

He opened his eyes then. No one would have known that he had been up all night.

'Have you really been up all night?' asked Mary Jane. She blinked at the sudden cold stare.

'I have many faults, but I don't lie.' His voice was as cold as his eyes and she made haste to make amends.

'I'm sorry, I wasn't doubting you, only you look so— so tidy!' she finished lamely.

'Tidy? I have showered and shaved and put on a clean shirt. Is that being tidy?' He lifted Brimble gently from his knee and stood up, towering over her. His gaze swept over her person. 'Most suitably dressed for the weather,' he observed, and she bore his scrutiny silently, aware that the hat, while practical, did nothing for her at all.

She turned the sign to 'Closed', coaxed Brimble into his basket, shut windows and locked doors and pronounced herself ready. The rain was still sheeting down. 'You'll get wet,' she told him. 'I've an umbrella…'

He smiled and took the key from her and locked the tea-room door and went to unlock the car door, bundled her in, gave himself a shake and got in beside her. 'Oxford?' he asked and, when she nodded happily, smiled.

Mary Jane, suddenly shy, was relieved when he started an undemanding conversation, and he, versed in the art of putting people at their ease, kept up a flow of small talk until they reached Oxford. The rain had eased a little, and, with the car safely parked, they set out on a walk around the colleges.

'Did you come here?' asked Mary Jane, craning her neck to see Tom Tower.

'I was at Trinity.'

'Before you trained as a doctor—no, surgeon.'

'I took my MD, and then went over to surgery—orthopaedics.'

She lowered her gaze from Tom Tower to her companion. 'I expect you're very clever.'

'Everyone is clever at something,' he told her, and took her arm and walked her to the Radcliffe Camera.

'May we go inside?'

'To the reading rooms if you like. It houses the Bodleian Library.'

He took her to the Eastgate Hotel and gave her coffee in the bar, a cheerful place, crowded with students, and then walked her briskly down to the river before popping her back into the car.

'There's a rather nice place for lunch,' he told her casually, 'a few miles away.'

An understatement, Mary Jane decided when they reached Le Manoir aux Quat' Saisons at Great Milton; it was definitely a grand place and the jersey dress was quite inadequate. However, she was given no time to worry about that. She was whisked inside, led away to tidy herself and then settled in the bar with a glass of sherry while Sir Thomas, very much at his ease, sat opposite her studying the menu. He glanced at her presently.

'Dublin Bay prawns?' he suggested. 'And what about *poulet Normand*?'

Mary Jane agreed, she had never tasted Dublin Bay prawns but she was hungry enough to try anything; as for the chicken, she had read the recipe for that in her cookery book—egg yolks and thick cream and brandy, butter and onions—it sounded delicious.

It was. She washed it down with spa water and, when invited, chose an orange cream soufflé—more cream, and Curaçao this time. Over coffee she said, in her sensible way, 'This is a delightful place and that was the most gorgeous meal I've had for a long time. You're very kind.'

She caught his eye and went a little pink. 'Oh, dear, I've made it sound like a half-term treat with an…' She stopped just in time and the pink deepened.

'Uncle? Godfather?' he suggested, and she let out a sigh of relief when he laughed. 'I've enjoyed my day too, Mary Jane, you are a very restful companion; you haven't rearranged your hair once or powdered your nose or put on more lipstick and you really enjoyed Oxford, didn't you?'

'Oh, very much. It's a long time since I was there.' She fell silent, remembering how her father used to take Felicity and her there, walking the streets, pointing out the lovely old buildings, and Sir Thomas watched her with faint amusement and vague pity. So independent, he reflected, making a life for herself, and so different from her rather beautiful sister. He must remember to mention her funny little tea-room to his family and friends; drum up some customers for her so that she would have some money to spend on herself. A new hat for a start. No rain hat was becoming but at least it need not be quite as awful as the one she had been wearing all day.

Her quiet voice interrupted his thoughts. 'If you are to be back in London this evening ought we not to be going? I don't want to go,' she added childishly and smiled at him, her violet eyes glowing because she was happy.

'I don't want to go either, but you are quite right.' He had uttered the words almost without thinking and realised to his surprise that he had meant them; he had really enjoyed her company, undemanding, ready to be pleased with everything they had seen and done.

He drove her back to the tea-room, talking about nothing much, at ease with each other, but when she offered him tea he refused. 'I've played truant for long enough. It has been a delightful day, Mary Jane—thank you for your company.'

She offered a small gloved hand. 'Thank you for asking me. It was a treat and so much nicer because I hadn't expected one. I hope you're not too busy this evening so that you can get a good night's sleep, Sir Thomas.'

He concealed a smile. The evening clinic was always busy and there was a pile of work awaiting him on his desk at home.

'I have no doubt of it,' he told her cheerfully, and got into his car and drove away.

She stood at the door until he was out of sight and then took off her outdoor things, fed a peevish Brimble and put the kettle on. It had been a lovely day; she thought about it, minute by minute, while she sipped her tea. She had too much common sense to suppose that Sir Thomas had actually wished for her company—he had needed a companion to share his day and she had been handy and it was obvious that he had called that morning so that he might get Felicity's address. His invitation had been on the spur of the moment and she was quite sure that she fell far short of his usual companions. And she had seen the look he had cast at the rain hat. She got up and went to examine her face in the small looking glass on the kitchen wall. It was rosy from her day out of doors but she didn't see how her skin glowed with health and how her eyes shone. All she saw was her hair, damp around the edges where it had escaped from the hat, and the lack of make-up.

'You're a plain girl,' she told her reflection, and Brimble looked up from his grooming to mutter an agreement.

Promptly at six o'clock, Sir Thomas sat himself down behind his desk in the clinic consultation-room and listened patiently as one patient after the other took the seat opposite to him, to be led away in turn to be carefully examined by him, and then told, in the kindest possible way, what was wrong and what would have to be done. It was almost nine o'clock by the time the last patient had been shown out and he and his registrar and houseman prepared to leave too. Outpatients Sister stifled a yawn as she collected notes—she hated the evening clinic but she had worked with Sir Thomas for several years now and if he had decided to have a clinic at three o'clock in the morning, she would have agreed cheerfully. He was her—and almost all of the nursing staff's—ideal man, never hurried, always polite, unfailingly patient, apparently unaware of the devotion accorded him. For such a successful man he was singularly unconceited.

He bade everyone goodnight and drove himself to his home; a house in a row of similar elegant houses in Little Venice, facing the Grand Union Canal. It had stopped raining at last and the late evening was quiet. He opened his front door and as he did so an elderly man, rather stout and short, came into the hall.

'Evening, Tremble,' said Sir Thomas, and tossed his

coat on to an elbow chair beside a Georgian mahogany side-table.

Tremble picked up the coat and folded it carefully over one arm. 'Good evening, sir. Mrs Tremble has a nice little dinner all ready for you.'

'Thank you.' Sir Thomas was looking through his post. 'Give me ten minutes, will you?'

He took his post and his bag into the study at the back of the hall and sat down to read the letters before going up to his room, to return presently and sit by the fire in the big drawing-room at the front of the house. He was greeted here by a Labrador dog, who got to elderly feet and lumbered happily to meet him.

Sir Thomas sat down, a glass of whisky beside him, the dog's head on his knee. 'A pity you weren't with us, old fellow,' he said. 'I rather fancy you would have liked her.'

Tremble's voice reminded him that dinner was served and he crossed the hall with the dog to the dining-room, a room beautifully furnished with a Regency mahogany twin pedestal table surrounded by Hepplewhite chairs; there was an inlaid mahogany sideboard of the same period against one wall and the lighting was pleasantly subdued from the brass sconces on the walls. There were paintings too—Dutch flower studies and a number of portraits.

Sir Thomas, being a very large man, ate his dinner with good appetite, exchanging a casual conversation with Tremble as he was served and offering his dog the last morsel of his cheese.

'Watson had his supper an hour ago, sir,' said Tremble severely.

'We are told that cheese is good for the digestion,

Tremble; I suppose that applies to dogs as well as humans.'

'I really couldn't say, sir. Will you have your coffee in the drawing-room?'

'Please, and do tell Mrs Tremble that everything was delicious.'

He went to his study presently with Watson as company, and worked at his desk. He had quite forgotten Mary Jane.

Even if Mary Jane had wanted to forget him she wasn't given that chance. Naturally, in a village that size, she had been seen getting into Sir Thomas's Rolls-Royce, a news item flashed round the village in no time at all, so that when she got out of it again that late afternoon, several ladies living in the cottages on either side of her saw that too.

Trade was brisk the following morning and it was only after she had answered a few oblique questions that she realised why. Since some of the ladies in the tea-room were prone to embroider any titbit of news to make it more exciting, she told them about her day out in a sensible manner which revealed not a whiff of romance.

She was well-liked; disappointed as they were at her prosaic description of her day with Sir Thomas, they were pleased that she had enjoyed herself. She had little enough fun and no opportunity of getting away from the village and meeting young people of her own age. They lingered over their coffee and, when the Misses Potter joined them, the talk turned, naturally enough, to Sir Thomas.

'Such a nice man,' declared Miss Mabel. 'As mild as milk.'

'Even milk boils over from time to time,' muttered Mary Jane, offering a plate of digestive biscuits. The scones had all been eaten long-since.

Sir Thomas, arriving at his consulting-rooms in Wigmore Street the following morning, wished Miss Pink, his secretary and receptionist, a cheerful good morning and paused at her desk.

'What have I got this weekend?' he wanted to know.

'You're making a speech at that dinner on Saturday evening. Miss Thorley phoned and asked would you like to take her to dinner on Sunday evening; she suggested a day out somewhere first.' Miss Pink's voice was dry.

For a moment Mary Jane's happy face, crowned with the deplorable hat, floated before Sir Thomas's eyes. He said at once, 'I intend to go down to my mother's. Would you phone Miss Thorley and tell her I shall be away?'

Miss Pink gave him a thoughtful look and he returned it blandly. 'I'm far too busy to phone her myself.'

Miss Pink allowed herself a gentle smile as Sir Thomas went into his consulting-room; Miss Thorley, on the rare occasions when she had seen her, had looked at her as though she despised her and Miss Pink, of no discernible age, sharp-nosed and spectacled, objected strongly to that.

There was just time before the first patient was announced for Sir Thomas to phone his mother and invite himself for the weekend.

Her elderly, comfortable voice came clearly over the wires. 'How nice, dear. Are you bringing anyone with you?'

He said that no, he wasn't and the fleeting thought

that it would be interesting to see his mother and Mary
Jane together whisked through his head, to be instantly
dismissed as so much nonsense.

Mary Jane's day out, while not exactly a nine-day
wonder, kept the village interested for a few days until
the local postman's daughter's wedding. An event which
caused the village to turn out *en masse* to crowd into
the church and throw confetti afterwards. It brought
some welcome custom to Mary Jane, too, for somewhere was needed afterwards where the details of the
wedding, the bride's finery and speculation as to the
happy couple's future happiness could be mulled over.
She did a roaring trade in coffee and scones and, for
latecomers, sausage rolls.

She went to bed that night confident that, with luck,
she would be able to get a new winter coat.

It was almost midnight by the time Sir Thomas, re-
splendent in white tie and tails, returned from the banquet which he had been invited to attend. He had made
his speech, brief and to the point, and it had been well
received and now it was just a question of changing into
comfortable clothes, collecting a sleepy Watson and getting into his car once more. It would be late by the time
he reached his mother's house, but he had a key. At that
time of night, with the roads quiet and a good deal of
them motorway, he should be there in little over an hour.

Which he was; he slowed down as he entered the village, its inhabitants long since in bed, and took the car
slowly past the church and then, a few hundred yards
further, through the open gates of the house beyond.

The night was chilly with a hint of frost and there

was bright moonlight. The low, rambling house was in darkness save for a dim light shining through the transom over the door. Sir Thomas got out quietly, opened the door for Watson and stood for a moment while his companion trotted off into the shrubbery at the side of the house, to reappear shortly and, as silent as his master, enter the house.

The hall was square, low-ceilinged and pleasantly warm. There was a note by the lamp on the side-table. Someone had printed 'Coffee on the Aga' on a card and propped it against the elegant china base of the lamp. Sir Thomas smiled a little and went soft-footed to the baize door beside the staircase and so through to the kitchen door, where he poured his coffee, gave Watson a drink and presently took himself up to his bed, leaving Watson already asleep on the rug before the Aga.

Four hours later he was up and dressed, drinking tea in the kitchen and talking to his mother's housekeeper, Mrs Beaver.

'And how's that nasty old London?' she wanted to know.

'Well, I don't see a great deal of it, I spend most of my days either at the hospital or my rooms. I often wonder why I don't resign and come and live in peace and quiet here.'

'Go on with you, Sir Thomas, leaving that clever brain of yours to moulder away doing nothing but walking the dog and shooting pigeons. That's not you. Now if you was to ask me, I'd say get yourself a wife and a clutch of children—no question of you giving up then with all them mouths to feed.'

He put down his mug and gave her a hug, 'You old matchmaker,' he told her, and whistled to Watson. It was a fine, chilly morning; there was time to go for a walk before breakfast.

His mother was at the table when he got back, sitting behind the coffee pot; a small, slim woman with pepper and salt hair done in an old-fashioned bun and wearing a beautifully tailored suit.

'There you are, Thomas. How nice to see you, dear, I suppose you can't stay for a few days?'

He bent to kiss her. 'Afraid not, Mama—I'm rather booked up for the next week or so, I'll have to go back very early on Monday morning.'

He helped himself to bacon and eggs, added mushrooms and a tomato or two and sat down beside her. 'The garden looks pretty good...'

'Old Dodds knows his job, though he's a bit pernickety when I want to cut some flowers.' She handed him his coffee. 'Well, what have you been doing, my dear—other than work?'

'Nothing much. A banquet I couldn't miss yesterday evening and one or two dinner parties...'

'What happened to that gorgeous young woman who had begged a lift from you—oh, some weeks ago now?'

He speared a morsel of bacon and topped it neatly with a mushroom.

'Ingrid Bennett. I have no idea.' He smiled suddenly, remembering. 'She insisted on stopping for tea and we did, at a funny little tea-room in a village near Stow-on-the-Wold, run by a small tartar with a sharp tongue.'

'Pretty?'

'No. A great deal of mousy hair and violet eyes.'

His mother buttered toast. 'How unusual—I mean the eyes. One never knows the hidden delights of remote villages until one has a reason to go to them.' She peeped at him and found him watching her, smiling.

'She interested you?'

'As a person? Perhaps; she was so unlike the elegant young women I usually meet socially. But more than that, I imagine she scratches a bare living from the place and yet she seemed quite content with her lot.'

'No family?'

'A sister. A beautiful creature—a top model, flitting about the world and making a great deal of money, I should imagine.'

'Then she might give something to the tea-shop owner.'

Sir Thomas reached for the marmalade. 'Somehow, I don't think that has occurred to her. Do we have to go to church?'

'Of course. We will have a lovely afternoon reading the Sunday papers and having tea round the fire.'

Mary Jane, always hopeful of customers even on a Monday morning, was taking the first batch of teacakes from the oven when the doorbell rang. She glanced at the clock on the wall; half-past eight and she hadn't even turned the sign round to 'Open' yet. Perhaps it was the postman with a parcel…

Sir Thomas was standing with his back to the door, his hands in his pockets, but he turned round as she unlocked the door and opened it.

She would have turned the sign round too but he put a large hand over hers to prevent that. 'Good morning, Mary Jane. May I beg a cup of coffee from you? I know it's still early.' He sounded meek, not at all as he usually spoke and she jumped at once to the wrong conclusion as he had anticipated.

'You're on your way back to London? You've been up all night?'

Her lovely eyes were soft with sympathy. She didn't wait for an answer, which saved him from perjury, but went on briskly. 'Well, come on in. Coffee won't take more than a few minutes—I could make you some toast…'

'Something smells very appetising.' He followed her into the kitchen.

'Teacakes. I've just made some.' She looked at him over her shoulder. 'Do you want one?'

'Indeed I do.' He wandered back to the door. 'I have my dog with me. Might he come in? Would Brimble object?'

'A dog?' She looked surprised. 'Of course he can come in. Brimble isn't up yet, but I'll shut the stairs door anyway.'

Watson, his nose twitching at the prospect of something to eat, greeted her with gentle dignity. 'Whenever possible he goes everywhere with me,' said Sir Thomas.

Mary Jane fetched a bowl and filled it with water and offered a digestive biscuit. 'The poor lamb, he'll be glad to get home, I expect.' She added shyly, 'You too, Sir Thomas.'

'I'll drop him off before I go to my rooms.'

She poured his coffee, offered a plate of buttered teacakes and poured coffee for herself. 'But you'll have to have some rest—you can't possibly do a day's work if you've been up all night. You might make a wrong diagnosis.'

Sir Thomas swallowed a laugh. He should, he reflected, be feeling guilty at his deception, actually he was enjoying himself immensely.

Over his second cup of coffee he asked, 'How's business? And is that cousin of yours bothering you?'

'I make a living,' she told him seriously. 'Oliver hasn't been again—I think that was the second time I've seen him in years. He isn't likely to come again.'

'No other family?' he asked casually.

'No—there's just Felicity and me. He quite likes her though because she's quite famous.'

'And you, Mary Jane, have you no wish to be famous?'

'Me? Famous? What could I be famous for? And I wouldn't want to be, anyway.' She added with a touch of defiance, 'I am very happy here. I've got Brimble and I know almost everyone in the village.'

'You don't wish to marry?'

She got up to refill his cup. 'I've not met many men—not in a village as small as this one. It would be nice to marry but it would have to be someone I—I loved. Could you eat another teacake?'

'I could, but I won't. I must be on my way.'

She watched him drive away, Watson sitting beside him, and went back to make more teacakes and fresh coffee. She didn't expect to be busy on a Monday morning but it was nice to be prepared.

As it turned out, she had several customers; early though it was and after a brief lull the Misses Potter came—most unusually for them on a Monday, to tell her over coffee that their nephew from Canada would be coming to visit them. They in their turn were followed by Mrs Fellowes, to ask her over still more coffee if she would babysit for them on the following Saturday as

Dr Fellowes had got tickets for the theatre in Cheltenham. Mary Jane agreed cheerfully; the doctor's children were small and cuddly and once they were asleep they needed very little attention. Mrs Fellowes had been gone only a few moments before two cars stopped, disgorging children and parents and what looked like Granny and Grandpa. They ate all the teacakes and most of the scones, drank a gratifying amount of coffee and lemonade and went away again with noisy cheerfulness, leaving her to clear away, close the tea-room for the lunch-hour and, after a quick sandwich, start on another batch of scones.

No one came during the early afternoon and in a way she was glad for it gave her time to return everything to its usual pristine order. It was almost four o'clock and she was wondering if she should close for the day when a car drew up and a lady got out, opened the door and asked if she might have tea.

'Have a table by the window,' invited Mary Jane. 'It's a nice afternoon and I like this time of day, don't you? Indian or China, and would you like scones or teacakes?'

'China and scones, please. What a charming village.' The lady smiled at her and Mary Jane smiled back; her customer wasn't young but she was dressed in the kind of tweeds Mary Jane would have liked to be able to afford and her pepper and salt hair was stylishly dressed. She had a very kind face, full of laughter lines.

Mary Jane brought the tea and a plate of scones, butter and a dish of strawberry jam, and Sir Thomas's mother engaged her in idle talk while she studied her. So this was the girl with the violet eyes; the tartar with a sharp tongue. She approved of what she saw and the eyes were certainly startlingly lovely.

'I don't suppose you get many customers at this time of year?' she asked casually.

'Well, no, although today I've been quite busy...'

'You don't open until mid-morning, I suppose,' asked Mrs Latimer, following a train of thought.

'About nine o'clock—I opened early today, though—someone who had been up all night and needed a hot drink.'

Mary Jane's cheeks went nicely pink at the thought of Sir Thomas. To cover her sudden confusion at the thought of him, she went on lightly, 'He had a dog with him—he was called Watson...'

'What an unusual name,' said Mrs Latimer, and silently congratulated herself on her maternal instincts. 'For a dog, I mean. What delicious scones.' She smiled at Mary Jane. 'I am so glad I came here.'

Chapter 4

The evenings were closing in and the mornings were crisp. Mary Jane, locking the door after another day almost devoid of customers, thought of Felicity in London, from whom she had had a card that morning. The Paris show had been a resounding success and she was having a few days off before another week or so of modelling, this time in the Seychelles. Mary Jane, reading it without envy, wondered why they had to go so far to take photos of clothes which only a tiny percentage of women wore. She wondered who paid for it all—perhaps that was why the clothes were so wildly expensive.

She fed Brimble, had her supper and spent the evening shortening the hem of the jersey dress. Short skirts were the fashion and she had nice legs even if there was no one to notice that.

* * *

The morning brought several customers, the last of whom, an elderly man, looked so ill she gave him a second cup of coffee without charging for it. He had a dreadful cough, too, watering eyes and a face as white as paper.

As he got up to go she said diffidently, 'You have got a frightful cold; should you be out?'

'Got a job to do,' he said hoarsely. 'No good giving in, miss.'

Poor fellow, thought Mary Jane, and then forgot him. Closing up for the day later, she peered out into the cold, wet evening and thought with sympathy of Dr and Mrs Fellowes, who had gone to London for a few days. It was no weather for a holiday.

She woke up in the night with a sore throat and when she got up she had a headache. There were no customers all day and for once she was glad because she was beginning to feel peculiar. She closed early, locking the door thankfully against persistent rain and a rising wind and, since she wasn't hungry, she fed Brimble, made herself a hot drink and went to bed after a hot bath, but even its warmth and that of the hot water bottle she clasped to her made no difference to the icy shivers running down her spine. Brimble, that most understanding of cats, got on to the bed presently and stretched out against her and soon she slept, fitfully, relieved when it was morning. A cup of tea teamed with a couple of Panadol would make her feel better. She crept downstairs, gave Brimble his breakfast, drank her tea and went back to bed. The weather had worsened during the night and there was no one about; there would certainly be no customers. She went to sleep again, to wake every few hours with a blinding headache and a chest which hurt when she breathed. It was late afternoon when she crawled out of bed again to feed Brimble, wash her face and put on a clean nightie. A night's sleep would surely get her back on her feet, she thought. She ought to make herself a drink, but the very idea of going downstairs again made her feel ill. She got back into bed…

She woke several times aware that she was thirsty, that she should feed Brimble, put on some clothes and knock on Mrs Adams's door and get her to ask Dr Fellowes's locum to come, but somehow she couldn't be bothered to do anything about things. She was dimly aware that Brimble was mewing but she was by now so muddled that she quite thought she had been downstairs to put out his food. She fell into an uneasy doze, not heeding the rain and the wind rattling at the windows.

Sir Thomas, driving himself back from a consultation in Bristol, turned off the motorway at Swindon. He would have to stop for lunch somewhere and he might as well go a little out of his way and have it at Mary Jane's. He had no appointments for the rest of the day and driving was tiring in the appalling weather. It was more than a little out of his way; from the village he would have to drive to Oxford but he had reasoned that he could pick up the M40 there, a mere fifty miles or so from London.

It was just after one o'clock when he stopped at the tea-room. There was no one around and no traffic, not that there was ever very much of that and he wasn't surprised to see the 'Closed' sign on the door. Mary Jane would be having her lunch. He got out of the car and went to the door and rang the bell and, since no one came, peered into the little room. Brimble was sitting on the little counter at the back, looking anxious, and when Sir Thomas tapped on the glass he jumped down and came to the door, standing on his hind legs, mewing urgently.

Sir Thomas rang again and knocked for good measure, standing patiently in his Burberry, the rain drenching his head. He stood back from the door and looked up to the windows above but there was no sign of anyone and after a moment he walked to the end of the little terrace and went down the narrow alley which led to the back gardens. Mary Jane's cottage was halfway along, he opened the flimsy gate, crossed the small garden and went to peer through the kitchen window. The kitchen was untidy, not at all in its usual state with a pan full of milk on the stove and the kettle and dishes and cutlery lying around. As he looked, Brimble jumped on to the draining board by the sink and scratched at the window, which, since he had his own cat-flap, seemed unnecessary. The cottages on either side were unlit and silent; Sir Thomas took out his Swiss Army penknife, selected one of its versatile components and eased it into the window frame.

The window opened easily for the hasp was loose, and he swung it wide so that Brimble might go out. He didn't want to. Instead he jumped down and went to the door leading to the stairs standing half-open.

Sir Thomas took off his Burberry, threw it into the kitchen and squeezed through the window, no easy task for a man of his splendid size. He gained the floor and stood for a moment, listening. When he called, 'Mary

Jane,' in a quiet voice, there was silence and he started up the narrow little stairs.

As he reached the tiny landing Mary Jane came wobbling out of the bedroom. She was barefoot and in her nightie and her hair hung down her back and over her shoulders in an appalling tangle. Her pinched face was a nasty colour and her eyelids puffy. Not a pretty sight.

'Oh, it's you,' she said in a hoarse whisper.

Sir Thomas bit back strong language, scooped her up and laid her back in the tumbled bedclothes. She was in no state to answer questions; he went back downstairs, out of the door this time, fetched his bag from the car, paused long enough to fill Brimble's bowl with what he took to be cold milk-pudding in the top of the fridge and took the stairs two at a time.

Mary Jane hadn't moved but she opened her eyes as he sat down on the side of the bed. She was too weary to speak, which was just as well, for he popped a thermometer under her tongue and took her wrist in his large cool hand. It felt comforting and she curled her hot fingers round it and closed her eyes again.

Her temperature was high and her breaths rapid and so was her pulse. He said with reassuring calm, 'You have a nasty bout of flu, Mary Jane. Who's your doctor?'

She opened an eye. 'He's away.'

'Is there anyone to look after you?'

She frowned, not wanting to bother to answer him. 'No.'

He tucked her in firmly. 'I'll be back,' he told her and went out of the back door again and round to the front, to bang on the doors on either side of the tea-room. No one came to answer his thumps and he went to his car and picked up the phone.

Back in the cottage he set to work with quiet speed, clearing the kitchen, shutting and locking the kitchen door, fastening the window and then going upstairs again to fetch his bag. Mary Jane opened her eyes once more. 'Do go away,' she begged. 'I've such a headache.'

'You'll feel better presently,' he assured her, and then asked, 'Have you a box or basket for Brimble?'

'On top of the wardrobe.' She sat up suddenly. 'Why? He's all right, he's not ill?'

'No, but you are. I'm taking you to someone who will look after you both for a day or two. Now be a good girl and stay quiet until I get organised.'

Brimble wasn't pleased to be stuffed gently into his basket, but the hands which picked him up and stowed him away were gentle and he had been easily mellowed by the milk-pudding. He was borne into the tea-room and the basket put on top of one of the tables, next to the bag Sir Thomas had brought downstairs. He unlocked the shop door next and went back upstairs, rolled Mary Jane in the quilt and carried her downstairs. The stairs, being narrow, made things a bit difficult, but Mary Jane was small and slight even if the quilt was bulky. He opened the tea-room door and with some difficulty the car door and arranged his bundle beside his seat, strapped her in and went back for Brimble and his bag before locking the door of the tea-room. He was very wet by now since he hadn't bothered to put his Burberry on again but thrown it into the back of the car, but before he got into the car he stood a moment looking up and down the street. There was no sign of anyone; presumably everyone was indoors, sitting cosily by the fire, no doubt with the TV on very loud to drown the sound of the wind and the rain. He got in, gave a quick look at Mary Jane's sickly face and drove off.

After a minute or so Mary Jane opened her eyes. She felt very ill but she knew vaguely that there were some things she needed to know.

'Not hospital,' she muttered. 'Brimble…'

'Don't fuss,' advised Sir Thomas. 'You're going somewhere so that you can lie in bed for a day or two and get well, and Brimble will be right by you.'

'Oh, good,' said Mary Jane, and, remembering her manners, 'thank you, so sorry to be such a nuisance.'

She dozed off, lulled by his grunt, a reassuring commonplace sound which soothed her. She stirred only slightly when he stopped before his mother's front door and lifted her out as though she had been a bundle of feathers and carried her in. Mrs Latimer, waiting in the hall, took one look at Mary Jane. 'Oh, the poor child. Upstairs, Thomas, the garden room—there's a balcony for the cat.'

He paused for a second by her. 'Bless you, you've thought of everything.'

He went on up the staircase and she received Brimble in his basket and went up after him at a more leisurely pace.

Sir Thomas laid Mary Jane on the bed and carefully unrolled her out of the quilt and Mrs Beaver tucked the bedclothes around her. 'There, there,' she said comfortably, 'the poor young thing. Just you go away, Sir Thomas, and I'll have her put to rights in no time at all. A nice wash and a clean nightie and some of my lemonade.'

Mrs Latimer, coming into the room, nodded her

head, set Brimble's basket down on the covered balcony and put a hand on her son's sleeve. 'Shall I get Dr Finney?'

'I'll have a look at her when you've tidied her up. The sooner I get her on to antibiotics the better. You might get him up tomorrow if you would, Mother.'

'Yes, dear. Now go away and have a drink or something and we'll let you know when we are ready for you.'

When he went upstairs again Mary Jane was awake; save for her eyes there was no colour in her face but her hair had been brushed and hung, neatly plaited, over one shoulder and she was wearing one of Mrs Latimer's nighties.

'That's better.' He came and sat on the edge of the bed and felt her pulse. It was galloping along at a fine rate and he frowned a little. 'I'm going to start you off on an antibiotic,' he told her. He spoke with pleasant remoteness, a doctor visiting his patient. 'An injection. I'll get it ready while Mrs Beaver turns you over.'

She couldn't be bothered to answer him; now that she was clean and in a warm bed all she wanted to do was sleep. 'Where's Brimble?' she asked suddenly, and rolled over obedient to Mrs Beaver's kind hands.

'Having a snack on the balcony,' said Sir Thomas, sliding in the needle as Mrs Beaver drew back the bedclothes and ignoring Mary Jane's startled yelp.

'There, dearie, all over,' said Mrs Beaver. 'You just turn over on to the other side and have a little nap.'

'It's sore.' Mary Jane's hoarse voice sounded aggrieved; tears weren't far off.

'Here's Brimble,' said Sir Thomas. She heard his voice, remote and kind and felt Brimble's small furry body beside her, closed her eyes on threatening tears and went to sleep.

Sir Thomas stood for a moment looking down at her. She looked not a day over fifteen…

Downstairs he found his mother sitting in the drawing-room. 'I think I will ring Finney,' he told her, 'explain the circumstances.'

She agreed, 'Yes, dear. I'll take good care of her—it is flu?'

'Yes, but I suspect that there's a mild pneumonia as well. I have no idea how long she was lying there ill.'

'You would have thought that the neighbours would have noticed that the tea-room was closed.'

'Normally, yes, but with this bad weather it would seem normal enough for her not to open, don't you think?'

When he came back from phoning they went to a be-lated lunch and as they drank their coffee Mrs Latimer asked, 'Has she no family at all? Did you not mention a sister? She should be told.'

'Felicity—yes, of course, if she is in London. I gather that she seldom is, but I have her address and phone number.' He saw his mother's look of surprise and smiled a little. 'I'll look her up. I'm free for the rest of today.'

'If you do see her, Thomas, and she is anxious about Mary Jane, do tell her that she is very welcome to come here and make sure that she is all right.'

'Thank you, dear.' They were back in the drawing-room and Mrs Latimer began to talk about other things until presently Sir Thomas said, 'I think I'll just take a quick look at Mary Jane before I go. Is Mrs Beaver in the kitchen or in her own room?'

Mrs Latimer glanced at the clock. 'In the kitchen getting the tea-tray ready.'

He went first to look at Mary Jane, deeply asleep now, one arm flung around Brimble. Her washed out face had a little colour now and her breathing was easier; he took her pulse and put a hand on her forehead and then went downstairs to find Mrs Beaver. 'Wake her and wash her and give her plenty to drink and something to eat if she fancies it—yoghurt or something similar. Dr Finney will come in the morning and give you fresh instructions. Thank you, Mrs Beaver—it will only be for a couple of days; I believe she is through the worst of it.'

He drank his tea, promised his mother that he would phone her that evening and drove back to London, leaving his parent thoughtful.

Mary Jane, unaware of his departure and indeed rather hazy as to whether she had seen him at all, woke to find Mrs Latimer sitting by the bed. She still felt ill and weary but her headache was better and she was warm.

When she tried to sit up Mrs Latimer said, 'No, dear, just lie still. We are going to wash your face and hands and make you comfortable and then you are going to eat a little something. Thomas told me to be sure that you did and presently he will telephone to find out if I have done as he asked.'

She smiled so kindly that Mary Jane, to her shame, felt tears fill her eyes and spill down her cheeks. Mrs Latimer said nothing, merely wiped them away and told her that she was getting better and then Mrs Beaver came in with a basin and towels and Brimble was coaxed away to eat his supper on the balcony while she was washed and her hair combed. She lay passive while the two ladies tidied her, fighting a fresh desire to burst into tears; she had looked after herself for so long that she had forgotten how marvellous it was to be cosseted with such care and gentleness.

Mrs Latimer saw the tears. 'Cry if you want to, my dear. I'm sure you're not a watering pot normally, it's just the flu. You're going to feel so much better in the morning.'

She was quite right. Mary Jane woke feeling as though she had been put through a mangle, but her head was clear; she even wished to get up, to be sternly discouraged by Mrs Beaver, standing over her while she drank her tea and ate some scrambled egg.

'If you would tell me,' began Mary Jane.

'All in good time, miss, you just lie there and get well—bless you, a day or two in bed'll do you all the good in the world and you could do with a bit of flesh on those bones.'

Sir Thomas telephoned as his mother was sitting down to breakfast; he had phoned on the previous evening to tell her that he had rung Felicity and was taking her out to dinner later; now he wanted to know how Mary Jane was and Mrs Latimer said carefully, 'Well, Thomas, I don't know much about it, but she seems better. Very limp and still rather hot but she's had several cups of tea and a few mouthfuls of scrambled egg. I gave her the pills you left for her to take. What did her sister say?'

He didn't answer at once. Felicity had been charming when he had phoned, expressed concern about Mary Jane and begged him to go and see her at her flat. He hadn't wanted to do that; instead he had arranged to take her out to dinner and over that meal he had told her about Mary Jane. She had listened for a few minutes and then smiled charmingly at him across the table. 'She'll be all right, she's awfully tough—it's very kind of you to bother.' She had put out a hand and touched his on the table. 'Could we go somewhere and dance?'

He had refused with beautiful manners, pleading patients to see and the hospital to visit and had driven her back to her flat, and when she had asked him where he lived he had evaded her question.

'She told me that Mary Jane would be all right, that she was tough—oh, and that it was kind of us to bother.'

'I see,' said Mrs Latimer, who didn't. 'Dr Finney will be here presently, will you be at your rooms? He could phone you there.'

'Yes, ask him to do that, will you? I'll phone you this evening— I don't think I'll have time before then.'

He rang off and Mrs Latimer finished her breakfast and went back to Mary Jane. 'My doctor is coming to see you presently; perhaps we can tidy you up first?'

'I could get up,' began Mary Jane. 'I feel much better. I'm giving you so much trouble and you are so kind…'

'It's delightful to have someone to fuss over, my dear. Thomas, as you can imagine, has long outgrown any attempts of mine to cosset him. How would you like a nice warm bath before Dr Finney comes and then pop back into bed?'

Mary Jane was sitting up very clean and fresh in another of her hostess's nighties, still pale and limp but doing her best to appear her normal self, when Dr Finney came. He was elderly and rather slow and very kind.

He examined Mary Jane very thoroughly, tapping her chest and thumping her gently and bidding her say 'nine nine nine' and put out her tongue. All these things done, he said thoughtfully, 'A narrow squeak, young lady; another day and you would have been in hospital with pneumonia. Most fortunate that Thomas found you and acted quickly. Another two days in bed and then you may return to your home. You don't have a job?'

'I run a tea-room.'

'Do you, indeed? How interesting. By all means return to it but don't attempt to exert yourself for a few more days. Take the pills which Thomas has left you and there's no reason why you shouldn't get out of bed from time to time and walk round.' His eye lighted on Brimble, who had just come in and had jumped on to the bed. 'A cat? Bless my soul!'

'He is mine, Sir Thomas brought him here with me.'

'Of course. I shall come and see you again in two days' time, young lady, and I expect to find you very much better.'

When Mrs Latimer came back presently Mary Jane said, 'I can't think why Sir Thomas brought me here. That sounds awfully rude but you do understand what I mean, Mrs Latimer. I could have gone to…' She paused because she couldn't think of anywhere, only Margaret, who wouldn't have had her anyway, and Miss Kemble, who would have had her and nursed her, too, but only because of a strong sense of duty. All her other friends lived in small houses with children or elderly grannies or grandpas in the spare bedrooms.

'I think,' said Mrs Latimer carefully, 'that Thomas realised that by the time he had found someone in the village who could spare the time to look after you you would have been fit only for the hospital and that would have been such an upheaval, wouldn't it, dear?'

'If I had some clothes I could go home as soon as Dr Finney says I may. I don't want to put you to any more trouble, I can never thank you enough.'

'We can talk about that in two days' time; now you are going to have a nap and presently Mrs Beaver will bring you a little lunch. Remember, my dear, that we are really enjoying having you here even though you aren't well. Allow two elderly ladies to spoil you.'

Mrs Latimer smiled at her and went away and Mary Jane closed her eyes and slept, with the faithful Brimble curled up against her.

It was amazing what two days of good food and ample rest did for Mary Jane. Her hair, washed by Mrs Beaver, shone with soft brown lights, her face lost its pinched look and its colour returned and her eyes regained their sparkle. Not pretty, but nice to look at, reflected Mrs Latimer.

After Dr Finney had been to see her again Mary Jane asked diffidently if someone could possibly get her clothes so that she might return home, 'For I have trespassed on your kindness too long,' she pointed out. 'If only I had the key, Mrs Adams could go and get me the clothes and send them at once.'

Mrs Latimer looked vague. 'Well, I suppose that Thomas has the key, my dear, but since he will be coming tomorrow, I'm sure he will know what is best to be done.'

So Mary Jane, wrapped in one of her hostess's quilted dressing-gowns, spent a happy day being shown round the house and sitting in Mrs Latimer's pretty little sitting-room at the back of the hall, listening to that lady talking about Thomas. She longed to ask why, at the age of thirty-four, he wasn't married. Perhaps he was divorced or loved someone already married to another man, perhaps she had died young… Mary Jane, with a lively imagination, allowed it to run riot.

He arrived the next day after lunch and he wasn't alone. Felicity got out of the car and accompanied him into the house, was introduced to his mother and made a pretty little speech to her; she had found that she had a couple of days free and on the spur of the moment she had telephoned to Sir Thomas and asked if she might accompany him if and when he next went to his home. 'I have been anxious about Mary Jane,' she added with one of her charming smiles. Mrs Latimer hid her doubts about that, welcomed her warmly and suggested that she might like to go and see Mary Jane at once.

'Oh, yes, please. She isn't infectious, is she? I have several bookings next week; I have to be careful…'

Mrs Latimer led her upstairs, leaving Sir Thomas to go into the drawing-room with Watson, where presently she joined him.

'What a very pretty girl,' she observed, sitting down by the fire. Her voice was dry and he looked at her, smiling a little.

'Beautiful. I'm sorry not to have let you know, but I had no time, I was on the point of leaving when she phoned. I could do nothing else but suggest that she could come.'

'Of course, dear. She expects to stay the night, I dare say.'

'She has an overnight bag with her—said something about putting up at the local pub.'

'No, no, she must stay here. I dare say Mary Jane is delighted to see her.' She didn't look at her son. 'The dear child is so anxious to go back to her tea-room but of course she has no clothes. What do you suggest?'

'I'll drive over presently, take Mrs Beaver with me and fetch what she needs. The place was in a mess; perhaps we could tidy it up a little before I take her back.'

'Do you suppose her sister will go with her and stay a day or two?'

'Unlikely...' He broke off as Felicity came into the room.

'May I come in? Mary Jane is resting so I didn't stay long. What a lovely house you have, Mrs Latimer. I do love old houses; I'd love to see round it.'

She sat down near Sir Thomas and smiled enchantingly at him, and he wondered how two sisters could be so unlike each other. 'I'll go and take a look at her,' he said blandly, 'see if she's fit to go home.'

'I'll come with you,' said Felicity.

'No, no. If she is resting, the fewer visitors she has, the better.'

He took no notice of her pretty little *moue* of disappointment and went away. First to the kitchen to see Mrs Beaver and then upstairs, where he found Mary Jane not resting at all but sitting in a chair with Brimble on her knee, looking out of the window at the dull weather outside.

'Not resting?' he asked, and pulled up a chair to sit beside her. 'Felicity said that you were. How are you?'

'I'm quite well, thank you, Sir Thomas. It was very kind of you to invite Felicity.'

He didn't answer that but observed, 'I hear that you would like to get back to your cottage. I'm going to take Mrs Beaver over there now. Make a list of what you need and we'll bring your things back and I'll drive you over first thing tomorrow morning.'

'I could go as soon as you come back…'

'And so you could, but you're not going to. Another night here won't do you any harm and my mother is loath to let you go.' He got out his pocket-book and a pen and handed them to her. 'Make your list. Mrs Beaver is waiting.'

He was brisk and businesslike so she did her best to be the same, making a careful list with directions as to where everything was. Handing it to him, she tried once more. 'I could go back this afternoon if you wouldn't mind taking me, really I could.'

'Don't be obstinate,' said Sir Thomas, and went away to come back within a few minutes with Mrs Beaver, hatted and coated in case Mary Jane had forgotten something. 'There's no reason why you shouldn't come downstairs and have tea with my mother and Felicity,' he said kindly, and pulled her gently out of her chair. 'Bring Brimble; it's time he and Watson met.'

So she went downstairs and met Watson waiting patiently at the bottom of the stairs for his master. He sniffed delicately at Brimble and Brimble eyed him from the shelter of Mary Jane's arms and muttered before they went into the drawing-room.

'Mary Jane's coming down for tea—we'll be back in good time for dinner.'

'You're not taking Mary Jane back?' Felicity sounded flurried. 'She hasn't any clothes here?'

'We're going to fetch them now.'

'Oh, then I'll come with you…' Felicity had jumped up.

'Mrs Beaver is coming, she knows what to get, but it's good of you to offer.'

He whistled to Watson and went away, leaving the three of them to chat over their tea. At least Felicity did most of the talking, relating titbits of gossip about the people she had met, the glamorous clothes she modelled and the delightful life she led. 'Of course,' she told Mrs Latimer airily, 'I shall give it all up when I marry but it will be so useful—I mean, knowing about clothes and make-up and being social.'

'You are engaged?' asked Mrs Latimer.

'No, not yet. I've had ever so many chances but I know the kind of man I intend to marry—plenty of money, because I'm used to that, a good social background, good looks.' She gave a little tinkling laugh. 'I'll make a good wife to a man with a successful career.'

All the while she talked Mary Jane sat quietly. Sir Thomas, she reflected, was exactly the kind of husband her sister intended to marry, and she was pretty and amusing enough for him to fall in love with her—and he had invited her to come to his mother's home, hadn't he? He had not answered her but he hadn't denied it either. Mrs Latimer quietly took the conversation into her own hands presently and suggested taking Felicity to her room so that she might tidy herself. 'We dine at eight o'clock,' she told her. 'I do hope you will be comfortable; if there is anything you need, do please ask.'

Mary Jane, left alone with Brimble, began making resolute plans for her return. There would be the baking to see to and the place to clean up, for as far as she could remember it had been in something of a pickle when Sir Thomas had fetched her away. He had been so kind and she had put him to a great deal of trouble, she hoped that Mrs Beaver had been able to find everything easily so that he hadn't had to wait too long. The cottage would be cold; she should have asked him to light the gas fire in the sitting-room and sit there...

He hadn't even been into the sitting-room. He and Mrs Beaver had gone into the cold tea-room and through to the kitchen which was indeed in a pickle.

'You go upstairs and get the clothes,' he told Mrs Beaver. 'I'll tidy up here.'

He had taken off his coat and his jacket and rolled up his shirt-sleeves and boiled several kettles of water, washed everything he could see that needed it, dried them and put them away, found a broom and swept the floor and looked in the cupboard. There was tea there, and sugar and a packet of biscuits, cat food and some porridge oats. The fridge held butter and lard, some rather hard cheese and a few rashers of bacon. He went to the foot of the stairs and called up to Mrs Beaver who was trotting to and fro and she peered down at him from the tiny landing. Before he could speak she observed, 'It's a shocking shame, Sir Thomas, that dear child— two of everything, beautifully washed and ironed and mended to death and a cupboard with almost nothing to wear in it. Good stuff, mind you, but dear knows when she went shopping last.' She drew a breath. 'And that sister of hers in them silks and satins—blood's thicker than water, I say and I don't care who hears me say it.'

'Perhaps something can be done about that. I'm going over to the village shop—it should be open still, there's almost no food in the house. Surely the milk-man calls...'

'Look outside the back door, sir...'

The milk was there; he fetched it in and put it in the

fridge, got into his coat and walked to the shop where
he bought what he hoped were the right groceries and
bore them back to stack them in the cupboard.

Mrs Beaver was ready by then; they got back into
the car and he half listened to Mrs Beaver's indignant
but respectful remarks about young girls being left to
fend for themselves. She paused for breath at last and
added apologetically, 'I do hope I've not put you out, sir,
letting me tongue run away with me like that and you
likely as not sweet on the young lady. I must own she's
pretty enough to catch any gentleman's eye.'

Sir Thomas agreed placidly.

He found his mother and Mary Jane in the drawing-
room, bent over a complicated piece of tapestry. They
looked up as he went in and Mary Jane got to her feet.
'I'll go and dress,' she said. 'And thank you very much
indeed, Sir Thomas.'

He smiled. 'You look very nice as you are, but I dare
say you will feel more yourself in a dress.' He held the
door for her as she went into the hall. 'Mrs Beaver's
taken your case upstairs. Would you like to leave Brimble here? Watson won't hurt him.'

He took the cat from her and watched her go up the
staircase before going back into the room.

'Where is our guest?' he asked.

'She went upstairs to tidy herself. Is the cottage all
right for Mary Jane to go back?'

'As clean and tidy as we could make it. I fetched some
food from the shop—the lady who owns it said they
were beginning to wonder where Mary Jane had gone—
no one had been out much because of the bad weather
and those that had had supposed that she had closed the

tea-room since there was no chance of customers. Her neighbours had been away and the Misses Potter, who call regularly, had been indoors with bad colds. A series of unfortunate events.' He sat down opposite her. 'I'm sure that once she is back the village will rally round— she is very well-liked.'

'I'm not surprised...' Mrs Latimer broke off as the door opened and Felicity came into the room. She had changed into a silk sheath of vivid green, its brevity allowing an excellent view of her shapely legs, its neckline, from Mrs Latimer's point of view, immodest. She walked slowly to join them, giving Sir Thomas time to study her charming if unsuitable appearance. It was a pity that he got to his feet almost without a glance and went to get her a drink.

Ten minutes later Mary Jane joined them, wearing the skirt of her suit and a Marks and Spencer blouse, and this time Sir Thomas allowed his gaze to dwell upon her prosaic person. What he thought was nobody's business; all he said was, 'Ah, Mary Jane, come and sit down and have a glass of sherry.'

Chapter 5

Mrs Latimer spoke. 'Come and sit by me, Mary Jane. How nice to see you dressed and well again. You have recovered so quickly, too. I'm glad for your sake but we shall miss you. Once you are settled in I shall drive over and have tea with you again.'

Mary Jane's quiet answer was drowned by Felicity's voice. 'How I wish that I could live away from London—I do love the country and the quiet life. Sometimes I wish that I would never need to travel so much again. How I envy you, Mary Jane.'

Not easily aroused to bad temper, Mary Jane found these sentiments too hard to swallow. 'Well, I don't suppose it would matter much if you gave up your modelling—there must be dozens of girls… I could do with some help, especially in the summer.' She spoke in a matter-of-fact voice, smiling a little. No one would have known that she was seething; first her dull, sensible clothes, highlighted pitilessly by Felicity's *couture* and now this nonsense about wanting to live in the country. Why, she had run away from it just as soon as she could... Sir Thomas, watching her quiet face from under his eyelids, had a shrewd idea of her thoughts. The contrast between her and her sister was too striking to overlook, especially the clothes; on the other hand, he conceded, Felicity hadn't beautiful eyes the colour of violets.

He said smoothly, 'You would probably find living in the country very dull, Felicity. Are you working at present?'

'Next week—here in London—perhaps we could meet? And then I'm off to New York for the shows. I was there last year and I had a marvellous time. The parties—you have no idea...'

She embarked on a colourful account of her visit and the three of them listened, Mary Jane with understandable wistfulness, Mrs Latimer with an apparent interest because she had never been ill-mannered in her life, and Sir Thomas with an inscrutable face which gave away nothing of his true feelings.

During dinner, however, Felicity was forced to curb her chatter; Sir Thomas kept the conversation firmly upon mundane matters, and, after drinking coffee with the ladies, he pleaded telephone calls to make and went away to the library, presumably not noticing Felicity's sulky face.

He returned just as Felicity, bored with her companions, declared herself ready for bed.

'Is eight o'clock too early for you?' asked Sir Thomas of Mary Jane. 'I need to be back in town by lunchtime.'

'That's fine,' said Mary Jane. 'But surely I could catch a bus or something…' She frowned. 'All the trouble…'

Felicity had been listening. 'I'll come with you…'

'It would mean getting up at half-past six,' Sir Thomas pointed out suavely.

She hesitated. 'Oh, well, perhaps not. It isn't as if Mary Jane needs anyone any more. I'll be waiting here for you when you get back.'

She smiled her most bewitching smile, quite lost on Sir Thomas who had turned away to speak to his mother.

It was one of those mornings in autumn when night was reluctant to give way to morning. It was raining, too. They left exactly at eight o'clock and Mrs Latimer had come down to see them off. She had embraced Mary Jane warmly and promised to see her again shortly, and now they were in the car driving back to the tea-room, she beside Sir Thomas, Brimble in his basket, indignantly silent on the back seat. There seemed no need for conversation; Mary Jane sensed that her companion had no wish to listen to chatter, not that she was much good at that and at that time of day small talk seemed out of place. However, although for the most part they were silent, it wasn't uneasy. She sat quietly, planning her week while Sir Thomas thought his own thoughts. Presumably they were amusing, for once or twice he smiled.

At the tea-room he took no notice of her protests that she was quite able to be left at its door. He got out, opened the door, reached into the car for Brimble's basket, took her key from her and ushered her into her home.

It was chilly and unwelcoming. 'Wait here,' he told her and went upstairs to light the gas fire, switch on the kitchen light and set Brimble's basket down on the table. He fetched her case then, took it upstairs and found her in the kitchen. 'How very clean and tidy it is,' she told him. 'I'm sure I left it in a frightful mess. Will you have a cup of coffee before you go?'

'I wish I could but I must get back.' He took her hand in his, smiling down at her very kindly. 'Take care of yourself, Mary Jane.'

She stared at him. 'You've been very kind, I can never thank you or Mrs Latimer enough, and thank you for bringing me back.' She offered a hand and he took it, bending to kiss her cheek as he did so. She watched him drive away, wondering if she would ever see him again. Probably not. On the other hand, if he should fall in love with Felicity, she would.

She went into the kitchen and released Brimble, made herself a pot of tea, unpacked her few things and put on her pinny. Customers were unlikely. On the other hand, she had to be ready for them if they did come. She went to turn the sign to 'Open' and only then saw the box on the table by the door. There was a bunch of flowers on it, too—chrysanthemums, the small ones which lasted for weeks, just what was needed to cheer up the tea-room...

She took the lid off the box then, and discovered a cooked chicken, straw potatoes and salad in a covered container, egg custard in a pottery dish and a crock of Stilton cheese; there was even a small bottle of wine.

Much cheered, she arranged the flowers on the ta-

bles, got the coffee going and got out her pastry board.
As soon as she had made some scones she would sit
down and write to Mrs Latimer—Mrs Beaver too—
and thank them for their kindness.

There was no sign of Felicity by the time Sir Thomas
reached his mother's house. He went to bid his mother
goodbye and went in search of Mrs Beaver. He found
her in the kitchen. 'Ask Rosie or Tracey—' the girls
who came from the village each day to help in the house
'—to go to Miss Seymour's room and tell her that I am
leaving in five minutes. If she is unable to be ready by
then, Mrs Latimer will get a taxi for her so that she can
get to Banbury and get a train to town.'

Felicity was in the hall with a minute to spare and
very put out. 'My make-up,' she moaned prettily, 'I
haven't had time, and I've thrown my things into my
case...' She pouted prettily at Sir Thomas who remained
impervious. 'Perhaps we could stop on the way...'

He had beautiful manners. 'I'm so sorry, but there
won't be time—I must be at the hospital. Shall we go?'

She bade Mrs Latimer goodbye with the hope that
she would see her again. 'For I haven't had time to see
your lovely home, have I?' But Mrs Beaver she ignored,
sweeping past her to get into the car.

'You'd never know that they were sisters,' declared
Mrs Beaver sourly. A thought echoed by Sir Thomas
as he swept the Rolls out of the gate and through the
village.

Felicity, accustomed to the admiration of the men she
met, worked hard to attract Sir Thomas, but although
he was a charming companion he remained aloof, and
when he stopped the car outside her flat she had the

feeling that she had made no impression on him whatsoever. It was a galling thought and a spur to her determination to get him interested in her. Obviously, he had no interest in her success as a model or the glamorous life she led. She would have to change her tactics. She bade him goodbye in a serious voice, with no suggestion that they might meet again and added a rider to the effect that she hoped Mary Jane would be all right. 'I shall take the first opportunity to go down and see her,' she assured him, and he murmured suitably, thinking that the likelihood of that seemed remote. One could never tell, however; beneath that frivolous manner there might be a heart of gold. He thought it unlikely, but he was a tolerant man, ready to think the best of everything and everyone. He dismissed her from his mind and drove to the hospital.

Mary Jane was taking the first batch of scones out of the oven when her first customers came in. A young couple barely on speaking terms, the girl having misread the map and directed her companion in entirely the wrong direction. They sat eyeing each other stormily over the little vase of flowers. Mary Jane brought the coffee and they wanted to know just where they were. She told them and the man muttered, 'We're miles out of our way thanks to my map-reader here.' He glared at the girl.

'No, you're not,' said Mary Jane. 'Just keep on this road and turn right at the first crossroads—you're only a few miles in the wrong direction.'

She left them to their coffee and presently the door opened and the Misses Potter came in.

'Not our usual time, my dear,' said Miss Emily, 'but

we were on our way to the stores and saw that you were back. Have you had a nice little break?'

Mary Jane said that, yes, she had and fetched the coffee pot just as Miss Kemble came in. 'I see you're back,' she said briskly. 'You have enjoyed your holiday, Mary Jane?'

It didn't seem worthwhile explaining. Mary Jane said that yes, she had, and poured more coffee. The young couple went presently, on speaking terms once more, and a tall, thin man with a drooping moustache came in and asked for lunch.

She hadn't had time to make sausage rolls and the demand for lunch during the winter was so small that she could only offer soup and sandwiches. She went to the kitchen to open the soup and slice bread, reflecting as she did so that someone had stocked up the fridge while she had been away. She would have to ask Mrs Latimer…

By one o'clock everyone had gone; she made herself some coffee, ate biscuits and cheese, fed Brimble and went upstairs. Beyond a quick look round she had had no time to put anything away and the bed would have to be made up.

That had been done and very neatly too, and so, when she looked, had her nightie been washed and ironed and folded away tidily. The bathroom was spotless and there wasn't a speck of dust anywhere. It was like having a fairy godmother.

She got into her outdoor things and went to the stores, exchanged the time of day with its owner and asked to use the phone. Mrs Latimer sounded pleased to hear from her and Mary Jane thanked her again for her kindness and then asked, 'Someone cleaned the cottage for me and the fridge is full of food and everything is washed and ironed. Did Sir Thomas…no sorry, I'm being silly, I'm sure he's never ironed anything in his life or bought groceries.'

Mrs Latimer chuckled. 'He certainly brought the food and I'm sure if he had to iron he would, and very well too. No, my dear, he took Mrs Beaver with him, she sorted out your things and together they tidied your cottage. Thomas is a dab hand at washing up.'

'Is he really?' said Mary Jane, much astonished. 'If I write him a note could you please send it on to him? And will you thank Mrs Beaver? As soon as I have time I'll write to you and her as well.'

'We look forward to that, my dear. Have you opened your tea-room yet?'

'Yes, and had customers too. I'm going back now to open until five o'clock although I don't expect any-one will come.'

They wished each other goodbye and she rang off and hurried back to her cottage. No one came that af-ternoon; she locked the door and went to get her sup-per, carrying the delicacies upstairs to the sitting-room to eat by the gas fire, with Brimble, on the lookout for morsels of chicken, sitting as close as he could get.

Her supper finished, she sat down to write her letters. Those to Mrs Latimer and Mrs Beaver were quickly done, but the note to Sir Thomas needed both time and thought. He had been kind and very helpful but not ex-actly friendly; it was hard to strike the right note and it took several wasted sheets of paper before she was sat-isfied with the result. By then it was time to go to bed.

She saw few customers during the following days. Doing her careful sums each evening, she decided that she was barely paying her way; there was certainly nothing to spare once her modest bills were paid. The winter always was a thin time, of course; it was just a question of hanging on until the spring. Looking out of the window at the dull autumn day, the spring looked a long way off. Luckily, there was Christmas; it might not bring more customers but those who came were usually full of the Christmas spirit and inclined to spend more. She was a neat-fingered girl and not easily depressed; in the tiny loft there was an old-fashioned trunk stuffed with old-fashioned clothes which had belonged to her mother. She got on to a chair and poked her head through the narrow opening. The loft was very small and cold and she wriggled into it and heard the scrabble of mouse feet, but mice or no mice she wasn't going to be put off. She leaned in as far as she was able and dragged the trunk over to the opening. She wouldn't be able to get it down into the cottage but she could open it and see if there was anything she could use.

There was. A gauzy scarf, yards of lace, bundles of ribbons, a watered silk petticoat, balls of wool still usable. She dragged them out, closed the trapdoor and examined her finds at her leisure. The wool was fine and in pale colours, splendid for dolls' clothes, even baby clothes, and the lace and ribbons and silk could be turned into the kinds of things people bought at Christmas: pincushions, lavender bags, beribboned nightdress cases—rather useless trifles but people bought them none the less. She went to bed that night, her head full of plans.

There was a card from Felicity in the morning: she was off to New York in two days' time and she had had a meal with Thomas—they would meet again when she got back. She didn't ask how Mary Jane was but Mary Jane hadn't expected that, anyway. She read the card again; she wasn't really surprised that Sir Thomas had been seeing Felicity, but it made her vaguely unhappy. 'And that's silly,' she told Brimble, his whiskered face buried in his breakfast saucer. 'For she's such a very pretty girl and her clothes are lovely. Perhaps she'll come and see us before Christmas,' and then, because that was what she had really been thinking about, she added, 'I wonder what meal it was and where they went?'

Sir Thomas could have told her if he had been there; he had been waylaid—there was no other word for it— by Felicity, who had taken pains to find out where he lived and had just happened to be walking past his house as he returned from the hospital. That she had done this three evenings running without success was something she didn't disclose but she evinced delighted surprise at seeing him again. 'Perhaps we could have dinner together?' she had suggested. 'You must need cheering up after a hard day's work.'

Sir Thomas had been tired, he had wanted his dinner and a peaceful evening with no one but Watson for company while he caught up with the medical journals, but his manners were too nice to have said so; instead he had suggested that they had a drink in a pleasant little bar not too far away, 'For I have to go back to the hospital shortly and I have any amount of work to do this evening.'

She had pouted prettily and agreed and jumped into the car; she had great faith in her charm and good looks, and had no doubt that once they sat down she could persuade him to take her on to dinner—let the hospital wait, he was an important man and must surely do what he wanted to do; he wasn't some junior doctor at everyone's beck and call.

She was, of course, mistaken, and half an hour later she had found herself being put into a taxi with no more than a brisk handshake and regrets that he must cut short an enjoyable meeting. 'I had hoped you could drive me to my flat,' she had complained prettily, and turned her lovely face up to his. 'I do hate going home alone.'

Sir Thomas had handed the cabby some money. 'You must have many friends, Felicity; I'm sure you won't be alone for long.' He had lifted a hand in casual salute as the taxi drove off.

Tremble had come fussing into the hall as he opened the door of his house and Watson had come to meet him.

'You're late, Sir Thomas—a bad day, perhaps?'

'No, no, Tremble, only the last hour or so. Give me ten minutes, will you, while I go through the post?'

He had gone into his study with the faithful Watson and leafed through his letters without paying much attention to them. He had had to waste part of an evening listening to Felicity's airy chatter, and he had found her tedious. 'A beautiful girl,' he told Watson. 'There's no denying that, and charming too. Perhaps I am getting middle-aged…'

It was much later that evening, standing by the French windows leading to the small garden behind the house, waiting for Watson to come in, that he had decided that he would drive down to see how Mary Jane was getting on. Her stiff little note of thanks had amused him, it had so obviously taken time and thought to compose, but she had given no hint as to how she was. It would, he told himself, be only civil to go and see her and make sure that she was quite well again. He was free on Sunday...

Customers had been thin on the ground that week; the Misses Potter came, as usual, of course, and one or two women from the village on their way home from shopping and the very occasional car. Mary Jane told herself that things would improve and started on her needlework. She had neat, clever fingers and a splendid imagination; in no time at all she had a row of mice, fashioned from the petticoat and wearing lace caps on their tiny heads and frilly beribboned skirts. Quite useless but pretty trifles that she hoped someone would buy. She was rather uncertain what she should ask for them and settled on fifty pence, which Miss Emily Potter told her was far too low a price. All the same she bought one and told Miss Kemble about them. That lady bought one too, declaring it was just the thing for a birthday present for her niece. Mary Jane thought it rather a poor sort of present but perhaps she didn't like the niece very much. Selling two of the mice so quickly gave her the heart to continue with her sewing. She sat them on the counter so that anyone paying for their coffee would see them and, very much encouraged by a passing motorist buying three of them, began on a series of frivolous heart-shaped pincushions.

When Sir Thomas drew up outside the tea-room she was standing on the counter stowing away the potted fern which was usually on it so that there was more room for the mice. She had left the 'Open' sign on the door in the hope that a customer or two might come and she turned round as the door was opened and the bell rang.

Sir Thomas's bulk, elegantly clothed in cashmere, filled the doorway. His, 'Good morning, Mary Jane,' was pleasantly casual, which gave her time to change the expression of delight on her face to one of nothing more than polite surprise. But not before Sir Thomas had seen it.

He wasn't a man to mince his words. 'I thought we might have lunch together; may I bring Watson in?'

'Of course bring him in. It's warm in the kitchen. Brimble's there.'

Sir Thomas fetched the dog, shut the door behind him and took off his coat. 'Where would you like to go?' he asked.

'Well, thank you all the same, but I've made a chicken casserole—Mrs Fellowes keeps poultry and she gave me one—already killed, of course. It's in the oven now and I wouldn't like to waste it. It's a French recipe, thyme and parsley and a bay leaf and a small onion. There should be brandy too, but I haven't any so I used the cooking sherry left over from last Christmas.'

Sir Thomas, who had never before had an invitation refused, listened, fascinated. His magnificent nose quivered at the faint aroma coming from the kitchen. With commendable promptness he said, 'Delicious. May I stay to lunch?'

Mary Jane was still standing on the counter. She looked down at him a little uncertainly. 'Well, if you would like to…'

'Indeed I would.' He crossed the room and stretched up and lifted her down, reflecting that she was a little too thin. He saw the mice then and picked one up. 'And what exactly are these bits of nonsense?'

'Well, I'm not very busy at this time of year, so I thought I'd make something to sell—for Christmas you know.'

He studied it and held it in the palm of his hand. 'My mother would love one, and Mrs Beaver. May I have two—how much are they?'

Mary Jane went very pink. 'I would prefer to give them to you, if you don't mind. If you will choose two I will wrap them up.'

He would have to be more careful, Sir Thomas told himself, watching her wrap the mice in tissue paper. Mary Jane was proud-hearted; she might have few possessions but she had the right kind of pride. He asked casually after the Misses Potter, wanted to know if her cousin had been annoying her lately and had her laughing presently over some of Watson's antics.

'Do you mind sitting in the kitchen?' She led the way to where the two animals were sitting amicably enough side by side before the cooking stove. 'I'll make some coffee and put the fire on upstairs.'

'I'll do that,' he said, and when he was downstairs again, he asked, 'Are there any odd jobs to be done while I'm here?'

'Would you reach up and get two plates from that top shelf? I don't often use them but they belonged to my mother.'

He reached up and put them on the table. 'Coalport— the Japan pattern—eighteenth-century? No, early nineteenth, isn't it? Delightful and very valuable, even just two plates.'

'Yes, we always used them when I was a little girl. I

never discovered what happened to them all when we came to live with Uncle Matthew. When I came here Cousin Oliver told me that I could take a few plates and cups and saucers with me so I took these. I found them at the back of the china pantry.'

'The casserole will taste twice as good on them. Do you want me to peel potatoes or clean these sprouts?'

She gave him an astonished look. 'But you can't do that. At least, what I mean is you mustn't, you might cut your hands and then you couldn't operate.'

'Then I'll make the coffee...'

The little kitchen was very crowded, what with Sir Thomas and his massive frame taking up most of it and Watson and Brimble getting under their feet. He made the coffee and carried it up to the sitting-room, closely followed by Watson, Mary Jane and Brimble. He had switched on the little reading lamp and the room looked cosy. Sir Thomas stretched out his long legs and drank his coffee. He thought that Mary Jane was very restful; there was no need to talk just for the sake of talking and she was quite unselfconscious. Presently he suggested, 'Would you like to drive around for a while this afternoon? Even in the winter the Cotswolds are always delightful.'

'That would be nice, but isn't there something else you'd rather do?'

He hid a smile, 'No, Mary Jane, there isn't.'

'Well, then, I'd like that very much.' She put down her mug. 'There's the bell.'

Three elderly ladies nipped with the cold, wanting coffee and biscuits and, when the aroma from the casserole reached them, wanting lunch as well. Sir Thomas could hear Mary Jane apologising in her pretty voice and reflected that if he hadn't been there she would have probably offered to share her dinner with them. As it was, she gave them very careful instructions as to how to get to Stow-on-the-Wold where, she assured them they could get an excellent lunch at the Union Crest.

When they had gone Sir Thomas went downstairs and locked the door and turned the notice to 'Closed'. 'For nothing,' he explained, 'must hinder my enjoyment of the casserole.'

It was certainly delicious; Mary Jane had creamed the potatoes and cooked the sprouts to exactly the right moment, grated nutmeg over them and added a dollop of butter, thus adding to the perfection of the chicken.

Mary Jane had laid the kitchen table with care and, although they drank water from the tap and everything was dished up from the stove, the meal was as elegant as any in a West End restaurant. Mary Jane didn't quite believe him when he said that, but it was nice of him to say so.

They washed up together while Watson and Brimble ate their own hearty meal and, since the days were getting short now and the evenings came all too quickly, Sir Thomas took Watson for a brisk walk while Mary Jane got into her elderly winter coat, made sure that Brimble was cosy in his basket and, being a good housewife, went round turning off everything that needed to be turned off, shut windows and locked the back door securely.

Sir Thomas ushered her into the car, settled Watson on the back seat and went to lock the tea-room door.

'Have you any preference as to where we should go?' he asked her.

Mary Jane, very comfortable in the leather seat and

quietly happy at the prospect of his company for an hour or so, had no preference at all.

He turned the car and went out of the village on the Gloucester road to turn off after a mile or so into the country. The road was narrow and there were few villages and almost no traffic. The big car went smoothly between the hedges, allowing them views on either side.

'You know this part of the country?' asked Sir Thomas.

'No, not well; I've never been on this road before. It's delightful.'

'It will take us to Broadway. There's another very quiet road from there to Pershore...'

At Pershore he turned south to Tewkesbury, where he stopped at the Bell and gave her a splendid tea with Watson under the table, gobbling up the morsels of crumpets and cake which came his way. 'Your scones are much better,' declared Sir Thomas.

She thanked him shyly and took another crumpet.

It was already dusk and, in the car once more, he turned for home, still keeping to the side-roads so that it was almost dark by the time they got back to the tearoom.

When she would have thanked him and got out of the car he put a hand over hers on the door-handle. 'No, wait.' And he took the key and went in to switch on the lights and go upstairs to turn on the fire. Only then did he come back to the car.

They went in together and Mary Jane said, 'I don't suppose you would like a cup of coffee?' And when he shook his head, 'I expect you've got something to do this evening.' She spoke cheerfully, thinking that he must have found her dull company. Perhaps he would have a delightful evening with some beautiful witty girl who would have him laugh. He hadn't laughed much all day, only smiled from time to time...

He stood watching her. Her unexpected outing had given her a pretty colour and her eyes shone. She offered her hand now. 'It was a lovely day—thank you very much. Please remember me to your mother and Mrs Beaver when you see them.' She smiled up at him. 'Did you have a pleasant evening with Felicity? She sent me a card. She's great fun.'

Sir Thomas, versed in the art of concealing his true feelings under a bland face, agreed pleasantly while reflecting that no two sisters could be more unlike each other and why had Felicity made a point of telling Mary Jane that she had spent the evening with him? A gross exaggeration to begin with, and what was the point? To make Mary Jane jealous? That seemed to him to be most unlikely; his friendship with her was of the most prosaic kind, brought about by circumstances.

He got into his car and drove back to London to his quiet house and a long evening in his study, making notes for a lecture he was to give during the coming week. But presently he put his pen down and sat back in his chair. 'You enjoyed your day?' he enquired of Watson, lying half-asleep before the fire. 'Delightful, wasn't it? I think that we must do it again.' He opened his diary. 'Let me see, when do I next go to Cheltenham?'

Watson opened an eye and thumped his tail. 'You agree? Good. Now let me see, whom do we know living not too far from the village?'

Mary Jane watched the tail-lights of the Rolls disappear down the village street and then locked the door and went to feed Brimble. She wasn't very hungry but supper would be something to do. She poached an egg and made some toast and a pot of tea and took the tray upstairs and sat by the gas fire while she ate her small meal. It had been a lovely day but she mustn't allow herself to get too interested in Sir Thomas. The thought occurred to her that perhaps since Felicity wasn't there to be taken out, he had taken the opportunity to see more of her. If he was falling in love with her sister then he would want to be on good terms with herself, wouldn't he? She should have talked more about Felicity so that if he had wanted to, he could have talked about her too. For some reason she began to feel unhappy, which was silly since Sir Thomas and Felicity would make a splendid couple. Perhaps she was being a bit premature in supposing that he had fallen in love, but he was bound to if he saw more of her sister; all the men she met fell in love with her sooner or later. Mary Jane was sure of that, for Felicity had told her so.

Autumn had given way to winter without putting up much of a fight and everyone was thinking about Christmas. The village stores stocked up on paper chains for the children to make and a shelf full of sweet biscuits and boxes of sweets. Mary Jane made a cake and iced it and stuck Father Christmas at its centre and put it in her window with two red candles and a 'Merry Christmas' stuck on to the window. Christmas was still a few weeks off, but with the red lampshades she had made the tea-room look welcoming. Surprisingly, for the next day or two she had more customers than she had had for weeks. She sold the mice too, stitching away each evening, replenishing her stock.

She had another card from Felicity. She was back in London to do some modelling for a glossy magazine but she intended to spend Christmas at her flat. There was no point in asking Mary Jane to join her there, she had written, for she knew how much she hated leaving the cottage. She wouldn't have gone, she told herself, even if she had been invited, for she knew none of Felicity's friends and hadn't the right clothes. All the same, it would have been nice to have been asked.

The next day Mrs Latimer came, bringing with her a little dumpling of a woman with a happy face. The Misses Potter were sitting at their usual place but there was no one else there. Mrs Latimer went over to the counter to where Mary Jane was getting out cups and saucers. 'How nice to see you again, my dear, and looking a lot better, too. I've come for tea—some of your nice scones? And come and meet someone who knows about you and your family…

'Mrs Bennett, this is Mary Jane Seymour—Mary Jane, Mrs Bennett was a friend of your mother's.'

The little lady beamed. 'You were a very little girl—you won't remember me, your mother and I lost touch. I heard that you and your sister had gone to live with your uncle and of course Felicity is quite famous, isn't she? However, I had no idea that you were here. I wrote once or twice to your uncle but he never answered. It's lovely to see you again, and with a career too!'

'Well, it's only a tea-room,' said Mary Jane, liking her new customer. 'Do sit down and I'll bring you your tea.'

The Misses Potter, too ladylike to stare, had been listening avidly. Now they had no excuse to stay any longer for the scones were eaten and the teapot drained.

They paid their bill, bowed to the two ladies and went home; news of any sort was welcome, and they looked forward to spreading it as soon as possible.

It was long after closing-time when Mrs Latimer and her friend left and the latter by then had wheedled Mary Jane into accepting her invitation to the buffet supper she was giving in ten days' time. It would mean a new dress, but Mary Jane, feeling reckless, had accepted.

That evening Mrs Latimer phoned her son. 'We had tea with Mary Jane—she's coming to Mrs Bennett's party. Tell me, Thomas, how did you discover that she had known Mary Jane's parents?' She paused. 'Or, for that matter, how did you discover Mrs Bennett? A most amiable woman, apparently not in the least surprised to have a visit from a friend of a friend…'

'Easily enough. Felicity mentioned her and I remembered the name—and phoned a few friends around that part of the country. Thank you for your help, my dear.'

Mrs Latimer was frowning as she put down the phone. Thomas was going to a good deal of trouble to liven up Mary Jane's sober life, she hoped it wasn't because he had fallen in love with Felicity. A man in love would go to great lengths to please a girl, and yet, somehow, he wasn't behaving as though he were. He could of course be sorry for Mary Jane. Mrs Latimer smiled suddenly. That young lady wouldn't thank him for that.

Chapter 6

The problems of a dress kept Mary Jane wakeful for a few nights. She would have to close the tea-room and go to Cheltenham. She couldn't afford to buy a dress; she would have to find the material and make it herself. There wasn't much time for that, especially as she hadn't a sewing-machine. Mrs Stokes had one and so did Mrs Fellowes and now was no time to be shy about asking to borrow from one of them.

Mrs Fellowes agreed to lend hers at once; moreover, when she heard why Mary Jane wanted it, she offered to give her a lift on the following day to Cheltenham.

She found what she wanted: ribbed silk in a soft dove-grey, just right for the pattern she had chosen, a simple dress with a full skirt, a modest neckline and elbow-length sleeves. She bought matching stockings and, in a fit of recklessness, some matching slippers in grey leather. They could be dyed black, she told herself, so they weren't an extravagance.

Customers were few and far between, which was a good thing, for she was able to cut out the dress and sew it. She had a talent for sewing and the dress, when it was finished, would pass muster just as long as it didn't come under the close scrutiny of someone in the world of fashion. She hung it in her bedroom and spent an evening doing her nails and washing her hair, half wishing that she weren't going to the party. Mrs Bennett seemed friendly and sweet but they didn't really know each other; she had said that there would be a lot of people there and Mary Jane wondered if there would be dancing. She loved to dance, but supposing no one wanted to dance with her?

She would be fetched, Mrs Bennett had told her in a letter; friends who lived in Shipton-under-Wychwood would collect her on their way to Bourton-on-the-Hill, where Mrs Bennett lived.

She was ready long before they arrived, wrapped in her elderly winter coat, cold with sudden panic at the idea of meeting a great many strange people. She need not have worried; the estate car which pulled up at her door was crammed with a cheerful family party, quite ready to absorb her into their number, and if they found the winter coat not quite in keeping with the occasion, no one said so. She was made to feel at home and by the time they arrived she had forgotten her sudden fright and went along to the bedroom set aside for their coats, to be further braced by the two girls and their mother admiring her dress. She needed their reassurance, for she could see that, compared with the dresses the other girls were wearing, hers, while quite suitable, was far too modest. Bare shoulders, tiny shoulder straps and bodices which stayed up by some magic of their own seemed to be the norm. She went down the staircase with the others and into the vast drawing-room in Mrs Bennett's house where her hostess was greeting her guests.

Sir Thomas, talking to his host, watched Mary Jane, a sober moth among the butterflies, pause by Mrs Bennett and exchange brief greetings. Her dress, he considered, suited her very well, although he surprised himself by wondering what she would look like in something pink and cut to show rather more of her person. No jewellery either. A pearl choker, he reflected, would look exactly right around her little neck. He listened attentively to his companion's opinion of modern politics, made suitable replies and presently made his way to where Mary Jane, swept along by her new acquaintances, stood with a group of other young people.

She saw him coming towards her and quite forgot to look cool and casual. Her gentle mouth curved into a wide smile and she flushed a little. He took her hand. 'Hello, Mary Jane, I didn't know that you knew the Bennetts.'

She didn't take her hand away. 'I didn't either. Your mother came the other day and brought Mrs Bennett with her. I think she's a friend of a friend and she remembered me when I was a little girl—she knew my mother.'

'What a delightful surprise for you,' said Sir Thomas gravely, not in the least surprised himself. 'Who brought you?'

'Mr and Mrs Elliott—they live at Shipton-under-

Wychwood and called for me. They've been very kind…'

'Ah, yes— I've met them. My mother's here—have you seen her yet?'

'No.' She added rather shyly, 'I don't know anyone here.'

'Soon remedied.' He took her arm and made his way round the room, greeting those he knew and introducing her and finally finding his mother.

'There you are, Thomas—and Mary Jane. How pretty you look, my dear, and what a charming dress—I have never seen so many exposed bosoms in all my life and many of them need covering.' She eyed Mary Jane and added, 'Although I don't think your bosom needs to be concealed; you have a pretty figure, my dear.'

Mary Jane, very pink in the cheeks, thanked her faintly and Sir Thomas, standing between them, stifled a laugh. His mother, a gentle soul by nature, could at times be quite outrageous.

'You agree, Thomas?' She smiled up at her son. 'No, probably you don't. Go away and talk to someone; I want a chat with Mary Jane.'

When they were alone she said, 'My dear, I wanted to ask you—where will you be at Christmas? Not alone, I hope?'

'Me? No, Mrs Latimer, Felicity is in London, you know, and I'm going there. I'm looking forward to it.' She told the lie, valiantly glad that Sir Thomas wasn't there to hear her. She was normally a truthful girl but this, she considered, was an occasion when she must bend the truth a little. After all, there was still time for Felicity to invite her…

'I'm glad to hear that. What do you do with your cat?'

Mary Jane was saved from replying by a dashing young man in a coloured waistcoat. 'I say, if I'm not interrupting, shall we dance? They're just starting up. Sir Thomas introduced us just now—Nick Soames? Remember?'

'Run along, dear,' said Mrs Latimer. 'But don't leave without coming to say goodbye, will you?'

So Mary Jane danced. Nick was a good partner and she had always loved dancing and when the dance finished he handed her over to someone called Bill, who didn't dance very well but made her laugh a lot. Now and then she saw Sir Thomas, head and shoulders above everyone else, circling the room with a succession of beautifully dressed girls. From the look of them he certainly hadn't agreed with his mother about the over-exposure of bosoms. They're not decent, decided Mary Jane, swanning round the room in the arms of someone called Matt, who talked of nothing but horses.

Mrs Bennett had drawn the line at a disco. It was her party, she had pointed out; the young ones could go somewhere and dance their kind of dancing whenever they liked; in her house they would foxtrot and waltz or not dance at all. The band was just striking up a nice old-fashioned waltz when Sir Thomas whisked Mary Jane away from an elderly gentleman who was on the point of asking her to dance with him.

'I was going to dance with that gentleman,' she pointed out tartly.

'Yes, I know, but he's a shocking dancer; your feet would have been black and blue.' He was going round the edge of the big room. 'Are you enjoying yourself?'

'Yes, very much, thank you. I—I was a bit doubtful at first, I mean, I don't know anyone, but Mrs Bennett has been so kind. She's coming to see me one day after Christmas so that we can talk about my mother and father. Uncle Matthew didn't talk to us much, you know; I dare say he didn't like children, although he was a very kind man.'

The music stopped but he didn't let her go and when it started again he went on dancing with her. She was a little flushed now, but her pale brown hair, pinned in its heavy coil, was as neat as when she had arrived and her small person, so demurely clad, was light in his arms.

He waltzed her expertly through an open door and into a small room, where a fire was burning and chairs grouped invitingly.

He sat her down by a small table with an inviting display of tasty bits and pieces in little dishes and a bottle of white wine in a cooler. 'Spare me five minutes of your time and tell me how you are.'

'I'm very well thank you, Sir Thomas.' She popped an olive into her mouth—she had had a sketchy lunch and almost no tea and the buffet supper was still an hour or so away.

'Busy?' He poured wine into two glasses. 'I suppose you will be going to Felicity's for Christmas?' His tone was casual though he watched her carefully from under his lids.

'Christmas.' Mary Jane stalled for a time while she thought up a good fib. 'Oh, yes, of course; I always go each year. It's great fun.'

He didn't believe her but nothing in his calm face showed that.

'How do you go?' he wanted to know, still casual.

'Oh, Felicity fetches me,' said Mary Jane, piling fib upon fib. She hadn't looked at him but had busied herself sampling the potato straws. She flashed him a brief smile. 'I expect you go to Mrs Latimer's?'

'Or she comes to stay with me with various other members of the family.'

He handed her a dish of little biscuits and she selected one carefully.

'I'm glad to see you looking so well.' Sir Thomas handed her her glass. 'Let us drink to your continued good health.'

The wine was delicious and very cold. 'And you,' said Mary Jane. 'I hope you have a very happy Christmas and don't have to work. I don't suppose you do, anyhow.'

'You suppose wrongly. People break arms and legs and fracture their skulls every day of the year, you know.'

'Well, yes, of course they do but surely you're too important...' She stopped because he was smiling.

'Not a bit of it; if I'm needed to operate or be consulted then I'm available.'

'Do you ever go to other countries?'

'Frequently.'

She had polished off the potato straws and most of the olives.

'May I have the supper dance?' asked Sir Thomas.

'Will that be soon? I'm awfully hungry...'

He glanced at his watch. 'Half an hour; that will soon pass if you are dancing.'

They went back to the drawing-room and he handed her over quite cheerfully to the horsey Matt, who danced her briskly round the room and gave her a detailed account of his last point-to-point. It was a relief when the music stopped and she was claimed by a tall young man with a melancholy face who had no idea how to dance but shambled round while he told her, in gruesome detail, about his anatomy classes. He was a medical student in his third year and anxious to impress her. 'I saw you dancing with Sir Thomas—do you know him?'

'We're acquainted.'

'He's great—you've no idea—to see him fit a prosthesis...'

'Yes, he seems well-known,' said Mary Jane quickly, anxious to avoid the details.

'Well-known? He's famous!' He trod on her foot and she hoped that he hadn't laddered her stockings or ruined her shoe. 'There's no one who can hold a candle to him. I watched him do a spinal graft last week...' He embarked on the details—every single drop of blood and splinter of bone. Sir Thomas, guiding his hostess round the floor, saw Mary Jane's face and grinned to himself.

The supper dance came next and he went to find her, still listening politely to her companion's description of the instruments needed for the grisly business. Sir Thomas put a large hand on her arm and nodded affably at the young man. 'Our dance, Mary Jane?' he said and led her away.

'It seems you're quite famous,' she observed, her small nose buried in his white shirt-front. 'You never talk about it.'

He said, seriously, 'I don't think I've ever met anyone who would want to hear.'

'How dreadful for you, having to keep it all to yourself.'

'Indeed it is at times but most of my companions

wouldn't wish to hear about anything to do with hospitals or patients.'

'No? Well, I wouldn't mind. I'm sure it couldn't be worse than that boy's description of a meni—mensis…'

'Meniscectomy—the removal of the cartilage of the knee. An operation performed with considerable success and not in the least dramatic.'

He smiled down at her. 'Next time I feel the urge to unburden myself I shall come and see you, Mary Jane.'

She didn't think that he was serious but she said cheerfully, 'You do—I'm not in the least squeamish.'

They went in to supper then, sharing a table with at least half a dozen other guests, eating lobster patties, tiny sausages, cheesey morsels and little squares of toast spread with pâtés and dainty trifles which left Mary Jane feeling hungry still. She drank two glasses of wine, though, and her eyes became an even deeper violet. She would have accepted a third glass of wine if Sir Thomas hadn't pulled her gently to her feet.

'A little exercise?' he suggested suavely, and danced her round the room in a leisurely manner, and when the music stopped took her to where his mother was sitting talking to Mrs Bennett.

'There you are, my dears.' Mrs Latimer beamed at them both. 'Thomas, go away and dance with some of the lovely girls here, I want to talk to Mary Jane.' She realised what she had said, and added, 'I put that very badly, didn't I? Mary Jane is lovely, too.'

Mary Jane smiled a little and sat down and didn't watch Sir Thomas as he went away. It was kind of Mrs Latimer to call her lovely, although it was quite untrue. It would have been nice if Sir Thomas had told her that but of course he never would; she had no illusions as to her mediocre face.

Presently, she was whisked away to dance once more—never mind her lack of looks, she danced well and the men had been quick to see that. She didn't lack partners and she was still full of energy when someone announced the last waltz and she found Sir Thomas beside her.

'I'll take you back,' he told her. 'Will you explain to the people who brought you?'

'Won't they mind?'

'I don't suppose so.' He was holding her very correctly, looking over her head with the air of a man who wasn't very interested in what he was doing. Most of the other couples were dancing very close together in a very romantic fashion but of course, she told herself, there was nothing about her to inspire romance. Perhaps he was wishing it was Felicity in his arms. He'd be holding her a lot tighter...!

She thanked him as the dance ended and after a few minutes of goodbyes went off to fetch her coat. It stood out like a sore thumb among the elegant shawls and cloaks in the hall and she wondered if he was ashamed of her and dismissed the thought as unworthy of him. His place was so sure in society that he had no need to worry about such things.

Mrs Latimer kissed her goodbye. 'We must see you again soon, Mary Jane,' a wish echoed by Mrs Bennett. 'We shall all be busy with Christmas,' she added, 'but in the New Year you must come and spend the day.'

Mary Jane thanked them both and got into the car and sat quietly as Sir Thomas drove away.

Clear of the village, he slowed the car. 'A pleasant

evening,' he observed. 'Do you go to many parties at this time of year?'

She couldn't remember when she had last attended a party—the church social evening, of course, and the Misses Potters' evening—parsnip wine and ginger nuts—but they were hardly parties.

'No.' She sought for some light-hearted remark to make and couldn't think of any.

He didn't seem to notice her reticence but began to talk about their evening, a casual rambling talk which needed very little reply.

It was profoundly dark when he drew up before her cottage. He said, 'Stay where you are, and give me the key,' and went and opened the door before coming back for her. At the door he said, 'Hot buttered toast and tea would be nice…'

She turned a startled face to his. 'It's half-past two in the morning.' She smiled suddenly. 'Come in, you can make the toast while I put the kettle on.'

They had it in the kitchen, with Brimble, refreshed by a sleep, sitting between them.

'You don't have to go back to London, do you?' asked Mary Jane.

'No, I'm spending the rest of the night at my mother's. I must be back in town by Monday morning, though. And you?'

'Me? Oh, I'm not doing anything. The tea-room will be open, of course, but there won't be many customers.'

'That will give you time to get ready for your trip to London,' he observed smoothly.

She agreed rather too quickly.

He bade her goodnight presently, bending to kiss her cheek with a casual friendliness. 'I dare say we shall

see each other again,' and when she looked puzzled,
'At Felicity's.'

She wished then that she could tell him that she
would not be there, that she had allowed him to suppose that she would be with her sister, but somehow she
couldn't think of the right words. He had gone before
she had conjured up another fib.

She had rather more customers than she had hoped
for in the last weeks before Christmas and the mice sold
well; she began to cherish the hope that she might go to
the January sales and look for a coat. The Misses Potter
had invited her for Christmas dinner as they had done
for several years now and the church bazaar gave her the
opportunity to bake some little cakes for Miss Kemble's
stall. And on Christmas Eve the postman handed in a
big cardboard box from Harrods. It contained caviar, a
variety of pâtés, a tin of ham, a small Christmas pudding and a box of crackers, chocolates and a half-bottle
of claret. The slip of paper with it contained a message
from Felicity; she knew that Mary Jane would have a
lovely Christmas, she herself was up to her ears in parties and there was a wonderful modelling job waiting
for her in Switzerland in the New Year. There was a PS
'Saw Thomas yesterday'.

Which was to be expected, reflected Mary Jane,
shaking off a sudden sadness.

She went to church at midnight on Christmas Eve
and lingered afterwards exchanging greetings with everyone there and then went back to the cottage to drink
hot cocoa and go to bed with Brimble heavy on her feet.
She wasn't sorry for herself, she told herself stoutly;
several people had given her small gifts and she was
going to spend the day with the Misses Potters'. She

wondered what Sir Thomas was doing, probably with Felicity… She fell into a troubled sleep which would have been less troubled had she known that he was bent over the operating table, carefully pinning and plating the legs of a young man who had, under the influence of the Christmas spirit, jumped out of a window on to a concrete pavement.

She took the wine, the crackers and the chocolates with her when she went to the Misses Potter. Brimble she had left snug in his basket, a saucer of his favourite food beside him. Her elderly friends liked her to stay for tea and by the time she had washed the delicate china they used on special occasions, it would be evening. She had put a little Christmas tree in the cottage window and switched on the lights before she left; it would be welcoming when she went home.

Miss Emily had roasted a capon and Miss Mabel had set the table in the small dining-room with a lace-edged cloth, the remnants of the family silver and china and wine glasses and had lighted a branched candlestick. Mary Jane wished them a happy Christmas, kissed their elderly cheeks and handed over the wine.

'Crackers,' declared Miss Emily. 'How delightful, my dear, and chocolates—Bendick's—the very best, too. Let us have a small glass of sherry before lunch.'

It had been a very pleasant day, thought Mary Jane, letting herself into the cottage. Tomorrow she would go for a good walk in the morning and then have a lazy afternoon reading by the fire.

It was raining in the morning and not a soul stirred in the village street. 'It'll be better out than in,' she told Brimble and got into her wellies, her elderly raincoat and tied a scarf over her hair, crammed her hands into woolly gloves and then set out. She took the country road to Icomb, past the old fort, on to Wick Rissington and then she turned for home, very wet and, despite her brisk walking, rather cold.

It was a relief to reach the path at the side of the church, a short cut which would bring her into the main street, opposite the tea-room. She nipped down it smartly and came to a sudden halt. The Rolls was standing before her door and Sir Thomas, apparently impervious to the wind and rain, was leaning against its bonnet, the faithful Watson beside him.

His, 'Good afternoon, Mary Jane,' was austere and she had the suspicion that he was concealing ill-humour behind his bland face. It was just bad luck that he should turn up; she was, after all, supposed to be in London, enjoying the high life with Felicity.

She stood in front of him, feeling at a disadvantage; she was wet and bedraggled and the sodden scarf did nothing for her looks.

'Hello, Sir Thomas—how unexpected…'

He took the key from her and opened the door and stood aside to let her enter before following her in. Watson shook himself thankfully and went straight through to the kitchen and Sir Thomas, without asking, took off his coat.

'I expect you'd like a cup of tea,' said Mary Jane, wringing out her headscarf over the sink and kicking off her wellies.

'I expect I would.' He took her raincoat from her and hung it on the hook behind the back door and she went to put on the kettle. It was a little unnerving, she reflected, being confronted like this; she would have to think something up.

She wasn't given the time. 'Well,' said Sir Thomas, 'perhaps you will explain.'

'Explain what?' She busied herself with cups and saucers, wondering if a few more fibs would help the situation. Apparently not.

'Why you are here alone when you should be with Felicity in London.'

'Well…' She spooned tea into the pot and couldn't think of anything to say.

'You told me that you were staying with your sister, and yet I find you here.'

'Yes, well,' began Mary Jane and was halted by his impatient response.

'For heaven's sake stop saying "Yes, well"—forget the nonsense and tell me the truth for once.'

She banged the teapot on to the table. 'I always tell you the truth…' She caught his cold stare. 'Well, almost always…'

She sat down opposite him and poured out their tea, handed him a plate of scones and offered Watson a biscuit as Brimble jumped on to her lap.

She decided to take the war into the enemies' camp. 'Why aren't you in London?'

His stern mouth twitched. 'I spent most of Christmas Day with my mother and I'm on my way back to town.'

'You're going the wrong way.'

'Don't be pert. I am well aware which way I am travelling. And now, Mary Jane, since you are unable to string two sentences together, perhaps you will answer my questions.'

'I don't see why I should…'

He ignored this. 'Did Felicity invite you to go to London for Christmas?'

'It's none of your business.' She gave him a defiant look and saw that he had become Sir Thomas Latimer, calm and impersonal and quite sure that he would be answered when he asked a question. She said in a small voice, 'Well, no.' She added idiotically, 'I expect she forgot—you know, she has so many friends and she leads a busy life.'

'Did you not hear from her at all?'

'Oh, yes. She sent me a hamper from Harrods. I don't expect that I would like to go to London anyway, I haven't the right clothes and her friends are awfully clever and witty and I'm not.'

'So why did you lie to me?'

'Well…'

'If you say well just once more, I shall shake you,' he observed pleasantly. 'Tell me, have you ever been to stay with Felicity?'

'W… Actually, no.'

'So why did you lie to me?'

'They were fibs,' she told him sharply. 'Lies hurt people but fibs are useful when you don't want—to interfere or make people feel that they have to help you if you're getting in the way.' She added anxiously, 'Have I made that clear?'

'Oh, yes, in a muddled way. Tell me, Mary Jane, why should you not wish me to know that you would be staying here on your own for Christmas?'

'I have just told you.'

'You think that I have fallen in love with Felicity?'

She looked at him then. 'Everyone falls in love with her, she's so beautiful and she is fun to be with and so successful. Whenever she sends me a card she mentions you so you must know her quite well by now. So you must…yes, I think you must love her.'

She wasn't sure if she liked his smile. 'Would you like me for a brother-in-law, Mary Jane?'

She wondered about the smile; she wouldn't like him for a brother-in-law; she would like him for a husband, and why should she suddenly discover that now of all times, sitting opposite him, being cross-examined as though she were in a witness-box and fighting a great wish to nip round the table and fling her arms round his neck and tell him that she loved him? She would have to say something, for he was watching her.

'Yes, oh, yes, that would be delightful.' She bent to pat Watson so that he shouldn't see her face and was surprised and relieved when Sir Thomas got up.

'Well, I must be off.' He added smoothly, 'Shall I give your love to Felicity when I see her?'

'Yes, please.' She went to the door with him and she held out her hand. 'Drive carefully,' she told him. 'Goodbye, Sir Thomas.'

His hand on the door, he paused. 'There is something you should know. Falling in love and loving are two quite different things. Goodbye.'

He drove away, Watson sitting beside him, and she went back to the kitchen and began to tidy up. She told herself that it was extremely silly to cry for no reason at all, but she went on weeping and Brimble, wanting his supper and jumping on to her lap to remind her of that, got a shockingly damp coat.

Presently she dried her eyes. 'Well—no, I mustn't say well; what I mean to say is I shall forget this afternoon and take care not to see Sir Thomas again unless I simply must.'

Brimble, drying his fur, agreed.

It was difficult, though, the tea-shop was open, but for several days no one came to drink the coffee or eat the scones she had ready, she filled her days with odd jobs around the cottage, turning out cupboards and drawers with tremendous zeal, making plans for the year ahead; perhaps she should branch out a bit—do hot lunches? But supposing no one ate them? She couldn't afford to waste uneaten meals and her freezer was too small to house more than bare necessities. Felicity, on one of her flying visits, had suggested, half laughingly, that she should sell the cottage and train for something. Mary Jane had asked what and she had said, carelessly, 'Oh, I don't know—something domestic—children's nurse or something worthy—a dietician at a hospital or a social worker, at least you would meet some people. This village is dead or hadn't you noticed?'

Mary Jane recalled the conversation clearly enough now and gave it her serious consideration, deciding that she didn't want to be any of the people Felicity had suggested and, moreover, that the village wasn't dead. Quiet, yes, but at least everyone knew everyone else…

It was the last day of December when Mrs Bennett came. She trotted in, her good natured face wreathed in smiles. 'I'm so glad I found you at home,' she declared, 'and I do so hope you are not doing anything exciting this evening, for I've come to take you back with me— to see the New Year in, my dear.'

She sat herself down and Mary Jane sat down on

the other side of the table. 'How very kind of you, Mrs Bennett, but you see it's a bit difficult—there's Brimble and I'd have to come home again...'

Mrs Bennett brushed this aside. 'Put on the coffee-pot, my dear, and we'll put our heads together.' She unbuttoned her coat and settled back in her chair. 'Someone will come over for you at about half-past seven and we'll dine at half-past eight, and I promise you that directly after midnight someone shall bring you back here. There won't be many people, just a few close friends and the family.' She added firmly, 'You can't possibly stay here by yourself, Mary Jane.' She glanced around. 'Your sister isn't here?'

Mary Jane brought the coffee and passed the sugar and milk. 'No, I'm not sure if she is in England—she travels all over the place, you know.'

'So, that settles it,' said Mrs Bennett comfortably. 'Wear that pretty dress you had on at the party, I dare say we shall all be feeling festive, and please don't disappoint me, my dear.'

'I'd love to come, Mrs Bennett, if it's not being too much of a bother collecting me and bringing me back. You're sure the grey dress will do?'

'Quite positive. Now I must be off home and make sure that everything is ready for this evening.'

Mary Jane wasted no time; the contents of a cupboard she had intended to turn out were ruthlessly returned higgledy-piggledy before she set about making her person fit for the evening's entertainment. Her hair washed and hanging still damp down her back, she studied her face, looking for spots. There were none, she had a lovely skin which needed little make-up which was a good thing for she couldn't have afforded it anyway. Her hands needed attention, too…

She was ready long before she needed to be, her hair shining, her small nose powdered, sitting by the little fire with her skirts carefully spread out and Brimble perched carefully on her silken knee. A cheerful tattoo on the door sent her downstairs to open the door to discover that the same family who had taken her to the dance were calling for her. They greeted her with a good deal of friendly noise, waited while she fetched her coat and bade Brimble goodbye and wedged her on to the back seat between the two girls and drove off all talking at once. Such fun, she was told, just a few of us, nothing like the Christmas party but Mrs Bennett always has a splendid meal and lashings of drinks.

They sat down sixteen to dinner and Mary Jane found herself between two faces she recognised, the horsey Matt, who it seemed was a nephew of Mrs Bennett's and the medical student, both of whom were in a festive mood and didn't lack for conversation. Dinner lasted a very long time and by the time they had had coffee it was getting on for eleven o'clock and more people were arriving. Mary Jane, listening to an elderly man with a very red face explaining the benefits of exactly the right mulch for roses, allowed her eyes to rove discreetly. It was silly, but she had hoped that perhaps Sir Thomas would be there…but he wasn't.

She was wrong. Calm and immaculate in his dinner-jacket, he arrived with five minutes to spare, just in nice time to take the glass of champagne he was offered and thread his way through the other guests to stand beside her.

Chapter 7

Mary Jane saw him coming, and delight at seeing him again swamped every other feeling. She could feel herself going pale, as indeed she was, and her heart thumped so strongly that she trembled so that the glass she was holding wobbled alarmingly. He reached her side, took the glass from her and wished her good evening, adding, 'Did you think that I would not be here?'

He was smiling down at her and she only stopped herself just in time from telling him how wonderful it was to see him. She said instead, 'Well, it's a long way from London and I dare say you've been busy with your patients and—and had lots of invitations to spend the evening there.'

'Oh, yes, indeed, but I wished to spend the evening with my mother—she came over with me.'

She followed her train of thought. 'Isn't Felicity in London?'

He was still smiling but his eyes were cold. 'Yes, she sent you her love.' He might have added that she had wanted him to take her to a party at one of the big hotels and he had made the excuse that he was going to his mother's home. She had said sharply, 'How dull for you, Thomas. I don't suppose you'll see Mary Jane, but if you do or if you meet anyone who knows her send my love, will you?'

Mary Jane said in a wooden voice, 'It's a pity she isn't here…' She was unable to finish for there was a sudden hush as Big Ben began to strike the hour. At its last stroke there were cries of 'Happy New Year!' as the champagne corks were popped and everyone started kissing everyone else. Mary Jane looked at the bland face beside her and said, meaning every word, 'I hope you have a very happy New Year, Sir Thomas.'

He smiled suddenly. 'I hope that we both shall, Mary Jane.' He bent and kissed her, a swift, hard kiss as unlike a conventional social peck as chalk from cheese. It took her breath but before she could get it back Matt had caught her by the hand and whirled her away to be kissed breathless by all the men there. She disentangled herself, laughing, and found Mrs Latimer standing close by.

'My dear, a happy New Year,' said Sir Thomas's mother, 'and how nice to see you enjoying yourself. You lead far too quiet a life.'

Mary Jane wished her a happy New Year in her turn. 'I've just been talking to Sir Thomas.' She blushed brightly, remembering his kiss, and Mrs Latimer just hid a smile.

'He drove down earlier this evening, and he will go

back early tomorrow morning—he had made up his mind to be here.'

'He shouldn't work so hard,' said Mary Jane, and blushed again, much to her annoyance. 'What I mean is, he must get so tired.' She added, 'It's none of my business, please forgive me.'

'You're quite right,' observed Mrs Latimer. 'His work is his whole life although I think, when he marries, his wife and children will always come first.'

The very thought hurt; Mary Jane murmured suitably and said that she would have to find her hostess. 'Mrs Bennett kindly said that someone would drive me back as soon after midnight as possible.' She wished her companion goodbye and found Mrs Bennett at the far end of the room talking to Sir Thomas. As Mary Jane got within hearing, she said, 'There you are, my dear. What a pity that you must go but I quite understand…was it fun?'

'I've had a marvellous evening, Mrs Bennett, and thank you very much. I'll get my coat. Shall I wait in the hall and would it be all right if you said goodbye to everyone for me?'

'Of course, child. Sir Thomas is taking you home.'

'Oh, but Mrs Latimer is here, he'll—that is, you will have to come back for her.' She looked at him and found him smiling.

'The Elliots are driving her back presently.' He spoke placidly but she couldn't very well argue with him. She fetched her coat and got into the Rolls without speaking, only when they were away from the house and out of the village she said, 'I'm sorry to break up your evening.'

He said coolly, 'Not at all, Mary Jane, I had no intention of staying and it is only a slight detour to drop you off before I go back.'

A damping remark which she found difficult to answer but when the silence got too long she tried again. 'Did you bring Watson with you?'

'No—I'm only away for the night and I'll be back to take him for his run tomorrow before I go to my rooms. Tremble will look after him.'

'Won't you be tired?' She added hastily, 'I don't mean to be nosy.'

'I appreciate your concern. I'm not operating tomorrow and I have only a handful of private patients to see later in the day.'

The conversation, she felt, was hardly scintillating. The silence lasted rather longer this time. Presently she ventured, 'It was a very nice party, wasn't it?'

He said mildly, 'Do stop making light conversation, Mary Jane…'

'With pleasure,' she snapped. 'There is nothing more—more boring than trying to be polite to someone who has no idea of the social niceties.' She paused to draw an indignant breath, rather pleased with the remark, and then doubtful as to whether she had been rather too outspoken. His low laugh gave her no clue. She turned her head away to look out at the dark nothingness outside. Where was her good sense, she thought wildly; how could she have fallen in love with this taciturn man who had no more interest in her than he might have in a row of pins? She would forget him the moment she could get into her cottage and shut the door on him.

He drew up gently before her small front door, took the key from her hand and got out and opened it before coming back to open the door of the car for her.

Switching on the tea-room lights, he remarked, 'A cup of tea would be nice.'

'No, it wouldn't,' said Mary Jane flatly. 'Thank you for bringing me home, although I wish you hadn't.' She put a hand on the door, encouraging him to leave, a useless gesture since the door wasn't over-sturdy and his vast person was as unyielding as a tree trunk.

He laughed suddenly. 'Why do you laugh?' she asked sharply.

'If I told you you wouldn't believe me. Tell me, Mary Jane, why did you wish that I hadn't brought you home?'

She said soberly, 'I can't tell you that.' She held out a hand. 'I'm sorry if I've been rude.'

He took her hand between his. 'Goodnight, Mary Jane.' His smile was so kind that she could have wept.

He went out to his car and got in and drove away and she locked up and turned off the lights, gave Brimble an extra supper and took herself off to bed. It was another year, she thought, lying in bed, warmed by the hot water bottle and Brimble's small body. She wondered what it might bring.

It brought, surprisingly, Felicity, sitting beside a rather plump young man with bags under his eyes in a Mercedes. Felicity flung open the tea-shop door with a flourish. 'I just had to wish you a happy New Year,' she cried, and then paused to look around her. The little place was empty except for Mary Jane, who was on her knees hammering down a strip of torn lino by the counter. She got to her feet and turned round and the young man, who had followed Felicity said, 'Good lord, is this your sister, darling?'

Mary Jane eyed him; this was not the beginning of

a beautiful friendship, she reflected, but all the same she wished him good morning politely and kissed her sister's cheek. 'I'm spring cleaning,' she explained.

Felicity tossed off the cashmere wrap she had flung over her *haute couture* suit. 'Darling, how awful for you, isn't there a char or someone in this dump to do it for you?'

There didn't seem much point in answering that. 'Would you like a cup of coffee?' She waved at two chairs upended on to one of the tables. 'If you'd like to sit down it won't take long.'

Felicity said carelessly, 'This is Monty.' She went over to the table. 'Well, darling, give me a chair to sit on…'

Mary Jane thought that he didn't look capable of lifting a cup of tea let alone a chair and certainly he did it unwillingly. She went into the kitchen and collected cups and saucers while the coffee brewed and presently she went back to ask. 'Are you going somewhere or just driving round?'

'Riding round. It's very flat in town after New Year and I've no bookings until next week. Then it will be Spain, thank heaven. I need the sun and the warmth.'

Mary Jane let that pass, poured the coffee and took the tray across to the table and poured it for the three of them, rather puzzled as to why Felicity had come. She didn't have to wonder for long. 'Have you seen anything of Thomas?' asked Felicity. 'Well, I don't suppose you have but you may have heard something of him—after all, his mother doesn't live so far away, does she? She made a great fuss of you when you had the flu.'

She didn't wait for an answer, which was a good

thing. 'I see quite a lot of him in town; I must say he's marvellous to go around with…'

'I say, steady on,' said Monty. 'I'm here, you know.'

Felicity gurgled with laughter. 'Of course you are, darling, and you're such fun.' She leaned across the table and patted his arm. 'But I do have my future to think of—a nice steady husband who adores me and can keep me in the style I've set my heart on…'

'You said you loved me,' complained Monty, and Mary Jane wondered if they had forgotten that she was there, sitting between them.

'Of course I do, Monty—marrying some well-heeled eminent surgeon won't make any difference to that.'

Mary Jane went into the kitchen. Felicity must be talking about Sir Thomas. If Felicity had been alone she might have talked to her about him and discovered if she were joking; her sister was selfish and uncaring of anyone but herself but there was affection between them; she could at least have discovered if she loved Sir Thomas. But the presence of Monty precluded that. She went back into the tea-room and found Felicity arranging the cashmere stole. 'Well, we're off, darling—lunch at that nice restaurant in Oxford, and then home to the bright lights.' She kissed Mary Jane. 'I'll send you a card from sunny Spain. I must try to see Thomas, I'm sure he could do with a day or two in the sun.'

Monty shook Mary Jane's hand. 'I would never have guessed that you two were sisters.' He shook his head. 'I mean to say…' He had a limp handshake.

Mary Jane put the 'Closed' sign on the door and went back to knocking in nails. Thoughts, most of them unhappy as well as angry, raced round her head. Surely, she told herself, Sir Thomas wasn't foolish enough to fall in love with Felicity, but of course if he really loved her—hadn't he said that loving and being in love were two different things? She forced herself to stop thinking about him.

After a few days customers began to trickle in; the Misses Potter came as usual for their tea and several ladies from the village popped in on their way to or from the January sales; life returned to its normal routine. Mary Jane sternly suppressed the thought of Sir Thomas, not altogether successfully, when a card from Felicity came. She had written on the back, 'Gorgeous weather, here for another week. Pity he has to return on Saturday. Be good. Felicity'.

Mary Jane ignored the last few words, she had no other choice but to be good, but, reading the rest of the scrawled words, she frowned. Felicity had hinted that she would see Sir Thomas and persuade him to go to Spain with her. It looked as though she had succeeded.

'I suppose the cleverer you are the sillier you get,' said Mary Jane in such a venomous tone that Brimble laid back his ears.

She was setting out the coffee-cups on Saturday morning when the first of the motorcyclists stopped before her door. He was joined by two others and the three of them came into the tea-room. Young men, encased in black leather and talking noisily. They took off their helmets and flung them down on one of the tables, pulled out chairs and sat down. They weren't local men and they stared at her until she felt uneasy.

'Coffee?' she asked. 'And anything to eat?'

'Coffee'll do, darlin', and a plate of whatever there is.' He laughed. 'And not much of that in this hole.' The other two laughed with him and she went into the kitchen to pour the coffee. Before doing so she picked up Brimble and popped him on the stairs and shut the door on him. She wasn't sure why she had done it; she wasn't a timid girl and the men would drink the coffee and go. She put the coffee on the table, then fetched a plate of scones and went back to the kitchen where she had been making pastry for the sausage rolls. She could see them from where she stood at the kitchen table and they seemed quiet enough, their heads close together, talking softly and sniggering. Presently they called for more coffee and ten minutes later they scraped back their chairs and put on their helmets. She took the bill over with an inward sigh of relief, but instead of taking it, the man she offered it to caught her hand and held it fast. 'Expect us to pay for that slop?' he wanted to know.

'Yes,' said Mary Jane calmly. 'I do, and please leave go of my hand.'

'Got a tongue in 'er 'ead, too. An' what'll you do if we don't pay up, Miss High and Mighty?'

'You will pay up. You asked for coffee and scones and I gave you them, so now you'll pay for what you've had.'

'Cor—got a sharp tongue, too, 'asn't she?' He tightened his grip. '"Ave ter teach 'er a lesson, won't we, boys?'

They swept the cups and saucers, the coffee-pot and the empty plates on to the floor and one of them went around treading on the bits of china, crushing them to fragments. The chairs went next, hurled across the room and then the tables. The little vases of dried flowers they threw at walls and all this was done without a word.

She was frightened but she was furiously angry too, she lifted a foot, laced into a sensible shoe, and kicked

the man holding her hand. It couldn't have hurt much
through all that leather, but it took him by surprise. He
wrenched her round with a bellow of rage.

'Why, you little…'

Sir Thomas, on his way to spend a weekend with
his mother and at the same time call upon Mary Jane,
slowed the car as the tea-room came into view and then
stopped at the sight of the motorbikes. He got out, saw
the anxious elderly faces peering from the cottages on
either side of Mary Jane's home, crossed the narrow
pavement in one stride and threw open her door. A man
who kept his feelings well under control, he allowed
them free rein at the sight of her white face…

Mary Jane wished very much to faint on to a comfortable sofa, but she sidled to the remains of the counter
and hung on to it. This was no time to faint; Sir Thomas
had his hands full and apparently he was enjoying it,
too. The little room seemed full of waving arms and
legs. The man who had been holding her was tripped
up neatly by one of Sir Thomas's elegantly shod feet
and landed with a crash into the debris of tables and
chairs which left Sir Thomas free to deal with the two
other men. Subdued and scared by this large, silent man
who knocked them around like ninepins, they huddled
in a corner by their fallen comrade, only anxious to be
left alone.

'Any one of you move and I'll break every bone in
his body,' observed Sir Thomas in the mildest of voices,
and turned his attention to Mary Jane.

His arm was large and comforting and as steady as
a rock. 'Don't, whatever you do, faint,' he begged her,
'for there's nowhere for you to lie down.' Nothing in

his kind, impersonal voice and his equally impersonal arm hinted at his great wish to pick her up and drive off with her and never let her go again. 'The police will be along presently; someone must have seen that something was wrong and warned them.' He looked down at the top of her head. 'I'll get a chair from the kitchen…'

She was dimly aware of someone coming to the door then, old Rob from his cottage by the church, where he lived with his two sons. 'The Coats lad came running to tell something was amiss. The police is coming and my two boys'll be along in a couple of shakes.' He cast an eye over the three men huddled together. 'Varmints!' He turned a shrewd eye upon Sir Thomas. 'Knock 'em out, did yer? Nice bit of work, I'd say.'

The police, Rob's two sons and the rector arrived together. Not that Mary Jane cared. Let them all come, she reflected; a cup of tea and her bed was all she wanted. The bed was out of the question, but the rector, a meek and kindly man, made tea which she drank with chattering teeth, spilling a good deal of it, thankful that Sir Thomas was dealing with the police so that she needed to answer only essential questions before they marched the three men away to the waiting van. 'You'll need to come to the station on Tuesday morning, miss,' the senior office said. 'Nine o'clock suit you? Have you got a car?'

'I'll bring Miss Seymour, Officer,' said Sir Thomas and he nodded an affable goodbye and turned to old Rob. 'Will you wait while I see Mary Jane up to her bed?'

'I do not want…' began Mary Jane pettishly, not knowing what she was wanting.

'No, of course you don't.' Sir Thomas's voice was

soothing. 'But in half an hour or so when you have got over the nasty shock you had, you will think clearly again. Besides, I want to have a look at that wrist.'

She went upstairs, urged on by a firm hand on her back, and found Brimble waiting anxiously on the tiny landing. The sight of his small furry face was too much; she burst into tears, sobbing and sniffing and grizzling into Sir Thomas's shoulder. He waited patiently until the sobs petered out, offered a handkerchief, observing that there was nothing like a good cry and at the same time tossing back the quilt on her bed.

'Half an hour,' he told her, tucking it around her and lifting Brimble on to the bed. 'I'll be back.'

Downstairs, he found old Rob and his sons waiting. 'Ah, yes, I wonder if I might have your help...?' He talked for a few minutes and when old Rob nodded, money changed hands and they bade him goodbye and went off down the village street. Sir Thomas watched them go and then went to let the patient Watson out of the car and get his bag, let himself into the tea-room again and go soft-footed upstairs with Watson hard on his heels.

Mary Jane had fallen asleep, her hair all over the place, her mouth slightly open. She had a little colour now and her nose was pink from crying. Sir Thomas studied her lovingly and then turned his attention to her hand lying outside the quilt. The wrist was discoloured and a little swollen. The man's grasp must have been brutal. He suppressed the wave of rage which shook him and sat down to wait for her to wake up.

Which she did presently, the long lashes sweeping up to reveal the glorious eyes. Sir Thomas spent a few seconds admiring them. 'Better now? I'd like to take a look at that wrist. Does it hurt?'

'Yes.' She sat up in bed and dragged the quilt away. 'But I'm perfectly all right now. Thank you very much for helping me. I mustn't keep you…'

He was holding her hand, examining her wrist. 'This is quite nasty. I'll put a crêpe bandage on for the time being and we'll see about it later. Can you manage to pack a bag with a few things? I'm taking you to stay with my mother for a few days.'

She sat up very straight. 'I can't possibly, there's such a lot to do here, I must get someone to help me clear up and I must see about tables and chairs and cups and saucers and…' She paused, struck by the thought that she had no money to buy these essentials and yet she would have to have them, they were her very livelihood. She would have to borrow, but from whom? Oliver? Certainly not Oliver. Felicity? She might offer to help if she knew about it.

Sir Thomas, watching her, guessed her thoughts and said bracingly, 'There is really nothing you can do for a day or two.' He added vaguely, 'The police, you know. Far better to spend a little time making up your mind what is to be done first.'

'But your mother…'

'She will be delighted to see you again.' He got up and reached down the case on the top of the wardrobe. 'Is Brimble's basket downstairs? I'll get it while you pack—just enough for a week will do. Do you want to leave any messages with anyone? What about the milk and so on?'

'Mrs Adams next door will tell him not to call, and there's food in the fridge…'

'Leave it to me.'

She changed into her suit, packed the jersey dress, undies and a dressing-gown, her few cosmetics, then she did her hair in a perfunctory fashion and found scarf and gloves, out-of-date black court shoes, well-polished, and she burrowed in the back of a drawer and got the few pounds she kept for an emergency. By then, Sir Thomas was calling up the stairs to see if she was ready. He came to fetch her case while she picked up Brimble, carried him down to his basket and fastened him in. She was swept through the ruins of the tea-room before she had time to look round her, popped into the car with the animals on the back seat while he went back to lock the door. He came over to the car then. 'I think it might be a good idea to leave the key with Mrs Adams,' he suggested and she agreed readily, her thoughts busy with ways and means.

A tap on the window made her turn her head. The rector was there, so was his sister, Miss Kemble and Mrs Stokes and hurrying up the street was the shop-keeper. Mary Jane opened the window and a stream of sympathy poured in. 'If only we had known,' declared Miss Kemble, 'we could have come to your assistance.'

'But you did, at least the rector did. A cup of tea was exactly what I needed most! It was all a bit of a shock.'

The shopkeeper poked her head round Mrs Stokes's shoulder. 'A proper shame it is,' she declared. 'No one is safe these days. A good thing you've got the doctor here to take you to his mum. You 'ave a good rest, love— the place'll be as good as new again, don't you worry.'

They clustered round Sir Thomas as he came back to the car and after a few minutes' talk he got into his seat, lifted a hand in farewell and drove away. 'I like your rector,' he observed, 'but his sister terrifies me.'

Which struck her as so absurd that she laughed, which was what he had meant her to do.

He didn't allow her to talk about the disastrous morning either but carried on a steady flow of remarks to which, out of politeness, she was obliged to reply. When they arrived at his mother's house, she was met by that lady with sincere pleasure and no mention as to why she had come. 'We've put you in the room you had when you were here,' she was told. 'And have you brought your nice cat with you?'

Mrs Latimer broke off to offer a cheek to her son and receive Watson's pleased greeting. 'Would you like to go up to your room straight away? Lunch will be in ten minutes or so. Come down and have a drink first.'

The house was warm and welcoming and Mrs Beaver, coming into the hall, beamed at her with heartwarming pleasure. It was like coming home, thought Mary Jane, skipping upstairs behind that lady, only of course it wasn't, but it was nice to pretend...

No one mentioned the morning's events at lunch. The talk was of the village, a forthcoming trip Sir Thomas was to make to the Middle East and whether Mrs Latimer should go to London to do some shopping. Somehow they contrived to include Mary Jane in their conversation so that presently she was emboldened to ask, 'Are you going away for a long time?'

'If all goes well, I should be away for a week, perhaps less. I've several good reasons for wanting to get back as soon as possible.'

Was one of them Felicity? wondered Mary Jane, and Mrs Latimer put the thought into words by asking, 'Have you seen anything of that glamorous sister of yours lately, Mary Jane?'

'No. I'm not sure where she is—she was in Spain but I don't know how long she will be there.'

Sir Thomas leaned back in his chair, his eyes on her face. 'Felicity is in London,' he observed casually.

It was quite true, thought Mary Jane, love did hurt, a physical pain which cut her like a knife. Somehow she was going to have to live with it. 'Perhaps you would like to go and see her?' Sir Thomas went on.

She spoke too quickly. 'No, no, there's no need, I mean, she's always so—that is, she works so hard she wouldn't be able to spare the time.'

She had gone rather red in the face and he said blandly, 'I don't suppose she could do much to help you,' and when his mother suggested that they have their coffee in the drawing-room she got up thankfully.

They had had their coffee and were sitting comfortably before the fire when Sir Thomas asked abruptly, 'Have you any money, Mary Jane?'

She was taken by surprise; there was no time to think up a fib and anyway, what would be the point of that? 'Well, no, I mean I have a few pounds—I keep them hidden at the cottage but I've brought them with me and there's about forty pounds in the post office.' She achieved a smile. 'I shall be able to borrow for the tea-room.' She added hastily, 'I'm not sure who yet, but I've friends in the village.'

'Good. As I said, there's nothing to be done for a day or two; besides, I think that wrist should be X-rayed. I'll take you up to town when I go on Monday morning—I'm operating all day but I'll bring you back in the evening. Someone can take you to my house and Mrs Tremble will look after you until I'm ready.'

He smiled at her. 'You are about to argue but I beg you not to; I'm not putting myself out in the least.'

'It only aches a little.'

'You may have got a cracked bone.' He glanced at her bandaged wrist. He asked mildly, 'What had you done to annoy the man?'

'I kicked him.'

'Quite right too,' said Mrs Latimer. 'What a sensible girl you are. I would have done the same. Do you suppose it hurt?'

He went away presently to make some phone calls and Mrs Latimer said cosily, 'Now, my dear, do tell me exactly what happened if you can bear to talk about it. What a brave girl you are. I should never have dared to ask for my money.'

So Mary Jane told her and discovered that talking about it made it seem less awful than she supposed. True, the problem of borrowing money and starting up again was at the moment impossible to solve but as her companion so bracingly remarked, things had a way of turning out better than one might expect. On this optimistic note she bore Mary Jane away to the conservatory at the back of the house to admire two camellias in full bloom.

The three of them had tea round the fire presently and sat talking until Sir Thomas was called to the phone and Mrs Latimer suggested that Mary Jane might like to unpack and then make sure that Mrs Beaver had prepared the right supper for Brimble, who had spent a day after his heart, curled up before the fire. Mary Jane went to her room, bearing him with her; there was some time before dinner and perhaps mother and son would like to be alone. So she stayed there, spending a lot of time before the looking-glass, trying out various hair-styles and then, disheartened by the fact that they didn't improve her looks in the slightest, pinning it in her usual fashion, applied lipstick and powder and, when the gong sounded, went downstairs, leaving Brimble asleep on the bed.

Sir Thomas and his mother were in the drawing-room and he got up at once and invited her to sit down and offered her a drink.

'But the gong's gone...'

He smiled. 'I don't suppose anything will spoil if we dine five minutes later. Did you fall asleep?'

He was making it easy for her and Mrs Latimer said comfortably, 'All that excitement—you must have an early night, my dear.'

They dined presently and Mary Jane discovered that she was hungry. The mushrooms in garlic sauce, beef Wellington and *crème brulée* were delicious and just right—as was the conversation; about nothing much, touching lightly upon any number of subjects and never once on her trying morning. As they got up from the table, Sir Thomas said casually, 'Shall we go for a walk tomorrow, Mary Jane? I enjoy walking at this time of year but perhaps you don't care for it?'

'Oh, but I do.' The prospect of being with him had sent the colour into her cheeks. 'I'd like that very much.'

'Good—after lunch, then. We go to church in the morning—come with us if you would like to.'

'I'd like that, too.'

'Splendid, I've fixed up an appointment for you on

Monday morning—half-past nine—we'll have to leave around seven o'clock. I'm operating at ten o'clock.'

'I get up early. Would someone mind feeding Brimble? He'll be quite good on the balcony.'

'Don't worry about him, my dear.' Mrs Latimer was bending her head over an embroidery frame. 'Mrs Beaver and I will keep an eye on him. Thomas, did you bring any work with you?'

'I'm afraid so—there's a paper I have to read at the next seminar.'

'Then go away and read it or write it, or whatever you need to do. Mary Jane and I are going to have a nice gossip—I want to tell her all about Mrs Bennett's daughter—she's just got engaged…'

The rest of the evening passed pleasantly. Sir Thomas reappeared after an hour or so and shortly afterwards, in the kindest possible manner, suggested that she might like to go to bed. 'Rather a dull evening for you,' he apologised.

'Dull? It was heavenly.' Had he any idea what it was like to spend almost every evening on one's own even if one were making pastry or polishing tables and chairs? Well, of course he hadn't, he would spend his evenings with friends, going to the theatre, dining out and probably seeing as much of Felicity as possible. The sadness of her face at the thought caused him to stare at her thoughtfully. He wanted to ask her why she was sad, but, not liking him enough to answer, she would give him a chilly look from those lovely eyes and murmur something. He still wasn't sure if she liked him, and even if she did, she had erected an invisible barrier between them. He was going to need a great deal of patience.

She hadn't been expected to sleep but she did, to be wakened in the morning by Mrs Beaver with a tray of tea and the news that it was a fine day but very cold. 'Breakfast in half an hour, miss, and take my advice and wear something warm; the church is like an ice-box.'

She had brought her winter coat with her but it wouldn't go over her suit. It would have to be the jersey dress. She dressed under Brimble's watchful eye and went down to breakfast.

That night, curled up in her comfortable bed, she reviewed her day. It had been even better that she had hoped for. The three of them had gone to church and, despite the chill from the ancient building, she had loved every minute of the service, standing between Sir Thomas and his mother, and after lunch she had put on her sensible shoes, tied a scarf over her head and gone with him on the promised walk. It was a pity, she reflected, that they had talked about rather dull matters: politics, the state of the turnip crop on a neighbouring farm, the weather, Watson. She had wanted to talk about Felicity but she hadn't dared and since he hadn't mentioned the tea-room she hadn't liked to say anything about it. After all, he had done a great deal to help her; she was a grown woman, used to being on her own, capable of dealing with things like loans and painting and papering. Women were supposed to be equal to men now, weren't they? She didn't feel equal to Sir Thomas, but she supposed that she would have to do her best. He had been kind and friendly in a detached way but she suspected that she wasn't the kind of girl he would choose for a companion. She would have to go to London with him in the morning to have her wrist X-rayed, although it didn't seem necessary to her, but once she was back here she would go back to her cottage and then she need never see him again. She went to sleep then, feeling sad, and woke in the small hours, suddenly afraid of the future. It would be hard to begin again and it would be even harder never to see Sir Thomas, or worse—if he married Felicity, she would have to see him from time to time. She wouldn't be able to bear that, but of course she would have to. She didn't go to sleep again but lay making plans as to how to open the tea-room as quickly as possible with the least possible expense. She would need a miracle.

Chapter 8

It was still dark when they left the next morning. They had breakfast together, wasting no time and, with Watson drowsing on the back seat, had driven away, with no one but Mrs Beaver to see them off. Until they reached the outskirts of the city there was little traffic and they sat in a companionable silence, making desultory conversation from time to time. Crawling through the London streets, Mary Jane thanked heaven that she lived in the country. How could Felicity bear to live in the midst of all the noise and bustle? She asked abruptly, 'Do you like living in London?'

'My work is here, at least for a good part of the time. I escape whenever I can.'

They were in the heart of the city now and the hospital loomed ahead of them. At its entrance he got out, led her across the entrance hall and down a long tiled passage to the X-ray department, where he handed her over to a nurse.

'I'll see you later at my house,' he told her as he prepared to leave.

'Oh, won't you be here?' She was suddenly uncertain.

'I am going home now, but I shall be back presently. By then you will be taken care of by someone. Then Mrs Tremble is expecting you.'

She wanted to ask more questions, but the nurse was watching them with interest and besides, she could see that he was concealing impatience. She said goodbye and went with the nurse to take off her coat and have the bandage taken off her wrist.

The radiographer was young and friendly and she was surprised to find that he knew how her wrist had been injured. 'Sir Thomas phoned,' he told her airily, 'and of course he had to give me a history of the injury. Said you were a brave young lady. Does it bother you at all?'

'It aches but it doesn't feel broken.'

'There may be a bone cracked, though. Let's get it X-rayed—I'll get the radiologist to take a look at it and let Sir Thomas know as soon as possible.'

That done, he bade her goodbye, handed her over to the nurse to have the bandage put on again and then be taken back to the entrance hall.

There was a short, stout man talking to the porter but as she hesitated he came towards her. 'Miss Seymour, Sir Thomas asked me to drive you to his house. I'm Tremble, his butler.'

She offered a hand. 'Thank you, I'm afraid I'm being a nuisance…'

'Not at all, miss. You just come with me. Mrs Tremble has coffee waiting for you. Sir Thomas asked me to tell you that he may be delayed this evening and he hopes that you will dine with him before he drives you back to Mrs Latimer.'

He had ushered her out to the forecourt and into a Jaguar motor car, and as they drove away she asked, 'Where are we going?'

'To Sir Thomas's home, miss.' He had a nice, fatherly manner. 'Me and my wife look after him, as you might say. Little Venice, that's where he lives, nice and quiet and not too far from the hospital.'

It wasn't the country, she reflected, but it was certainly quiet and even on a winter's day it was pleasant, with the water close by and the well-cared-for houses. Tremble ushered her in, took her coat and opened a door. Watson came to greet her as she went into the room.

She had found Mrs Latimer's house charming but this drawing-room was even more so. There were easychairs drawn up to a blazing fire, a vast sofa between them, covered as they were in a tawny red velvet. A Pembroke table stood behind it and on either wall were mahogany bow-fronted cabinets, filled with porcelain and silverware. At the window facing the street there was a Georgian library table, flanked by two side-chairs of the same period, and here and there, just where they would be needed, were tripod tables, bearing low tablelamps.

'Just you sit down,' said Tremble, 'and I'll bring you your coffee, miss.'

He went away, leaving her to inspect the room at her leisure with Watson pressed close to her, until she sat down in one of the chairs as Tremble came back. 'Sir Thomas said for you to make yourself at home, miss. There's the library across the hall if you should like to go there presently. Mrs Tremble will be along in a few minutes to make sure that what she's cooking for lunch suits you.'

'Please don't let her bother—I'm sure whatever it is will be delicious. I'm putting you to a great deal of trouble.'

'Not at all, miss. It's a pleasure to have you here. If Watson gets tiresome just open the French window and let him into the garden.'

Left alone, she drank her coffee, shared the biscuits with Watson and presently went to the French window at the back of the room to look out into the garden beyond. It was quite a good-sized garden with a high brick wall and, even on a grey winter day, was a pleasant oasis in the centre of the city. She went and sat down again and presently Mrs Tremble came into the room.

She was a tall, very thin woman with a sharp nose and a severe hairstyle, but she had a friendly smile and shrewd brown eyes. 'You'll be wanting to know where the cloakroom is, miss; I'm sure Tremble forgot to tell you. Forget his own head one day, he will! Now, as to your lunch; I've a nice little Dover sole and one of my castle puddings if that'll suit? Tremble will bring you a sherry and suggest a wine.'

So, later, Mary Jane sat down to her lunch and afterwards went to the library to choose something to read. The shelves were well-filled, mostly by ponderous volumes pertaining to Sir Thomas's work but she found a local history of that part of London and took it back to read by the fire. Her knowledge of London was scanty and it would be nice to know more about Sir Thomas's private life, even if it was only through reading about his house in a book.

Tremble brought her tea as dusk fell, and drew the red velvet curtains across the windows. 'I'll give Watson his tea now, miss, and take him for a quick run. When Sir Thomas is late home I do that, then the pair of them go for a walk later in the evening.'

Mary Jane ate her tea and, lulled by the warmth of the fire and the gentle lamp-light, she closed her eyes and went to sleep. Voices and Watson's bark woke her and she sat up as the door opened and Sir Thomas came in.

The thought of him had been at the back of her mind all day, mixed in with worried plans for the future of the tea-room. Now the sight of him, calm and self-assured, sent a wave of happiness through her insides.

She remembered just in time about Felicity and greeted him in a sober manner quite at variance with her sparkling eyes.

He wished her good evening in a friendly voice, enquired after her day and voiced the hope that she hadn't found it too tiresome that he had been delayed in driving her back to his mother's house.

'Tiresome? Heavens, no. I've had a lovely day. You can have no idea how delightful it is to eat a meal you haven't cooked for yourself. Such delicious food too! How lucky you are to have Mrs Tremble to cook for you, Sir Thomas—and I've done nothing all day, just lounged around with Watson.' She beamed at him. 'I expect you've been busy?'

He agreed that he had, in a bland voice which didn't betray a long session in Theatre, a ward round, outpatients clinic and two private patients he had seen when he should have been having lunch.

He had sat down opposite her. He had poured her a drink and was sitting with a glass of whisky on the table beside him. She looked exactly right sitting there in her unfashionable clothes; she would be nice to come home to. He dismissed the thought with a sigh; he wanted her for his wife, but only if she loved him, and he wasn't even sure if she liked him! She was grateful for his help, but gratitude was something he chose to ignore.

It was a pity that Mary Jane couldn't read his thoughts. She sat there, making polite conversation until Tremble came to tell them that dinner was served and at the table, sitting opposite him, she continued to make small talk while she ate her salmon mousse, beef *en croûte* and Mrs Tremble's lavish version of Queen of Puddings.

The excellent claret had loosened her tongue so that by the end of their meal she felt emboldened to ask, 'Will you be seeing Felicity? I expect—'

He said silkily, 'I do not know what you expect, Mary Jane, but rid yourself of the idea that I have any interest in your sister. Any meetings we have had have not been of my seeking.'

'Oh, I thought—that is, Felicity said…that you—that you got on well together.'

'In plain terms, that I had fallen in love with her, is that what you are trying to say?' He was suddenly coldly angry. 'You may believe me, Mary Jane, when I tell you that I have no wish to dangle after your sister. I am no longer a callow youth to be taken in by a pretty face.'

She had gone rather red. 'I'm sorry if I've annoyed

you. It's none of my business,' and, at his questioning raised eyebrows, she added, 'your private life.'

He debated whether to tell her how mistaken she was and decided not to, and the conversation lapsed while Tremble brought in the coffee tray. When he had gone again, Mary Jane, for some reason, probably the claret, allowed her tongue to run ahead of her good sense. 'Haven't you ever been in love?' she wanted to know.

'On innumerable occasions from the age of sixteen or so. It is a normal habit, you know.'

'Yes, I know. I fell in love with the gym instructor when I was at school and then with the man who came to tune the piano at home. I actually meant enough to want to marry someone...?'

He said gently, 'Yes, Mary Jane. And you?'

'Well, yes.'

'Still the piano-tuner?' He was laughing at her.

She said quickly, 'No,' and managed to laugh too; of course he had found her silly and rather rude, 'I dare say you're wedded to your work.' She spoke lightly.

'Certainly it keeps me fully occupied.' He glanced at his watch. 'Perhaps we had better go...'

She got up at once. 'Of course, I'm sorry, keeping you talking and you've had a long day already.'

She made short work of bidding the Trembles good-bye, saying just the right things in her quiet voice, shaking their hands and smiling a little when Tremble voiced the hope that he would see her again. 'Most unlikely.'

With Watson, drowsy after a good supper and a quick run, on the back seat, Sir Thomas drove away.

Mary Jane, still chatty from the claret, asked, 'Do you like driving?'

'Yes. It is an opportunity to think, especially at this time of night when the roads are fairly clear.'

She kept quiet after that. If he wanted to think then she wouldn't disturb him and if it came to that she had plenty to think about herself. She tore her eyes away from his hands on the wheel and stared ahead of her into the road, lit by the car's headlights. That way she could pretend that he wasn't there sitting beside her and concentrate on her own problems. When eventually he broke the silence it was to remind her that she had an interview with the police in the morning, something she had quite forgotten. 'I've arranged for an officer to come to Mother's house and interview you there,' he added.

'Thank you—I'd forgotten about it. Perhaps he could drive me back to the cottage? I really must start clearing up and getting it ready to open again.' A fanciful remark if ever there was one; she hadn't any idea at the moment how to find the money to start up once more, but he wasn't to know that.

Sir Thomas, who did know, gave a comforting rumble which might have meant anything and said briskly, 'Mother will be disappointed if you don't stay for a few days, and besides, although your wrist has no broken bones, it would be foolish of you to use it for anything more strenuous than lifting a tea-cup. Please do as I ask, Mary Jane, and wait another few days. If it won't bore you too much, I'll take you back home on Saturday morning.'

'Bored?' She was horrified at the thought. 'How could I possibly be bored in that lovely house, and your mother is so kind—I'd almost forgotten how nice mothers are.' There was a wistful note in her voice, and Sir Thomas sternly suppressed his wish to stop the car and

comfort her in a manner calculated to make her forget
her lack of a parent. Instead, he said in his quiet way,
'Good, that's settled, then.'

It was after ten o'clock when they reached Mrs Latimer's house and found the welcoming lights streaming
from the windows and her waiting for them. So was the
faithful Mrs Beaver, bustling in with a tray of coffee
and sandwiches. 'And there's your bed waiting for you,
Mary Jane, and you'd best be into it seeing that Constable Welch'll be here at nine o'clock sharp.'

Mary Jane drank her coffee obediently, ate a sandwich and, although she very much wanted to stay with
Sir Thomas, bade them both goodnight.

'I dare say you'll be gone in the morning,' she observed as they walked together to the door.

'I'll be gone in ten minutes or so,' he told her.

She stopped short. 'You're never going back now?
You can't—you mustn't, you've been at the hospital all
day and driven here and now you want to drive straight
back?'

He said placidly, 'I like driving at night and I promise you I'll go straight to bed when I get home.'

She put a hand on his coat sleeve. 'You'll take care,
Thomas, do be careful.'

His eyes glinted under their lids. 'I'll be very careful, Mary Jane.' He bent and kissed her then. It was a
quick, hard kiss, not at all like the very occasional peck
she received from friends. She didn't know much about
kisses, but this was definitely no peck. The look she
gave him was amethyst fire.

'Oh, Thomas,' she muttered, and flew across the hall
and upstairs, happily unaware that she had called him
Thomas twice. She woke in the night, however, and she

remembered. 'I am a fool,' she told Brimble, curled up on her feet. 'What a good thing he's not here and I must, simply must go away from here before he comes again.'

She had no chance against Mrs Latimer's gentle insistence that she should stay, or Mrs Beaver's more emphatic opinion that she needed more flesh on her bones and, over and above that, Constable Welch, when he came, assured her that there was no need for her return. 'Those men are to stay in custody for a few more days until we get things sorted out,' he told her. 'And there's nothing you can do for a bit.'

So she stayed in the nice old house, keeping Mrs Latimer company, eating the nourishing food Mrs Beaver insisted upon and discovering something of Sir Thomas. For his mother was quick to show her the family photo albums: Thomas as a baby, Thomas as a boy, Thomas as a student, Thomas receiving a knighthood...

'Why?' asked Mary Jane.

'Well, dear, he has done a great deal of work— around the world, I suppose I could say—teaching and getting clinics opened and lecturing, and, of course, operating. His father was a surgeon, too, you know.'

During the next few days she learnt a good deal about Sir Thomas, information freely given by his mother. By the time Saturday came around, Mary Jane felt that she knew quite a lot about him. At least, she told herself, she would have a lot to think about...

Watson's cheerful bark woke her the next morning and a few minutes later Mrs Beaver came in with her morning tea. 'He doesn't get enough rest,' she said, as she pulled back the curtains, revealing a grey February morning. 'Got here in the early hours, and he's up and outside before I could put the kettle on.' She shook her head. 'There's no holding him.'

When she had gone, Mary Jane got out of bed and went to look out of the window. Sir Thomas was at the end of the garden, throwing a ball for Watson. Whatever Mrs Beaver thought, he appeared to be well-rested and full of energy.

He wished her good morning with detached friendliness when she went down to breakfast, and asked if she would be ready to leave after breakfast and applied himself to his bacon and eggs. They had reached the toast and marmalade when he asked, casually, 'Have you any plans, Mary Jane?'

'I'll get cleared up,' she told him, summoning a cheerful voice. 'I can distemper the walls if they're marked, then I'll go to Cheltenham and borrow some money.' She didn't enlarge upon this and he didn't ask her to, which was just as well, because she had no idea how to set about it. She had spent several anxious hours during the nights going over her problems without much success and had come to the conclusion that if the solicitor who had attended to her uncle's affairs was unable to advise her there was nothing for it but to ask Felicity for some money.

They had almost finished when Mrs Latimer joined them. 'I shall miss you, dear,' she told Mary Jane. 'You must come and stay again soon—with Brimble, of course. Do take care of yourself. I shall come and see you and I'll bring Mrs Bennett with me.'

They left shortly after with Watson and Brimble sharing the back seat and Mary Jane very quiet beside Sir Thomas. There seemed nothing to say and since it was still only half light there was no point in admiring the scenery. It wasn't an awkward silence, though, she had the feeling that speech wasn't necessary, that he was content to drive silently, that to make conversation for its own sake was unnecessary. They were almost there when he observed casually, 'I shall be away all next week—Austria. I'll see you when I get back.'

He looked at her and smiled. It was a tender smile and a little amused and she looked away quickly. Then, for something to say, she asked, 'Have you been to Austria before?'

'Several times. Vienna this time—a seminar there.'

He had slowed the car down the village street and he stopped before her cottage, got out and opened the door and let Watson out as he reached in for Brimble's basket. Mary Jane stared.

'Someone's painted the outside—look...'

'So they have,' observed Sir Thomas, showing only a faint interest as he took the key from a pocket and opened the door.

She went in quickly and then stood quite still. 'Inside too,' she said. 'Look at the walls, and there's a new counter and tables and chairs.' She turned to look at him. 'Did you know? But how could...there's no money to pay for it.' She stared into his quiet face. 'It's you, isn't it? You arranged it all.'

'Mr Rob and his sons have done all the work, your friends in the village collected tables and chairs and I imagine that every house in the village contributed the china.'

'You arranged it, though, and you paid for it, too, didn't you?' She smiled widely at him. 'Oh, Sir Thomas, how can I ever thank you? And everyone else of course, and as soon as I've got started again I'll pay you back, every penny.'

'You called me Thomas.' He had come to stand very close to her.

'I expect I forgot,' she told him seriously. 'I hope you didn't mind.'

'On the contrary, I took it as a sign that we were becoming friends.'

She put a hand on his arm. 'How can I ever be anything else after all you've done for me?' She reached up and kissed his cheek. 'I'll never forget you.'

'I rather hope you won't!'

He stared down at her with such intensity that she said hurriedly, 'Will you have a cup of coffee? It won't take a minute.'

He went to fetch her case from the car and she let an impatient Brimble out of his basket and put on the kettle and saw that there were cups and saucers arranged on the kitchen table and an unopened tin of biscuits, sugar in a bowl and milk in the fridge. She knew the reason a moment later for when Sir Thomas came in he was followed by the rector, his sister, old Rob and his sons, the shopkeeper and the Misses Potter.

There was a chorus of, 'Welcome back, Mary Jane,' and a good deal of talk and laughter as she made the coffee and handed round the cups. No one intended to hurry away; they all sat around, admiring their efforts, telling Mary Jane that she had never looked so plump and well. 'And we would never have done any of this if it hadn't been for Sir Thomas,' declared Miss Emily in her penetrating voice. 'He had us all organised in no time.'

It was a pity that presently he declared that he had to go and in the general bustle of handshaking and goodbyes Mary Jane had no chance to speak to him. She did go out to the car with him and stood there on the pavement, impervious to the cold, her hands held in his.

'We can't talk now, Mary Jane, and perhaps it is just as well, but I'm coming to see you. You want to see me, too, don't you?'

'Yes, oh, yes, please, Thomas!'

His kiss was even better than the last one. She stood there watching the Rolls disappear out of sight and would have probably gone on standing, freezing slowly, if Miss Kemble hadn't opened the door and told her to come inside at once. Mary Jane, who never took any notice of Miss Kemble's bossy ways, meekly did as she was told.

She was borne away presently to eat her lunch at the rectory and to be given a great deal of unheeded advice by Miss Kemble. That lady said to her brother later in the day, 'I have never known Mary Jane to be so attentive and willing to take my advice.'

Mary Jane had heard perhaps one word in ten of Miss Kemble's lectures; her head was full of Sir Thomas, going over every word he had said, the way he had looked, his kiss.

Back in her cottage once more, she assured Brimble that she would be sensible, at least until she saw him again. He had said that he wanted to see her again... she forgot about being sensible and fell to daydreaming again.

She was up early the next morning, polishing and dusting, setting out cups and saucers and making a batch of scones. Sunday was a bad day usually, and she seldom opened, only in the height of the tourist season, but she had a feverish wish to get back to her old life as quickly as possible. Her efforts were rewarded, for several cars stopped and when she opened again after lunch there were more customers. It augured well for the future, she told herself, counting the takings at the end of the afternoon.

Her luck held for the first few days, and a steady trickle of customers came; if it continued so, she could make a start on paying back Sir Thomas. She had no idea how much it would be and probably she would be in his debt for years.

Thursday brought Oliver. He marched into the tea-room and stood looking around him. 'Who paid for all this?' he wanted to know.

Mary Jane, her hands floury from her pastry making, stood in the kitchen doorway, looking at him. 'So you did hear about the—incident? The rector told me that he had let you know...'

Oliver blew out his cheeks. 'Naturally, it was his duty to inform me.'

Mary Jane put her neat head on one side. 'And what did you do about it?'

'There was no necessity for me to do anything. The place was being put to rights.' He looked around him. 'It must have cost you a pretty penny. You borrowed, of course?'

'That's my business. Have you just come to see if I'm still here or do you want something?'

'Since your regrettable treatment of Margaret I would hesitate to ask any favours of you.'

'Quite right too, Oliver. So it's just curiosity.'

He said pompously, 'I felt it my duty to come and see how things were.'

'Oh, stuff,' said Mary Jane rudely. 'Do go away, Oliver, you're wasting my time.'

'You've wasted enough time with that surgeon,' he sneered. 'We hear the village gossip as well as everyone else. Hoping to catch him, are you? Well, I'll tell you something—even if you were pretty, and knew how to dress you wouldn't stand a chance. That sister of yours has him hooked. We've been to town and met her—just back from Vienna. She means to marry him, and I must say this for the girl, she always gets what she wants.'

She put her hands behind her back because they were shaking and, although she had gone pale, she said steadily enough, 'Felicity is beautiful and famous and she works hard at her job. She deserves to have whatever she wants.'

'Well, from all accounts he's a great catch—loaded, well-known and handsome. What more could a girl want?' He laughed nastily. 'So you can stop your silly dreaming and look around for someone who's not too fussy about looks.'

'Oh, do go. I'm busy.' She added, 'You're getting fat, Oliver—you ought to go on a diet.'

If he didn't go quickly, she reflected, she would scream the place down. He was sly and mean and she had no doubt at all that he had come intending to tell her about Felicity and Sir Thomas; he had obviously known all about the tea-room being vandalised and what Sir Thomas had done to help her. Thankfully, he went with a last, sniggering, 'I don't expect Felicity will ask you to be a bridesmaid, but you wouldn't like that, would you? Seeing the man of your dreams marrying your sister.'

It was too much; she had been cutting up lard to make the puff pastry for the sausage rolls, and she scooped up a handful and threw it at him as he opened the door. It caught him on the side of his head and slid down his cheek, oozed over his collar and down on to his overcoat.

Rage and surprise rendered him speechless. 'Bye bye, Oliver,' said Mary Jane cheerfully.

She locked the door when he had gone, turned the sign to 'Closed' and went upstairs, where she sat down and had a good cry. It had been foolish of her, she told Brimble, to imagine, even for a moment, that Sir Thomas had any deeper feelings for her than those of friendliness and—regrettably—pity, but he could have told her...and he was coming to see her; he wanted to talk. Well, of course he did, he wanted to tell her about Felicity and himself, didn't he? But why couldn't he have told her sooner and only kissed her in a casual manner, so that she couldn't get silly ideas into her head? She blew her red nose, bathed her eyes and went back to her pastry making. Perhaps Oliver had been lying; he was quite capable of that. The thought cheered her so that by the time she had taken the sausage rolls from the oven she felt quite cheerful again.

She had some more customers calling in for coffee and sausage rolls. Several of them remarked upon her heavy cold and she agreed quickly, conscious that her eyes were still puffy and her nose still pink.

Sir Thomas had thoughtfully caused a telephone to be installed when the tea-room had been done up, arguing that as she lived alone it was a sensible thing to have. She had thanked him nicely, wondering how she was going to pay for its rental, let alone any calls she might make.

When it rang just before closing time she lifted the

receiver—only he and possibly Mrs Latimer would know the number and, even if her friends in the village knew it, too, they would hardly waste money ringing her up when they only needed to nip down the road. 'Thomas,' she said happily to Brimble, disturbed from a refreshing nap.

It was Felicity.

'Felicity,' said Mary Jane. 'How did you know I had a phone?'

'Thomas told me. Back with your nose to the pastry-board again? What a thrill for you, darling. I'm just back from Vienna and in an absolute daze of happiness, darling. I told you I'd marry when I found the right man—good looks, darling, lots of lovely money and dotes on me.'

Mary Jane found her voice. 'What wonderful news and how exciting. When will you get married?'

'I've one or two modelling dates I can't break but very soon—a few weeks. I wanted to move in with him, but he wouldn't hear of it.' She giggled. 'He's very old-fashioned.'

Mary Jane wasn't sure about Sir Thomas being old-fashioned but she was quite sure that allowing Felicity to move in with him would be something he would never agree to.

'Will you have a big wedding?'

'As big as I am able to arrange in a few weeks. There's a nice little church close by—we've dozens of friends between us and I shall wear white, of course. Bridesmaids, too. A pity you're so far away, darling.'

Which remark Mary Jane took, quite rightly, to be a kinder way of saying that she wasn't expected to be a bridesmaid or even a guest.

'What would you like for a wedding present?'

Felicity laughed. 'Oh, darling, don't bother, I'm sending a list to Harrods. Besides, you haven't any money.'

Mary Jane was pleased to hear how bright and cheerful her voice sounded. 'Let me know the date of the wedding, anyway,' she begged. 'And I'm so glad you're happy, dear.' She was going to burst into tears any minute now. 'I must go, I've scones in the oven.'

'You and your scones,' laughed Felicity, and rang off. Just in time. She locked the door and turned the notice round and switched off the lights, not forgetting to put the milk bottles outside the back door and checking the fridge before polishing the tables ready for the morning. All the while she was weeping quietly. Oliver, with his nasty, snide remarks, had been bad enough and she had almost persuaded herself that he had just been malicious, but now Felicity had told her the same story.

Moping would do no good, she told herself presently, and started to clean the stove—a job she hated, but anything was better than having time to think.

She pushed her supper round and round her plate and went to bed. It was a well-known adage that things were always better in the morning.

They were exactly the same, except that now she never wanted to see Thomas again. He had been amusing himself while Felicity was away, playing at being the Good Samaritan. She ground her little white teeth at the thought. If it took her the rest of her life she would pay him back every penny. How dared he kiss her like that, as though he actually wanted to…?

He had said that he would be away for the whole of the week and it was still only Friday; she would have the weekend to decide how she would behave and even if he had to go to the hospital or see his patients he might not come for some days. He might not come at all.

'Which, of course, would be far the best thing,' she told Brimble.

He came the next day just as she was handing a bill to the last of the few people who had been in for tea. She stared at him across the room, her heart somersaulting against her ribs. He looked as he always did, calm and detached, but he was smiling a little. Well he might, reflected Mary Jane, ushering her customers out of the door which Sir Thomas promptly closed, turning the sign round.

'It is not yet five o'clock,' said Mary Jane frostily. Talking to him wasn't going to be difficult at all because she was so angry.

'I got back a day early,' said Sir Thomas, still standing by the door. 'It has been a long week simply because I want to talk to you.'

'Well, you need not have hurried. Felicity phoned me. She's—she's very happy, I hope you will be too.' Despite her efforts her voice began to spiral. 'You could have told me... You've been very kind, more than kind, but I can understand that you wanted to please her.'

'What exactly are you talking about?' he wanted to know, his voice very quiet.

'Oh, do stop pretending you don't know,' she snapped. 'I knew that you would fall in love with her but you didn't tell me, you let me think...did you have a nice time together in Vienna?'

His voice was still quiet but now it was cold as well. 'You believe that I went straight from you to be with Felicity? That I am going to marry her? That I was amusing myself with you?'

'Of course I do. Oliver told me and I didn't quite be-lieve him and then she phoned.'

'Is that what you think of me, Mary Jane?' And when she nodded dumbly he gave her a look of such icy rage that she stepped back. If only he would go, she thought miserably, and had her wish.

Chapter 9

Mary Jane stood in the middle of the sitting-room, listening to the faint whisper of the Rolls-Royce's departure, regretting every word she had uttered. She hadn't given Sir Thomas a chance to speak, and her ingratitude must have shocked him. She should have behaved like a future sister-in-law, congratulated him and expressed her delight. All she had done was to let him see that she had taken him seriously when all the time he was merely being kind. Well, it was too late now. She had cooked her goose, burnt her boats, made her bed and must lie on it. She uttered these wise sayings out loud, but they brought her no comfort.

She felt an icy despair too deep for tears. The thought of a lifetime of serving tea and coffee and baking cakes almost choked her. She could, of course, sell the cottage and go right away, but that would be running away, wouldn't it? Besides, she must owe him a great deal of money...

Leaving church the next morning, Miss Kemble took her aside. 'You must have your lunch with us,' she insisted, overriding Mary Jane's reasons for not doing so. 'Of course you must come, you are still too pale. Do you not sleep? Perhaps you are nervous of being alone?'

Mary Jane said very quickly that she wasn't in the least nervous—only at the thought of Miss Kemble moving in to keep her company. 'Besides,' she pointed out, 'I have a telephone now.'

'Ah, yes, that charming Sir Thomas Latimer, what a good friend he has been to you. I hear from all sides how thoughtful he is of others—always helping lame dogs over stiles.' An unfortunate remark unintentionally made.

They were kind at the rectory. She was given a glass of Miss Kemble's beetroot wine and the rector piled her plate with underdone roast beef which she swallowed down, wishing that Brimble were there to finish it for her. I don't mean to be ungrateful, she reflected, but why does Miss Kemble always make me feel as if I were an object for charity?

She left shortly after their meal with the excuse that she intended to go for a brisk walk. 'For I don't get out a great deal,' she explained, and then wished that she hadn't said that, for Miss Kemble might decide to go with her.

However, there was a visiting parson coming to tea and staying the night, so Miss Kemble was fully occupied. Mary Jane thanked the pair of them sincerely; they had been kind and going to the rectory had filled in some of the long day. Sunday was always a bad day with time lying heavy on her hands, and today was worse than usual. She tired herself out with a long walk; as the days went by it would get easier to forget Sir Thomas and the chances of seeing much of him were slight; Felicity didn't like a country life. She let herself into her cottage, shed her coat and scarf, fed Brimble and spent a long time cooking a supper she hardly touched.

There was a spate of customers on Monday morning to keep her busy and she had promised to make a cake for the Women's Institute meeting during the week, so the baking of it took most of the afternoon.

'Another day gone,' said Mary Jane to Brimble.

Mrs Latimer and Mrs Bennett came the next day. 'We thought we would have a little drive round, dear,' explained Mrs Latimer, 'and we'd love a cup of coffee.'

They sat down, her only customers—and begged her to join them.

'I must say I'm disappointed,' observed Mrs Latimer. 'You don't look at all well, dear. You were quite bonny when I last saw you. Are you working too hard? A few days' rest perhaps? Thomas is back from wherever it was he went to…'

'Vienna.'

'That's right. Has he been to see you?'

Mrs Latimer's blue eyes were guileless.

'Yes.'

For the life of her, Mary Jane couldn't think of anything to add to that. And if Mrs Latimer expected it she gave no sign but made some observation about the life her son led. 'It is really time he settled down,' she declared, which gave Mrs Bennett the chance to talk about her recently engaged daughter, so that any chance

Mary Jane had of finding out more about Thomas and Felicity was squashed.

'You must come and see us,' said Mrs Bennett. 'On a Sunday, when you're free. How nice that you're on the telephone—very thoughtful of Thomas to have it put in. I must say it has all been beautifully redecorated.'

'He's been very kind,' said Mary Jane woodenly. 'And the village gave me the china and the tables and chairs. I don't think I could have managed to start again without help. I'm very grateful.'

'My dear child,' said Mrs Latimer, 'I don't know of many girls who would have carved themselves a living out of an old cottage and the pittance your uncle left you, and as for that wretched cousin of yours...'

'I don't see Oliver very often,' said Mary Jane, adding silently, Only when he wants something or has news which he knows might upset me.

The two ladies left presently and, save for a man on a scooter who had taken a wrong turning, she had no more customers that day.

Sir Thomas immersed himself in his work, as calm and courteous and unflappable as he always was, only Tremble was disturbed. 'There's something up,' he confided to Mrs Tremble. 'Don't ask me what, for I don't know, but there's something wrong somewhere.'

'That nice young lady...' began his wife.

'Now don't go getting sentimental ideas in your head,' begged Tremble.

'Mark my words,' said Mrs Tremble, who always managed to have the last word.

That same evening Felicity arrived on Thomas's doorstep. Tremble, opening the door to her, tried not to look disapproving; he didn't like flighty young ladies with forward manners but he begged her to go into the small sitting-room behind the little dining-room while he enquired if Sir Thomas was free.

Thomas was at his desk writing, with Watson at his feet. He looked up with a frown as Tremble went in. 'Something important, Tremble?'

'A young lady to see you, sir, a Miss Seymour.'

The look on his master's face forced him to remember his wife's words. If this was the young lady who was giving all the trouble then he for one was disappointed. There was no accounting for taste, of course, but somehow she didn't seem right for Sir Thomas.

He followed his master into the hall and opened the sitting-room door and let out a sigh of relief when Sir Thomas exclaimed, 'Felicity—I thought it was Mary Jane.'

'Mary Jane? Whatever would she be doing in London? You might at least look pleased to see me, Thomas. I've news for you—it will be in the papers tomorrow but I thought you might like to know before then. I'm engaged, isn't it fun? A marvellous man—a film director, no less. I've had him dangling for weeks—a girl has to think very carefully about her future, after all. He went to Vienna with me and I decided he'd do. He is in the States now, coming back tomorrow. You'll come to the wedding, of course. I phoned Mary Jane—she won't be coming, she'd be like a fish out of water and she hasn't the right clothes.'

Sir Thomas was still standing, looking down at her, sitting gracefully in a high-backed chair. He said evenly, 'I think it is unlikely that I shall be free to come to your wedding, Felicity. I hope that you will both be very happy. I expect Mary Jane was surprised.'

Felicity shrugged. 'Probably. You were in Vienna, too, were you not? We might have met but I suppose you were lecturing or something dull.'

'Yes. May I offer you a drink?'

'No, thanks, I'm on my way to dine with friends.' She smiled charmingly. 'Do you know, Thomas, I considered you for a husband for a while but it would never have done; all you ever think of is your work.'

He smiled. He didn't choose to tell her how mistaken she was.

On Thursday afternoon the Misses Potter came for tea, as usual. There had been a handful of customers but now the tea-room was empty and Miss Emily said in a satisfied voice, 'I am glad to find that you have no one else here, Mary Jane, for we have brought the newspaper for you to read. There is something of great interest in it. Of course, the *Telegraph* only mentions it, but I persuaded Mrs Stokes to let me have her *Daily Mirror* which has more details.'

The ladies sat themselves down at their usual table and Mary Jane fetched tea and scones and waited patiently while the ladies poured their tea and buttered their scones. This done, Miss Emily took the newspapers from her shopping basket and handed them to her. The *Telegraph* first, the page folded back on 'Forthcoming Marriages'.

Mary Jane's eyes lighted on the announcement at once. 'Mr Theobald Coryman, of New York, to Miss Felicity Seymour of London.' She read it twice just to make sure, and then said, 'I don't understand—is it a mistake?'

'In the *Telegraph*?' Miss Emily was shocked. 'A most reputable newspaper.' She handed over the *Daily Mirror*, which confirmed the *Telegraph*'s genteel announcement in a more flamboyant manner. 'Famous Model to Wed Film Director' said the front-page and under that a large photo of Felicity and a man in horn-rimmed glasses and a wide-brimmed hat. They were arm in arm and Felicity was displaying the ring on her finger.

'It must be a mistake,' said Mary Jane. 'Felicity said…!'

She remembered with clarity what her sister had said—word for word, and Thomas's name had not been mentioned. It was she herself who had made the mistake, jumped to the wrong conclusion and accused Sir Thomas of behaviour in a manner which had been nothing short of that of a virago. She had indeed cooked her goose; worse, she had wronged him in a manner he wasn't likely to forgive or forget. She hadn't given him a chance to say anything, either.

The Misses Potter were looking at her in some astonishment. 'You are pleased? Felicity seems to have done very well for herself.'

'Yes, I'm delighted,' said Mary Jane wildly. 'It's marvellous news. I'm sure she'll—they—will be very happy. He looks…!' She paused, at a loss to describe her sister's future husband; there wasn't much of him to see other than the hat and the glasses. 'Very nice,' she finished lamely.

'They seem very suitable,' remarked Miss Emily drily. 'He is, so they say, extremely rich.'

'Yes, well, Felicity likes nice things.'

The elderly sisters gave her a thoughtful glance. 'I think we all do, dear,' said Miss Mabel. 'You look a bit peaked—have a cup of tea with us.'

Which Mary Jane did; a cup of tea was the panacea for all ills, at least in the United Kingdom, and it gave her time to pull herself together.

The Misses Potter went presently, and she was left with her unhappy thoughts. Would it be a good idea, she wondered, to write to Sir Thomas and apologise; on the other hand, would it be better to do nothing about it? Had she the courage, she wondered, to write and tell him that she loved him and would he forgive her? She went upstairs and found paper and pen and sat down to compose a letter. An hour later, with the wastepaper basket overflowing, she gave up the attempt. Somehow her feelings couldn't be expressed with pen and ink. 'In any case,' she told Brimble, 'I don't suppose he has given me a thought.'

In this she was mistaken; Sir Thomas had thought about her a great deal. Although he shut her away to the back of his mind while he went about his work, sitting in Sister's office after a ward round, apparently giving all his attention to her tart remarks about lack of staff, the modern nurse, the difficulties she experienced in getting enough linen from the laundry—all of which he had heard a hundred times before, he was thinking that he would like to wring Mary Jane's small neck and then, illogically, toss her into his car and drive away to some quiet spot and marry her out of hand. How dared she imagine for one moment that he was amusing himself with her when he loved her to distraction? That he had never allowed his feelings to show was something he hadn't considered.

He promised Sister that he would speak to the hospital committee next time it met, and wandered off to be joined presently by his registrar wanting his opinion about a patient. Stanley Wetherspoon was a good surgeon and his right hand, but a bit prosy. Halfway through his carefully expressed opinion, Sir Thomas said suddenly, 'Why didn't I think of it before? Of course, we were in Vienna at the same time. Naturally...'

Stanley paused in mid-flow and Sir Thomas said hastily, 'So sorry, I've lost the thread—this prosthesis—what do you suggest that we do?'

Presently, Stanley went on his way, reassured, wondering all the same if his boss was overworking and needed a holiday.

Sir Thomas, outwardly his normal pleasantly assured self, went to his rooms, saw several patients and then requested Miss Pink to come into his consulting-room.

'How soon can I get away for a day?'

'Well, it's your weekend on call, Sir Thomas—I could ask your patients booked for Monday to come on Saturday morning—since you'll be here anyway—if you saw them then you could have Monday off.'

'And Tuesday? I know I've got a couple of cases in the afternoon, but is the morning free?'

'It will be if I get Mrs Collyer and Colonel Gregg to come in the afternoon—after three o'clock? That'll give you time to get back to your rooms from hospital and have a meal.'

'Miss Pink, you are a gem of real value to me. Do all that, will you? Then let me know when you've fixed things.'

At the door she asked, 'You'll leave an address, Sir Thomas?'

'Yes. I'll go very early in the morning; if you need anything, get hold of Tremble.'

'Well, well,' said Miss Pink, peering out of the window to watch him getting into his car, and she went in search of his nurse, tidying up in the examination-room. A lady of uncertain age, just as she was, and devoted, just as she was, to Sir Thomas's welfare.

'He looked so happy,' said Miss Pink, and, after a cosy chat of a romantic nature, she went away to reorganise his days for him. A task which necessitated a good deal of wheedling and coaxing, both of which she did most willingly; Sir Thomas had the gift of inspiring loyalty and, in Miss Pink's case, an abiding devotion.

Mary Jane spent the next three days composing letters in her head to Sir Thomas, but somehow when she wrote them down they didn't seem the same. By Sunday evening she had a headache, made worse by a visit from Oliver.

'Well, what do you think of Felicity?' he wanted to know when she opened the door to him.

'I'm very pleased for her, Oliver. You had it all wrong, didn't you?'

He gave her a nasty look. 'I may have been mistaken with the name of her future husband, but there's no denying that she has done very well for herself.'

'Why have you come?' asked Mary Jane, not beating about the bush and anxious for him to go again.

'Margaret and I have had a chat—now that this place is tarted up and equipped again, we think that it might be a good idea if we were to buy you out. You can stay here, of course—the cottage is yours anyway, more's the pity—you can run the place and we will pay you a salary. A little judicial advertising and it should make it worth our while.' He added smugly, 'We can use the connection with Felicity—marvellous publicity.'

'Over my dead body,' said Mary Jane fiercely. 'Whatever will you dream up next? And, if that is why you came, I'll not keep you.'

She opened the door and ushered him out while he was still arguing.

When he had gone, however, she wondered if that wouldn't have solved her problem. Not that she would have stayed in the cottage. There was no doubt that he would buy the place from her even if it meant getting someone in to run it. She would have money and be free to go where she wanted. She couldn't think of anywhere at the moment, but no doubt she would if she gave her mind to it. The trouble was, she thought only of Sir Thomas.

The sun was shining when she got up on Monday morning; February had allowed a spring day with its blue sky and feathery clouds to sneak in. Mary Jane turned the door sign to 'Open', arranged cups and saucers on the four tables and made a batch of scones. The fine weather might tempt some out-of-season tourist to explore and come her way. Her optimism was rewarded: first one table, then a second and finally a third were occupied. Eight persons drinking coffee at fifty-five pence a cup and eating their way through the scones. She did some mental arithmetic, not quite accurate, but heartening none the less, and made plans to bake another batch of scones during the lunch hour. It was still only mid-morning and there might be other customers.

The family of four at one of the tables called for more coffee and she was pouring it when the door opened and Sir Thomas came in, Watson at his heels. It was difficult not to spill the coffee, but she managed it somehow, put the percolator down on the table and, heedless of the customers' stares, stood gaping at him. He sat down at the remaining empty table, looking quite at his ease, and requested coffee. Watson, eager to greet Mary Jane, had, at a quiet word from his master, subsided under the table. Sir Thomas nodded vaguely at the other customers and looked at Mary Jane as though he had never seen her before, lifting his eyebrows a little because of her tardy response to his request.

The wave of delight and happiness at the sight of him which had engulfed her was swamped by sudden rage. How could he walk in as though he were a complete stranger and look through her in that casual manner? Coffee, indeed. She would like to throw the coffee-pot at him…

She poured his coffee with a shaky hand, not looking at him but stooping to pat the expectant Watson's head, and then, just to show him that he was only a customer like anyone else, she made out the bill, laid it on the table and held out her hand for the money.

He picked the hand up gently. It was a little red and rough from her chores, but it was a pretty shape and small. He kissed it on its palm and folded her fingers over it and gave the hand back to her.

What would have happened next was anybody's guess, but the two women who had arrived in a small car, having taken a wrong turning, asked loudly for their bill. When they had gone, Mary Jane made herself as small as possible behind the counter, taking care not to look at Sir Thomas, very aware that he was looking at her. The young couple on a walking holiday went next, looking at her curiously as they went out, frankly staring at Sir Thomas, and that left the family of four, a hearty, youngish man, his cheerful loud-voiced wife and two small children. They had watched Sir Thomas with avid interest, in no hurry to be gone, hoping perhaps for further developments. Sir Thomas sat, quite at his ease, silent, his face a blank mask, his eyes on Mary Jane. Unable to spin out their meal any longer, they paid their bill and prepared to go. His wife, looking up from fastening the children's coats, beamed at Mary Jane. 'You'll be glad to see the back of us, love—I dare say he's dying to pop the question—can't take his eyes off you, can he?'

They all went to the door and she turned round as they went out. 'Good luck to you both, bye bye.'

They got into their car and Sir Thomas got up, turned the sign to 'Closed', locked the door and stood leaning against it, his hands in his pockets.

Mary Jane, standing in the middle of the room, waited for him to speak; after a while, when the silence became unbearable, she said the first thing to come into her head.

'Shouldn't you be at the hospital?'

'Indeed I should, but, owing to Miss Pink's zealous juggling of my appointments book, I have given myself the day off.' He smiled suddenly and her heart turned over. 'To see you, my dearest Mary Jane.'

'Me?'

'You believed that I had gone to Vienna to be with Felicity?' He asked the question gravely.

'Well, you see, Oliver told me and then Felicity phoned and she didn't say who it was and I thought it would be you—she said you were famous and rich and good-looking and you are, aren't you? It sounded like you.'

'And then?' he prompted gently.

'Miss Emily showed me two newspapers and one of them had a photo of Felicity and—I've forgotten his name, but he wears a funny hat, and I tried to write you a letter but it was too difficult...'

'You supposed that I had helped you to set this place to rights because you are Felicity's sister?'

She nodded. 'I was a bit upset.'

'And why were you upset, Mary Jane?'

She met his eyes with an effort. 'I'd much rather not say, if you don't mind.'

'I mind very much. I mind about everything you say and do and think. I am deeply in love with you, my dearest girl, you have become part—no, my whole life. I want you with me, to come home to, to talk to, to love.'

Mary Jane was filled with a delicious excitement, and a thankful surprise that sometimes dreams really did come true. She said in a small voice, 'Are you quite sure, Thomas? I love you very much, but Oliver...'

Sir Thomas left the door and caught her close. 'Oliver can go to the devil. Say that again, my darling.'

She began obediently, 'Are you quite sure...?' She peeped at him and saw the look on his face. 'I love you very much.'

'That's what I thought you said, but I had to make sure.'

'But I must tell you...'

'Not another word,' said Sir Thomas, and kissed her. Presently, Mary Jane, a little out of breath, lifted her face to his. 'That was awfully nice,' she told him.

'In which case...'

'Thomas, there's a batch of scones in the oven.' She added hastily, 'It isn't that I don't want you to kiss me, I do, very much, but they'll burn.'

Sir Thomas, quite rightly, took no notice of this remark but presently he said, 'Pack a bag, my love, and urge Brimble into his basket. You may have ten minutes. I will see to things here. No, don't argue, there isn't time—you may argue as much as you wish once we're married.'

She reached up and kissed his chin. 'I'll remember that,' she said and slipped away up the stairs to do as she was told.

He watched her go before going into the kitchen and rescuing the scones, the faithful Watson beside him. Brimble was on the kitchen table, waiting.

'What must I take with me, Thomas?' Mary Jane's voice floated down the little stairs. 'You didn't say where we are going?'

He stood looking up at her anxious face. 'Why, home, of course, my love.' And saw her lovely smile.

* * * * *

STARS THROUGH THE MIST

Chapter 1

The operating theatre was a hive of industry, its usual hush giving way to sudden utterances of annoyance or impatience as the nurses went briskly to and fro about their business. Sister Deborah Culpeper, arranging her instruments with efficient speed on the trolley before her, found time to listen to the plaintive wail of her most junior nurse, who was unable to find the Langenbeck retractors she had been sent to fetch, while at the same time keeping an eye on Bob, the theatre technician, who was trying out the electrical equipment needed for the various drills which would presently be needed. She calmed the nurse, nodded approval of Bob's efforts, begged Staff Nurse Perkins to get the dressings laid out in their correct order and glanced at the clock.

One minute to nine o'clock, and as far as she could see, everything was ready. She swung the trolley round with an expert kick and then stood, relaxed and calm, behind it, knowing that in a few minutes the rest of the staff would follow suit; she never badgered them or urged them on, merely saw to it that each nurse had her fair share of the work and time enough in which to do it. She looked ahead of her now, apparently at the tiled wall opposite her, aware of every last move being made, nothing of her visible beneath the green gown which enveloped her, only her dark eyes showing above the mask. She looked the picture of calm self-assurance, and her nurses, aware of their own hurried breath and rapid pulses, envied her. A quite unwarranted feeling, as it happened, for despite her outward tranquillity, Deborah's heart had quickened its pace to an alarming rate, and her breath, despite her efforts to keep it firmly under her control, had run mad. She gave her head a tiny, vexed shake, for it annoyed her very much that she should behave so stupidly whenever Mr van Doorninck was operating; she had tried every means in her power to remain uncaring of his presence and had mastered her feelings so well that she could present a placid front to him when they met and subdue those same feelings so sternly that she could scarcely be faulted as a perfect Theatre Sister; only on his operating days did her feelings get a little out of hand, something which she thanked heaven she could conceal behind her mask. She looked up now as the patient was wheeled in, arranged with nicety upon the operating table and covered with a blanket, to be followed immediately by the opening of the swing doors at the further end of the theatre and the appearance of two men.

Deborah's lovely eyes swept over the shorter, younger man—the Registrar, Peter Jackson—and rested briefly upon Mr van Doorninck. He was a very tall man with broad shoulders shrouded, as was every one else, in green theatre garb. His eyes above the mask swept round the theatre now, missing nothing as he walked to the table. His good morning to Sister Culpeper was affable if somewhat reserved, and his glance from under heavy lids was brief. She returned his greeting in a quiet, detached voice and turned at once to her trolley, wondering for the hundredth time how it was possible for a sensible woman of twenty-seven to be so hopelessly and foolishly in love with a consultant surgeon who had never uttered more than a few brief conventional phrases to her. But in love she was, and during the two years in which she had worked for him, it had strengthened into a depth of feeling which had caused her to refuse two proposals of marriage. She sighed soundlessly and began the familiar ritual of arranging the sterile sheets and towels over the unconscious form on the table.

She worked with speed and care, knowing exactly how the silent man on the other side of the table liked them arranged; in two years she had got to know quite a lot about him—that he was even-tempered but never easy-going, that when the occasion warranted it, he could display a cold anger, that he was kind and considerate and reticent about himself—almost taciturn. But of his life outside the theatre she knew very little; he was yearned over by the student nurses to whom he gave lectures, sought after by the more senior female staff, and openly laid siege to by the prettier, younger nurses. No one knew where he lived or what he did with his spare time; from time to time he let drop the information that he was either going to Holland or had just returned. The one fact which emerged from the wealth of rumour which surrounded him was that he was not married—an interesting detail which had increased the efforts of the young women who rather fancied themselves as his wife. And once or twice he had mentioned to Deborah that he had parents in Holland, as well as brothers and a sister who had been to England to visit him. Deborah had longed to ask questions and had restrained herself, knowing that if she did he would probably never tell her anything again.

She finished the preliminaries, glanced at him, and at his 'Ready, Sister?' gave her usual placid 'Yes, sir,' and handed him the towel clips which he liked to arrange for himself. After that she kept her thoughts strictly upon her job—scalpel, artery forceps, retractors, and then as he reached the bone, the lion forceps, the Langenbeck retractors, the rugines, the bone levers—she handed each in turn a second or so before he put out his hand to receive them, admiring, as she always did, his smooth technique and the sureness of his work. Not for nothing had he won a place on the top rung of the orthopaedic surgeon's ladder.

The patient was a young man with a malignant tumour of the femur; his only chance of recovery was extensive excision, a proceeding which Mr van Doorninck was undertaking now. Beyond a muttered word now and then to his registrar or a request for some special instrument, he spoke little; only when the operation was three parts completed and they were stitching up did he remark: 'There's a good chance of complete recovery here—as soon as he's fit we'll get him fitted with a leg—remind me to talk to Sister Prosser about him, Peter.'

He turned away from the table and took off his gloves to fling them into one of the bowls and walked out of the theatre, back into the scrubbing-up room, leaving Peter to supervise the removal of the patient and Deborah to organise the preparation of the theatre for the next case, reflecting as she did so that Sister Prosser, plain and plump and fifty if she was a day, was the most envied member of the nursing staff, because she saw Mr van Doorninck every day, and not only that, he took coffee with her frequently, and was known to have a great respect for her opinion of his patients' conditions.

The morning wore on; a child next with a Ewing's tumour over which the surgeon frowned and muttered to Peter, knowing that his careful surgery offered little hope of a permanent cure, then an old lady whose broken thigh was to be pinned and plated. It was like a carpenter's shop, thought Deborah, expertly changing drills and listening to the high whine of the electric equipment Bob was obediently switching on and off; what with drills and saws and mallets, it was a noisy way to spend a morning, although after five years of it she should be used to it. She had always been interested in bones and when she had finished her training and had had an opportunity of taking the post of staff nurse in the orthopaedic theatre, she had jumped at the chance, and a year later, when the Theatre Sister had retired, she had taken over her job, content with her lot—there was time enough to think about getting married in a year or two, in the meantime she would make a success of her new post, something she had done in a very short time so that there still seemed no urgency to take the idea of marriage seriously.

She was twenty-five when Mr van Doorninck walked into the theatre unit one day, to be introduced as the new orthopaedic consultant, and from that moment she had felt no desire to marry anyone at all, only him. She had realised how hopeless her wish was within a short time, and being a girl with common sense, had told herself to stop being a fool, and had accepted numerous invitations from a number of the younger doctors in the hospital. She had taken trips in fast sports cars, attended classical concerts, and visited cinemas and theatres, according to her escorts' tastes, but it hadn't helped in the least; she was left with the feeling that she had wasted her time as well as that of all the young men who had taken her out, for Mr van Doorninck's image remained clearly imprinted inside her head and refused to be budged.

She had come to realise over the last few months that there was only one way of escape from his unconscious toils; she would have to leave Clare's and start all over again somewhere else. Indeed she had already put this plan into effect, searching the *Nursing Times* for a suitable post, preferably situated at the furthest possible point from London.

They had a break for coffee after the old lady's fragile bones had been reinforced by Mr van Doorninck's expert carpentry. The talk was of the patients, naturally enough, but with their second cups, the two men began a discussion on the merits of the Registrar's new car and Deborah slipped away to scrub and relieve Staff for her own elevenses. They were still discussing cars when the theatre party reassembled around the table again to tackle a nasty shattered elbow, which Mr van Doorninck patiently fitted together like a jigsaw puzzle with

Peter's help, several lengths of wire, a screw or two, and the electric drill again. That done to his satisfaction, he turned his attention to the last case, added hastily to the list at the last minute, because the patient had only been admitted early that morning with a fractured pelvis after he had crashed on his motor bike. It took longer than Deborah had expected. Half way through the operation she signed to Staff and one of the nurses to go to lunch, which left her with Bob and a very junior nurse, who, though willing and eager to please, was inclined to blunder around. It was long past two o'clock when the case left the theatre, and Mr van Doorninck, with a politely worded apology for running so far over his usual time, went too. She wouldn't see him again until Thursday; he operated three times a week and today was Monday.

The afternoon was spent doing the washdown in the theatre, and Deborah, on duty until Staff should relieve her at five o'clock, retired to her office to attend to the paper work. She had discarded her theatre gown and mask and donned her muslin cap in order to go to the dining room for her late dinner; now she spent a few moments repairing the ravages of a busy morning—not that they showed overmuch; her very slightly tiptilted nose shone just a little, her hair, which she wore drawn back above a wide forehead, still retained the smooth wings above each cheek and the heavy coil in her neck was still firmly skewered. She applied lipstick to her large, well-shaped mouth, passed a wetted fingertip across her dark brows, put her cap back on, and stared at the result.

She had been told times out of number that she was a very pretty girl, indeed, one or two of her more ardent admirers had gone so far as to say that she was beautiful. She herself, while not conceited, found her face passably good-looking but nothing out of the ordinary, but she, of course, was unaware of the delight of her smile, or the way her eyes crinkled so nicely at their corners when she laughed, and those same eyes were unusually dark, the colour of pansies, fringed with long curling lashes which were the envy of her friends. She pulled a face at her reflection and turned her back on it to sit at the desk and apply herself to the miscellany upon it, but after ten minutes or so she laid down her pen and picked up the latest copy of the *Nursing Times*; perhaps there would be a job in it which might suit her.

There was—miles away in Scotland. The hospital was small, it was true, but busy, and they wanted an energetic working Sister, able to organise and teach student nurses the secrets of orthopaedics. She marked it with a cross and went back to her writing, telling herself that it was just exactly what she had been looking for, but as she applied herself once more to the delicate task of giving days off to her staff without disrupting the even flow of work, several doubts crept into her mind; not only was the hospital a satisfying distance from Mr van Doorninck, it was also, unfortunately, an unsatisfying distance from her own home. Holidays, not to mention days off, would be an almost impossible undertaking. She went home to Somerset several times a year now, and once a month, when she had her long weekend, she drove herself down in the Fiat 500 she had bought cheap from one of the housemen. She frowned, trying to remember her geography, wondering if Somerset was further away from the northern coasts of Scotland than was London. She could always spend a night

with her Aunt Mary who lived on the edge of a ham-
let rejoicing in the incredible name of Twice Brewed,
hard by Hadrian's Wall, but even then she would have
to spend another night on the road. And what was she
going to tell her friends when they found out that she
intended to leave? She had no good reason for doing
so, she had never been anything but happy until Mr
van Doorninck turned up and destroyed her peace of
mind, and even now she was happy in a way because
she was sure of seeing him three times a week at least.
She frowned. Put like that, it sounded ridiculous—she
would have to find some really sensible reason for giving in her notice. She picked up her pen once more; she
would puzzle it out later, when she was off duty.

But there was no opportunity; she had forgotten that
it was Jenny Reed's birthday and that they were all
going out together to the cinema, so she spent the rest
of the evening with half a dozen of the younger Sisters
and shelved her problems.

There wasn't much time to think next day either,
for the three victims of a car crash were admitted in
the early hours of the morning and she was summoned
early to go on duty and open up the theatre. Staff was
already there when she arrived and so was the junior
nurse, her eyes round with excitement as she began the
humbler routine tasks which fell to her lot.

'Oh, Sister,' she breathed, 'they're in an awful bad
way! Lottie Jones—she's on nights in the Accident
Room, she says they've broken every bone in their
bodies.'

Deborah was putting out the sharps and needles and
collecting the electrical equipment. 'In which case we're

going to be here for a very long time,' she remarked cheerfully. 'Where's Nurse Patterson?'

That young lady, only half awake, crept through the door as she put the question, wished her superior a sleepy good morning and went on to say: 'They're mincemeat, Sister, so rumour has it, and where's the night staff? Couldn't they have at least started…?'

'It's not only our three,' Deborah pointed out crisply. 'They've had a busy night, the general theatre has been on the go since midnight. Get the plaster room ready, will you, Nurse, and then see to the bowls.'

She was on the point of scrubbing up, ready to start her trolleys, when Mr van Doorninck walked in. She looked at him twice, because she was accustomed to seeing him either in his theatre gown and trousers, or a selection of sober, beautifully cut grey suits, and now he was in slacks and a rather elderly sweater. It made him look younger and much more approachable and it seemed to have the same effect on him as well, for he said cheerfully, 'Hullo—sorry we had to get you up early, but I wanted you here. Do you suppose they could send up some coffee—I can tell you what I intend doing while we drink it.' He glanced around him. 'These three look as though they could do with a hot drink, too,' a remark which sent Patterson scurrying to the telephone to order coffee in the consultant's name, adding a gleeful rider that it was for five people and was to be sent up at once.

Deborah led the way to her office, offered Mr van Doorninck a chair, which he declined, and sat down herself behind her desk. She had taken off her cap and had her theatre cap and mask in her hand, but she put these down now and rather absent-mindedly began to thrust the pins more securely into the great bundle of hair she had twisted up in such a hurry. She did it with a lack of self-consciousness of which she was unaware and when she looked up and caught his eye, she said, 'Sorry about this—there wasn't much time, but I'm listening.'

'Three cases,' he began. 'The first is a young man—a boy, I should say, fractured pelvis, left and right fractured femurs, I'm afraid, and a fractured patella—fragmented, I shall have to remove the whole thing. The other two aren't quite so bad—fractured neck of femur, compound tib and fib and a few ribs; the third one has got off comparatively lightly with a comminuted fracture of left femur and a Potts'. I think if we work the first case off, stop for a quick breakfast, and get the other two done afterwards—have you a list for Mr Squires this morning? Doesn't he usually start at eleven o'clock?'

Deborah nodded. 'But it's a short list and I'm sure he'll agree to start half an hour later if he were asked.'

'How are you placed for staff? Will you be able to cover both theatres? You'll be running late.'

It was Staff's half day before her days off, but he wouldn't know about that. Deborah said positively: 'I can manage very well; Bob will be on at eight o'clock and both part-time staff nurses come in.'

She made a show of consulting the off-duty book before her. She wouldn't be able to go off duty herself, for she was to be relieved by one of the part-time staff nurses; she would have to telephone her now, and get her to come in at one o'clock instead.

'When would you like to start?' she wanted to know calmly.

He glanced at his watch. 'Ten minutes, if you can.'

She got up from her chair. 'We'll be ready—you'll want the Smith-Petersen nails, and shall I put out the McLaughlin pin-plate as well? And will you want to do a bone graft on the tib and fib?'

'Very probably. Put out everything we've got, will you? I'll pick what I want, we can't really assess the damage until I can get the bone fragments away.'

He followed her out of the office and they walked together down the wide corridor to the scrubbing-up room, where Peter was already at one of the basins. Deborah wished him good morning and went to her own basin to scrub—ten minutes wasn't long and she had quite a lot to do still.

The operation lasted for hours, and unlike other jobs, there was no question of hurrying it up; the broken bones had to be exposed, tidied up, blood vessels tied, tissue cut away and then the pieces brought together before they were joined by means of pins or wires, and only then after they had been X-rayed.

Mr van Doorninck worked steadily and with the absorption of a man doing a difficult jigsaw puzzle, oblivious of time or anything else. Deborah, with an eye on the clock, sent a nurse down to breakfast with the whispered warning to look sharp about it; Staff went next and when Bob came on at eight o'clock and with him the other two student nurses, she breathed more freely. She still had to telephone Mrs Rudge, the part-time staff nurse, but she lived close by and with any luck she would be able to change her duty hours; she would worry about that later. She nodded to Bob to be ready with the drill, checked swabs with the junior nurse, and tidied her trolleys.

The case was wheeled away at long last, and as the

patient disappeared through one door, Mr van Doorninck and Peter started off in the opposite direction.
'Twenty minutes?' said Mr van Doorninck over his
shoulder as he went, not waiting for her reply.

'You must be joking,' Deborah muttered crossly,
and picked up a handful of instruments, to freeze into
immobility as he stopped abruptly. 'You're right, of
course—is half an hour better?'

She said 'Yes, sir,' in a small meek voice and plunged
into the ordered maelstrom which was the theatre.
Twenty minutes later she was in her office, her theatre
cap pushed to the back of her head, drinking the tea
Staff had whistled up for her and wolfing down buttered
toast; heaven knew when she would get her next meal…

She certainly didn't get it at dinnertime, for although
the second case proved plain sailing, even if slow, the
third presented every small complication under the sun;
the femur was in fragments, anyone less sure of himself than Mr van Doorninck might have felt justified
in amputating below the knee, but he, having made
up his mind that he could save the limb, set to work
to do so, and a long and tedious business it was, ne-
cessitating Deborah sending Mrs Rudge to the second
theatre to take care of Mr Squires who had obligingly
agreed to take his list there, and she had taken two of
the nurses with her, a circumstance which had caused
Staff Nurse Perkins to hesitate about taking her half
day, but it was impossible to argue about it in theatre;
she went, reluctantly.

The operation lasted another hour. Deborah had contrived to send the nurses to their dinners, but Bob she
didn't dare to send; he was far too useful and understood the electric drills and the diathermy machine even

better than she did herself—besides, she was scrubbed, and at this stage of the operation there was no question of hampering Mr van Doorninck for a single second.

It was half past two when he finally straightened his back, thanked her politely for her services and walked away. She sent Bob to his belated dinner, and when Mrs Rudge arrived from the other theatre, went downstairs herself to cold beef and salad. There was certainly no hope of off-duty for her now. Mrs Rudge would go at four o'clock and that would leave herself and two student nurses when Bob went at five. She sighed, eating almost nothing, and presently went over to the Nurses' Home and tidied herself in a perfunctory manner, a little horrified at the untidiness of her appearance— luckily it had all been hidden under her cap and mask.

It had just turned four o'clock when the Accident Room telephoned to say that there was a small child coming up within minutes with a nasty compound fracture of upper arm. Deborah raced round collecting instruments, scrubbing to lay the trolley while telling the nurses, a little fearful at having to get on with it without Staff to breathe reassuringly down their necks, what to do next. All the same, they did so well that she was behind her trolley, scrubbed and threading needles when the patient was wheeled in, followed by Mr van Doorninck and Peter.

'Oh,' said Deborah, taken delightfully by surprise, 'I didn't know that it would be you, sir.'

'I was in the building, Sister,' he informed her, and accepted the towel clip she was holding out. 'You have been off duty?'

She passed him a scalpel. 'No.'

'You will be going this evening?'

She took the forceps off the Mayo table and held them ready for Peter to take. 'No,' then added hastily, in case he should think she was vexed about it, 'It doesn't matter in the least.'

He said 'Um' behind his mask and didn't speak again during the operation, which went without a hitch. All the same, it was almost six o'clock when they were finished and it would be another hour before the theatre was restored to its pristine state. It was a great pity that Peter had to put a plaster on a Pott's fracture—it was a simple one and he did it in the little plaster room, but he made a good deal of mess and Deborah, squeezing out plaster bandages in warm water for him to wind round the broken leg, found her temper wearing thin. It had been a long day, she was famished and tired and she must look a sight by now and there were still the books to write up. She glanced at the clock. In ten minutes the nurses were due off duty; she would have to stay and do her writing before she closed the theatre. She sighed and Peter cocked an eyebrow at her and asked: 'Worn out, Deb?'

'Not really, just hungry, and I haven't had time to do my hair properly or see to my face all day. I feel a fright.' She could hear her voice sounding cross, but he ignored it and agreed cheerfully:

'You look pretty awful—luckily you're so gorgeous, it doesn't matter, though the hair is a trifle wild.'

She giggled and slapped a wet bandage into his outstretched hand.

'Well, it doesn't matter, there's no one to see me. I shall eat an enormous supper and fall into bed.'

'Lucky girl—I'm on until midnight.'

She was instantly sympathetic. 'Oh, Peter, how

awful, but there's not much of a list for Mr Squires tomorrow afternoon and only a handful of replasters and
walking irons—you might be able to get someone to
give you a hand.'

He nodded. 'We're on call, aren't we?'

That was true; Clare's was on call until Thursday.
'I'll keep my fingers crossed,' she promised him. 'And
now be off with you, I want to clear up.'

It was very quiet when the nurses had gone. Deborah
tugged her cap off her dreadfully untidy hair, kicked off
her shoes, and sat down at her desk. Another ten minutes or so and she would be free herself. She dragged
her thoughts away from the tantalising prospect of supper and a hot bath and set to on the operation book. She
was neatly penning in the last name when the unit doors
swung open and her tired mind registered the disturbing
fact that it was Mr van Doorninck's large feet coming
down the corridor, and she looking like something the
sea had washed up. She was still frantically searching
for her shoes when he came in the door. She rose to her
stockinged feet, feeling even worse than she looked because he was, by contrast, quite immaculate—no one,
looking at him now, would know that he had been bent
over the operating table for the entire day. He didn't
look tired either; his handsome face, with its straight
nose and firm mouth, looked as good-humoured and
relaxed as it usually did.

Deborah spoke her thoughts aloud and quite involuntarily. 'Oh, dear—I wasn't expecting anyone and I
simply…' She broke off because he was smiling nicely
at her. 'I must look quite awful,' she muttered, and when
he laughed softly: 'Is it another case?' He shook his

head. 'You want to borrow some instruments—half a minute while I find my shoes...'

He laughed again. 'You won't need your shoes and I don't want any instruments.' He came a little further into the room and stood looking at her. She looked back at him, bewildered, her mind noting that his Dutch accent seemed more pronounced than usual although his English was faultless.

'How do you feel about marrying me?' he wanted to know blandly.

Chapter 2

She was so amazed that she couldn't speak. Just for one blissful moment she savoured the delightful idea that he had fallen in love with her, and then common sense took over. Men in love, however awkward about the business, weren't likely to employ such a cool manner as his. He had sounded for all the world as though he wanted her to fit in an extra case on his next list or something equally prosaic. She found her voice at last and was surprised at its steadiness. 'Why do you ask me?' she wanted to know.

She watched his nod of approval. The light over the desk showed up the grey hair at his temples and served to highlight the extreme fairness of the rest. His voice was unhurried as he said pleasantly:

'What a sensible girl you are—most women would have been demanding to know if I were joking. I have noticed your calm manner when we have worked together, and I am delighted to see that it isn't only in the operating theatre that you are unflurried.'

He was silent for so long that Deborah, desperate for something, anything to do, sat down again and began to stack the various notebooks and papers neatly together. That there was no need to do this, and indeed it would merely give her more work in the morning sorting them all out again, escaped her notice. He might think her sensible and calm; inside, happily concealed by her dark blue uniform, she was bubbling like a cauldron on the boil.

Presently, in the same pleasant voice, he went on: 'I will explain. I am returning to Holland to live very shortly; my father died recently and it is necessary for me to live there—there are various obligations—' he dismissed them with a wave of his hand and she wondered what they might be. 'I shall continue with my work, naturally, but we are a large family and I have a great many friends, so there will be entertaining and social occasions, you understand. I have neither the time nor the inclination to arrange such things, neither do I have the slightest idea how to run a household. I need a wife, someone who will do these things and welcome my friends.'

He paused, but she wasn't looking at him. There were some retractors on the desk, put there for repair; she had picked them up and was polishing their handles vigorously with the cloth in which they were wrapped. He leaned across the desk and took them from her without a word and went on: 'I should tell you that I have been married. My wife died eight years ago and I have had no wish to become deeply involved with any woman since;

I do not want to become deeply involved with you, but I see very little likelihood of this; we have worked together now for two years and I believe that I understand you very well. I would wish for your companionship and friendship and nothing more. I am aware that women set great store by marrying for love and that they are frequently unhappy as a consequence. Perhaps you do not consider what I am offering enough, and yet it seems to me that we are ideally suited, for you have plenty of common sense, a delightful manner and, I think, similar tastes to my own. I can promise you that your life will be pleasant enough.' His blue eyes stared down at her from under half-closed lids. 'You're twenty-seven,' he told her, 'and pretty enough to have had several chances of marrying and settling down with a husband and children, but you have not wanted this—am I right?'

She nodded wordlessly, squashing a fleeting, nonsensical dream of little flaxen-haired van Doornincks as soon as it had been born. Because she simply had to know, she asked: 'Have you any children?'

'No,' his voice was so remote that she wished she hadn't spoken, 'I have two brothers and a sister, all married—there are children enough in the family.'

Deborah waited for him to ask her if she liked children, but he didn't, so after a minute or two's silence she said in a quiet little voice:

'May I have some time to think about it? You see, I've always imagined that I would marry someone I…' She stopped because she wasn't sure of her voice any more.

'Loved?' he finished for her in a depressingly matter-of-fact tone. 'I imagine most girls do, but I think that is not always the best way. A liking for each other, consid-

eration for one's partner, shared interests—these things
make a good marriage.'

She stared at him, her lovely eyes round. She hadn't
supposed him to be a cold man, although he was talking like one now. Either he had been unhappy in his
first marriage or he had loved his wife so dearly that
the idea of loving any other woman was unthinkable to
him. She found either possibility unsatisfactory. With a
tremendous effort she made herself be as businesslike as
he was. 'So you don't want children—or—or a wife?'

He smiled. 'Shall we discuss that later? Perhaps I
haven't made myself quite plain; I admire and like you,
but I'm not in love with you and I believe that we can
be happy together. We are sensible, mature people and
you are not, I believe, a romantic girl...'

She longed to tell him how wrong he was. Instead:
'You don't believe in falling in love, then?'

He smiled so charmingly that her outraged heart
cracked a little.

'And nor, I think, do you, Deborah, otherwise you
would have been married long ago—you must be single from choice.'

So that was what he thought; that she cared nothing
for marriage and children and a home of her own. She
kept her angry eyes on the desk and said nothing at all.

Presently he said, 'I have offended you. I'm sorry,
but I find myself quite unable to be anything but honest with you.'

She looked up at that and encountered his blue stare.
'I've had chances to marry,' she told him, at the same
time wondering what would happen if she told him just
why she had given up those same chances. 'Did you
love your wife?' The question had popped out before

she had been able to stop it and she watched the bleak look on his face as it slowly chilled her.

He said with a bitter little sneer which hurt her, 'All women are curious...'

'Well, I'm not all women,' she assured him sharply, 'and I'm not in the least curious'—another lie—'but it's something I should have to know—you said you wanted to be honest.'

He looked at her thoughtfully. 'You're quite right. One day we will talk about her. Will it suffice for the moment if I tell you that our marriage was a mistake?' He became his usual slightly reserved self again. 'Now that I have told you so much about myself, I do not see that you can do anything else but marry me.'

She answered his smile and was tempted to say yes at once, but common sense still had a firm place inside her lovely head; she would have to think about it. She told him so and he agreed unconcernedly. 'I shall see you on Thursday,' he observed as he went to the door. 'I'll leave you to finish your writing. Good night, Deborah.'

She achieved a calm 'Good night, Mr van Doorninck,' and he paused on the way out to say: 'My name is Gerard, by the way, but perhaps I shouldn't have told you that until Thursday.'

Deborah did no more writing; she waited until she heard the swing doors close after him and then shovelled the books and papers into a drawer, pell-mell. They could wait until tomorrow—she had far too much on her mind to be bothered with stupid matters like off-duty and laundry and instruments which needed repairing. She pinned on her cap anyhow, found her shoes at last, locked the theatre, hung the keys on the hook above the door, and went down to supper. Several of her friends were as late as she was; they greeted her with tired good nature and broke into a babble of talk to which she didn't listen until the Accident Room Sister startled her by saying, 'Deb, whatever is the matter? I've asked you at least three times what van Doorninck did with those three cases we sent up, and you just sit there in a world of your own.'

'Sorry,' said Deborah, 'I was thinking,' a remark which called forth a little ripple of weary laughter from everyone at the table. She smiled round at them all and plunged obligingly into the complexities of the three patients' operations.

'No off-duty?' someone asked when she had finished.

Deborah shook her head. 'No—I'll make it up some time.'

'He works you too hard,' said a pretty dark girl from the other side of the table. 'Cunning wretch, I suppose he turned on the charm and you fell for it.'

The Accident Room Sister said half-jokingly, 'And what wouldn't you give to have the chance of doing just that, my girl? The handsome Mr van Doorninck is a confirmed bachelor, to the sorrow of us all, and the only reason Deb has lasted so long in theatre is because she never shows the least interest in him, so he feels safe with her. Isn't that right, Deb?'

Deborah blushed seldom; by a great effort of will she prevented herself from doing so now. She agreed airily, her fingers crossed on her lap, and started on the nourishing rice pudding which had been set before her. She wouldn't have rice pudding, she promised herself. Perhaps the Dutch…she pulled her thoughts up sharply; she hadn't decided yet, had she? It would be ridiculous to accept his offer, for it wouldn't be the kind of marriage she would want in the first place, on the other hand there was the awful certainty that if she refused him she would never see him again, which meant that she would either remain single all her days or marry someone else without loving him. So wasn't it better to marry Mr van Doorninck even if he didn't love her? At least she would be with him for the rest of her life and he need never find out that she loved him; he hadn't discovered it so far, so why should he later on?

She spooned the last of the despised pudding, and decided to marry him, and if she had regrets in the years to come she would only have herself to blame. It was a relief to have made up her mind, although perhaps it had been already made up from the very moment when he had startled her with his proposal, for hadn't it been the fulfilment of her wildest dreams?

She retired to her room early on the plea of a hard day and the beginnings of a headache, determined to go to bed and think the whole preposterous idea over rationally. Instead of which she fell sound asleep within a few minutes of putting her head on the pillow, her thoughts an uncontrollable and delicious jumble.

She had time enough to think the next day, though. Wednesday was always a slack day in theatre even though they had to be prepared for emergencies. But there were no lists; Deborah spent the greater part of the day in the office, catching up on the administrative side, only sallying forth from time to time to make sure that the nurses knew what they were about. She went off duty at five o'clock, secretly disappointed that Mr van Doorninck hadn't put in an appearance—true, he hadn't said that he would, but surely he would feel some impatience? Upon reflection she decided that probably he wouldn't, or if he did, he would take care not to let it show. She spent the evening washing her hair and doing her nails, with the vague idea that she needed to look her best when he arrived at ten o'clock the next morning.

Only he didn't come at ten. She was in theatre, on her knees under the operating table because one of the nurses had reported a small fault in its mechanism. She had her back to the door and didn't hear him enter; it was the sight of his large well-polished shoes which caused her to start up, knocking her cap crooked as she did so. He put out a hand and helped her to her feet without effort, rather as though she had been some small slip of a girl, and Deborah exclaimed involuntarily, 'Oh—I'm quite heavy. I'm too tall, you must have noticed.' Her eyes were on his tie as she babbled on: 'I'm so big…!'

'Which should make us a well-suited couple,' he answered equably. 'At least, I hope you will agree with me, Deborah.'

She put a hand up to her cap to straighten it, not quite sure what she should answer, and he caught her puzzled look. 'Not quite romantic enough?' he quizzed her gently. 'Have dinner with me tonight and I'll try and make amends.'

She was standing before him now, her lovely eyes on a level with his chin. 'I don't know—that is, I haven't said…'

His heavy-lidded eyes searched hers. 'Then say it now,' he commanded her gently. It seemed absurd to accept a proposal of marriage in an operating theatre, but there seemed no help for it. She drew breath:

'Yes, I'll marry you, Mr van Doorninck.' She uttered the absurd remark in a quiet, sensible voice and he laughed gently.

'Gerard, don't you think? Can you manage seven o'clock?'

Her eyes left his chin reluctantly and met his. 'Yes, I think so.'

'Good. I'll fetch you—we'll go to the Empress if you would like that.'

Somewhere very super, she remembered vaguely. 'That will be nice.' An inadequate answer, she knew, but he didn't appear to find it amiss; he took her two hands lightly in his and said: 'We'll have a quiet talk together—it is essential that we should understand each other from the beginning, don't you agree?'

It sounded very businesslike and cool to her; perhaps she was making a terrible mistake, but was there a worse mistake than letting him go away for ever? She thought not. For want of anything better to say, she repeated, 'That will be nice,' and added, 'I must go and scrub, you have a list as long as your arm.'

It stretched longer than an arm, however, by the time they had finished. The second case held them up; the patient's unexpected cardiac arrest was a surprise which, while to be coped with, flung a decided spanner in the works. Not that Mr van Doorninck allowed it to impede his activities—he continued unhurriedly about his urgent business and Deborah, after despatching Staff to the other end of the table to help the anaesthetist in any way he wished, concentrated upon supplying her future husband's wants. The patient rallied, she heard Mr van Doorninck's satisfied grunt and relaxed herself; for a patient to die on the table was something to be avoided at all costs. The operation was concluded and the patient, still unconscious and happily unaware of his frustrated attempts to die, was borne away and it was decided that a break for coffee would do everyone some good. Deborah, crowding into her office with the three men and sharing the contents of the coffee pot with them, was less lucky with the biscuit tin, for it was emptied with a rapidity she wouldn't have prevented even if she could have done so; the sight of grown men munching Rich Tea biscuits as though they had eaten nothing for days touched her heart. She poured herself a second cup of coffee and made a mental note to wheedle the stores into letting her have an extra supply.

The rest of the morning went well, although they finished more than an hour late. Mr van Doorninck was meticulously drawing the muscle sheath together, oblivious of time. He lifted an eyebrow at Peter to remove the clamps and swab the wound ready for him to stitch and put out an outsize gloved hand for the needleholder which Deborah was holding ready. He took it without a glance and paused to straighten his back. 'Anything for this afternoon, Sister?' he enquired conversationally.

'Not until three o'clock, sir.' She glanced at Peter, who would be taking the cases. 'A baby for a gallows frame and a couple of Colles.'

'So you will be free for our evening together?'

'Yes, sir.' Hadn't she already said so? she asked herself vexedly, and threaded another needle, aware of the pricked ears and held breaths around her and Peter's swift, astonished look.

Mr van Doorninck held out his needleholder for her to insert the newly threaded needle. He said deliberately so that everyone could hear, 'Sister Culpeper and

I are engaged to be married, so we are—er—celebrating this evening.'

He put out a hand again and Deborah slapped the stitch scissors into it with a certain amount of force, her fine bosom swelling with annoyance—giving out the news like that without so much as a word to her beforehand! Just wait until we're alone, she cautioned him silently, her smouldering look quite lost upon his downbent, intent head. And even if she had wanted to speak her mind, it would have been impossible in the little chorus of good wishes and congratulations. She made suitable murmurs in reply and scowled behind her mask.

But if she had hoped to have had a few words with him she was unlucky; the patient was no sooner stitched than he threw down his instruments, ripped off his gloves and made off with the long, leisurely stride which could only have been matched on her part by a frank run. She watched him go, fuming, and turned away to fob off the nurses' excited questions.

Her temper had improved very little by the time she went off duty. The news had spread, as such news always did; she was telephoned, stopped in the corridors and besieged by the other Sisters when she went down to tea. That they were envious was obvious, but they were pleased too, for she was well liked at Clare's, and each one of them marvelled at the way she had kept the exciting news such a close secret.

'He'll be a honey,' sighed Women's Surgical Sister. 'Just imagine living with him!' She stared at Deborah. 'Is he very rich, Deb?'

'I—I don't really know.' Deborah was by now quite peevish and struggling not to show it. It was a relief, on the pretext of dressing up for the evening, when she could escape. All the same, despite her ill-humour, she dressed with care in a pinafore dress of green ribbed silk, worn over a white lawn blouse with ballooning sleeves and a fetching choirboy frill under her chin, and she did her hair carefully too, its smooth wings on her cheeks and the complicated chignon at the back of her neck setting off the dress to its greatest advantage. Luckily it was late August and warm, for she had no suitable coat to cover this finery; she rummaged around in her cupboard and found a gossamer wool scarf which she flung over her arm—and if he didn't like it, she told her reflection crossly, he could lump it.

Still buoyed up by indignation, she swept down the Home stairs, looking queenly and still slightly peevish, but she stopped in full sail in the hall because Mr van Doorninck was there, standing by the door, watching her. He crossed the polished floor and when he reached her said the wrong thing. 'I had no idea,' he commented, 'that you were such a handsome young woman.'

His words conjured up an outsize, tightly corseted Titanic, when her heart's wish was to be frail and small and clinging. She lifted pansy eyes to his and said tartly, 'My theatre gowns are a good disguise...' and stopped because she could see that he was laughing silently.

'I beg your pardon, Deborah—you see how necessary it is for me to take a wife? I have become so inept at paying compliments. I like you exactly as you are and I hope that you will believe that. But tell me, why were you looking so put out as you came downstairs?'

She felt mollified and a little ashamed too. 'I was annoyed because you told everyone in theatre that we were engaged—I didn't know you were going to.'

He chose to misunderstand her. 'I had no idea that

you wished it to remain a secret.' He smiled so nicely
at her that her heart hurried its beat.

'Well—of course I didn't.'

'Then why were you annoyed?'

An impossible question to answer. She smiled reluctantly and said:

'Oh, I don't know—perhaps I haven't quite got used
to the idea.'

His blue eyes searched hers calmly. 'You have had
second thoughts, perhaps?'

'No—oh, no.'

He smiled again. 'Good. Shall we go?'

They went through the Home door together, and she
was very conscious of the unseen eyes peering at them
from the net-covered windows, but she forgot all about
them when she saw the car drawn up waiting for them.
She had wondered from time to time what sort of car
he drove, and here it was—a BMW 3 OCSL, a sleek,
powerful coupé which looked as though it could do an
enormous speed if it were allowed to. She paused by
its door and asked: 'Yours?'

'Yes. I could use a larger car really, but once I'm in
it it's OK, and she goes like a bird. We'll change her,
though, if you prefer something roomier.'

Deborah had settled herself in her seat. 'She's super,
you mustn't dream of changing her.' She turned to look
at him as he got in beside her. 'I always imagined that
you would drive something stately.'

He laughed. 'I'm flattered that you spared even such
thoughts as those upon me. I've a Citroën at home, an
SM, plenty of room but not so fast as this one. I take it
that you drive?'

He had eased the car into the evening traffic and

was travelling westward. 'Well,' said Deborah, 'I drive, but I'm not what you would call a good driver, though I haven't had much opportunity...'

'Then we must find opportunity for you—you will need a car of your own.'

In Piccadilly, where the traffic was faster and thinner, he turned off into Berkeley Street and stopped outside the Empress Restaurant. A truly imposing place, she discovered, peeping discreetly about her as they went in—grandly Victorian with its red plush and its candelabra. When they were seated she said with disarming frankness: 'It rather takes my breath away.'

His mouth twitched. 'Worthy of the occasion, I hope.' He opened his eyes wide and she was surprised, as she always was, by their intense blue. 'For it is an occasion, is it not?'

She studied him; he was really extraordinarily handsome and very distinguished in his dinner jacket. After a moment he said softly:

'I hope I pass muster?'

She blinked and smiled rather shyly. 'I beg your pardon—I didn't mean to stare. It's just that—well, you never see a person properly in theatre, do you?'

He studied her in his turn. 'No—and I made a mistake just now. I called you handsome, and you're not, you're beautiful.'

She flushed delicately under his gaze and he went on blandly: 'But let us make no mistake, I'm not getting sentimental or falling in love with you, Deborah.' His voice had a faint edge which she was quick to hear.

She forced her own voice to normality. 'You explained about that, but supposing you should meet someone with whom you do fall in love? And you might, you're not old, are you?'

'I'm thirty-seven,' he informed her, still bland, 'and I have had a number of years in which to fall in and out of love since Sasja's death.' He saw her look and smiled slightly. 'And by that I mean exactly what I said; I must confess I've been attracted to a number of women, but I didn't like them—there is a difference. I like you, Deborah.'

She sipped the drink he had ordered and studied the menu card and tried not to mind too much that he was talking to her as though she were an old friend who had just applied for a job he had going. In a way she was. She put the idea out of her head and chose Suprême de Turbot Mogador and settled for caviare for starters, then applied herself to a lighthearted conversation which gave him no opportunity of turning the talk back to themselves. But that didn't last long; with the coming of the Vacherin Glacé he cut easily into her flow of small talk with:

'As to our marriage—have you any objection if it takes place soon? I want to return to Holland as quickly as possible and I have arranged to leave Clare's in ten days' time. I thought we might get married then.'

Deborah sat with her fork poised midway between plate and mouth. 'Ten days' time?' she uttered. 'But that's not possible! I have to give a month's notice.'

'Oh, don't concern yourself with that. I can arrange something. Is that your only objection?'

'You don't know my family.'

'You live in Somerset, don't you? We might go down there and see them before we go to Holland—unless you wish to be married from your home?'

It was like being swept along a fast-moving river with not even a twig in sight. 'I—I hadn't thought about it.'

'Then how would it be if we marry quietly here in London and then go to see your parents?'

'You mean surprise them?'

'I'll be guided by you,' he murmured.

She thought this rather unlikely; all the same it was a good idea.

'Father's an historian,' she explained, 'and rather wrapped up in his work, and Mother—Mother is never surprised about anything. They wouldn't mind. I'd like a quiet wedding, but in church.'

He looked surprised. 'Naturally. I am a Calvinist myself and you are presumably Church of England. If you care to choose your church I'll see about the licence and make the arrangements. Do you want any guests?'

She shook her head; it didn't seem quite right to invite people to a marriage which was, after all, a friendly arrangement between two people who were marrying for all the wrong reasons—although there was nothing wrong with her reason; surely loving someone was sufficiently strong grounds for marrying them? And as for Gerard, his reasons, though very different, held a strong element of practical common sense. Besides, he believed her to be in complete agreement with him over the suitability of a marriage between two persons who, presumably, had no intention of allowing their hearts to run away with their feelings. She wondered idly just what kind of a girl might steal his heart. Certainly not herself—had he not said that he liked her, and that, as far as she could see, was as far as it went.

She drank her coffee and agreed with every show

of pleasure to his suggestion that they should go somewhere and dance.

He took her to the Savoy, where they danced for an
hour or more between pleasant little interludes at the
table he had secured well away from the dance floor.
She was an excellent dancer and Gerard, she discovered, danced well too, if a trifle conservatively. Just
for a space she forgot her problems and gave herself to
the enjoyment of the evening, and presently, drinking
champagne, her face prettily flushed, she found herself
agreeing that a light supper would be delightful before
he took her back to Clare's. It was almost three o'clock
when he stopped the car outside the Home. He got out
of the car with her and opened the heavy door with the
latch key she gave him and then stood idly swinging
it in his hand.

'Thank you for a delightful evening,' said Deborah,
and tried to remember that she was going to marry this
large, quiet man standing beside her, and in ten days,
too. She felt sudden panic swamp the tenuous happiness inspired by the champagne and the dancing, and
raised her eyes to his face, her mouth already open to
give utterance to a variety of thoughts which, largely
because of that same champagne, no longer made sense.

The eyes which met hers were very kind. 'Don't
worry, Deborah,' he urged her in his deep, placid voice.
'It's only reaction; in the morning everything will be
quite all right again. You must believe me.'

He bent and kissed her cheek, much as though he
were comforting a child, and told her to go to bed. 'And
I'll see you tomorrow before I go to Holland.'

And because she was bewildered and a little afraid
and her head had begun to ache, she did as he bade her.

With a whispered good night she went slowly up the stairs without looking back to see if he was watching her, undressed and got into bed, and fell at once into a dreamless sleep which was only ended by her alarm clock warning her to get up and dress, astonished to find that what Gerard had said was quite true; everything did seem all right. She went down to breakfast and in response to the urgent enquiries of her companions, gave a detailed account of her evening and then, fortified by several cups of strong tea, made her way to the theatre unit.

There wasn't much doing. Mr Squires had a couple of Smith-Petersen pins to insert, a bone graft to do, and there was a Carpal Tunnel—an easy enough list, for he kept strictly to straightforward bone work, leaving the bone tumours to Gerard van Doorninck. They were finished by one o'clock and Deborah had time to go down to dinner before sending Staff off duty. The theatre would have to be washed down that afternoon and she wanted to go through the sharps; some of the chisels needed attention, as did the grooved awl and one or two of the rugines. She would go down to the surgical stores and see what could be done. She had them neatly wrapped and was on the point of making her way through the labyrinth of semi-underground passages to the stores, when Gerard walked in. 'Hullo,' he said. 'Going somewhere?'

She explained about the sharps, and even as she was speaking he had taken them from her and put them on the desk. 'Later. I have to go again in a few minutes. I just wanted to make sure...' he paused and studied her with cool leisure. Apparently her calm demeanour pleased him, for he said: 'I told you that everything

would be all right, didn't I?' and when she nodded, longing to tell him that indeed nothing was right at all, he
went on: 'I've seen about the licence—there's a small
church round the corner, St Joram's. Would you like to
go and see it and tell me if you will marry me there?'

Her heart jumped because she still wasn't used to the
idea of marrying him, although her face remained tranquil enough. 'I know St Joram's very well, I go there
sometimes. I should like to be married there.'

He gave a small satisfied sound, like a man who had
had a finicky job to do and had succeeded with it sooner
than he had expected.

'I'll be back on Monday—there's a list at ten o'clock,
isn't there? I'll see you before we start.'

He took her hand briefly, said goodbye even more
briefly, and retraced his steps. Deborah stood in the
empty corridor, listening to his unhurried stride melt
into the distance and then merge into the multitude of
hospital sounds. Presently she picked up the instruments
and started on her way to the surgical stores.

Chapter 3

The warmth of the early September morning had barely penetrated the dim cool of the little church. Deborah, standing in its porch, peered down its length; in a very few minutes she was going to walk down the aisle with Gerard beside her and become his wife. She wished suddenly that he hadn't left her there while he returned to lock the car parked outside, because then she wouldn't have time to think. Now her head seethed with the events of the last ten days; the interview with Miss Bright, the Principal Nursing Officer, and the astonishing ease with which she found herself free to leave exactly when Gerard had wanted her to; the delight and curiosity of her friends, who even at that very moment had no idea that she was getting married this very morning; she had allowed them to think that she and Gerard were going down to her parents in Somerset. She had even allowed them to discuss her wedding dress, with a good deal of friendly bickering as to which style and material would suit her best, and had quietly gone out and shopped around for a pale blue dress and jacket and a wisp of a hat which she had only put on in the car, in case someone in the hospital should have seen it and guessed what it might be, for it was that sort of a hat. But the hat was the only frivolous thing about her; she looked completely composed, and when she heard Gerard's step behind her, she turned a tranquil face to greet him, very much at variance with her heart's secret thudding.

He had flowers in his hand, a small spray of roses and orange blossom and green leaves. 'For you,' he said. 'I know that you should have a bouquet, but it might have been difficult to hide from your friends.' He spoke easily with no sign of discomposure and proceeded to fasten them on to her dress in a matter-of-fact manner. When he had done so, he stood back to look at her. 'Very nice,' was his verdict. 'How lucky that we have such a glorious morning.' He looked at his watch. 'We're a few minutes early, shall we stroll round the church?'

They wandered off, examining the memorials on the walls and the gravestones at their feet, for all the world, thought Deborah, slightly light-headed, as though they were a pair of tourists. It was when they reached the pulpit that she noticed the flowers beautifully arranged around the chancel. She stopped before one particularly fine mass of blooms and remarked: 'How beautiful these are, and so many of them. I shouldn't have thought that the parish was rich enough to afford anything like this.'

She turned to look at her companion as she spoke and exclaimed:

'Oh, you had them put here. How—how thoughtful!'

'I'm glad you like them. I found the church a little bare when I came the other day—the vicar's wife was only too glad to see to them for me.'

'Thank you,' said Deborah. She touched the flowers on her dress. 'And for these too.'

They had reached the chancel at exactly the right moment; the vicar was waiting for them with two people—his wife, apparently, and someone who might have been the daily help, pressed into the more romantic role of witness.

The service was short. Deborah listened to every word of it and heard nothing, and even when the plain gold ring had been put upon her finger she felt as though it was someone else standing there, being married. She signed the register in a composed manner, received her husband's kiss with the same calm, and shook hands with the vicar and the two ladies, then walked out of the little church with Gerard. He was holding her hand lightly, talking quietly as they went, and she said not a word, only noticed every small detail about him—his grey suit, the gold cuff links in his silk shirt, the perfection of his polished shoes—who polished them? she wondered stupidly—and his imperturbable face. He turned to smile at her as they reached the door and she smiled back while hope, reinforced by her love, flooded through her. She was young still and pretty, some said beautiful, men liked her, some enough to have wanted to marry her; surely there was a chance that Gerard might fall in love with her? She would be seeing much more of him now, take an interest in his life, make herself indispensable, wear pretty clothes...

'My dear girl,' said Gerard kindly, 'how distraite you have become—quite lost in thought—happy ones, I hope?'

They were standing by the car and he had unlocked the door as he spoke and was holding it open for her, his glance as kind as his voice. She got in, strangely vexed by his kindness, and said too brightly: 'It was a nice wedding. I—I was thinking about it.'

He nodded and swung the car into the street. 'Yes, one hears the words during a simple ceremony—I have always thought that big social weddings are slightly unreal.'

It was on the tip of her tongue to ask him if his previous wedding had been just such a one, but it seemed hardly a fitting time to do so. She launched into a steady flow of small talk which lasted until they were clear of the centre of the city and heading west.

But presently she fell silent, staring out at the passing traffic as the car gathered speed, casting around in her mind for something to talk about. There was so much to say, and yet nothing. She was on the point of remarking—for the second time—about the weather when Gerard spoke. 'I think we'll lunch at Nately Scures—there's a good pub there, the Baredown. I don't know about you, Deborah, but getting married seems to have given me a good appetite.'

His manner was so completely at ease that she lost her awkwardness too. 'I'm hungry too,' she agreed, 'and I didn't realise that it was already one o'clock. We should be home by tea time.'

It was during lunch that one or two notions, not altogether pleasant, entered her head and quite unknown to her, reflected their disquiet in her face. They were sitting back at their ease, drinking their coffee in a companionable silence which Gerard broke. 'What's on your mind, Deborah?'

She put some more sugar into her cup although she didn't want it, and stirred it because it gave her something to do. She began uncertainly: 'I was just thinking—hoping that Mike, my elder brother, you know, will be home for a day or two with Helen—his wife.'

He smiled very faintly. 'Why?'

'Well, I was thinking about—about rooms. You see, the house is very old and there aren't…' She tried again. 'There is Mother and Father's room and a big guest room, all the other bedrooms are small. If Mike and Helen are there they'll be in the guest room, which makes it easy for us, because then we shall have our own rooms and there won't be any need for me to make an excuse—I mean for us not sharing a room.' She gave him a determinedly matter-of-fact look which he returned with an urbane one of his own. 'I don't suppose you had thought about it?'

'Indeed I had—I thought a migraine would fill the bill.'

'Do you have migraine?'

'Good God, girl, no! You.'

She said indignantly: 'I've never had migraine in my life, I don't even know what it feels like. I really don't think…'

He gave her an amused glance. 'Well, it seems the situation isn't likely to arise, doesn't it? We can hardly turn your brother and his wife out of their room just for one night.' He had spoken casually, now he changed the subject abruptly, as they got up to go.

'It was nice of you not to mind about going straight back to Holland. We'll go away for a holiday as soon as I can get everything sorted out at the Grotehof.'

She nodded. 'Oh, the hospital, yes. Have you many private patients too?'

He sent the car tearing past a lorry. 'Yes, and shall have many more, I think. I'm looking forward to meeting your family.'

She stirred in her seat. 'Father is a little absent-minded; he doesn't live in the present when he's busy on a book, and Mother—Mother's a darling. Neither of them notices much what's going on around them, but Mother never questions anything I do. Then there's Mike—and Helen, of course, and John and Billy, they're fourteen and sixteen, and Maureen who's eleven. There are great gaps between us, but it's never seemed to matter.'

They were almost at Salisbury when she ventured to remark: 'I don't know anything about your family and I'm terrified of meeting them.'

He slowed the car down and stopped on the grass verge and turned to look at her. 'My dear Deborah— you, terrified? Why? My mother is like any other mother, perhaps a little older than yours; she must be, let me see, almost sixty. My two brothers, Pieter and Willem, are younger than I, my sister Lia comes between us—she's married to an architect and they live near Hilversum. Pieter is a pathologist in Utrecht, Willem is a lawyer—he lives in den Haag.'

'And your mother, does she live with you?'

'No, she didn't wish to go on living in the house after

my father died—I'm not sure of the reason. She has a flat close by. We see each other often.'

'So you live alone?'

'There is Wim, who sees to everything—I suppose you would call him a houseman, but he's more than that; he's been with us for so long, and there is Marijke who cooks and keeps house and Mevrouw Smit who comes in to clean. Mother took Leen, who has been with us ever since I can remember, with her when she moved to the flat.'

'Is your house large?'

'Large?' he considered her question. 'No—but it is old and full of passages and small staircases; delightful to live in but the very devil to keep clean.' He gave her a quick, sidelong glance. 'Marijke and Mevrouw Smit see to that, of course. You will be busy enough in other ways.'

'What other ways?' asked Deborah with vague suspicion.

'I told you, did I not, that I need to entertain quite a lot—oh, not riotous parties night after night, but various colleagues who come to the hospital for one reason or the other—sometimes they bring their wives, sometimes they come on their own. And there is the occasional dinner party, and we shall be asked out ourselves.'

'Oh. How did you manage before?'

He shrugged. 'Marijke coped with the odd visitor well enough, my mother acted as hostess from time to time. Remember I have been away for two years; I spent only a short time in Amsterdam each month or so, but now I am going back to live I shall be expected to do my share of entertaining. You will be of the greatest help to me if you will deal with that side of our life.'

'I'll do my best, though it's rather different from handing instruments…'

He laughed. 'Very. But if you do it half as well you will be a great success and earn my undying gratitude.'

She didn't want his gratitude; she wanted his love, but nothing seemed further from his thoughts. Dinner parties, though, would give her the opportunity to wear pretty clothes and make the most of herself—he might at least notice her as a person. She began to plan a suitable wardrobe…

The road was surprisingly empty after they had left Salisbury behind. At Warminster they turned off on to the Frome road and then, at Deborah's direction, turned off again into the byroads, through the small village of Nunney and then the still smaller one of Chantry. Her home lay a mile beyond, a Somerset farmhouse, with its back tucked cosily into the hills behind it, and beautifully restored and tended by Mr Culpeper and his wife. It looked delightful now in the afternoon sun, its windows open as was its front door, its garden a mass of colour and nothing but the open country around it. Deborah gave a small sigh of pleasure as she saw it. 'That's it,' she told Gerard.

'Charming,' he commented. 'I hope your parents will ask us back for a visit. I can see that it is a most interesting house—those windows'—he nodded towards the side of the house—'their pediments appear most interesting.'

He brought the car to a halt before the door and as he helped her out she said with something like relief: 'Father will be delighted that you noticed them, they're very unusual. Probably he'll talk of nothing else and quite forget that we're married.' They were walking to the door. 'Do you really know something of sixteenth-century building?'

'A little.' He smiled down at her and said unexpectedly: 'You look very pretty in that blue dress. Shall I ring the bell?'

For answer she shook her head and let out a piercing whistle, answered almost immediately by an equally piercing reply followed by: 'Debby, is it really you? I'm in the sitting room. Come in, darling. I can't leave this…'

The hall was cool, flagstoned and bare of furniture save for an old oak chest against one wall and a grandfather clock. Deborah went through one of the open doors leading out of it and walked across the faded, still beautiful carpet to where her mother was kneeling on the floor surrounded by quantities of manuscript.

'Your father dropped the lot,' she began, preparing to get up. 'I simply have to get them into some sort of order.'

She was a great deal smaller than her daughter, but they shared the same lovely face and pansy eyes. She leaned up to hug her daughter with a happy: 'This is a lovely surprise. Are you on holiday or is it just a couple of days?' Her eyes lighted upon Gerard. 'You've had a lift—who's this?' She added thoughtfully, just as though he wasn't there: 'He's very good-looking.' She smiled at him and he returned her smile with such charm that she got to her feet, holding out a hand.

'Mother,' said Deborah with the kind of cheerful resignation her children had acquired over the years, 'this is Gerard van Doorninck. We got married this morning.'

Her parent remained blissfully calm and shook hands. 'Well now,' she exclaimed, not in the least put out, 'isn't that nice? Debby always has known her own mind since she could handle a spoon. I should have loved to have been at the wedding, but since I wasn't we'll have a little celebration here.' She studied the tall quiet man before her. 'If I'm your mother-in-law, you're quite entitled to kiss me.'

And when he had: 'I hope Debby warned you about us. You see, my husband and I seldom go out, we're far too happy here and it's so quiet he can work undisturbed—and as for me, the days are never long enough. What do you do for a living?' she shot at him without pause.

'I'm an orthopaedic surgeon—I've been at Clare's for two years now. Deborah was my Theatre Sister.'

Mrs Culpeper nodded her slightly untidy head. 'Nasty places, operating theatres, but I suppose one can fall in love in one just as easily as anywhere else.' She spun round and addressed her daughter. 'Darling, how long are you staying, and when did you get married?'

'Just tonight, Mother, and we got married this morning.'

'In church, I hope?'

'Yes—that little one, St Joram's, just round the corner from Clare's.'

'Quite right too. Your brother's here with Helen—they're in the guest room, of course.' She handed Gerard the manuscript in an absentminded manner. 'Where am I to put you both?'

'Don't worry, Mother,' said Deborah in a hurry. 'I'll have my own room and Gerard can have Billy's—it's only for tonight—we couldn't think of turning Mike and Helen out.'

Her mother gave her a long, thoughtful look. 'Of course not, dear, and after all, you have the rest of your lives together.'

Deborah agreed with her calmly, not looking at Gerard.

'Good, that's settled—two such sensible people. Gerard, will you take these papers into the study across the hall and tell my husband that you're here? You may have to say it twice before he pays any attention; he found an interesting stone in the garden this morning—I believe it's called a shepherd's counting stone. You have a Dutch name.'

'I am Dutch, Mrs Culpeper.' And Deborah, stealing a look, was glad to see that Gerard wasn't in the least discomposed.

'I saw Queen Wilhelmina once,' Mrs Culpeper went on chattily, 'in London, during the war.' She turned to Deborah. 'Your father will be most interested, Debby. Come and put the kettle on for tea, dear.'

Deborah tucked her arm into her mother's. 'Yes, dearest, but wouldn't it be nicer if Gerard had me with him when he meets Father?'

'He looks perfectly able to introduce himself,' declared her volatile parent. 'I meant to have had tea hours ago. Come along, dear.'

Deborah looked across the room to where Gerard was standing, his arms full of papers. 'Do you mind?' she asked him.

'Not in the least. In fact it's an eminently sensible suggestion.' He smiled at her and she realised with astonishment that he was enjoying himself.

They all met again ten minutes later. She was standing at the table in the large, low-ceilinged kitchen, cutting sandwiches and listening to her mother's happy rambling talk while she arranged the best Spode tea service on a tray, when the door opened and the two men came in. Mr Culpeper was a tall man, almost as tall as his new son-in-law, with a thin upright body and a good-looking face which wore its usual abstracted expression. He was almost bald, but his moustache and neat Van Dyck beard were still brown and thick. He came across the room to where Deborah stood and flung an arm around her shoulders and kissed her with fondness. He said without preamble: 'I like your husband, Debby—no nonsense about him, and thank God I've at last found someone in the family who is interested in pediments.'

His eyes lighted upon the plate of sandwiches before her and he helped himself to one and bit into it with relish. 'Mike and Helen won't be back just yet, so let's have tea.' He took the tray from his wife and led the way to the sitting room.

Tea was a success, largely because Gerard joined in the conversation with an ease of manner which made him seem like an old friend of the family, and later, when they had been left together in her room—'for of course you will want to unpack for Gerard', her mother had said—Deborah asked him: 'You aren't bored? You see, we all love them very much and we don't in the least mind when they forget things and or start talking as though we weren't there...'

He took her hands in his. 'No, Deborah, I'm not bored, nor would I ever be here with your parents. They are charming people and they have found the secret of

being happy, haven't they? I envy someone like your
mother, who can cast down her teacup and dash into
the garden because a thrush is singing particularly
sweetly—and your father…they are a devoted couple,
I believe.'

She was very conscious of his hands. 'Yes, they are. I
suppose that's why they view the world with such kindness and tolerance and at the same time when they want
to, the two of them just retire into a—a sort of shell together—they're very unworldly.' She looked at him a little anxiously. 'I'm not a bit like them,' she assured him.
'We're all very practical and sensible; we've looked after
them all our lives.' She smiled. 'Even little Maureen!'

He bent his head to kiss her cheek gently. 'That's
why you're such a nice person, I expect. You know, I
had forgotten that people could live like this. Perhaps
the rest of us have our values wrong, working too hard,
making money we have to worry about, going on holidays we don't enjoy—just because everyone else does.'

'But you're not like that.' She was quite certain of it.

'Thank you for saying that. I hope I'm not, but I'm
often discontented with my life, though perhaps now
that I have you for a companion I shall find more pleasure in it.'

She was breathless, but it would never do to let him
see that. She moved her hands ever so slightly and he
let them go at once. She turned away, saying lightly: 'I
shall do my best, only you must tell me what you like
and what you don't like—but you must never think
that I shall be bored or find life dull. There's always
so much to see and do and I love walking and staring
round at things.'

He laughed. 'How restful that sounds—I like that

too. We'll walk and stare as often as we can spare the time. I have a small house in Friesland and several good friends living nearby. We must spend some weekends there.'

Deborah turned to face him again, once more quite composed. 'Another house? Gerard, I've never asked you because there hasn't been much time to talk and it didn't seem important, but now I want to know. You haven't a lot of money or anything like that, have you?'

The corners of his mouth twitched. 'As to that, Deborah, I must plead guilty, for I do have a good deal of money and I own a fair amount of land besides.' He studied her face. 'Would you have married me if you had known?'

'I don't know. Yes, I do—I should have married you just the same because you would have known that I wasn't doing it for your money—at least, I hope you would.'

She saw the bleak look erase all expression from his face and wondered what she had said to cause it. 'Oh dear, have I annoyed you?'

The look had gone; perhaps she had imagined it. 'No, Deborah, and I'm glad to hear that is how you feel about it. Now supposing I take my case to Billy's room and unpack what I need, and then do you suppose we might have a stroll in your father's delightful garden?'

A suggestion to which she agreed happily enough.

It was good to see Mike and Helen again, and even if they were surprised at her news, it was only to be expected. The evening was passed pleasantly, with some of Mr Culpeper's prized Madeira brought out to drink the bride's health and a buzz of family talk interrupted by excited telephone conversations with Maureen and her brothers. And as for Deborah, the evening had become a happy dream because when they had walked in the garden, Gerard had given her a ring with the matter-of-fact observation that she should have had it before they were married; he had gone to Holland to fetch it and had forgotten to give it to her. It was a beautiful ring, a diamond, an enormous one, in a strange old-fashioned setting of two pairs of hands supporting the stone on either side. She had exclaimed over its beauty, watching its rainbow colours as she turned her hand from side to side in order to see it better, thanking him nicely, trying to forget that he himself had forgotten.

He told her that it was the traditional betrothal ring of his family. 'At least,' he had explained, 'there are two, exactly alike. My grandmother left this one to me as I was the eldest grandson, and—' he became silent and she, anxious to help him out, said: 'What a sensible idea! The other ring will be left to—to whoever is your heir—that means,' she hurried on, 'that the wives don't have to give up their engagement rings. I wonder how that all started?'

He replied casually, 'Oh, an ancestor of mine—he had a very youthful wife, and when their son married she was still a young woman and flatly refused to give up her ring, so because he loved her to distraction he had another made just like it.'

They had laughed about it together, although secretly she thought it a charming story, and later the ring had been admired and discussed and admired again. Only when she was at last in her own room lying in her white-painted bed amidst her small, familiar possessions, did she allow herself to shed a few tears because the dream would never come true, of course; she would have to be sensible and make Gerard a good wife and be thankful that he at least liked her. But at the same time, she promised herself fiercely through her tears, she would never give up trying to make him love her.

She wakened early by reason of the early morning sun shining in through the open window and was on the point of getting up when there was a tap on the door and Gerard came in. His good morning was friendly, his manner as matter-of-fact as it had been the previous evening.

'I hoped you would be awake,' he said. 'I have been wondering if you would like to pay lightning visits to your brothers and sister before we leave for Holland? The boys are at Wells, aren't they? Twelve miles, no further, and Wells to Sherborne is under twenty-five and on our way, in any case, for we can pick up the Winchester road from there. The ferry doesn't sail until midnight, so as long as we don't linger over meals, we should have ample time.' He sat down on the end of her bed. 'Would you like that?'

Deborah smiled her pleasure. 'Oh, Gerard, how kind of you to think of it! I'd simply love it—you're sure there's time?'

'Positive.' He looked at his watch. 'It's half past six—a little early perhaps...?'

'Mother always gets up at seven. I'll go down and make the tea and tell her. We can have breakfast when we want, no one will mind. When do you want to leave?'

'Half past eight. I'll come down with you—better still,' he got off the bed, 'I'll go down and put the kettle on.'

By the time Deborah reached the kitchen he had the kettle boiling and a tray laid with cups and saucers and milk and sugar, which surprised her very much, for she hadn't supposed him to be the kind of man who would be handy about the house, indeed, even now, in need of a shave and in a dressing gown of great magnificence, he contrived to look more than elegant and the making of early morning tea seemed alien to his nature. There was, she guessed, a great deal to his character of which she knew nothing.

She took the tea upstairs, whispered their plans to her mother, who thought it a splendid idea and accepted them without demur, and then went back to the kitchen to drink her tea with Gerard, and because the morning was such a beautiful one, they wandered through the back door and strolled round the garden admiring the flowers, their tea cups in their hands, stopping to take an occasional sip.

'What a delightful way in which to start the day,' commented Gerard, back in the kitchen.

Deborah agreed. 'And one can do it almost any-where,' she pointed out, 'provided there's a strip of grass and a few flowers, or a pleasant walk nearby... have you a dog?'

'Yes, though he hasn't seen a great deal of me lately; Wim stands proxy for me, though. And there are two cats, but they belong to Marijke.'

'What do you call your dog?'

'Smith, he's a Jack Russell. He goes everywhere with me when I'm home.'

'I hope he'll like me; I could take him for walks.'

'You shall.' He took her cup from her and put it ti-dily in the sink. 'Shall we get dressed? What do we do about breakfast? Shall we get our own?'

'Everyone will be down—but we can always start if they're not.'

They left exactly on time amidst a chorus of good wishes and goodbyes and urgings to return as soon as possible, coupled with a great many messages from Mrs Culpeper for the boys and Maureen.

All of which Deborah faithfully passed on, although her listeners were all far too excited to pay any attention to them; the boys, naturally enough, were much more interested in the car than in their sister, and she was agreeably surprised to find how well Gerard got on with them. Her notions of him were sadly out, she admitted to herself as they took a boisterous leave of Billy and John and tore down the Fosse Way towards Sherborne and Maureen. She had always thought of him as being a perfect darling, of course, because she loved him, but also a little reserved as well as being a quiet man. He was still quiet, of course, but he obviously enjoyed the boys' company and she hadn't expected that.

It was mid-morning by now and Maureen came dancing out of her class to cast herself into her elder sister's embrace. 'Debby,' she shrilled, 'how lovely—tell me all about the wedding and what did you wear...?' She stopped to smile at Gerard and then throw herself with enthusiasm at him. 'Oh, you do look nice,' she assured him. 'Just wait till I tell the girls—can I come and stay with you soon?' She plucked impatiently at his arm. 'You're very good-looking, aren't you? Which is a good thing because Debby's quite beautiful, isn't she, and thank heavens you're so tall because now she can wear high heels if she wants to.' She didn't wait for him to answer but turned her attention to Deborah again. 'You haven't told me what you wore.'

'This dress I'm wearing—it was a very quiet wedding, darling.'

Deborah smiled at her small sister; she and the boys were all so large, but Maureen took after her mother in her smallness, although at the moment she had no looks at all, only a great deal of charm.

'Shall I come and have lunch with you?' she wanted to know.

It was Gerard who answered her. 'Sorry, Maureen. We're on our way home to Holland, but how about paying us a visit in the holidays? We'll come over and fetch you.'

She flung her arms around him. 'Oh, will you? Will you really? Promise?'

'Promise.' He bent and kissed her small elfin face and looked at Deborah. 'We must go, my dear,' and he smiled half-humorously over the child's head.

They had time and to spare when they reached Dover, for the big car had eaten up the miles and they had stopped only briefly on the way. Gerard parked the car in the queue and invited Deborah to get out.

'There's an hotel just outside the dock gates,' he told her. 'We have ample time to have dinner before we go on board.'

When they reached the hotel it was long past the time that dinner was served, but Gerard seemed to have little difficulty in persuading the waiter that just this once he might stretch a point. They dined simply, watching the harbour below from their table in the window.

Deborah was surprised to find that there was a cabin booked for her when they got on board; the crossing was barely four hours and she wasn't in the least tired, but when she said so, Gerard merely smiled and told her that it would be a good idea if she were to get some sleep. 'It can be very noisy,' he explained. 'Even if you don't sleep, you can read—I'll get you some magazines. And my cabin is next to yours, so you have only to knock if you want anything.'

She thanked him, wishing that they could have spent the time together talking, for she suspected that once they got to his home he would be swallowed up in his work almost at once and she might see very little of him. He was going to take up the appointment which had been waiting for him in the hospital where he had been a consultant for some years; she felt sure that he would want to start at once.

She lay down on her bunk and pulled a blanket over her and opened the first of the magazines. Long before the ferry sailed, she was asleep.

Chapter 4

Deborah was called with a cup of tea and a polite request from the steward that she would join her husband in the lounge as soon as she was ready. Gerard was waiting for her, looking, at four-fifteen in the morning, quite immaculate, so that she was glad that she had taken trouble with her own appearance; her face nicely made up, her hair as neat as it always was, her blue outfit fresh and creaseless from its careful hanging while she slept.

It was still dark when they landed, but Gerard shot away as though he knew the road blindfold, which, she conceded, was probably the case. But although he drove fast he didn't allow it to interfere with the casual conversation which he carried on, explaining in which direction they were going, pointing out the towns as they passed through them and warning her when they approached the frontier between Belgium and Holland.

It was growing lighter now. They passed through the small town of Sluis with its narrow, twisting streets, still so quiet in the early morning and then out again on to the straight tree-lined road, making for the ferry at Breskens. 'There is another route,' he told her, 'through Antwerp and Breda, but it's usually loaded with traffic. Even with a possible delay on the ferry I find this way shorter now that the new bridges and roads are open to Rotterdam.'

It was light enough to see by now and Deborah, wide awake, asked endless questions and could barely wait to drink the coffee he fetched for her on board the ferry, because she wanted to see everything at once as they crossed the great river. She thought Flushing disappointingly dull, although the sea-front, which she could see in the distance, was probably delightful with its long line of hotels facing the beach. But she had little enough chance to do more than glimpse it, for Gerard skirted the town and took the motorway to Goes, past factories and shipyards and a great deal of dreary flat country. She would have liked to have commented upon this, for after Somerset she found it depressing, but she held her tongue, and presently, once they were past Goes, on the fine road crossing the islands, speeding towards Rotterdam, she cheered up, for here the country was green and pretty in the morning sunlight and the houses with their steep red roofs and the solid farms looked delightful enough. Even Rotterdam, even though there was little to see but towering flats and factories and docks, was interesting and bustling with early workers, and the more so because Gerard told her a great deal about it as he eased the car through the ever-increasing traffic with a patience and good humour she was sure she would never have had.

Once through the city and on the motorway once more, Gerard remarked: 'We could have crossed the river lower down and gone through Europoort on the new road to Delft, but you have already seen so many factories and blast furnaces—this way is more interesting and we can stop in Delft and have breakfast. Reyndorp's Prinsenhof will be open by now.'

Delft, Deborah discovered at once, was quite a different kettle of fish. Gerard parked the car in one of the main streets of the picturesque little town and led her across the road to the restaurant, where they obligingly served them with an ample breakfast at a table in a window overlooking the street. There were already plenty of people going to work on their bicycles, milk carts, bread carts, carts loaded with vegetables and weaving in and out of them, hordes of schoolchildren on their motorised bikes.

'Everything seems to start very early,' Deborah exclaimed. 'Look, there's a shop open already.'

'A good many open at eight o'clock, sometimes earlier. I suppose we breakfast earlier than they do in England—we lunch at midday, and most people have an evening meal about six o'clock.'

'That makes a very long evening.'

His blue eyes twinkled. 'Ah, yes—but the Dutchman likes to sit at home reading his paper, drinking his glass of gin and surrounded by his wife and children. Perhaps you find that dull, but we don't think so.'

Deborah shook her head; it didn't sound dull at all. She enjoyed for a fleeting moment a vivid picture of Gerard and herself on either side of the hearth with a clutch of small van Doornincks between them. She brushed the dream aside briskly; he had told her that he had a great many friends and entertained quite frequently and that they would go out fairly often, and perhaps, as there were to be no little van Doornincks, that was a very good thing.

They were less than forty miles from Amsterdam now and once back on the motorway it seemed even less. They seemed to come upon the city suddenly, rising abruptly from the flat fields around it and Gerard had perforce to slow down, turning and twisting through narrow streets and along canals which looked so charming that she wished that they might stop so that she might take a better look. Presently he turned into a busy main street, only to cross it and turn down another narrow street bordering a canal.

'Where are we now?' she ventured to ask.

'The Keizersgracht. It's a canal which runs almost in a full circle round the city. There are other canals which follow its line exactly, rather like a spider's web. All of them contain beautiful old houses, most of which are embassies or warehouses or offices now.'

She peered around her; the houses were large, tall and built on noble lines with big square windows and great front doors, and despite this they contrived to look homelike. She said so and heard him laugh. 'I'm glad you like them, for here we are at my—our home.'

He had slowed the car and stopped outside a double-fronted, red brick house, its front door reached by a double row of steps, its windows, in orderly rows, large and square, its roof, Deborah could see, craning her pretty neck, ended in a rounded gable which leaned, very slightly, forward. She would have liked to have stood and stared, just as she would have paused by the canals, but Gerard was waiting for her. He took her hand as she got out of the car and drew it under his arm and mounted the steps to the door which opened as they reached it.

This would be Wim, she guessed, a short, thick-set man with grizzled hair and blue eyes set in a round, cheerful face. He shook Gerard's proffered hand with pleasure and when Gerard introduced him to Deborah, took her hand too and said in heavily accented, difficult English:

'I am happy, Mevrouw. It is a moment to rejoice. My felicitations.'

She thanked him, and without knowing it pleased him mightily by remarking on his knowledge of English, adding the rider that she hoped that her Dutch would be as good. Upon this small wave of mutual friendliness they entered the hall, while Wim closed the door behind them.

The hall was narrow, although it had two deep alcoves, each with a wall table and a mirror hanging above. Along one side, between them, was a double door, carved and arched, and beyond them a carved wooden staircase. On the other side of the hall there were three doors and an arched opening reached by several descending steps, coming up which now was a tall, thin, middle-aged woman, with pale hair which could have been flaxen or equally well grey. She wore a rather old-fashioned black dress and a large print apron and although her face seemed severe she was smiling broadly now. She broke at once into speech and then turned to Deborah, her hand held out, and began all over again. When she finally stopped Deborah smiled and nodded and asked Gerard urgently: 'Please will you tell Marijke that I'll learn Dutch just as soon as I can, so that we can have the pleasure of talking to each other?'

She watched him as he repeated what she had said in his own language. It sounded like nonsense to her, but she supposed that if she worked hard enough at it, she would at least learn the bare bones of it in a few weeks, and anyway, it seemed that she had said the right thing, for Marijke was smiling more broadly than ever. She shook Deborah's hand again, said something to Gerard in which the word coffee was easily recognisable, and went back down the steps while Wim opened the first of the doors in the hall for them to enter.

The room had a very high ceiling of ornamental plaster work and panelled walls ending in a shelf two thirds of the way up, upon which rested a collection of china which Deborah supposed was Delft. The furniture was comfortable, upholstered in a russet velvet which went well with the deep blues and greens and ambers of the vast carpet. The lampstands were delicate china figures holding aloft cream and russet shades. She found the room delightful, although it was a good deal more splendid than she had expected.

They had their coffee sitting side by side upon a small settee covered in exquisite needlework, and somehow the sight of the old, beautifully simple silver coffee service on its heavy tray flanked by cups which should by rights have been in some museum, so old and fragile were they, depressed her; she had expected comfort, certainly, but this was more than comfort, it was an ageless way of life which she would have to learn to live. She shivered a little, thinking of the dinner parties; possibly the guests would dislike her...

'It's all strange, isn't it?' Gerard was at his most placid. 'But it's home. All this'—he waved a large, square hand—'has been handed down from one son to the next, whether we have wanted it or not, though to be honest, I love every stick and stone of the place, and I hope that you will too.' He put down his coffee cup. 'You will be tired. Would you like to go to bed?'

She was quite taken aback. 'Oh, no, thank you, I'm not in the least tired. If I might just go to my room, I could unpack and change my clothes. I expect you have a great deal to do.'

She saw at once that she had said the right thing, for the relief on his face, quickly suppressed, was real enough. 'Yes, I have. Shall we meet again for lunch? I've asked Mother round.' He smiled nicely. 'You'll feel better once you have met her.'

She got to her feet and he walked with her to the door, opened it and called for Marijke. Even as Deborah started up the staircase in the wake of the older woman, she heard him cross the hall to the front door.

Her room was at the back of the house and her luggage was already in it. As soon as Marijke had left her she went to the window, to discover a small garden below, with a fountain in its centre and tubs of flowers grouped round it. There was grass too, only a very small circle of it, but it looked green and fresh, and brooding over the cheerful little plot was a copper beech, rustling faintly in the wind.

Deborah turned her back on the pleasant scene presently to survey the room; large and airy and furnished in the style of Chippendale, probably genuine pieces, she thought, caressing the delicate lines of the dressing table. There was a vast cupboard along one wall with a door beside it and on the opposite wall a tall-boy. The bed was wide and covered with the same pastel pale chintz as the curtains, the carpet was a deep cream and the lamps and small armchair were covered in pink striped silk. A beautiful room. She sighed her content and hastened to open the first of its three doors. A bathroom with another door leading back on to the landing, she glanced quickly at its luxury and crossed the room. The second door opened on to a short corridor lined with cupboards and lighted by a window on its other side, there was a door at its end and she opened that too and went in. Gerard's luggage was there, so this was his room, smaller than her own and a little severe but just as comfortable. It, too, had a door leading on to the landing and a bathroom built into a deep alcove.

She went back the way she had come and had a bath and put on a plain cotton jersey dress the colour of apricots, then sat down at the dressing table and did her face with great care and arranged her hair in its smooth wings with the chignon at the back, put her engagement ring back on her finger and, after a long look at herself in the handsome mirror, made her way downstairs.

There were voices in the sitting room and she heard Gerard's laugh. His mother had arrived. She trod firmly down the staircase and had almost reached the bottom when he appeared in the sitting room doorway.

'I thought I heard you,' he greeted her smilingly, and whistled briefly. A small dog scampered past him and across the hall. 'Here's Smith, I've just fetched him from the vet.'

Smith had halted in front of her and she sat down on the stairs and put out a gentle hand. 'Hullo, Smith,' she said, 'I hope we're going to be friends.' The dog stared at her with bright black eyes, and after a moment wagged his tail and allowed her to stroke him, and when she got to her feet, walked quite soberly beside her to where Gerard was waiting.

He took her arm as they went into the sitting room and led her over to the window where his mother sat. She wasn't at all what Deborah had imagined she would be; small for a start, almost as small as her own mother, and her eyes were brown and kind. Her nose was an autocratic little beak, but the mouth below it was as kind as the eyes. She stood up as they reached her and said in excellent English:

'Deborah, my dear, welcome to the family. You do not know how happy I am to see Gerard married, and to such a lovely girl. I must say that he described you very well, but I have been longing to meet you. Gerard, bring a chair over here so that I can talk to Deborah— and pour us all a drink.'

And when Deborah was seated and he had gone to the other end of the room where the drinks were laid out on a Pembroke table: 'You must not think that I order him about, my dear. Indeed, I would not dream of doing any such thing, but just now and again I pretend to do so and he pretends to do as I wish. It works very well for us both. And now tell me, what do you think of this house?'

'I've only seen a very little of it; Gerard had things to do... What I have seen I find quite beautiful.'

The older lady nodded complacently. 'I knew you would like it—love it, I hope. I did, still do, but my husband and I were devoted and without him it doesn't seem the same—besides, I was determined to leave it the moment Gerard told me about you.' She smiled faintly. 'I think I guessed before that.' She gave Deborah a long, thoughtful look and Deborah looked back at her, her eyes quiet.

'Then he lived in a huge flat,' his mother explained, taking it for granted that Deborah knew what she was talking about. She shuddered delicately. 'He loathed it, although he never said so...' she broke off as Gerard came towards them.

'Champagne,' he announced, 'as befits an occasion,' and he lifted his glass to Deborah.

They lunched without haste, although the moment they had finished Gerard excused himself on the pretext of a visit to the hospital as well as his consulting rooms to see what his secretary had got for him. 'Mother will love to show you the house,' he told Deborah as he prepared to leave. 'Don't wait tea—I don't expect to be back much before six.'

She smiled and nodded because that was what she would have to learn to do cheerfully from now on; watch him go through the front door and then wonder where he had gone to and what he was doing and who he was with...it didn't bear thinking about. She turned to her mother-in-law with a too-bright smile and professed herself eager to explore the house.

Gerard had been right when he had described it as being full of narrow passages and old staircases, and some of the rooms were very small, although all were charmingly furnished. Deborah wandered up and down with Mevrouw van Doorninck, stopping to peer at family portraits or admire a mirror or one of the trifles of silver or china with which the house was filled. When they had finally completed their tour, she said: 'I feel as though I had turned you out, Mevrouw van Doorninck. How could you bear to leave?'

'It was a wrench, Deborah, but I have some of the furniture in the flat and all my personal treasures. I had made up my mind before Gerard's father died that I would leave, although Gerard didn't want it. You see, I wanted him to marry again, and if I had stayed here, he might never have done so. But living on his own, without a wife to greet his guests and arrange his dinner parties and run the house…that sounds all wrong, my dear, but I don't mean it to be. He talked about you several times when he came home from Clare's, you know. He told me what a quiet, sensible girl you were and how capable and charming, and I hoped that he would ask you to marry him, and you see that I have my wish.' She patted Deborah's hand. 'You must come and see me very soon—tomorrow if Gerard can spare the time, and then in a day or so I shall give a small dinner party for you so that you can meet the family. You will feel a little strange at first, but I'm sure that Gerard will arrange for you to have Dutch lessons and show you round Amsterdam and show you off to his friends. Very soon you will settle down quite nicely.'

And indeed, to all intents and purposes Deborah did settle down. To the world around her she presented a calm, unruffled face, charming manners and a smiling acceptance of her new way of life. True to her promise, Mevrouw van Doorninck had given her dinner party, where she had met Gerard's sister and brothers; three nice people anxious to make her feel at home. They were considerably younger than he and she liked them at once. She met the children too; Lia had two boys, and Pieter and Willem had a boy and a girl each, all

rather alike with pale flaxen hair and blue eyes and just
as willing as their parents to absorb her into the family, the older ones trying out their school English on
her, the toddlers not caring what language she spoke.

And because Gerard had done nothing about it,
she had asked Wim's advice and found herself an old
dry-as-dust professor, long retired from his university
chair at Leiden, and applied herself assiduously to her
Dutch—a disheartening task, she soon discovered, what
with the verbs coming at the end of a sentence instead
of the middle and the terrible grammar, but at least she
had learned a few dozen words, correctly pronounced—
the old professor had seen to that. It was amazing the
amount one could learn when one applied oneself and
one had, sadly enough, time idle on one's hands.

But there was one person amongst the many whom
she met whom she could not like—Claude van Trapp,
a man younger than Gerard and a friend of the family
since their boyhood days. He was good-looking, and
what she would suppose could be described as good
fun. He was certainly an intelligent man, and yet Deborah mistrusted him; she found his charm false, and
the snide remarks he let fall from time to time seemed
to her to be spiteful more than witty. It surprised her
that Gerard tolerated him with a careless good humour
which annoyed her, and when the opportunity occurred
she had, in a roundabout way, tried to discover the reason for this. But he had only laughed and shrugged his
great shoulders. 'A little sharp in the tongue, perhaps,'
he conceded, 'but we have known each other since our
pram days, you know.'

She hadn't pursued the subject, for it was apparent
that Gerard was so tolerant of Claude's comings and

goings to the house that he hardly noticed him and indeed probably believed him to be the boy he had known. She knew him to be incapable of pettiness or meanness himself, so he certainly wouldn't expect it or look for it in his friends. He was, in fact, blinded by familiarity and she could do nothing about it. But after the first few meetings, she contrived to slip away on some pretext or other when Claude came to the house; easily enough done, for she was taking her duties seriously and there was always something to do around the house, and when his company was unavoidable she behaved with an impeccable politeness towards him, meeting his malicious titbits of gossip and innuendoes with a charming vagueness, ignoring his thinly veiled contempt for her apparent dimness, just as she ignored his admiring glances and sly looks.

It was after she had been in Holland a bare three weeks that Claude called one afternoon. She was in the little garden with Smith, sitting under the shade of the copper beech while she learned the lesson Professor de Wit had set her. It was a beautiful day and she felt a little drowsy, for the night before they had given their first dinner party, quite a small one but nerve-racking. All the same, it had been a success and she had been elated by Gerard's pleased comments afterwards; she had even allowed herself the satisfaction of knowing that he had admired her in the new dress she had bought for the occasion, a pale green silk sheath. She had worn the thick gold chain his mother had given her and of course, her lovely ring. After the guests had gone home, he had followed her into the drawing room and leaned against the wall, watching her as she went round plumping up cushions, restoring chairs to their

original places and moving the small tables carefully.
It was a room she already loved, its grandeur mitigated
by a pleasant homeliness, brought about, she was sure,
by the fact that it was lived in. She moved a priceless
Rockingham vase to a place of safety and said with satisfaction: 'There, now it looks like itself again—I think
your friends must love coming here, Gerard.'

'I daresay.' He sauntered across the pale Aubusson
carpet towards her. 'A pleasant and successful evening,
Deborah, and you were a perfect hostess. I knew that
you would make me an excellent wife—you are also a
very charming and beautiful one.' He bent and kissed
her. 'Thank you, my dear.'

She had waited, hoping foolishly that he might say
more; that he found her attractive, even that he was falling a little in love with her, but his bland: 'What a wise
choice I have made,' gave her little consolation. She had
said a little woodenly that she was pleased that she was
living up to his good opinion of her and wished him a
good night, to go to her room and lie very wide awake
in her vast bed until the early hours of the morning.
Three weeks, she had reminded herself, and that was
only a fraction of the lifetime ahead of her, playing the
hostess to Gerard's friends, helping him in every way
she could, keeping his home just as he wanted it, taking an interest in his work on those all too rare occasions when he talked about it.

She remembered that she didn't even know where the
hospital was, nor for that matter, his consulting rooms,
and when she had asked him he had said kindly that
he imagined she had enough to fill her days without
bothering her head about such things, and then, sens-

ing her hurt, had offered to take her to the hospital and show her round.

It was almost as though he were keeping her at arms' length…and yet he had been good to her and very kind; she had a more than generous allowance, and true to his promise, Maureen was to visit them in a week's time and when Deborah had admired a crocodile handbag he had bought it for her without hesitation. He had bought her a car too—a Fiat 500—and opened accounts at all the larger shops for her. He was generous to a fault, and she repaid him in the only ways she knew how; by breakfasting with him each morning even though he was immersed in his post which she opened for him, and after he had gone, sorted for his secretary to attend to when she came during the morning. And she was always waiting for him when he got home in the evenings, sitting with Smith in the garden or reading in the sitting room. She wasn't sure if this was what he wanted her to do, and it was difficult to tell because he was unfailingly courteous to her, but at least she was there if he should want to talk. In a week or two, when she knew him a little better, she would ask him.

She applied herself to her Dutch grammar again and twiddled Smith's ears gently. There was still an hour before Wim would bring the tea and Gerard had said that he would be late that evening. She sighed and began to worry her way through the past tense of the verb *to be*.

Her earnest efforts were interrupted by the appearance of Claude. She looked up in some surprise as he lounged across the little plot of grass.

'Oh, hullo, Claude,' she forced her voice to politeness. 'I didn't hear the bell.'

'I walked in,' he told her coolly. 'A lovely afternoon and nothing to do—I thought I might invite myself to tea.'

She closed her book. 'Why, of course,' and felt irritated when he sat down beside her and took it from her.

'What's this? Dutch grammar—my goodness, you are trying hard, aren't you? Does Gerard know, or did he fix it up for you?'

She became evasive. 'I have lessons from a dear old professor—it's a difficult language, but I know quite a few words already, as well as one or two sentences.'

'"I love you," for instance, or should it be "do you love me?"' he asked, and added: 'Oh, I've annoyed you—I must apologise, but the idea of Gerard loving anyone is so amusing that I can't help wondering.'

Deborah turned to look at him, amazed at the fury of the rage she was bottling up. 'I know that you are a very old friend of Gerard's, but I don't care to discuss him with anyone. I hope you understand that.'

'Lord, yes,' he said easily. 'You have my fullest admiration, Debby—it must be hellishly difficult.'

'I prefer you not to call me Debby,' she told him austerely, and then, her curiosity getting the better of her good sense: 'What must be difficult?'

He grinned. 'Why, to be married to Gerard, of course. Everyone knows what a mess he made of his first marriage—no wonder the poor girl died...'

She had had enough; if he had intended to anger her, he had succeeded; her fury bubbled over as she got up, restraining herself with difficulty from slapping his smiling face. She said in a voice which shook with anger: 'I was told you were Gerard's friend, but you aren't behaving like a friend! I haven't the least idea what you're talking about, and I don't want to know. I think you should go—now!'

He didn't budge, but sat looking up at her, grinning still. 'If only I knew you better there would be a number of interesting questions I should like to ask, though I daresay you wouldn't answer them. I had no idea that you had such a nasty temper. Does Gerard know about it, I wonder?'

'Does Gerard know what?' asked Gerard from the shadow of the door, and Deborah jumped at the sound of his quiet voice, hating herself for doing it, whereas Claude didn't move, merely said: 'Hullo, there—early home, aren't you? The newly married man and all that?'

Deborah suddenly didn't care if Claude was an old family friend or not; she said hotly: 'I was just asking Claude to leave the house, but now you're here, Gerard, I think he should tell you why.'

'No need, my dear.' Gerard sounded almost placid. 'I'm afraid I have been guilty of eavesdropping—it was such an interesting conversation and I couldn't bring myself to break it up.'

He strolled across the grass to join them. 'Get up,' he ordered Claude, and his voice was no longer placid, but cold and contemptuous. 'It is a strange thing,' he commented to no one in particular, 'how blind one becomes to one's friends, though perhaps friends isn't quite the operative word. Deborah is quite right; I think you should leave my house—this instant, Claude, and not come back.'

Claude had got to his feet. 'You're joking...'

'No.'

'Just because I was going to tell Debby'—he turned

to look at her—'Deborah—about Sasja? Don't be ridiculous, Gerard, if I don't tell her someone else will.'

'Possibly, but they would tell the truth. What were
you going to tell her, Claude?' The coldness of his voice
was tinged with interest.

'I—? Only that...'

Deborah had had enough; she interrupted sharply:
'I'm going to my room.'

Her husband put out a hand and took her arm in a
gentle grip which kept her just where she was, but he
didn't look at her.

'Get out,' he advised Claude softly, 'get out before
I remember that you were once a friend of mine, and
if you come here again, annoying my wife, I'll make
mincemeat of you.'

Deborah watched Claude go, taking no notice of his
derisive goodbye. She didn't look at Gerard either, only
after the faint slam of the front door signalled the last
of Claude van Trapp did she say once more: 'If you
don't mind—I've a headache... I'll get Wim to bring
you out some tea.'

'Wait, Deborah.' Gerard had turned her round to
face him, his hands on her shoulders. 'I'm sorry about
this—I had no idea that Claude...thank you for being
loyal, and in such circumstances. You have every right
to be angry, for I should have told you the whole sorry
story before our marriage, but it is one I have tried to
forget over the years, and very nearly succeeded—the
idea of digging it all up again...'

'Then I don't want to hear it,' declared Deborah.
'What possible difference could it make anyway? It
isn't as though we're—we're...'

'In love?' he finished for her. 'No, but we are friends,

companions if you like, sharing our lives, and you have the right to know—and I should like to tell you.' He had pulled her close and his arms were very comforting— but that was all they were. She leaned her head against his shoulder and said steadily: 'I'm listening.'

'I married Sasja when I was twenty-eight. She was nineteen and gay and pretty and so young. I was studying for my fellowship and determined to be a success because I loved—still love—my work and nothing less than success would do. It was my fault, I suppose, working night after night when we should have been out dancing, or going to parties or the theatre. Perhaps I loved her, but it wasn't the right kind of love, and I couldn't understand why she hadn't the patience to wait until I had got my feet on the bottom rung of the ladder, just as she couldn't understand why I should choose to spend hour after hour working when I could have been taking her out.' He sighed. 'You see, I had thought that she would be content looking after our home—we had a modern flat in Amsterdam—and having our children.' His even voice became tinged with bitterness. 'She didn't want or like children and she had no interest in my work. After a year she found someone else and I, God forgive me, didn't discover it until she was killed, with the other man, in a plane crash.'

Deborah said into the superfine cloth of his shoulder: 'I'm sorry, Gerard, but I'm glad I know.' She lifted her face to meet his. 'I wanted to slap Claude—I wish I had!'

She was rewarded by his faint smile. 'He was right in a way, you know—I was really responsible for Sasja's death.'

'He was not! He made it sound underhand and

beastly—quite horrible—and it wasn't like that, nor was it your fault.'

'Yes, it was, Deborah—I married the wrong girl just because I was, for a very short time, in love with her. Now you know why I don't want to become involved again—why I married you.'

'And if that's a compliment, it's a mighty odd one,' she told herself silently, and swallowed back the tears tearing at her throat.

Out loud, she said matter-of-factly: 'Well, now you've told me, we won't talk about Sasja again.' She took a heartening breath. 'You don't still love her?'

His voice was nicely reassuring. 'Quite sure. My love wore thin after a very few months—when she died I had none left.'

And Deborah's heart gave a guilty skip of joy; she was sorry about Sasja, but it was a long time ago, and she hadn't treated Gerard very well. She registered a mental resolve to find out more about her from her mother-in-law when the occasion was right, for it seemed to her that Gerard was very likely taking a blame which wasn't his. She drew away from him and said briskly: 'I'll get the tea, shall I? Would you like it out here?'

She was glad of the few minutes' respite to compose herself once more into the quiet companion he expected when he came home; she and Wim took the tea out between them and when she sat down again under the copper beech she saw that Gerard was leafing through her Dutch grammar.

She poured the tea and waited for him to speak. 'Something I forgot,' he said slowly. 'I should have arranged lessons for you.'

'As a matter of fact,' she began carefully, sugaring his tea and handing him the cup, 'I do have lessons. I asked around and I go to a dear old man called Professor de Wit four times a week. He's very good and fearfully stern. I've had eight lessons so far. He gives me a great deal of homework.'

Gerard put the book down. 'I have underestimated you, Deborah,' he observed wryly. 'Tell me, why are you going to all this trouble?'

She was taken aback. 'Trouble? It's no trouble, it's something to do. Besides, how can I be a good wife if I can't even understand my husband's language? Not all your friends speak English.'

He was staring at her, frowning a little. 'You regard our marriage as a job to be done well—is that how you think of it, Deborah?'

She took a sandwich with a hand which trembled very slightly; it would never do for him to get even an inkling. 'Yes,' she declared brightly. 'Isn't that what you wanted?' and when he didn't reply, went on: 'Maureen will be here next week. I know you won't have any time to spare, but will you suggest the best outings for her? I thought I'd take her to Volendam in the Fiat—all those costumes, you know—and then we can go to the Rijksmuseum and the shops and go round the canals in one of those boats. I'm longing to go—and the Palace, if it's open.'

'My poor Deborah, I've neglected you.'

'No. I knew that you were going to be busy, you told me so. Besides, I've had several weeks in which to find my own feet.'

He smiled. 'You're as efficient a wife and hostess as you were a Theatre Sister,' he told her. And because she thought he expected it of her, she laughed gaily and assured him that that had been her ambition.

Presently he got to his feet. 'I've a couple of patients to see at my consulting rooms,' he told her, 'but I'll be back within the hour. Are we doing anything this evening?'

She shook her head. Perhaps he would take her out—she would wear the new dress...

'Good. Could we dine a little earlier? I've a mass of work to do; a couple of quiet hours in the study would be a godsend to me.'

Deborah even managed a smile. 'Of course—half past six? That will give you a lovely long evening.'

He hesitated. 'And you?'

She gave him a calm smiling look from her lovely eyes. 'I've simply masses of letters to write,' she lied.

Chapter 5

They fetched Maureen the following week, travelling overnight to arrive at Sherborne in the early morning, picking up an ecstatic child beside herself with excitement, and driving on to Deborah's home for lunch. The boys were home for the half-term holiday too and it was a noisy hilarious meal, with the whole family talking at once, although Mr Culpeper confined his conversation to Gerard, because, as he remarked a little severely to the rest of his family, he appeared to be the only calm person present. He had, it was true, greeted his various children with pleasure, but as he had just finished translating an Anglo-Saxon document of some rarity, and wished to discuss it with someone intelligent, he took little part in the rather excited talk. Deborah could hear various snatches of her learned parent's rambling dissertation from time to time and wondered if Gerard was enjoying it as much as he appeared to be. She decided that he was; he was even holding his own with her father, something not many people were able to do. They exchanged brief smiles and she turned back to Maureen's endless questions.

They left shortly afterwards, driving fast to catch the night ferry, and Maureen, who had sat in front with Gerard, had to be persuaded to go to the cabin with Deborah when they got on board; the idea of staying up all night, and on a boat, was an alluring one, only the pleasures in store in the morning, dangled before her sleepy eyes by Gerard, convinced her that a few hours of sleep was a small price to pay for the novelty of driving through a foreign country at half past four in the morning.

The weather was fine, although it was still dark when they landed. Maureen, refreshed by a splendid nap, sat beside Gerard once more, talking without pause. Deborah wondered if he minded, although it was hard to tell from his manner, which was one of amused tolerance towards his small sister-in-law. Once or twice he turned to speak to her and she thought that there was more warmth in his voice when he spoke, but that could be wishful thinking, for after the unpleasant business with Claude and all that he had told her about his marriage to Sasja, she had hoped that perhaps his feelings might have deepened from friendship to even the mildest of affection.

She was to think that on several occasions during the next few days, but never with certainty. Gerard, it seemed, could spare the time to take his small relative round and about where he had not found it possible with herself, and Deborah caught herself wondering if he was seizing the opportunity to get upon a closer footing with herself. He drove them to Volendam, obligingly helped Maureen purchase postcards and souvenirs, admired the costumed villagers, standing ready to have their photos taken by the tourists, and when Maureen wished that she had a camera so that she could take her own pictures, purchased one for her. And what was more, he showed nothing but pleasure when she flung her arms around him and thanked him extravagantly for it.

They lunched that day at Wieringerwerf, after the briefest of visits to Hoorn. The restaurant was on the main road, a large, bustling place, colourful with flags and brightly painted chairs and tables on its terraces; not at all the sort of place Gerard would choose to go to for himself, Deborah suspected, but Maureen, eyeing the coloured umbrellas and the comfortable restaurant, pronounced it super. She chose her lunch from an enormous menu card and told Gerard that he was super too, and when he laughed, said:

'But it's true, you are super. I'm not surprised that Debby married you. If you could have waited a year or two, I'd have married you myself. Perhaps you have some younger brothers?'

'Married, I'm afraid, my dear—but I have a number of cousins. I'll arrange for you to meet them next time you come and you can look them over.' Deborah saw no mockery in his face and loved him for it.

Maureen agreed to this. 'Though I don't suppose you'll want me again for a little while. I mean, there are so many of us, aren't there? You'll only want a few at a time.'

Gerard glanced at Deborah. 'Oh, I don't know,' he said easily. 'I think it would be rather fun if all of you were to come over and spend Christmas. There's plenty of room.'

She beamed at him. 'I say, you really are the greatest! I'll tell Mother, so's she can remind Father about it, then it won't come as a surprise to him—he forgets, you know.'

She polished off an enormous ice cream embellished with whipped cream, chocolate, nuts and fruit, and sighed blissfully. 'Where do we go next?' she wanted to know.

Gerard glanced at his watch. 'I'm afraid back home. I have a list this afternoon at four o'clock.'

'You won't be home for dinner?' asked Deborah, trying to sound casual.

'I very much doubt it. Can you amuse yourselves?'

'Of course.' Had she not been amusing herself times without number all these weeks? 'Shall I get you something cooked when you come in?'

'Would you? It could be any time.'

It was late when he got back, Marijke had gone to bed, leaving Wim to lay a tray for his master. So it was Deborah who went down to the kitchen and heated soup and made an omelette and a fresh fruit salad and carried them up to the dining room.

She arranged everything on the table and when Gerard was seated went to sit herself in one of the great armchairs against the wall.

'I hope it was successful,' she essayed, not knowing if he was too tired to talk or if he wanted to talk about it.

He spooned his soup. 'Entirely successful. You're referring to the case this afternoon—I had no idea that you knew about it.'

'I didn't. You always have a list on Thursday afternoons, but you have never been later than eight o'clock, so I guessed…'

He laughed. 'I keep forgetting that you've worked for me for two years. It was an important patient and he had come a long way in the hope that I could help him, but he refused utterly to allow me to begin the operation until his wife had arrived.'

'Was it a chondroma?'

'Yes.'

'Poor man, but I'm glad you could help him. His wife must be so thankful.'

Gerard began on the omelette. 'I imagine so,' and when he didn't say anything else she said presently: 'Thank you for spending so much time with us today. Maureen loved it.'

'And you?'

'I loved it too; it's all foreign to me, even though I live here now.'

He frowned. 'I keep forgetting that too. I shan't have a minute to spare tomorrow, but I'll manage an afternoon the day after—have you any plans?'

'Could we go somewhere for tea? Maureen loves going out to tea, especially if it's combined with sightseeing. I could take her on a round of the canals tomorrow.'

He speared the last of the omelette, complimented her upon her cooking and observed: 'I know I'm booked up for tomorrow, but how would it be if you both came to the hospital and had a look round? I'll get one of the housemen to take you round. Go to the—no, better still, I'll come home and pick you up, only you mustn't keep me waiting. Paul van Goor can look after you and see you into a taxi afterwards. Would you like that?'

She said very quietly: 'Enormously,' wondering if he was being kind to Maureen or if he was allowing her to share his life just a little at last. 'If you'll tell us what time you want us to be ready, we'll be waiting.' She got up. 'Would you like the brandy? I'm going to fetch the coffee.'

'Shall we go into the sitting room and share the pot between us?'

She loathed coffee so late at night, but she would gladly swallow pints of it if he wanted her to talk to. Perhaps the operation had been a bit of a strain—she had no idea who the important patient might be and she had too much sense to ask. All the same, when she had poured coffee for them both she asked him: 'I'd love to hear about the op if it wouldn't bore you—which method did you use?'

She had done the right thing, she could sense that. He told her, using terms he had no need to explain, describing techniques she understood and could comment upon with intelligence. It was very late when he had finished, and when he apologised for keeping her up she waved a careless hand and said in a carefully matter-of-fact voice: 'I enjoyed it.'

She took the tray back to the kitchen, wished him good night and went quickly upstairs, because she couldn't trust herself to preserve her careful, tranquil manner any longer.

She and Maureen were to be ready at half past one on the following afternoon, and at exactly that time Gerard came for them. He was preoccupied but, as always, courteous during the short drive. The Grotehof hospital was in the centre of the city, tucked away behind some of its oldest houses. The building was old too, but had been extended and modernised until it was difficult to see where the old ended and the new began. The entrance was in the old part, through a large, important door leading to a vast tiled hall. It was here that Gerard, with a muttered word of apology, handed them over with a hasty word of introduction to a young and cheerful houseman, Paul van Goor, who, obviously primed as to his task, led them through a labyrinth of corridors to the children's ward, talking all the time in excellent English.

From there they went to the surgical block, the medical block, the recreation rooms, the Accident Room, the dining room for the staff and lastly the theatre block, the newest addition to the hospital, he told them proudly. It consisted of six theatres, two for general surgery, one for ENT, one for cardio-thoracic work and two for orthopaedics. They couldn't go inside, of course, although Deborah longed to do so, and when she peered through the round window in the swing doors she felt a pang of regret that it was no longer her world; she amended that—the regret was because it was still Gerard's world and she no longer had a share in it, for at least at Clare's she worked with him. Now she was a figurehead in his house, running it smoothly and efficiently, dressing to do him credit, living with him and yet not sharing his life.

She sighed, and Paul asked her if she was tired and when she said no, suggested that they might like to go back through the hospital garden, very small but lovingly tended. They returned via lengthy staircases and roundabout passages, Deborah deep in thought, Maureen and Paul talking earnestly. They were passing a great arched doorway when a nurse flung it open and

coming towards them from the other side was Gerard,
a different Gerard, surrounded by a group of housemen
and students, his registrar, the Ward Sister and a handful of nurses. If he saw them he took no notice; Deborah hadn't expected him to. She managed to snatch at
Maureen's hand as she lifted it to wave to him.

'No, you can't, darling,' she said urgently. 'Not here,
it wouldn't do. I'll explain later.'

She had done her best to do so on their way to Mevrouw van Doorninck's flat in the taxi Paul had got for
them, but all Maureen said was: 'Oh, Debby, how stuffy
you are—he's my brother-in-law, and you're married to
him, of course he can wave to us if he wants to; important people do just what they like and no one minds.'

She was inclined to argue about it; fortunately she
was kept too occupied for the rest of the afternoon, for
Gerard's mother had gathered the family together to
meet Maureen and the party was a merry one. 'Only,' as
Mevrouw van Doorninck declared to Deborah, as they
drank their tea and nibbled the thin sugary biscuits, 'it's
such a pity that Gerard can't be here too. I had hoped
now that he was married...it is as though he is afraid
to be happy again.' She glanced at Deborah, who said
nothing at all, and went on presently: 'He seems very
fond of Maureen, such a sweet child. I look forward to
meeting the rest of your family, my dear.'

'I'm sure they're just as eager to meet you, Mevrouw
van Doorninck.' Deborah was relieved that they had
left the subject of Gerard. 'They're all coming over to
spend Christmas.'

'Christmas?' Her companion gave her another sharp
look. 'A great deal could happen by then.'

Deborah would have liked to ask her mother-in-law what, in heaven's name, could happen in this well-ordered, well-organised world in which she now lived. A flaming row, she told herself vulgarly, would relieve the monotony, but Gerard was difficult to quarrel with—he became at once blandly courteous, placidly indifferent, a sign, she had decided forlornly, that he didn't consider her of sufficient importance in his life to warrant a loss of temper.

She and Maureen got up to go presently, walking back to the house in the Keizersgracht, to curl up in the comfortable chairs in the sitting room and discuss the delights of Christmas and the not so distant pleasures of the next day when Gerard had promised to take them out.

He telephoned just before dinner, to say that he was detained at the hospital and would dine with a colleague and she wasn't to wait for him. All the same she sat on, long after Maureen had gone to bed and Wim and Marijke had gone to their rooms. But when the clock struck midnight and there was no sign of him, she went to bed too, but not to sleep. She heard his quiet steps going through the quiet house in the early hours of the morning and lay awake until daylight, wondering where he had been and with whom.

He was at breakfast when she got down in the morning, looking, Deborah thought, a little tired but as impeccably dressed as he always was, and although she wanted very much to ask him why he had come home so very late the night before, she held her tongue, remarked on the pleasant morning and read her letters. She was rewarded for this circumspect behaviour by him saying presently:

'I promised to take you both out this afternoon. I'm

sorry, but it won't be possible. Could you find something to do, do you suppose?'

She wouldn't let him see her disappointment. 'Of course—there are a hundred and one things on Maureen's list. She'll be disappointed, though.'

'And you.' His glance was thoughtful.

'Oh, I'll be disappointed too; I love sightseeing. As it's her last day, I'll take her to Schevingenen. She'll love it there, and your mother was telling me of a lovely tea-room near the sea.'

She smiled at him, a friendly, casual smile, to let him see that it was of no importance whatever that he had had to cry off, and picked up the rest of her post, only to put it down again as a thought struck her.

'Gerard, would you rather not take Maureen back tomorrow? I can easily take her in the Fiat. Rather a comedown for her after the BMW and the Citroën, I know, but I've been on the road several times now and you said yourself that my driving had improved…'

He frowned at her across the table. 'I don't like the idea of you going that distance, though I must confess that it would be awkward for me to leave.'

'That's settled, then,' she said briskly. 'Only if you don't mind, I think I'll spend a night at home; I don't think I'd be much good at turning round and coming straight back.'

'An excellent idea.' He was still frowning. 'I wonder if there's someone who could drive you—Wim's taking Mother up to Friesland or he could have gone; there may be someone at the hospital.'

'Don't bother,' said Deborah quickly, 'you've enough to do without that. I'll be quite all right, you know, you don't need to give it another thought.'

'Very well. I won't, though if it had been anyone else but you…'

She was left to decide for herself if he had intended that as a compliment or not.

They were on their way back from Schevingenen that afternoon when she found herself behind her husband's car. He was driving the Citroën, and seated beside him was a small, dark, and very attractive woman, a circumstance which made Deborah thankful that Maureen was so taken up with a large street organ in the opposite direction that she saw nothing.

Presently the traffic allowed her to slip past him. Without looking she was aware of his sudden stare as she raced the little car ahead of the Citroën while Maureen chattered on, still craning her neck to see the last of the organ. Deborah answered her small sister's questions mechanically while her thoughts were busy. So Gerard couldn't spare the time to take them out, though seemingly he had leisure enough to drive around with a pretty woman during an afternoon which was to have been so busy. She had, she told herself savagely, two minds to stay home for a good deal longer than one night. There were, if her memory served her right, several social engagements within the next week or so—let him attend them alone, or better still, with his charming companion. She frowned so fiercely at the very idea that Maureen, turning to speak to her, wanted to know if she had a headache.

Gerard was home for dinner. Deborah greeted him with her usual calm friendliness, hoped that his day hadn't been too busy and plunged into an account of their outing that afternoon, pausing at the end of it to give him time to tell her that he had seen her, and explain his companion. But he said nothing about it at all, only had a short and lively conversation with Maureen and joined her in a game with Smith before shutting himself up in his study.

Deborah exerted herself to be entertaining during dinner, and if her manner was over-bright, her companions didn't seem to notice. After the meal, when Gerard declared himself ready to take Maureen on a boat tour of the lighted canals, even though it was almost dark and getting chilly, she pleaded a headache and stayed at home, working pettishly at a petit-point handbag intended for her mother-in-law's Christmas present.

She and Maureen left after breakfast the next morning to catch the midday ferry from Zeebrugge and Gerard had left the house even earlier; over breakfast he had had very little to say to her, save to advise her to take care and wish her a pleasant journey, but with Maureen he had laughed and joked and given her an enormous box of chocolates as a farewell present and responded suitably to her uninhibited hugs.

They made good time to the ferry, and once on board, repaired to the restaurant where, over her enormous lunch, Maureen talked so much that she didn't notice that Deborah was eating almost nothing.

The drive to Somerset was uneventful. By now the little girl was getting tired; she dozed from time to time, assuring Deborah that she did so only to ensure that she would be wide awake when they reached home. Which left Deborah with her thoughts, running round and round inside her head like mice in a wheel. None of them were happy and all of them were of Gerard.

They reached home at about midnight, to find her

parents waiting for them with hot drinks and sandwiches and a host of questions.

Deborah was answering them rather sleepily when the telephone rang and Mr Culpeper, annoyed at the interruption, answered it testily. But his sharp voice shouting, 'Hullo, hullo' in peremptory tones changed to a more friendly accent. 'It's Gerard,' he announced, 'wants to speak to you, Deb.'

She had telephoned the house in Amsterdam on their arrival at Dover, knowing very well that he wouldn't be home and leaving nothing but a brief message with Wim. She picked up the receiver now, schooling her voice to its usual calm and said: 'Hullo, Gerard.'

His voice was quiet and distinct. 'Hullo, Deborah. Wim gave me your message, but I wanted to hear for myself that you had got home safely. I hope I haven't got you out of bed.'

'No. You're up late yourself.'

His 'Yes' was terse. He went on quickly: 'I won't keep you. Have a good night's sleep and drive carefully tomorrow. Good night, Debby.'

She said good night and replaced the receiver. He had never called her Debby before; she wondered about it, but she was really too tired to think. Presently they all went to bed and she slept without waking until she was called in the morning.

She was to take Maureen back to school after breakfast and then continue on her return journey. It seemed lonely after she had left her little sister, still talking and quite revived by a good night's sleep. There hadn't been much time to talk to her mother while she had been home, and perhaps that was a good thing; she might have let slip some small thing...all the same, it had been a cheerful few hours. Her parents, naturally enough, took it for granted that she was happy and beyond asking after Gerard and agreeing eagerly to the Christmas visit they had said little more; there had been no chance because Maureen had so much to talk about. It would have been nice to have confided in someone, thought Deborah, pushing the little car hard along the road towards the Winchester bypass, but perhaps not quite loyal to Gerard. The thought of seeing him again made her happy, but the happiness slowly wilted as the day wore on. There had been brilliant sunshine to start with, but now clouds were piling up behind her and long before she reached Dover, it was raining, and out at sea the sky showed a uniform greyness which looked as though it might be there for ever.

She slept for most of the crossing, sitting in a chair in the half-filled ship; she was tired and had been nervous of getting the car on board. Somehow with Maureen she hadn't found it frightening, but going up the steep ramp to the upper car deck she had quaked with fright; it was a relief to sit down for a few hours and recover her cool. She fetched herself a cup of coffee, brought a paperback and settled back. They were within sight of land when she woke and feeling tired still, she tidied herself and after a hasty cup of tea, went to the car deck. ...ng down the ramp wasn't too bad, although her ... stalled when she reached the bottom. Deborah ... herself trembling as she followed the cars ahead of her towards the Customs booth in the middle of the docks road. Suddenly the drive to Amsterdam didn't seem the easy journey she had made it out to be when she had offered to take Maureen home. It stretched before her in her mind's eye, dark and wet, with the

Breskens ferry to negotiate and the long-drawn-out, lonely road across the islands, and Rotterdam…she had forgotten what a long way it was; somehow she hadn't noticed that when she was with Gerard, or even when she had taken Maureen back, but then it had been broad daylight.

She came to a halt by the Customs, proffered her passport and shivered in the chilly night air as she wound down the window. The man smiled at her. 'You will go to the left, please, Mevrouw.' He waved an arm towards a road leading off from the main docks road.

Deborah was puzzled; all the cars in front of her were keeping straight on. She said slowly so that he would be sure to understand: 'I'm going to Holland—don't I keep straight on to the main road?'

He was still smiling but quite firm. 'To the left, Mevrouw, if you will be so good.'

She went to the left; possibly they were diverting the traffic; she would find out in good time, she supposed. She was going slowly because the arc lights hardly penetrated this smaller side road and she had no idea where it was leading her, nor was there a car in front of her. She was on the point of stopping and going back to make sure that she hadn't misunderstood the Customs man, when her headlights picked out the BMW parked at the side of the road and Gerard leaning against its boot. In the bad light he looked enormous and very reassuring too; she hadn't realised just how much she had wanted to be reassured until she saw him there, standing in the pouring rain, the collar of his Burberry turned up to his ears, a hat pulled down over his eyes. She pulled up then and he walked over to her and when she wound down the window, said: 'Hullo, my dear. I thought it might be a good idea to come and meet you and drive you back—the weather, you know...'

She was still getting over her surprise and joy at seeing him. Her 'hullo' was faint, as was her protesting: 'But I can't leave the Fiat here?'

She became aware that Wim was there too, standing discreetly in the background by his master's car. Gerard nodded towards him. 'I brought Wim with me, he'll take the Fiat back.' He opened the car door. 'Come along, Deborah, we shall be home in no time at all.'

She got out silently and allowed herself to be tucked up snugly beside him in the BMW, pausing only to greet Wim and hope that he didn't mind driving the Fiat home.

'A pleasure, Mevrouw,' grinned Wim cheerfully, 'but I think that you will be there first.' He put out a hand to take the car keys from her and raised it in salute as he walked back to her car.

As Gerard reversed his own car and swept back the way she had come Deborah asked: 'Oh, is that why he told me to come this way and not out of the main gate?'

'Yes—I was afraid that we might miss you once you got past the Customs. Did you have a good trip back?'

For a variety of reasons and to her great shame her voice was drowned in a sudden flood of tears. She swallowed them back frantically and they poured down her cheeks instead. She stared out of the window at the outskirts of the town—flat land, dotted here and there with houses, it looked untidy even in the dim light of the overhead street lamps—and willed herself to be calm. After a minute Gerard said 'Deborah?' and because she would have to say something sooner or later she managed a 'Yes, thank you,' and spoilt it with a dreary snivel.

He slid the car to the side of the road on to a patch of waste land and switched off the engine. He had tossed off his hat when he got into the car; now he turned his handsome head and looked down at her in the semi-dark. 'What happened?' he asked gently, and then: 'Debby, I've never seen you cry before.'

She sniffed, struggled to get herself under control and managed:

'I hardly ever do—n-nothing's the m-matter, it's just that I'm tired, I expect.' She added on a small wail: 'I was t-terrified—those ramps on the ferry, they were ghastly—I thought I'd never reach the top and I didn't notice with Maureen, but when I was by m-myself it was awful, and the engine stalled and it was raining and when I got off the ferry it s-seemed s-such a long way to get home.' She hiccoughed, blew her nose and mopped her wet cheeks.

'I should never have let you go alone, I must have been mad. My poor girl, what a thoughtless man I am! You see, you are—always have been—so calm and efficient and able to cope, and then last night when I telephoned you, you sounded so tired—I rearranged my work to come and meet you. I remembered this long dark road too, Deborah, and in the Fiat it would be even longer. Forgive me, Deborah.'

She sniffed. His arm, flung along the back of the seat and holding her shoulders lightly, was comforting, and she was rapidly regaining her self-control. Later, she knew, she would be furious with herself for breaking down in this stupid fashion. She said in a voice which was nearly normal: 'Thank you very much, Gerard. It was only because it was raining and so very dark.'

She felt his arm slide away. 'I've some coffee here—Marijke always regards any journey more than ten miles distant from Amsterdam as being fraught with danger and probable starvation and provides accordingly. Sandwiches, too.'

They ate and drank in a companionable silence and presently Gerard began to talk, soothing nothings about her parents and her home and Smith—perhaps he talked to his more nervous patients like that, she thought sleepily, before he told them that he would have to operate. He took her cup from her presently and said: 'Go to sleep, Deborah, there's nothing to look at at this time of night—I'll wake you when we reach Amsterdam.'

She started to tell him that she wasn't tired any more, and fell asleep saying it.

She wakened to the touch of his hand on her arm. 'A few minutes,' he told her, and she was astonished to see the still lighted, now familiar streets of the city all around them. But the Keizersgracht was only dimly lit, its water gleaming dimly through the bare trees lining the road. It was still raining, but softly now, and there were a few lights from the houses they passed. As they drew up before their own front door, she saw that the great chandelier in the hall was beaming its light through the glass transom over the door and the sitting room was lighted too so that the wet pavement glistened in its glow. Gerard helped her out of the car and took her arm and they crossed the cobbles together as the front door was flung open and Marijke, with a wildly barking Smith, stood framed within it.

Going through the door Deborah knew at that moment just how much she loved the old house; it welcomed her, just as Marijke and Smith were welcoming her, as though she had returned from a long and arduous journey. She smiled a little mistily at Marijke and bent to catch Smith up into her arms. They went into the sitting room and Gerard took her coat, then Marijke was there almost at once with more hot coffee and a plate of paper-thin sandwiches. She talked volubly to Gerard while she set them out on the silver tray and carried it over to put on the table by Deborah's chair. When she had gone, Deborah asked: 'What was all that about?'

He came to sit opposite her and now she could see the lines of fatigue on his face, so that before he could answer she asked: 'Have you had a hard day?'

He smiled faintly. 'Yes.'

'You've been busy—too busy, lately.'

'That is no excuse for letting you go all that way alone.'

She said firmly: 'It was splendid for my driving. I'll not mind again.'

'There won't be an again,' he told her briefly, 'and Marijke was talking about you.'

'Oh—I recognised one word—stomach.'

It was nice to see him laugh like that. 'She said that you look tired and that beautiful women should never look other than beautiful. She strongly advised nourishment for your—er—stomach so that you would sleep like a rose.'

Deborah said softly: 'What a charming thing to say, about the rose, I mean. Dear Marijke—she and Wim, they're like the house, aren't they?' And was sorry that she had said it, because he might not understand. But he did; the look he gave her was one of complete understanding. She smiled at him and then couldn't look away from his intent gaze. 'You saw me the other afternoon,' he stated the fact simply. 'You have been wondering why I couldn't find the time to take you and Maureen on a promised trip and yet have the leisure to drive around with a very attractive woman—she was attractive, did you not think so?'

'Yes.'

'I don't discuss my patients with you, you know that, I think—although I must confess I have frequently wished to do so—but I do not wish you to misunderstand. The patient upon whom I operated the other evening was...' he named someone and Deborah sat up with a jerk, although she said nothing. 'Yes, you see why I have been so worried and—secretive. The lady with me was his wife. She had been to Schiphol to meet her daughter, who was breaking her journey on her way home to get news of her father. At the last moment his wife declared that she was unable to tell her and asked me to do it. We were on our way back to the hospital when you saw us. I should have told you sooner. I'm not sure why I didn't, perhaps I was piqued at the way you ignored the situation. Any other woman—wife—would have asked.'

'It was none of my business,' she said stiffly. 'I didn't know...'

'You mean that you suspected me of having a girl-friend?' He was smiling, but she sensed his controlled anger.

There was no point in being anything but honest with him. 'Yes, I think I did, but it still wouldn't be my business, and it shouldn't matter, should it?'

He hadn't taken his eyes off her. 'I believe you said

that once before. You think that? But do you not know me well enough to know that I would have been quite honest with you before I married you?'

Her head had begun to ache. 'Oh, yes, indeed, but that wasn't what I meant. What I'm trying to say is that I've no right to mind, have I?'

Gerard got to his feet and pulled her gently to hers. 'You have every right in the world,' he assured her. 'I don't think our bargain included that kind of treatment of each other, Deborah. I don't cheat the people I like.'

She didn't look at him. 'No, I know that, truly I do. I'm sorry I was beastly. I think I'm tired.'

They walked together out of the room and in the hall he kissed her cheek. 'I'll wait for Wim, he shouldn't be much longer now. And by the way, I've taken some time off. In a couple of days I'll take you to the house in Friesland, and we might go and see some friends of mine who live close by—she's English, too.'

Deborah was half way up the stairs. 'That sounds lovely,' she told him and then turned round to say: 'Thank you for coming all that way, it must have been a bind after a hard day's work.'

He didn't answer her, but she was conscious of his eyes on her as she climbed the stairs.

Chapter 6

But before they went to Friesland Deborah met some other friends of Gerard's. She had spent a quiet day after her return, arranging the menu for a dinner party they were to give during the following week, paying a morning visit to her mother-in-law, telephoning her own mother and writing a few letters before taking Smith for a walk. She was back home, waiting for Gerard's return from the Grotehof after tea, when the telephone rang.

It was a woman's voice, light and sweet, enquiring if Mijnheer van Doorninck was home. 'No,' said Deborah, and wondered who it was, 'I'm sorry—perhaps I could take a message?' She spoke in the careful Dutch the professor had taught her, and hoped that the conversation wasn't going to get too involved.

'Is that Gerard's wife?' asked the voice, in English now, and when Deborah said a little uncertainly: 'Why, yes—' went on: 'Oh, good. I'm Adelaide van Essen. My husband's a paediatrician at the Grotehof and a friend of Gerard. We got back from England last night and Coenraad telephoned me just now and told me about you. You don't mind me ringing you up?'

'I'm delighted—I don't know any English people here yet.'

'Well, come and meet me—us, for a start. Come this evening. I know it's short notice, but I told Coenraad to ask Gerard to bring you to dinner—you will come?'

'I'd love to.' Deborah paused. 'I'm not sure about Gerard, he works late quite a lot and often works at home.'

She had the impression that the girl at the other end of the line was concealing surprise. Then: 'I'm sure he'll make time. We haven't seen each other for ages and the men are old friends. We live quite near you, in the Herengracht—is seven o'clock too early? Oh, and here's our number in case you want to ring back. Till seven, then. I'm so looking forward to meeting you.'

Deborah went back to her chair. The voice had sounded nice, soft and gentle and friendly. She spent the next ten minutes or so in deciding what she should wear and still hadn't made up her mind when Gerard came in.

His hullo was friendly and after he had enquired about her day, he took a chair near her. 'I met a friend of mine at the Grotehof this afternoon,' he told her. 'Coenraad van Essen—he's married to an English girl. They're just back from England and they want us to go round for dinner this evening. Would you like to go? It's short notice and I don't know if it will upset any arrangements you may have made?'

She chose a strand of silk and threaded her needle.

'His wife telephoned a few minutes ago. I'd like to go very much. She suggested seven o'clock, so I had better go and talk to Marijke.'

Marijke hadn't started the cutlets and the cheese soufflé; Deborah, in her laborious Dutch and helped by a few words here and there from Wim, suggested that they should have them the following day instead and apologised for the short notice. To which Marijke had a whole lot to say in reply, her face all smiles. Deborah turned to Wim. 'I don't quite understand…'

'Marijke is saying that it is good for you to see a lady of your own age and also English. She wishes you a merry evening.' He beamed at her. 'Me, I wish the same also, Mevrouw.'

She wore the pink silk jersey dress she had been unable to resist the last time she had visited Metz, the fashionable dress shop within walking distance of the house, and went downstairs to find Gerard waiting for her. 'I'm not late?' she asked anxiously as she crossed the hall.

'No—I wanted a few minutes with you. Shall we go into the sitting room?'

Deborah's heart dropped to her elegant shoes. What was he going to tell her? That he was going away on one of his teaching trips—that he wouldn't be able to take her to Friesland after all? She arranged her face into a suitable composure and turned to face him.

'Did you never wonder why I had not given you a wedding gift?' he asked her. 'Not because I had given no thought to it; there were certain alterations I wanted done, and only today are they finished.'

He took a small velvet case from his pocket and opened it. There were earrings inside on its thick satin lining; elaborate pearl drops in a diamond setting. She looked at them with something like awe. 'My goodness,' she uttered, 'they're—they're beautiful! I've never seen anything like them.'

He had taken them from their box. 'Try them on,' he invited her. 'They're very old, but the setting was clumsy; I've had them re-set to my own design. You are tall enough to take such a style, I think.'

She had gone to the mirror over the sofa table and hooked them in and stood looking at them. They were exquisite, and he was right, they suited her admirably. She turned her lovely head and watched the diamonds take fire. 'I don't know how to thank you,' she began. 'They're magnificent!'

Thanking him didn't seem quite enough, so she went to him and rather hesitantly kissed his cheek. 'Do you suppose I might wear them this evening?' she asked.

'Why not?' He had gone over to the small secretaire by one of the windows and was opening one of its drawers. He returned with another, larger case in his hand. 'This has been in the family for quite some time too,' he observed as he gave it to her. 'I've had it re-strung and the clasp re-set to match the earrings.'

Deborah opened the case slowly. There were pearls in it, a double row with a diamond and pearl clasp which followed the exact pattern of the earrings. She stared at it and all she could manage was an ecstatic 'Oh!' Gerard took them from her and fastened them round her neck and she went back to the mirror and had another look; they were quite superb. 'I don't know how to thank you,' she repeated, quite at a loss for words. 'It's the most wonderful wedding present anyone could dream of having.'

He was standing behind her, staring at her reflection.

After a moment he smiled faintly. 'You are my wife,' he pointed out. 'You are entitled to them.' He spoke lightly as he turned away.

He need not have said that, she thought unhappily, looking at her suddenly downcast face in the mirror. It took her a few moments to fix a smile on to it before she turned away and picked up her coat.

'Do we walk or go in the car?' she asked brightly.

He helped her into her coat and she could have been his sister, she thought bitterly, for all the impression she made upon him. 'The car,' he told her cheerfully. 'It's almost seven, perhaps we had better go at once.'

The house in the Herengracht was bigger than Gerard's but very similar in style. Its vast front door was opened as they reached it and an elderly man greeted them with a 'Good evening, Mevrouw—Mijnheer.'

Gerard slapped him on the shoulder. 'Tweedle, how are you? You haven't called me Mijnheer for many a long day.' He looked at Deborah, smiling. 'This is Tweedle, my dear, who has been with Coenraad since he was a toddler. I daresay you will meet Mrs Tweedle presently.'

'Indeed, she will be delighted,' Tweedle informed them gravely, adding: 'The Baron and Baroness are in the small sitting room, Mr Gerard.'

He led the way across the panelled hall and opened a door, announcing them as he did so, and Deborah, with Gerard's hand under her elbow urging her gently on, went in.

The room was hardly small and she saw at a glance that it was furnished with some magnificent pieces worthy of a museum, yet it was decidedly lived in; there was a mass of knitting cast down carelessly on a small drum table, a pile of magazines were tumbled on to the sofa table behind the big settee before the chimneypiece, and there was a pleasant scent of flowers, tobacco and—very faint—beeswax polish. There were two people in the room, a man as tall as Gerard but somewhat older, his dark hair greying at the temples, horn-rimmed glasses astride his handsome beaky nose. It was a kind face as well as a good-looking one, and Deborah decided then and there that she was going to like Gerard's friend. The girl who got up with him was small, slim and very pretty, with huge dark eyes and a mass of bright red hair piled high. She was wearing a very simple dress of cream silk and some of the loveliest sapphires Deborah had ever set eyes on. She felt Gerard's hand on her arm again and went forward to receive the Baron's quiet welcome and the charming enthusiasm of his small wife, who, after kissing Gerard in a sisterly fashion, led her to a small sofa and sat down beside her.

'You really are a dear to come at a moment's notice,' she declared. 'You didn't mind?'

Deborah shook her head, smiling. She was going to like this small vivid creature. 'It was kind of you to ask us. I'm so glad to meet another English girl. Gerard has been so busy and—and we haven't been married very long. I've met a great many of his colleagues, though.'

Her companion glanced at her quickly. 'Duty dinners,' she murmured, 'and the rest of the time they're immersed in their work. Coenraad says you were Gerard's Theatre Sister.'

'Yes. I worked for him for two years while he was at Clare's.' She felt she should have been able to say more about it than that, but she could think of nothing. There was a pause before her hostess asked: 'Do you like Amsterdam? I love it. We've a house in Dorset and we go there whenever we can, and to my parents, of course. The children love it.'

She didn't look old enough to have children. 'How many have you?' Deborah asked.

'Two.' Adelaide turned to her husband and he corrected her smilingly: 'Two and a half, my love.'

Deborah watched him exchange a loving glance, full of content and happiness, and swallowed envy as she heard her host say: 'Do you hear that, Gerard? You're going to be a godfather again—some time in the New Year.' And when Gerard joined them, he added: 'We'll do the same for you, of course.'

Everyone laughed; this was the sort of occasion, Deborah told herself bitterly, that she hadn't reckoned with. She made haste to ask the children's names and was at once invited to visit them in their beds.

'They won't be asleep,' their doting mother assured her, 'at least Champers won't. Lisa's only eighteen months old and drops off in seconds. Champers likes to lie and think.'

She led the way up the curving staircase and into the night nursery where an elderly woman was tidying away a pile of clothes. She was introduced as Nanny Best, the family treasure, before she trotted softly away with a bright nod. The two girls went to the cot first; the small girl in it was a miniature of her mother, the same fiery hair and preposterous lashes, the same small nose. She was asleep, her mother dropped a kiss on one fat pink cheek and crossed the room to the small bed against the opposite wall. There was no doubt at all that the small boy in it was the baron's son. Here was the dark hair, the beaky nose and the calm expression. He grinned widely at his mother, offered a hand to Deborah and after kissing them both good night, declared his intention of going to sleep.

They went back downstairs and were met in the hall by the Labrador dogs. 'Castor and Pollux,' Adelaide introduced them, and tucked an arm into Deborah's. 'Call me Adelaide,' she begged in her sweet voice. 'I'm going to call you Deborah.' She paused to look at her companion. 'You're quite beautiful, you know, no wonder Gerard married you.' Her eyes lingered on the earrings. 'I like these,' she said, touching them with a gentle finger, 'and the pearls, they suit you. How lucky you are to be tall and curvy, you can wear all the jewels Gerard will doubtless give you, but look at me—one pearl necklace and I'm smothered!'

They laughed together as they entered the room and the two men looked up. Coenraad said: 'There you are, darling.'

The meal was a splendid one. Deborah, looking round the large, well appointed dining room, reflected how well the patrician families lived with their large old houses, their priceless antique furniture, their china and glass and silver and most important of all, their trusted servants who were devoted to them and looked after their possessions with as much pride as that of their owners.

She was recalled to her surroundings by Adelaide. 'So you're going to Friesland,' she commented. 'I expect Gerard will take you to see Dominic and Abigail—she's English, too—they live close by. They're both dears. They've a house in Amsterdam, of course, but they go to Friesland when they can. Abigail is expecting a baby in about six months.' She grinned happily. 'Won't it be fun, all of us living near enough to pop in and visit, and so nice for the children—they can all play together.'

Deborah agreed, aware that Gerard had stopped talking and was listening too. 'What are the schools like?' she heard herself ask in a voice which sounded as though she really wanted to know.

They stayed late; when they got back home the house was quiet, for Wim and Marijke had long since gone to bed, but the great chandelier in the hall still blazed and there were a couple of lamps invitingly lighting the sitting room. Deborah wandered in and perched on the side of a chair.

'You enjoyed the evening?' Gerard wanted to know, following her.

'Very much—what a nice person Adelaide is, and so is Coenraad. I hope I did the right thing, I asked them to join our dinner party next week.'

'Splendid. Coenraad and I have known each other for a very long time.' He went on: 'He and Addy are very devoted.'

'Yes.' Deborah didn't want to talk about that, it hurt too much. 'I'm looking forward to meeting Abigail too.'

'Ah, yes, on Saturday. We'll leave fairly early in the morning, shall we, go to the house first and then go on to Dominic's place in the afternoon. Probably they'll want us to stay for dinner, but as I'm not going in to the Grotehof in the morning, it won't matter if we're late back.'

She got up. 'It sounds delightful. I think I'll go to bed.' She put a hand up to the pearl necklace. 'Thank you again for my present, Gerard. I'll treasure it, and the earrings.'

He was switching off the lamps. 'But of course,' he told her blandly. 'They have been treasured for generations of van Doorninck brides, and I hope will continue to be treasured for a long time to come.'

She went upstairs wondering why he had to remind her so constantly that married though they were, she was an—she hesitated for a word—outsider.

Deborah half expected that something would turn up to prevent them going to Friesland, but it didn't. They left soon after eight o'clock, travelling at a great pace through Hoorn and Den Oever and over the Afsluitdijk and so into Friesland. Once on the land again, Gerard turned the car away from the Leeuwarden road, to go through Bolsward and presently Sneek and into the open country beyond. Deborah was enchanted with what she saw; there seemed to be water everywhere.

'Do you sail at all?' she wanted to know of Gerard.

He slowed the car and turned into a narrow road running along the top of a dyke. He looked years younger that morning, perhaps because he was wearing slacks and a sweater with a gay scarf tucked in its neck, perhaps because he had a whole day in which to do as he liked.

'I've a small yacht, a van der Stadt design, around ten tons displacement—she sails like a dream.'

She wasn't sure what ten tons displacement meant. 'Where do you keep her?'

'Why, at Domwier—I can sail her down the canal to the lake. I've had no time this summer to do much sailing, though, and it's getting late in the year now, though with this lovely autumn we might have a chance— would you like to come with me?'

'Oh, please, if I wouldn't be a nuisance; I don't know a thing about boats, but I'm willing to learn.'

'Good—that's a dare, if the weather holds. We're almost at Domwier—it's a very small village; a church, a shop and a handful of houses. The house is a mile further on.'

The sun sparkled on the lake as they approached it, the opposite shore looked green and pleasant with its trees and thickets, even though there weren't many leaves left. They drove through a thick curtain of birch and pine and saw the lake, much nearer now, beyond rough grass. She barely had time to look at it before Gerard turned into a short sandy lane and there was the house before them. It looked like a farmhouse without the barn behind it, built square and solid with no-nonsense windows and an outsize door surmounted by a carving of two white swans. The sweep before the house was bordered by flower beds, still colourful with dahlias and chrysanthemums, and beyond them, grass and a thick screen of trees and bushes through which she glimpsed the water again. Smith tumbled out of the car to tear round the garden, barking ecstatically, while they made their way rather more soberly to the front door. It stood open on to a tiled hall with a door on either side and another at its end through which came a stout woman, almost as tall as Gerard. That she was delighted to see them was obvious, although Deborah could discover nothing of what she was saying. It was only when Gerard said: 'Forgive us, we're speaking Fries, because Sien dislikes speaking anything else,' that she realised that they were speaking another language altogether. Her heart sank a little; now she would have to learn this language too! As though he had read her thoughts, Gerard added: 'Don't worry, you won't be expected to speak it, though Sien would love you for ever if you could learn to understand just a little of what she says.'

'Then I'll do that, I promise. Do you come up here often?'

He corrected her gently: 'We shall, I hope, come up here often. Once things are exactly as I want them at the hospital, I shall have a good deal more time. I have been away for two years, remember, with only brief visits.'

'Yes, I know, but must you work so hard every day? I mean, you're not often home…' She wished she hadn't said it, for she sensed his withdrawal.

'I'm afraid you must accept that, Deborah.' He was smiling nicely, but his eyes were cool. He turned back to Sien and said something to her and she shook Deborah's hand and, still talking, went back to the kitchen.

Gerard flung an arm round Deborah's shoulders and led her to the sitting room. 'Coffee,' he invited her, 'and then we'll go round the place.' His manner was friendly, just as though he had forgotten their slight discord.

The room was simply furnished in the traditional Friesian style, with painted cupboards against the walls, rush-seated chairs, a stove with a tiled surround and a nicely balanced selection of large, comfortable chairs. There was a telephone too and a portable television tucked discreetly in a corner. 'It's simple'—Gerard had seen her glance—'but we have comfort and convenience.'

Most decidedly, she agreed silently, as Sien came in with a heavy silver tray with its accompanying silver pot and milk jug and delicate cups. The coffee was delicious and so was the spiced cake which accompanied

it. They sat over it and Deborah, determined to keep the
conversation on safe ground, asked questions about the
house and the furniture and the small paintings hung
each side of the stove. She found them enchanting, just
as beautiful in their way as the priceless portraits in
the Amsterdam house; the ancestors who had sat for
Paulus Potter, the street scene by Hendrik Sorgh and
the two by Gerrit Berckheyde; she had admired them
greatly, almost nervous of the fact that she was now in
part responsible for them. But these delicate sketches
and paintings were much smaller and perfect to the
last hair and whisker—fieldmice mostly, small animals
of all kinds, depicted with a precise detail which she
found amazing.

'They're by Jacob de Gheyn,' Gerard told her. 'An
ancestress of mine loved small animals, so her husband
commissioned these for her, and they have been there
ever since. I agree with you, they're quite delightful.
Come and see the rest of the house.'

The dining room was on the other side of the hall,
with a great square bay window built out to take in the
view of the lake beyond, comfortably furnished with
enormous chairs covered in bright patterned damask.
There was a Dutch dresser against one wall, decked
with enormous covered tureens and rows of old Delft-
ware. There was a similar dresser in the kitchen too
which Deborah could see was as up-to-date as the latest model at the Ideal Home Exhibition, and upstairs the
two bathrooms, tiled and cosily carpeted, each with its
pile of brightly coloured towels and a galaxy of matching soaps and powders, rivalled the luxury of the town
house. By contrast the bedrooms were simply furnished
while still offering every comfort, even the two small

attic rooms, reached by an almost perpendicular flight of miniature stairs, were as thickly carpeted and as delightfully furnished as the large rooms on the floor below.

As they went downstairs again she said a little shyly: 'This is a lovely house, Gerard—how wonderful to come here when you want peace and quiet. I love the house in Amsterdam, but I could love this one as much.'

He gave her an approving glance. 'You feel that? I'm glad, I have a great fondness for it. Mother too, she comes here frequently. It's quiet in the winter, of course.'

'I think I should like it then—does the lake freeze over?'

They had strolled into the dining room and found Sien busy putting the finishing touches to the lunch table. 'Yes, though not always hard enough for skating. I can remember skating across to Dominic's house during some of the really cold winters, though.'

'But it's miles…'

He poured her a glass of sherry. 'Not quite. Round about a mile, I should suppose. We shall have to drive back to the road presently, of course, and go round the head of the lake. It's no distance.'

They set off after a lunch which Deborah had thoroughly enjoyed because Gerard had been amusing and gay and relaxed; and she had never felt so close, and she wondered if he felt it too. It was on the tip of her tongue to try and explain a little to him of how she felt—oh, not to tell him that she loved him; she had the good sense to see that such a statement would cook her goose for ever, but to let him see, if she could, that she was happy and contented and anxious to please him. But there was no chance to say any of these things; they left immediately after lunch and the journey was too short to start a serious talk.

Dominic's house, when they reached it, was a good deal larger than their own but furnished in a similar style. Dominic had come to meet them as they got out of the car, his arm around his wife's shoulders. He was another large man. Deborah found him attractive and almost as good-looking as Gerard, and as for his wife, she was a small girl who would have been plain if happiness hadn't turned her into a beauty. She shook hands now and said in a pretty voice:

'This is a lovely surprise—we heard that Gerard had married and we had planned to come and see you when we got back to Amsterdam. We were returning this week, but the weather's so marvellous, and once the winter starts it goes on and on.'

Inside they talked until tea came, and presently when Gerard suggested that they should go, there was no question of it. 'You'll stay to dinner,' said Abigail. 'Besides'—and now she was smiling—'I mustn't be thwarted, because of my condition.' There was a general laugh and she turned to Deborah. 'Well, I'm not the only one, I hear Adelaide van Essen is having another baby—isn't she a dear?'

Deborah agreed. 'It's wonderful to find some other English girls living so close by.' She added hastily, 'Not that I'm lonely, but I find Dutch rather difficult, though I am having lessons.'

'Professor de Wit?' asked Abigail. 'Adelaide went to him. I nursed his brother before I married Dominic.' The two girls plunged into an interesting chat which was only broken by Dominic suggesting mildly that perhaps Abigail should let Bollinger know that there would be two more for dinner.

Abigail got up. 'Oh, darling, I forgot. Deborah, come and meet Bolly—he came over from England with me, and he's part of the household now.'

She smiled at her husband as they left the room, and Deborah, seeing it, felt a pang of sadness. It seemed that everyone else but herself and Gerard was happily married. Walking to the kitchen, half listening to Abigail's happy voice, she wondered if she had tried hard enough, or perhaps she had tried too much. Perhaps she annoyed him in some way, or worse, bored him. She would have to know. She resolved to ask him.

She did so, buoyed up by a false courage induced by Dominic's excellent wine. They were half way home, tearing along the Afsluitdijk with no traffic problems to occupy him.

'Do I bore you, Gerard?' she asked, and heard the small sound he made. Annoyance? Impatience? Surprise, perhaps.

But when he answered her his voice was as cool and casually friendly as usual. 'Not in the least. What put such an idea into your head?'

'N-nothing. I just wondered if you were quite satisfied—I mean with our marriage; if I'm being the kind of wife you wanted. You see, we're not much together and I don't know a great deal about you—perhaps when you get home in the evening and you're tired you'd rather be left in peace with the paper and a drink. I wouldn't mind a bit...'

They were almost at the end of the dyke, approaching the great sluices at its end. Gerard slowed down and gave her a quick look in the dark of the car.

He said on a laugh: 'I do believe you're trying to turn me into a Dutchman with my gin and my paper after a hard day's work!' His voice changed. 'I'm quite satisfied, Deborah. You are the wife I wanted, you certainly don't bore me, I'm always glad to see you when I get home, however tired I am.' His voice became kind. 'Surely that is enough to settle your doubts?'

Quite enough, she told him silently, and quite hopeless too. An irrational desire to drum her heels on the floorboards and scream loudly took possession of her. She overcame it firmly. 'Yes, thank you, Gerard,' and began at once to talk about the house in Friesland. The subject was threadbare by the time they reached Amsterdam, but at least she had managed not to mention themselves again.

It was late and she went straight to bed, leaving Gerard to take Smith for his last perambulation and lock up, and in the morning when she came down it was to hear from Wim that he had been called to the hospital in the very early morning and hadn't returned. It was almost lunchtime when he did, and as his mother had been invited for that meal, it was impossible to ask him about it; in any case, even if they had been alone, he would probably not have told her anything. She applied herself to her mother-in-law's comfort and after lunch sat in the drawing room with her, listening to tales of the family and making suitable comments from time to time, all the while wondering where Gerard had got to. He had gone to his study—she knew that, because he had said that he had a telephone call to make, but that was more than two hours ago. The two ladies had tea together and Deborah had just persuaded the older lady to stay to dinner when Gerard joined them with the hope that they had spent a pleasant afternoon and never a word about his own doings.

He told her the reason for his absence that evening after he had driven his mother back to her flat.

'Before you ask me any of the questions I feel sure are seething inside your head, I'll apologise most humbly.'

'Apologise? Whatever for?' She put down the book she had been reading and stared at him in astonishment.

'Leaving you with Mother for the entire afternoon.'

'But you had some calls to make—some work to do, didn't you?'

He grinned suddenly and her heart thumped against her ribs because he looked as she knew he might look if he were happy and carefree and not chained to the hospital by chains of his own forging. 'I went to sleep.' And when she goggled at him: 'I know, I'm sorry, but the fact is, I had some work to do after we got home last night and I stayed up until two o'clock or thereabouts, and I had to go to the Grotehof for an emergency op at five.'

'Gerard, you must have been worn out! Why on earth didn't you tell me, why won't you let me help you...' That wouldn't do at all, so she went on briskly: 'And there was I telling your mother that you never had a minute to call your own, working at your desk even on a Sunday afternoon.'

He was staring hard at her. 'You're a loyal wife,' he said quietly, and she flushed faintly under his eyes.

'I expect all wives are,' she began, and saw the expression on his face. It had become remote again; he was remembering Sasja, she supposed, who hadn't been loyal at all. 'Shall we have dinner early tomorrow eve-

ning so that you can get your work done in good time?
Have you a heavy list in the morning?'

'That was something I was going to tell you. I've
changed the list to the afternoon—two o'clock, because
I thought we might go for a run in the morning.'

A little colour crept into her cheeks again, but she
kept her voice as ordinary as possible. 'That sounds
nice. Where shall we go?'

'Not too far. The river Vecht, perhaps—we could
keep off the motorway and there won't be much traffic
about this time of the year.'

Deborah agreed happily, and later, in bed, thinking
about it, she dared to hope that perhaps Gerard's first
rigid ideas about their marriage weren't as rigid as they
had been. She slept peacefully on that happy thought.

They were out of Amsterdam by nine o'clock the next
morning, driving through the crisp autumn air. Gerard
took the road to Naarden and then turned off on to the
narrow road following the Vecht, going slowly so that
Deborah could inspect the houses on its banks, built
by the merchant princes in the eighteenth century, and
because she found them so fascinating he obligingly
turned the car at the end of the road and drove back
again the same way, patiently answering her questions
about them. They had coffee in Loenen and because
there was still plenty of time before they had to return to
Amsterdam he didn't follow the road to Naarden again,
but turned off into the byroads which would lead them
eventually back to the city.

The road they were on stretched apparently unend-
ing between the flat fields, and save for a group of farm
cottages half a mile away, and ahead of them the vague
outline of a farmhouse, there was nothing moving ex-

cept a farm tractor being driven across a ploughed field. Deborah watched the driver idly as they came level with him. 'He must be lonely,' she said idly, and then urgently: 'Gerard, that tractor's going to turn over!'

She was glad that he wasn't one of those men who asked needless questions; they weren't travelling fast, so he slid to a halt and had the door open as the tractor, some way off, reared itself up like an angry monster and crashed down on to its hapless driver.

Even in his hurry, it warmed Deborah's heart when Gerard leaned across her to undo her door and snap back her safety belt so that she could get out quickly. There was a narrow ditch between the road and the field; he bridged it easily with his long legs and then turned to give her a hand before they started to run as best they might across the newly turned earth.

The man had made no sound. When they reached him he was unconscious, trapped by the bonnet of the tractor, its edge biting across the lower half of his body.

It was like being back in theatre, thought Deborah wildly, working in a silent agreed pattern which needed no speech. She found a pulse and counted it with care while Gerard's hands began a careful search over the man's body.

'Nasty crack on his head on this side,' she offered, and peered at the eyes under their closed lids. 'Pupil reaction is equal.'

Gerard grunted, his fingers probing and feeling and probing again.

'I'm pretty sure his pelvis is fractured, God knows what's happened to his legs—how's his pulse?' She told him and he nodded. 'Not too bad,' and examined more closely the wound on the man's head. 'Can't feel a fracture, though I think there may be a crack. We've got to get this thing eased off him, even if it's only a centimetre.'

He slid a powerful arm as far as it would go and heaved with great caution and slowness. 'Half an inch would do it.' He was talking to himself. 'Your belt, Debby—if we could budge this thing just a shade and stuff your belt in...'

She had her belt off while he was still speaking. 'How about trying to scoop the earth from under him and slip the belt in?'

He had understood her at once. He crouched beside the man, the belt in his hand, his arm ready to thrust it between the bonnet's rim and the man's body. Deborah dug with speedy calm; there was nothing to use but her hands. She felt the nails crack and tear and saw, in a detached way, the front of her expensive tweed two-piece gradually disappear under an encrustation of damp earth, but presently she was able to say: 'Try now, Gerard.'

It worked, albeit the pressure was eased fractionally and wouldn't last long. Gerard withdrew his arm with great care and said: 'We have to get help.' His voice was as calm as though he was commenting upon the weather. 'Take the keys and drive the car to that farm we saw ahead of us and ask...no, that'll take too long, I'll go. Stay here—there's nothing much you can do. Push the belt in further if you get the chance.' He got to his feet. 'Thank heaven you're a strapping girl with plenty of strength and common sense!'

He started to run back towards the car, leaving her smouldering; did he really regard her as strapping? He had made her sound like some muscly creature with no feminine attributes at all! Deborah chuckled and the chuckle changed to a sob which she sternly swallowed; now was no time to be feminine. She took the man's pulse once more and wondered how long she would have to wait before Gerard got back.

Not long—she saw the car racing down the road and prayed silently that there would be nothing in the way. The next minutes seemed like eternity. Deborah turned her head at length to see Gerard with four or five men, coming towards her. They were carrying ropes and when he was near enough she said in the matter-of-fact voice he would expect of her: 'His pulse is going up, but it's steady. What are you going to do?'

'Get ropes round this infernal thing and try and drag it off.'

'You'll get double hernias,' she warned him seriously.

Gerard gave a crack of laughter. 'A risk we must all take. I fear, there's no other tractor for miles around.'

He turned away from her and became immersed in the task before him. They had the ropes in place and were heaving on them steadily when the first police car arrived, disgorging two men to join the team of sweating, swearing men. The tractor shuddered and rolled over with a thud, leaving the man free just as the second police car and an ambulance arrived.

Gerard scarcely heeded them; he was on his knees, examining the man's legs. 'By some miracle,' he said quietly to Deborah, 'they're not pulped. I may be able to do something about them provided we can get at him quickly enough. Get me some splints.'

She went to meet the ambulance men, making all the speed they could over the soft earth. She had no idea what the word splint was in Dutch, but luckily they were carrying an armful, so she took several from one rather astonished man, smiled at him and raced back to Gerard. He took them without a word and then said: 'Good lord, girl, what am I supposed to tie them with?'

She raced back again and this time the ambulance man ran to meet her and kept beside her as she ran back with the calico slings. There was help enough now, she stood back and waited patiently. It took a long time to get the man on to the stretcher and carry him, with infinite caution, across the field to the waiting ambulance. She waited until the little procession had reached it before following it and when she reached the car there was no sign of Gerard, so she got in and sat waiting with the patience she had learned during her years of nursing. The ambulance drove off presently and one of the policemen leaned through the car window and proffered her a note—from Gerard, scribbled in his almost undecipherable scrawl. 'I must go with the ambulance to the Grotehof,' he had written on a sheet torn out of his pocket book. 'Drive the car back and wait in the hospital courtyard.' He had signed it 'G' and added a postscript: 'The BMW is just like the Fiat, only larger.'

All the same, reading these heartening words, Deborah felt a pang of nervousness; she had never driven the BMW; if she thought about it for too long she would be terrified of doing so. She thanked the policeman who saluted politely, and happily ignorant of the fact that she was almost sick with fright, drove away. It was quite five minutes before she could summon up the courage to press the self-starter.

She was still shaking when she stopped the car cautiously before the entrance to the hospital, wondering what she was supposed to do next. But Gerard had thought of that; Deborah was sitting back in her seat, taking a few calming breaths when the Medical Ward Sister, whom she had already met, popped her head through the window. 'Mevrouw van Doorninck, you will come with me, please.'

'Hullo,' said Deborah, and then: 'Why, Zuster?'

'It is the wish of Mijnheer van Doorninck.' Her tone implied that there was sufficient reason there without the need for any more questions.

'Where is he?' asked Deborah, sitting stubbornly where she was.

'In theatre, already scrubbed. But he wishes most earnestly that you will come with me.' She added plaintively: 'I am so busy, Mevrouw.'

Deborah got out of the car at once, locked it and put the keys in her handbag. She would have to get them to Gerard somehow; she had no intention of driving through Amsterdam in the BMW—getting to the hospital had been bad enough. She shuddered and followed the Sister to the lift.

They got out on the Medical floor and she was bustled through several corridors and finally through a door. 'So—we are here,' murmured the Sister, said something to whoever was in the room, gave Deborah a smile and tore away. Deborah watched her go, knowing just how she felt; probably she was saying the Dutch equivalent of 'I'll never get finished,' as she went; even the simple task of escorting someone through the hospital could make a mockery of a tight and well-planned schedule of work.

It was Doctor Schipper inside the room waiting for her. Deborah had met him before; she and Gerard had had dinner with him and his wife only the week before.

She wished him a good afternoon, a little puzzled, and he came across the little room to shake her hand.

'You are surprised, Mevrouw van Doorninck, but Gerard wishes most urgently that you should have a check-up without delay. He fears that you may have strained yourself in some way—even a small cut...'

'I'm fine,' she declared, aware of sore hands. 'Well, I've broken a few fingernails and I was scared stiff!'

A young nurse had slid into the room, so Deborah, submitting to the inevitable, allowed herself to be helped out of her deplorable dress and examined with thoroughness by Doctor Schipper. He stood back at length. 'Quite OK,' he assured her. 'A rapid pulse, but I imagine you had an unpleasant shock—the accident was distressing...'

'Yes, but I think it was having to drive the car which scared me stiff. I only drive a Fiat 500, you know— there's quite a difference. Can I go home now?'

'Of course. Nurse will arrange for you to have a taxi, but first she will clean up your hands, and perhaps an injection of ATS to be on the safe side—all that earth...'

She submitted to the nurse's attentions and remembered the car keys just as she was ready to go. 'Shall I leave them at the front door?' she asked Doctor Schipper.

He held out a hand. 'Leave them with me—I'll get them to Gerard. He won't want them just yet, I imagine.'

Deborah thanked him, reminded him that he and his wife were dining with them in a few days' time and set off for the entrance with the nurse, where she climbed into a taxi and went home to find Wim and Marijke, worried about their non-appearance for lunch, waiting anxiously.

She was herself again by the evening, presenting a

bandbox freshness to the world marred only by her deplorable nails and an odd bruise or two. She had deliberately put on a softly clinging dress and used her perfume with discreet lavishness; studying herself in the mirror, she decided that despite her height and curves, she looked almost fragile. She patted a stray wisp of hair into position, and much comforted by the thought, went downstairs to wait for Gerard.

He came just before dinner, gave her a brief greeting and went on: 'Well, we've saved the legs and I've done what I could with the pelvis—he's in a double hip spica.' He poured their drinks and handed her hers, at the same time looking her over with what she could only describe to herself as a professional eye. 'Schipper told me that you were none the worse—you've recovered very well. Thank heaven you were with me!'

'Yes,' she spoke lightly without looking at him. 'There's nothing like beef and brawn...'

His eyes strayed over her, slowly this time and to her satisfaction, not in the least professionally. 'Did I say that? I must have been mad! Anyone less like beef and brawn I have yet to see—you look charming.'

Deborah thanked him in a level voice while her heart bounced happily. When he asked to see her hands she came and stood before him, holding them out. There were some scratches and the bruises on her knuckles were beginning to show, and the nails made her shudder. He put his drink down and stood up and surprised her very much by picking up first one hand and then the other and kissing them, and then, as if that wasn't enough, he bent his head and kissed her cheek too.

Chapter 7

Deborah had gone to sleep that night in a state of mind very far removed from her usual matter-of-factness. She wakened after hours of dreaming, shreds and tatters with no beginning and no end and went downstairs with the remnants of those same dreams still in her eyes. Nothing could have brought her down to earth more quickly than Gerard's brief good morning before he plunged into a list of things he begged her, if she had time, to do for him during the day—small errands which she knew quite well he would have no time to see to for himself, but it made her feel like a secretary, and from his businesslike manner he must think of her as that, or was he letting her know that his behaviour on the previous evening was a momentary weakness, not to be taken as a precedent for the future?

She went round to see her mother-in-law in the afternoon. The morning had been nicely filled with Gerard's commissions and a lesson with the professor, and now, burdened with her homework, she made her way to Mevrouw van Doorninck's flat, walking briskly because the weather, although fine, was decidedly chilly. She paused to look at one or two shops as she went; the two-piece she had worn the day before was a write-off; the earth had been ground into its fine fabric and when she had shown it to Marijke that good soul had given her opinion, with the aid of Wim, that no dry-cleaner would touch it. She would have to buy another outfit to replace it, Deborah decided, and rang the bell.

Mevrouw van Doorninck was pleased to see her. They got on very well, for the older woman had accepted her as a member of the family although she had never invited Deborah's confidence. She was urged to sit down now and tell all that had happened on the previous day.

'I didn't know you knew about it,' observed Deborah as she accepted a cup of tea.

'Gerard telephoned me in the evening—he was so proud of you.'

Deborah managed to laugh. 'Was he? I only know that he thanked heaven that I was a strong young woman and not a—a delicate feminine creature.'

She turned her head away as she spoke; it was amazing how that still hurt. Her mother-in-law's reply was vigorous. 'You may not be delicate, my dear, but you are certainly very feminine. I can't imagine Gerard falling in love with any other type of woman.'

Deborah drank some tea. 'What about Sasja?' she asked boldly. 'Gerard told me a little about her, but what was she really like—he said that she was very pretty.'

'Very pretty—like a doll, she was also a heartless and immoral young woman and wildly extravagant. She made life for Gerard quite unbearable. And don't think, my dear,' she went on dryly, 'that I tried to interfere or influence Gerard in any way, although I longed to do so. I had to stand aside and watch Gerard make the terrible mistake of marrying her. Infatuation is far worse than love, Deborah, it blinds one to reality; it destroys...fortunately he had his work.' She sighed. 'It is a pity that work has become such a habit with him that he hardly knows how to enjoy life any more.' She looked at Deborah, who stared back with no expression at all. 'You have found that, perhaps?'

'I know he's very busy getting everything just as he wants it at the Grotehof—I daresay when he is satisfied he'll have more time to spare.'

'Yes, dear.' Mevrouw van Doorninck's voice had that same dryness again, and Deborah wondered uneasily if she had guessed about Gerard and herself. It would be unlikely, for he always behaved beautifully towards her when there were guests or family present—he always behaved beautifully, she amended, even when they were alone. Her mother-in-law nodded. 'I'm sure you are right, my dear. Tell me, who is coming to the dinner party tomorrow evening?'

Deborah recited the names. She had met most of the guests already, there were one or two, visiting specialists, whose acquaintance she had yet to make; one of them would be spending the night. She told her mother-in-law what she intended wearing and got up to go. When she bent to kiss the older lady's cheek she was surprised at the warmth of the kiss she received in return and still more surprised when she said: 'If ever you need help or advice, Deborah, and once or twice I have thought…no matter. If you do, come to me and I will try and help you.'

Deborah stammered her thanks and beat a hasty retreat, wondering just what Gerard's mother had meant.

She dressed early for the dinner party because she wanted to go downstairs and make sure that the table was just so, the flowers as they should be and the lamps lighted. It was to be rather a grand occasion this time because the Medical Director of the hospital was coming as well as the *Burgemeester* of the city, who, she was given to understand, was a very important person indeed. She was wearing a new dress for the occasion, a soft lavender chiffon with long full sleeves, tight cuffed with a plunging neckline discreetly veiled by pleated frills. There was a frill round the hem of the skirt too and a swathed belt which made the most of her waist. She had added the pearls and the earrings and hoped that she looked just as a successful consultant's wife should look.

'Neat but not gaudy,' she told herself aloud, inspecting her person in the big mirror on the landing, not because she hadn't seen it already in her room where there were mirrors enough, but because this particular mirror, with its elaborate gilded frame somehow enhanced her appearance.

'That's a decidedly misleading statement.' Gerard's voice came from the head of the stairs and she whirled round in a cloud of chiffon to face him.

'You're early, how nice! Everything's ready for you—I'm going down to see about the table.'

'This first.' He held out a large old-fashioned plush casket. 'You told me the colour of your dress and it seemed to me that Great-aunt Emmiline's garnets might be just the thing to go with it.'

Deborah sat down on the top tread of the staircase, her skirts billowing around her, and opened the box. Great-aunt Emmiline must have liked garnets very much; there were rings and brooches and two heavy gold bracelets set with large stones, earrings and a thick gold necklace with garnets set in it.

'They're lovely—may I really borrow them? I'll take great care...'

He had come to sit beside her. 'They're yours, Deborah. I've just given them to you. I imagine you can't wear the whole lot at once, but there must be something there you like?'

'Oh, yes—yes. Thank you, Gerard, you give me so much.' She smiled at him shyly and picked out one of the bracelets and fastened it round a wrist. It looked just right; she added the necklace, putting the precious pearls in her lap. She wasn't going to take off her engagement ring; she added two of the simpler rings to the other hand and found a pair of drop earrings. She added her pearl earrings to the necklace in her lap and hooked in the garnets instead and went to look in the mirror. Gerard was right, they were exactly right with the dress. 'Have I got too much on?' she asked anxiously.

'No—just right, I should say. That's a pretty dress. What happened to the one you spoilt?'

'It's ruined. I showed it to Marijke—the stain has gone right through.'

'I'm sorry. Buy yourself another one. I'll pay for it.'

Deborah was standing with the casket clasped to her breast. 'Oh, there's no need, I've got heaps of money from my allowance.'

'Nevertheless you will allow me to pay for another dress,' he insisted blandly.

'Well—all right, thank you. I'll just put these away.'

When she came out of her room he had gone. There was nothing to do downstairs, she had seen to everything during the day and she knew that Marijke and Wim needed no prompting from her. She went and sat by the log fire Wim had lighted in the drawing room and Smith, moving with a kind of slow-motion stealth, insinuated himself on to her silken lap. But he got down again as Gerard joined them, pattering across the room when his master went to fetch the drinks and then pattering back again to arrange himself on Gerard's shoes once he had sat down. A cosy family group, thought Deborah, eyeing Gerard covertly. He looked super in a black tie—he was a man who would never lose his good looks, even when he was old. She had seen photos of his father, who in his mid-seventies had been quite something—just like his son, sitting there, stroking Smith with the toe of his shoe and talking about nothing in particular. It was a relief when the doorbell signalled the arrival of the first of their guests, because she had discovered all at once that she could not bear to sit there looking at him and loving him so much.

The evening was a success, as it could hardly have failed to have been, for Deborah had planned it carefully; the food was delicious and the guests knew and liked each other. She had felt a little flustered when the *Burgemeester* had arrived, an imposing, youngish man with a small, plump wife with no looks to speak of but with a delightful smile and a charming voice. She greeted Deborah kindly, wished her happiness upon her recent marriage and in her rather schoolgirl English wanted to know if she spoke any Dutch. It was a chance to pay tribute to the professor's teaching; Deborah made a few halting remarks, shocking as to grammar but faultless as to accent. There was a good deal of kindly laughter and when the *Burgemeester* boomed: 'Your Dutch is a delight to my ear, dear lady,' her evening was made.

She had had no time to do more than say hullo to Coenraad and Adelaide, but after dinner, with the company sitting around the drawing room, the two girls managed to get ten minutes together.

'Very nice,' said Adelaide at once, 'I can see that you're going to be a wonderful wife for Gerard—it's a great drawback to a successful man if he hasn't got a wife to see to the social side. When I first married I thought it all rather a waste of time, but I was wrong. They talk shop—oh, very discreetly, but they do—and arrange visits to seminars and who shall play host when so-and-so comes, and they ask each other's advice... I like your dress, and the garnets are just the thing for it—another van Doorninck heirloom, I expect? I've got some too, only I have to be careful—my hair, you know.' She grinned engagingly. 'Did you go to Friesland?'

Deborah nodded. 'Yes, I loved the house, we had lunch there and then we went to see Dominic and Abigail. It's lovely there by the lake.'

'And what's all this about an accident? The hospital was positively humming with it. Coenraad told me about it, but you know what men are.'

They spent five minutes more together before Deborah, with a promise to telephone Adelaide in a few days, moved across the room to engage her mother-in-law in conversation.

It was after everyone had gone, and Doctor de Joufferie, their guest for the night, had retired to his room, that Gerard, on his way to let Smith out into the garden, told her that Claude was back in Amsterdam after a visit to Nice. 'I hear he's sold his house here and intends to live in France permanently.'

'Oh.' She paused uncertainly on her way to bed. 'He won't come here?'

'Most unlikely—if he does, would you mind?'

Deborah shook her head. 'Not in the least,' she assured her husband stoutly, minding very much.

Her answer was what he had expected, for he remarked casually. 'No, you're far too sensible for that and I have no doubt that you would deal with him should he have the temerity to call.' He turned away. 'That's a pretty dress,' he told her for the second time that evening.

She thanked him nicely, wishing that he had thought her pretty enough to remark upon that too; apparently he was satisfied enough that she was sensible.

She ruminated so deeply upon this unsatisfactory state of affairs that she hardly heard his thanks for the success of the evening, but she heard him out, murmured something inaudible about being tired, and went to bed.

Doctor de Joufferie joined them for breakfast in the morning, speaking an English almost as perfect as Gerard's. The two men spent most of the time discussing the possibility of Gerard going to Paris for some conference or other: 'And I hope very much that you will accompany your husband,' their visitor interrupted himself to say. 'My wife would be delighted to show you a little of Paris while we are at the various sessions.'

Deborah gave him a vague, gracious answer; she didn't want to hurt the doctor's feelings, but on the other hand she wasn't sure whether Gerard would want her to go with him; he had never suggested, even remotely, such a possibility. She led the conversation carefully back to the safe ground of Paris and its delights, at the same time glancing at her husband to see how he was reacting. He wasn't, his expression was politely attentive and nothing more, but then it nearly always was; even if he had no wish to take her, he would never dream of saying so.

The two men left together and she accompanied them to the door, to be pleasantly surprised at the admiration in the Frenchman's eyes as he kissed her hand with the hope that they might meet again soon. She glowed pleasantly under his look, but the glow was damped immediately by Gerard's brief, cool kiss which just brushed her cheek.

She spent an hour or so pottering round the house, getting in Wim's way, and then went to sit with her Dutch lesson, but she was in no mood to learn. She flung the books pettishly from her and went out. Gerard had told her to buy a new dress—all right, so she would, and take good care not to look too closely at the price tag. She walked along the Keizersgracht until she came to that emporium of high fashion, Metz, and once inside, buoyed up by strong feelings which she didn't bother to define, she went straight to the couture department. She had in mind another tweed outfit, or perhaps one of the thicker jersey suits. She examined one or two, a little shocked at their prices, although even after so short a time married to Gerard, she found that her shock was lessening.

It was while she was prowling through the thickly carpeted alcove which held the cream of the Autumn collection that she saw the dress—a Gina Fratini model for the evening—white silk, high-necked and long-sleeved, pin-tucked and gathered and edged with antique lace. Deborah examined it more closely; it wouldn't be her size, of course, and even if it were, when would she wear it, and what astronomical price would it be? She circled round it once more; it would do very well for the big ball Gerard had casually mentioned would take place at the hospital before Christmas, and what about the *Burgemeester's* reception? But the size? The saleswoman, who had been hovering discreetly, pounced delicately. She even remembered Deborah's name, so that she felt like an old and valued customer, and what was more, her English was good.

'A lovely gown, Mevrouw van Doorninck,' she said persuasively, 'and so right for you, and I fancy it is your size.' She had it over her arm now, yards and yards of soft silk. 'Would you care to try it on?'

'Well,' said Deborah weakly, 'I really came in for something in tweed or jersey.' She caught the woman's eye and smiled. 'Yes, I'll try it on.'

It was a perfect fit and utterly lovely. She didn't need the saleswoman's flattering remarks to know it. The dress did something for her, although she wasn't sure what. She said quickly, before she should change her mind: 'I'll take it—will you charge it to my husband, please?'

It was when she was dressed again, watching it being lovingly packed, that she asked the price. She had expected it to be expensive, but the figure the saleswoman mentioned so casually almost took her breath. Deborah waited for a feeling of guilt to creep over her, and felt nothing; Gerard had insisted on paying for a dress, hadn't he? Declining an offer to have it delivered, she carried her precious box home.

She would have tried it on then and there, but Wim met her in the hall with the news that Marijke had a delicious soufflé only waiting to be eaten within a few minutes. But eating lunch by herself was something quickly done with, so she flew upstairs to her room and unpacked the dress. It looked even more super than it had done in the shop. She put it on and went to turn and twist before the great mirror—she had put on the pearls and the earrings and a pair of satin slippers; excepting for the faint untidiness of the heavy chignon, she looked ready for a ball.

'Cinderella, and more beautiful than ever,' said Claude from the stairs.

Deborah turned round slowly, not quite believing that he was there, but he was, smiling and debonair, for all the world as though Gerard had never told him not to enter the house again.

'What are you doing here?' she asked, and tried to keep the angry shake from her voice.

'Why, come to pay you a farewell visit. I'm leaving this city, thank heaven, surely you've heard that? But I couldn't go until I had said goodbye to you, but don't worry, I telephoned the hospital and they told me that Gerard was busy, so I knew that it was safe to come, and very glad I am that I did. A ball so early in the day? Or is the boyfriend coming?'

Her hand itched to slap his smiling face. 'How silly

you are,' she remarked scathingly. 'And you have no right to walk into the house as though it were your own. Why didn't you ring the bell?'

'Ah, I came in through the little door in the garden. You forget, my lovely Deborah, that I have known this house since many years; many a time I've used that door.' He was lounging against the wall, laughing at her, so that her carefully held patience deserted her.

'Well, you can go, and out of the front door this time. I've nothing to say to you, and I'm sure Gerard would be furious if he knew that you had come here.'

He snapped his fingers airily. 'My dear good girl, let us be honest, you have no idea whether Gerard would be annoyed or not; you have no idea about anything he does or thinks or plans, have you? I don't suppose he tells you anything. Shall I tell you what I think? Why, that you're a figurehead to adorn his table, a hostess for his guests and a competent housekeeper to look after his home while he's away—and where does he go, I wonder? Have you ever wondered? Hours in the Grotehof—little trips to Paris, Brussels, Vienna, operating here, lecturing there while you sit at home thinking what thoughts?'

He stopped speaking and stared at her pinched face. 'I'm right, aren't I? I have hit the nail on its English head, have I not? Poor beautiful Deborah.' He laughed softly and came closer. 'Leave him, my lovely, and come to Nice with me—why not? We could have a good time together.'

She wasn't prepared for his sudden swoop; she was a strong girl, but he had hold of her tightly, and besides, at the back of her stunned mind was the thought that if she struggled too much her beautiful dress would be ruined. She turned her face away as he bent to kiss her and brought up a hand to box him soundly on the ear. But he laughed the more as she strained away from him, her head drawn back. So that she didn't see or hear Gerard coming up the stairs, although Claude did. She felt his hold tighten as he spoke.

'Gerard—hullo, *jongen*, I knew you wouldn't mind me calling in to say goodbye to Deborah, and bless her heart, she wouldn't let me go without one last kiss.'

She felt him plucked from her, heard, as in a dream, his apology, no doubt induced by the painful grip Gerard had upon him, and watched in a detached way as he was marched down the stairs across the hall to disappear in the direction of the front door, which presently shut with some force. Gerard wasn't even breathing rapidly when he rejoined her, only his eyes blazed in his set face.

'You knew he was coming?' His tone was conversational but icy.

'Of course not.' She was furious to find that she was trembling.

'How did he get in? Doesn't Wim open the door?'

'Of course he does—when the bell rings. He—he came in through the door in the garden. I had no idea that he was in the house until he spoke to me here.' She essayed a smile which wavered a little. 'I'm glad you came home.'

'Yes?' His eyebrows rose in faint mockery. 'You didn't appear to be resisting Claude with any great show of determination.'

She fired up at that. 'He took me by surprise. I slapped his cheek.'

'Did you call Wim?'

Deborah shook her head. Truth to tell, it hadn't entered her head.

Her husband stared at her thoughtfully. 'A great strapping girl like you,' he commented nastily. 'No kicking? No struggling?'

She hated him, mostly because he had called her a strapping girl. She wanted to cry too, but the tears were in a hard knot in her chest. She said sullenly: 'I was trying on this dress—it's new...' He laughed then and she said desperately: 'You don't believe me, do you? You actually think that I would encourage him.' Her voice rose with the strength of her feelings. 'Well, if that's what you want to believe, you may do so!'

She swept to her bedroom door and remembered something as she reached it. 'I bought this dress because you told me to and I've charged it to you—it's a model and it cost over a thousand gulden, and I'm glad!' She stamped her foot. 'I wish it had cost twice as much!'

She banged the door behind her and locked it, which was a silly action anyway, for when had he ever tried the door handle?

She took the dress off carefully and hung it away and put on a sober grey dress, then combed her hair and put on too much lipstick and went downstairs. She was crossing the hall when Gerard opened his study door and invited her to join him in a quiet voice which she felt would be wiser to obey. She went past him with her head in the air and didn't sit down when he asked her to.

'I came home to pack a bag,' he told her mildly, all trace of ill-humour vanished. 'There is an urgent case I have to see in Geneva and probably operate on. I intend to catch the five o'clock flight and I daresay I shall be away for two days. I'm sorry to spring it on you like this, but there's nothing important for a few days, is there?'

'Nothing.' Wild horses wouldn't have dragged from her the information that it was her birthday in two days' time. She had never mentioned it to him and he had never tried to find out.

He nodded. 'Good—' he broke off as Wim came in with a sheaf of flowers which he gave to Deborah. 'Just delivered, Mevrouw,' he told her happily, and went away, leaving a heavy silence behind him.

Deborah started to open the envelope pinned to its elaborate wrapping and then stopped; supposing it was from Claude? It was the sort of diabolical joke he would dream up...

She looked up and found Gerard watching her with a speculative eye and picked up the flowers and walked to the door. 'I'll pack you a case,' she told him. 'Will you want a black tie, or is it to be strictly work?'

His eyes narrowed. 'Oh, strictly work,' he assured her in a silky voice, 'and even if it weren't, a black tie isn't always essential in order to—er—enjoy yourself.'

He gave her a look of such mockery that she winced under it; it was almost as if Claude's poisoned remarks held a grain of truth.

Outside she tore open the little envelope and read the card; the flowers were from Doctor de Joufferie. She suppressed her strong desire to run straight back to Gerard and show it to him, and went to pack his bag instead.

It was quiet in the house after he had gone. Deborah spent the long evening working at her Dutch, playing with Smith and leafing through magazines, and went to bed at last with a bad headache. She had expected

Gerard to telephone, but he didn't, which made the headache worse. There was no call in the morning either; she hung around until lunchtime and then went out with Smith trotting beside her on his lead. She walked for a long time, and it was on her way back, close to the house, that she stopped to pick up a very small child who had fallen over, the last in a line of equally small uniformed children, walking ahead of her. She had seen them before, and supposed that they went to some nursery school or other in one of the narrow streets leading from the Keizersgracht. She comforted the little girl, mopped up a grazed knee and carried her towards the straggling line of her companions. She had almost reached it when a nun darted back towards them, breaking into voluble Dutch as she did so.

Deborah stood still. 'So sorry,' she managed, 'my Dutch is bad.'

The nun smiled. 'Then I will speak my bad English to you. Thank you for helping the little one—there are so many of them and my companion has gone on to the Weeshuis with a message.'

Deborah glanced across the road to where an old building stood under the shadow of the great Catholic church. 'Oh,' she said, and remembered that a Weeshuis was an orphanage. 'They're little orphans.'

The nun smiled again. 'Yes. We have many of them. The older ones go to school, but these are still too small. We go now to play and sing a little after their walk. Once we had a lady who came each week and told them stories and played games with them. They liked that.' She held out her arms for the child and said: 'I thank you again, Mevrouw,' and walked rapidly away to where the obedient line of children waited. Deborah watched them disappear inside the orphanage before she went home.

It was after her lonely tea that she had an idea. Without pausing to change her mind, she left the house and went back to the orphanage and rang the bell, and when an old nun came to peer at her through the grille, she asked to see the Mother Superior. Half an hour later she was back home again after an interview with that rather surprised lady; she might go once a week and play with the children until such time as a permanent helper could be found. She had pointed out hesitantly that she wasn't a Catholic herself, but the Mother Superior didn't seem to mind. Thursday evenings, she had suggested, and any time Deborah found the little orphans too much for her, she had only to say so.

The morning post brought a number of cards and parcels for her. She read them while she ate her breakfast and was just getting up from the table when Wim came in with a great bouquet of flowers and a gaily tied box.

'Mijnheer told me to give you these, Mevrouw,' he informed her in a fatherly fashion, 'and Marijke and I wish you a very happy birthday.' He produced a small parcel with the air of a magician and she opened it at once. Handkerchiefs, dainty, lace-trimmed ones. She thanked him nicely, promised that she would go to the kitchen within a few minutes so that she could thank Marijke, and was left to examine her flowers. They were exquisite; roses and carnations and sweet peas and lilies, out of season and delicate and fragrant. She sniffed at them with pleasure and read the card which accompanied them. It bore the austere message: With best wishes, G. So he had known all the time! She opened the box slowly; it contained a set of dressing table sil-

ver, elegantly plain with her initials on each piece surmounted by the family crest. There was another card
too, less austere than its fellow. This one said: 'To Deborah, wishing you a happy birthday.'

She went upstairs and arranged the silver on her
dressing table, and stood admiring it until she remembered that she had to see Marijke. She spent a long time
arranging the flowers so that she was a little late for her
lesson and Professor de Wit was a little put out, but she
had learnt her lesson well, which mollified him sufficiently for him to offer her a cup of coffee when they
had finished wrestling with the Dutch verbs for the day.
She went back home presently to push the food around
her plate and then go upstairs to her room. Her mother-
in-law was in Hilversum, she could hardly telephone
Adelaide and tell her that it was her birthday and she
was utterly miserable. Thank heaven it was Thursday; at
least she had her visit to the orphans to look forward to.

There was still no word from Gerard. Deborah told
Wim that she was going for a walk and would be back
for dinner at half past seven as usual, and set out. The
evenings were chilly now and the streets were crowded
with people on their way home or going out to enjoy
themselves, but the narrow street where the orphanage
was was quiet as she rang the bell.

The orphans assembled for their weekly junketings
in a large, empty room overlooking the street, reached
through a long narrow passage and a flight of steps, and
one of the dreariest rooms Deborah had ever seen, but
there was a piano and plenty of room for twenty-eight
small children. It was when she had thrown off her coat
and turned to survey them that she remembered that her
Dutch was, to say the least, very indifferent. But she

had reckoned without the children; within five minutes they had discovered the delights of 'Hunt the Slipper' and were screaming their heads off.

At the end of the hour they had mastered Grandmother's Steps too as well as Twos and Threes, and for the last ten minutes or so, in order that they might calm down a little, she began to tell them a story, mostly in English of course, with a few Dutch words thrown in here and there and a great deal of mime. It seemed to go down very well, as did the toffees Deborah produced just before the nun came to fetch them away to their supper and bed. An hour had never gone so quickly. She kissed them good night, one by one, and when they had gone the empty room seemed emptier and drearier than ever. She tidied it up quickly and went home.

Indoors, it was to hear from Wim that Gerard had telephoned, but only to leave a message that he would be home the following evening. Deborah thanked him and went to eat her dinner, choking it down as best she could because Marijke had thought up a splendid one for her birthday. Afterwards, with Smith on her lap, she watched TV. It was a film she had already seen several times in England, but she watched it to its end before going to bed.

Gerard came home late the following afternoon. Deborah had spent the day wondering how to greet him. As though nothing had happened? With an apology? She ruled this one out, for she had nothing to apologise for—with a dignified statement pointing out how unfair he had been? She was still rehearsing a variety of opening speeches when she heard his key in the door.

There was no need for her to make a speech of any kind; it riled her to find that his manner was exactly as it always was, quiet, pleasant—he was even smiling. Taken aback, Deborah replied to his cheerful hullo with a rather uncertain one followed by the hope that he had had a good trip and that everything had been successful. And would he like something to eat?

He declined her offer on his way to the door. 'I've some telephoning to do,' he told her. 'The post is in the study, I suppose?'

She said that yes, it was and as he reached the door, said in a rush: 'Thank you for the lovely flowers and your present—it's quite super—I didn't know that you knew...'

'Our marriage certificate,' he pointed out briefly. 'I'm sorry I was not here to celebrate it in the usual Dutch manner—another year, perhaps.'

'No, well—it didn't matter. It's a marvellous present.'

Gerard was almost through the door. He paused long enough to remark:

'I'm glad you like it. It seemed to me to be a suitable gift.' He didn't look at her and his voice sounded cold. He closed the door very quietly behind him.

Deborah threw a cushion at it. 'I hate him,' she raged, 'hate him! He's pompous and cold and he doesn't care a cent for me, not one cent—a suitable present indeed! And just what was he doing in Geneva?' she demanded of the room at large. She plucked a slightly outraged Smith from the floor and hugged him to her. 'None of that's true,' she assured him fiercely, and opened the door and let him into the hall. She heard him scratching on the study door and after a few moments it was opened for him.

They dined together later, apparently on the best of terms; Deborah told Gerard one or two items which she thought might interest him, but never a word about the orphans. The van Doornincks were Calvinists; several ancestors had been put to death rather nastily by the Spaniards during their occupation of the Netherlands. It was a very long time ago, but the Dutch had long memories for such things. She didn't think that Gerard would approve of her helping, even for an hour, in a convent. Her conscience pricked her a little because she was being disloyal to him; on the other hand, she wasn't a Catholic either, but that hadn't made any difference to her wish to help the children in some small way. She put the matter out of her mind and asked him as casually as possible about his trip to Geneva.

She might have saved her breath, for although he talked about Switzerland and Geneva in particular, not one crumb of information as to his activities while he was there did he offer her. She rose from the table feeling frustrated and ill-tempered and spent the rest of the evening sitting opposite him in the sitting room, doing her embroidery all wrong. Just the same, when she went to bed she said quite humbly: 'I'm really very sorry to have bought such an expensive dress, Gerard—I'll pay you back out of my next quarter's allowance.'

'I offered you a new dress,' he reminded her suavely. 'I don't remember telling you to buy the cheapest one you saw. Shall we say no more about it?'

Upon which unsatisfactory remark she went to bed.

It didn't seem possible that they could go on as before, with no mention of Claude, no coolness between them, no avoiding of each other's company, but it was. Deborah found that life went on exactly as before, with occasional dinner parties, drinks with friends, visits to her mother-in-law and Gerard's family and an occasional quiet evening at home with Gerard—and of course the weekly visit to the orphans.

It was getting colder now, although the autumn had stretched itself almost into winter with its warm days and blue skies. But now the trees by the canal were without leaves and the water looked lifeless; it was surprising what a week or so would do at that time of year, and that particular evening, coming home from the convent, there was an edge of winter in the air.

Deborah found Gerard at home. He was always late on Thursdays and when she walked into the sitting room and found him there she was surprised into saying so.

'I've been out,' she explained a little inadequately. 'It was such a nice evening,' and then could have bitten out her tongue, for there was a nasty wind blowing and the beginnings of a fine, cold rain. She put a guilty hand up to her hair and felt its dampness.

'I'll tell Marijke to serve dinner at once,' she told him, 'and change my dress.'

That had been a silly thing to say too, for the jersey suit she was wearing was decidedly crumpled from the many small hands which had clung to it. But Gerard said nothing and if his hooded eyes noticed anything, they gave nothing away. She joined him again presently and spent the evening waiting for him to ask her where she had been, and when he didn't, went to bed in a fine state of nervous tension.

Several days later he told her that he would be going away again for a day and possibly the night as well.

'Not Geneva?' asked Deborah, too quickly.

He was in the garden, brushing Smith. 'No—Arnhem.'

'But Arnhem is only a short distance away,' she pointed out, 'surely you could come home?'

He raised his eyes to hers. 'If I should come home, it would be after ten o'clock,' he told her suavely. 'That is a certainty, so that you can safely make any plans you wish for the evening.'

She stared at him, puzzled. 'But I haven't any plans—where should I want to go?'

He shrugged. 'Where do you go on Thursday evenings?' he asked blandly, and when she hesitated, 'That was unfair of me—I'm sorry. I only learned of it through overhearing something Wim said. Perhaps you would rather not tell me.'

'No—that is, no,' she answered miserably. 'I don't think so.'

Gerard flashed her a quizzical glance. 'Quid pro quo?' he asked softly.

She flushed and lifted her chin. 'When I married you, you made it very clear what you expected of me. Maybe I've fallen short of—of your expectations, but I have done my best, but I wouldn't stoop to paying you back in your own coin!'

She flounced out of the room before he could speak and went to her room and banged the door. They were going out that evening to dinner with a colleague of Gerard's. She came downstairs at exactly the moment when it was necessary to leave the house, looking quite magnificent in the pink silk jersey dress and the pearls and with such a haughty expression upon her lovely face that Gerard, after the briefest of glances, forbore from speaking. When she peeped at him his face was impassive, but she had the ridiculous feeling that he was laughing at her.

He had left the house when she got down in the morning. She had breakfast, did a few chores around the house and prepared to go out. She was actually at the front door when the telephone rang and when she answered it, it was to hear Sien's voice, a little agitated, asking for Gerard.

'Wim,' called Deborah urgently, and made placating noises to Sien, and when he came: 'It's Sien—I can't understand her very well, but I think there's something wrong.'

Sien had cut her hand, Wim translated, and it was the local doctor's day off and no one near enough to help; the season was over, the houses, and they were only a few, within reach were closed for the winter. She had tied her hand up, but it had bled a great deal. Perhaps she needed stitches? and would Mevrouw forgive her for telephoning, but she wasn't sure what she should do.

'Ask her where the cut is,' commanded Deborah, 'and if it's still bleeding.' And when Wim had told her, gave careful instructions: 'And tell her to sit down and try and keep her arm up, and that I'm on my way now— I'll be with her in less than two hours.'

She was already crossing the hall to Gerard's study where she knew there was a well-stocked cupboard of all she might require. She chose what she needed and went to the front door. 'I don't know how long I shall be, Wim,' she said. 'You'd better keep Smith here. I expect I may have to take Sien to hospital for some stitches and then try and find someone who would stay a day or two with her—she can't be alone.'

'Very good, Mevrouw,' said Wim in his fatherly fashion, 'and I beg you to be careful on the road.'

She smiled at him—he was such an old dear. 'Of course, Wim, I'll be home later.'

'And if the master should come home?'

Deborah didn't look at him. 'He said after ten this evening, or even tomorrow, Wim.'

She drove the Fiat fast and without any hold-ups, for the tourists had gone and the roads were fairly empty; as she slowed to turn into the little lane leading to the house she thought how lovely it looked against the pale sky and the wide country around it, but she didn't waste time looking around her; she parked the car and ran inside.

Sien had done exactly as she had been told. She looked a little pale and the rough bandage was heavily bloodstained, but she greeted Deborah cheerfully and submitted to having the cut examined.

'A stitch or two,' explained Deborah in her thread-bare Dutch, knowing that it would need far more than that, for the cut was deep and long, across the palm.

'Coffee,' she said hearteningly, and made it for both of them, then helped Sien to put on her coat and best hat—for was she not going to hospital to see a doctor, she wanted to know when Deborah brought the wrong one—locked the door and settled her companion in the little car. It wasn't far to Leeuwarden and Sien knew where the hospital was.

She hadn't known that Gerard was known there too. She only had to give her name and admit to being his wife for Sien to be given VIP treatment. She was stitched, given ATS, told when to come again and given another cup of coffee while Deborah had a little talk with the Casualty Officer.

'Can I help you at all?' he wanted to know as he handed her coffee too.

She explained thankfully about Sien being alone. 'If someone could find out if she has a friend or family nearby who would go back with her for a day or two, I could collect them on the way back. If not, I think I should take her back with me to Amsterdam or stay here myself.'

She waited patiently while Sien was questioned. 'There's a niece,' the young doctor told her, 'she lives at Warga, quite close to your house. Your housekeeper says that she will be pleased to stay with her for a few days.'

'You're very kind,' said Deborah gratefully. 'It's a great hindrance not being able to speak the language, you know. My husband will be very grateful when he hears how helpful you have been.'

The young man went a dusky red. 'Your husband is a great surgeon, Mevrouw. We would all wish to be like him.'

She shook hands. 'I expect you will be,' she assured him, and was rewarded by his delighted smile.

Sien's niece was a young edition of her aunt, just as tall and plump and just as sensible. Deborah drove the two of them back to the house, gave instructions that they were to telephone the house at Amsterdam if they were in doubt about anything, asked them if they had money enough, made sure that Sien understood about the pills she was to take if her hand got too painful, wished them goodbye, and got into the Fiat again. It was early afternoon, she would be home for tea.

Chapter 8

But she wasn't home for tea; it began to rain as she reached the outskirts of the city, picking her careful way through streets which became progressively narrower and busier as she neared the heart of the city. The cobbles glistened in the rain, their surface made treacherous; Deborah had no chance at all when a heavy lorry skidded across the street, sweeping her little car along with it. By some miracle the Fiat stayed upright despite the ominous crunching noises it was making. Indeed, the bonnet was a shapeless mass by the time the lorry came to a precarious halt with Deborah's car inextricably welded to it.

She climbed out at once, white and shaking but quite unhurt except for one or two sharp knocks. The driver of the lorry got out too to engage her immediately in earnest conversation, not one word of which did she understand. Dutch, she had discovered long since, wasn't too bad provided one had the time and the circumstances were favourable. They were, at the moment, very unfavourable. She looked round helplessly, not at all sure what to do—there were a dozen or more people milling about them, all seemingly proffering advice.

'Can't anyone speak English?' she asked her growing audience. Apparently not; there was a short pause before they all burst out again, even more eager to help. It was a relief when Deborah glimpsed the top of a policeman's cap above the heads, forging its way with steady authority towards her. Presently he came into full view, a grizzled man with a harsh face. Her heart sank; awful visions of spending the night in prison and no one any the wiser were floating through her bemused brain. When he spoke to her she asked, without any hope at all: 'I suppose you don't speak English?'

He smiled and his face wasn't harsh any more. 'A little,' he admitted. 'I will speak to this man first, Mevrouw.'

The discussion was lengthy with a good deal of argument. When at length the police officer turned to her she hastened to tell him:

'It wasn't anyone's fault—the road was slippery—he skidded, he wasn't driving fast at all.'

The man answered in a laboured English which was more than adequate. 'He tells me that also, Mevrouw. You have your papers?'

She managed to open the car's battered door and find them out of her handbag. He examined her licence and then looked at her. 'You are wife of Mijnheer Doorninck, *chirurg* at the Grotehof hospital.'

She nodded.

'You are not injured, Mevrouw?'

'I don't think so—I feel a little shaky.' She smiled. 'I was scared stiff!'

'Stiff?' He eyed her anxiously.

'Sorry—I was frightened.'

'I shall take you to the hospital in one moment.' He was writing in his notebook. 'You will sit in your car, please.'

Deborah did as she was told and he went back to talk some more to the lorry driver, who presently got into his cab and drove away.

'It will be arranged that your car'—his eye swept over the poor remnant of it—'will be taken to a garage. Do not concern yourself about it, Mevrouw. Now you will come with me, please.'

'I'm quite all right,' she assured him, and then at his look, followed him obediently to the police car behind the crowd, glad to sit down now, for her legs were suddenly jelly and one arm was aching.

They were close to the hospital. She was whisked there, swept from the car and ushered into the Accident Room where Gerard's name acted like a magic wand; she barely had time to thank the policeman warmly before she was spirited away to be meticulously examined from head to foot. There was nothing wrong, the Casualty Officer decided, save for a few painful bruises on her arm and the nasty shock she had had.

'I will telephone and inform Mijnheer van Doorninck,' he told her, and she stifled a giggle, for Gerard's name had been uttered with such reverence. 'He's not home,' she told him, 'not until late this evening or tomorrow morning—he's in Arnhem. In any case, I'm perfectly all right.'

She should have suspected him when he agreed with her so readily, suggesting that she should drink a cup of tea and have a short rest, then he would come back and pronounce her fit to go home.

She drank the tea gratefully. There was no milk with it, but it was hot and sweet and it pulled her together and calmed her down. She lay back and closed her eyes and wondered what Gerard would say when he got back. She was asleep in five minutes.

She slept for just over an hour and when she wakened Gerard was there, staring down at her, his blue eyes blazing from a white face. She wondered, only half awake, why he looked so furiously angry, and then remembered where she was.

She exclaimed unhappily: 'Oh, dear—were you home after all? But I did tell them not to telephone the house…'

'I was telephoned at Arnhem. How do you feel?'

Deborah ignored that. 'The fools,' she said crossly, 'I told them you were busy, that there was no need to bother you.'

'They quite rightly ignored such a foolish remark. How do you feel?' he repeated.

She swung her legs off the couch to let him see just how normal she was. 'Perfectly all right, thank you— such a fuss about nothing.' She gulped suddenly. 'I'm so sorry, Gerard, I've made you angry, haven't I? You didn't have to give up the case or anything awful like that?'

His grim mouth relaxed into the faintest of smiles. 'No—I had intended returning home this evening, anyway. And I am not angry.'

She eyed him uncertainly. 'You look…' She wasn't

sure how he looked; probably he was tired after a long-drawn-out operation. She forced her voice to calm. 'I'm perfectly able to go home now, Gerard, if that's convenient for you.'

He said slowly, studying his hands: 'Is that how you think of me? As someone whose wishes come before everything else? Who doesn't give a damn when his wife is almost killed—a heartless tyrant?'

She was sitting on the side of the couch, conscious that her hair was an untidy mop halfway down her neck and that she had lost the heel of a shoe and her stockings were laddered. 'You're not a heartless tyrant,' she protested hotly. 'You're not—you're a kind and considerate husband. Can't you see that's why I hate to hinder you in any way? It's the least I can do—I'd rather die…'

She had said too much, she realised that too late.

'Just what do you mean by that?' he asked her sharply.

Deborah opened her mouth, not having any idea what to say and was saved from making matters worse by the entry of the Casualty Officer, eager to know if she felt up to going home and obviously pleased with himself because he had come under the notice of one of the most eminent consultants in the hospital and treated his wife to boot. He was a worthy young man, his thoughts were written clearly on his face, Deborah thanked him cordially and was pleased when Gerard added his own thanks with a warmth to make the young man flush with pleasure. She hadn't realised that Gerard was held in such veneration by the hospital staff; the things she didn't know about him were so many that it was a little frightening—certainly they were seen to the entrance by an imposing number of people.

The BMW was parked right in front of the steps; anyone else, she felt sure would have been ordered to move their car, for no one could get near the entrance, but no one seemed to find anything amiss. Gerard helped her in and she sat back with a sigh. As he drove through the hospital gateway she said apologetically: 'The police said they would take the Fiat away and they'd let you know about it. It—it's a bit battered.'

'It can be scrapped.' His voice was curt. 'I'll get you a new car.'

That was all he said on the way home and she could think of nothing suitable to talk about herself. Besides, her head had begun to ache. Wim and Marijke were both hovering in the hall when they got in. Gerard said something to them in Dutch and Marijke came forward, talking volubly.

'Marijke will help you to bed,' Gerard explained. 'I suggest that you have something to eat there and then get a good sleep—you'll feel quite the thing by the morning.' His searching eyes rested for a brief, professional minute on her face. 'You have a headache, I daresay, I'll give you something for that presently. Go up to bed now.'

She would have liked to have disputed his order, but when she considered it, bed was the one place where she most wanted to be. She thanked him in a subdued voice and went upstairs, Marijke in close attendance.

She wasn't hungry, she discovered, when she was tucked up against her pillows and Marijke had brought in a tray of soup and chicken. She took a few mouthfuls, put the tray on the side table and lay back and closed her eyes, to open them at once as Gerard came in after the most perfunctory of knocks. He walked over to the bed, took her pulse, studied the bruises beginning to show on her arm, and then stood looking down at her with the expression she imagined he must wear when he was examining his patients—a kind of reserved kindliness. 'You've not eaten anything,' he observed.

'I'm not very hungry.'

He nodded, shook some pills out of the box he held, fetched water from the carafe on the table and said: 'Swallow these down—they'll take care of that headache and send you to sleep.'

She did as she was bid and lay back again against the pillows.

'Ten minutes?' she wanted to know. 'Pills always seem to take so long to work.'

'Then we might as well talk while we're waiting,' he said easily, and sat down on the end of the bed. 'Tell me, what is all this about Sien? Wim tells me that you went up to Domwier because she had cut her hand.'

'Yes—the doctor wasn't there and it sounded as though it might have needed a stitch or two—she had six, actually. I—I thought you would want me to look after her as you weren't home.'

He took her hand lying on the coverlet and his touch was gentle. 'Yes, of course that was exactly what I should have wanted you to do, Deborah. Was it a bad cut?'

She told him; she told him about their visit to the hospital at Leeuwarden too, adding: 'They knew you quite well there—I didn't know...' There was such a lot she didn't know, she thought wearily. 'I got the doctor there to find out if Sien had any friends or family—I fetched her niece, they seemed quite happy together.' She blinked huge, drowsy eyes. 'I forgot—I said I would telephone and make sure that Sien was all right. Could someone…?'

'I'll see to it. Thank you, my dear. What a competent girl you are, but you always were in theatre and you're just as reliable now.'

She was really very sleepy, but she had to answer that. 'No, I'm not. I bought that terribly expensive dress just to annoy you—and what about Claude? Have you forgotten him? You thought I was quite unreliable with him, didn't you?'

She was aware that her tongue was running away with her, but she seemed unable to help herself. 'Don't you know that I…?' She fell asleep, just in time.

She was perfectly all right in the morning except for a badly discoloured arm. All the same, Marijke brought her breakfast up on a tray with the injunction, given with motherly sternness, to eat it up, and she was closely followed by Gerard, who wished her a placid good morning and cast a quick eye over her. 'I've told Wim,' he said as he was leaving after the briefest of stays, 'that if anyone telephones about the Fiat that he is to refer them to me. And by the way, Sien is quite all right. I telephoned last night and again this morning. She sends her respects.'

Deborah smiled. 'How very old-fashioned that sounds, and how nice! But she's a nice person, isn't she? I can't wait to learn a little of her language so that we can really talk.'

He smiled. 'She would like that. But first your Dutch—it's coming along very nicely, Deborah—your grammar is a little wild, but your accent is impeccable.'

She flushed with pleasure. 'Oh, do you really mean that? Professor de Wit is so loath to praise. I sometimes feel that I'm making no headway at all.' She smiled at him. 'I'm glad you're pleased.'

He opened the door without answering her. 'I shouldn't do too much today,' was all he said as he went.

If he had been there for her to say it to, she would have told him that she didn't do too much anyway because there was nothing for her to do, but that would have sounded ungrateful; he had given her everything she could possibly want—a lovely home, clothes beyond her wildest dreams, a car, an allowance which she secretly felt was far too generous—all these, and none of them worth a cent without his love and interest. She had sometimes wondered idly what the term 'an empty life' had meant. Now she knew, although it wouldn't be empty if he loved her; then everything which they did would be shared—the dinner parties, the concerts, the visits to friends, just as he would share the burden of his work with her. Deborah sighed and got out of bed and went to look out of the window. It was a cold, clear morning. She got dressed and presently telephoned Adelaide van Essen and invited her round for coffee.

It was two days later that Deborah mentioned at breakfast that she had never seen Gerard's consulting rooms and, to her surprise, was invited to visit them that very day.

'I shan't be there,' he explained with his usual courtesy. 'I don't see patients there on a Thursday afternoon—it's my heavy afternoon list at the Grotehof, but go along by all means. Trudi, my secretary, will be there—her English is just about as good as your Dutch, so you should get on very well together.'

He had left soon afterwards, leaving her a prey to a variety of feelings, not the least of which was the sobering one that he had shown no visible regret at not being able to take her himself. Still, it would be something to do.

She went after lunch, in a new tweed suit because the sun was shining, albeit weakly. She was conscious that she looked rather dishy and consoled herself with the thought that at last she was being allowed to see another small, very small, facet of Gerard's life.

The consulting rooms were within walking distance, in a quiet square lined with tall brick houses, almost all of which had brass plates on their doors—a kind of Dutch Harley Street, she gathered, and found Gerard's name quickly enough. His rooms were on the first floor and Deborah was impressed by their unobtrusive luxury; pale grey carpet, solid, comfortable chairs, small tables with flowers, and in one corner a desk where Trudi sat.

Trudi was young and pretty and dressed discreetly in grey to match the carpet. She welcomed Deborah a little nervously in an English as bad as her Dutch and showed her round, leaving Gerard's own room till last. It too was luxurious, deliberately comfortable and relaxing so that the patient might feel at ease. She smiled and nodded as Trudi rattled on, not liking to ask too many questions because, as Gerard's wife, she should already know the answers. They had a cup of tea together presently and because Trudi kept looking anxiously at the clock, Deborah got up to go. Probably the poor girl had a great deal of work to do before she could leave. She was halfway across the sea of carpet when the door opened and Claude came in. She was so surprised that she came to a halt, her mouth open, but even in her surprise she saw that he was taken aback, annoyed too. He cast a lightning glance at Trudi and then back to Deborah. 'Hullo, my beauty,' he said.

She ignored that. 'What are you doing here?' she demanded, 'I'm quite sure that Gerard doesn't know. What do you want?'

He still looked shaken, although he replied airily enough. 'Oh, nothing much. Trudi has something for me, haven't you, darling?'

The girl looked so guilty that Deborah felt sorry for her. 'Yes—yes, I have. It's downstairs, I'll get it.'

She fled through the door leaving Deborah frowning at Claude's now smiling face. 'What are you up to?' she wanted to know.

'I?' he smiled even more widely. 'My dear girl, nothing. Surely I can come and see my friends without you playing the schoolmarm over me?'

'But this is Gerard's office…'

'We do meet in the oddest places, don't we?' He came a step nearer. 'Jealous, by any chance? Gerard would never dream of looking for us here…'

'You underestimate my powers,' said Gerard in a dangerously quiet voice. 'And really, this time, Claude, my patience is exhausted.'

He had been standing in the open doorway. Now he crossed the room without haste, knocked Claude down in a businesslike fashion, picked him up again and frogmarched him out of the room. Deborah, ice-cold with the unexpectedness of it all, listened to the muddle of feet going down the stairs. It sounded as though Claude was having difficulty in keeping his balance. The front door was shut with quiet finality and Gerard came back upstairs. He looked as placid as usual and yet quite murderous.

'Is this why you wanted to visit these rooms?' he asked silkily.

She had never seen him look like that before. 'No, you know that.'

'Why is Trudi not here?'

'Trudi?' She had forgotten the girl, she hadn't the least idea where she had gone. 'She went to fetch something for Claude—he didn't say what it was.'

'She is downstairs, very upset,' he informed her coldly. 'She told me that she hadn't been expecting anyone else—only you.'

Deborah gaped at him. 'She said that? But…' But what, she thought frantically—perhaps what Trudi had said was true, perhaps she hadn't expected Claude. But on the other hand he had told her that he had come to fetch something and that Trudi was an old friend.

'Oh, please, do let me try and explain,' she begged, and met with a decided: 'No, Deborah—there is really no need.'

She stared at him wordlessly. No, she supposed, of course there was no need: his very indifference made that plain enough. It just didn't matter; she didn't matter either. She closed her eyes on the bitter thought, all the more bitter because she had thought, just once or twice lately, that she was beginning to matter just a little to him.

She opened her eyes again and went past him and down the stairs. Trudi was in the hall. Deborah gave her a look empty of all expression and opened the door on to the square. It looked peaceful and quiet under the late afternoon sky, but she didn't notice that; she didn't notice anything.

Once in the house, she raced up to her room and

dragged out a case and started to stuff it with clothes.
There was money in her purse, enough to get her to
England—she couldn't go home, not just yet at any rate,
not until she had sorted her thoughts out. She would go
to Aunt Mary; her remote house by Hadrian's Wall was
exactly the sort of place she wanted—a long, long way
from Amsterdam, and Gerard.

She was on her way downstairs with her case when
the front door opened and Gerard came in. He shut it
carefully and stood with his back to it.

'I must talk to you, Deborah,' his voice was quiet
and compelling. 'There's plenty of time if you're going
for the night boat train. I'll drive you to the station—if
you still want to go.'

Deborah swept across the hall, taking no notice, but
at the door, of course, she was forced to stop; only then
did she say: 'I'll get a taxi, thank you—perhaps you
will let me pass.'

'No, I won't, my dear. You'll stay and hear what I
have to say. Afterwards, if you still wish it, you shall go.
But first I must explain.' He took the case from her and
set it on the floor and then went back to lean against the
door. 'Deborah, I have been very much at fault—I'm not
sure what I thought when I saw Claude this afternoon.
I only know that I was more angry than I have ever
been before in my life, and my anger blinded me. After
you had gone Trudi told me the truth—that Claude had
come to see her. She is going to Nice with him, but they
had planned it otherwise—I was to know nothing about
it until I arrived in the morning and found a letter from
her on my desk.' He smiled thinly. 'It seems that since
Claude could not have my wife, he must make do with
my secretary. None of this is an excuse for my treat-

ment of you, Deborah, for which I am both ashamed and sorry. What would you like to do?'

'Go away,' said Deborah, her voice thick with tears she would rather have died than shed. 'I've an aunt—if I could go and stay with her, just for a little while, just to—to… I've not been much of a success—I'd do better to go back to my old job.'

He said urgently: 'No, that's not true. No man could have had a more loyal and understanding wife. It is I who have failed you and I am only just beginning to see…perhaps we could start again. You really want to go?' He paused and went on briskly: 'Come then, I'll take you to the station.'

If only he would say that he would miss her— She thought of a dozen excuses for staying and came up with the silliest. 'What about your dinner, and Wim—and Sien?'

'I'll see to everything,' he told her comfortably. 'You're sure that you have enough clothes with you?'

Deborah looked at him in despair; he was relieved that she was going. She nodded without speaking, having not the least idea what she had packed and not caring, and followed him out to the car. At the station he bought her ticket, stuffed some money into her handbag and saw her on to the train. She thought her heart would break as it slid silently away from the platform, leaving him standing there.

By the time she reached Aunt Mary's she was tired out and so unhappy that nothing mattered at all any more. She greeted her surprised relation with a story in which fact and fiction were so hopelessly jumbled together that they made no sense at all, and then burst into tears. She felt better after that and Aunt Mary being a sensible woman not given to asking silly questions, she was led to the small bedroom at the back of the little house, told to unpack, given a nourishing meal and ordered with mild authority to go to bed and sleep the clock round. Which she did, to wake to the firm conviction that she had been an utter fool to leave Gerard—perhaps he wouldn't want her back; he'd positively encouraged her to go, hadn't he? Could he be in love with some girl at long last and wish to put an end to their marriage and she not there to stop, if she were able, such nonsense? The idea so terrified her that she jumped out of bed and dressed at a great speed as though that would help in some way, but when she got downstairs and Aunt Mary took one look at her strained face, she said: 'You can't rush things, my dear, nor must you imagine things. Now all you need is patience, for although I'm not clear exactly what the matter is, you can be certain that it will all come right in the end if only you will give it time. Now go for a good long walk and come back with an appetite.'

Aunt Mary was right, of course. After three days of long walks, gentle talk over simple meals and the dreamless sleep her tiredness induced, Deborah began to feel better; she was still dreadfully unhappy, but at least she could be calm about it now. It would have been nice to have given way to tears whenever she thought about Gerard, which was every minute of the day, but that would not do, she could see that without Aunt Mary telling her so. In a day or two she would write a letter to him, asking him—she didn't know what she would ask him; perhaps inspiration would come when she picked up her pen.

The weather changed on the fourth day; layers of

low cloud covered the moors, the heather lost its colour, the empty countryside looked almost frightening. There was next to no traffic on the road any more and even the few cottages which could be seen from Aunt Mary's windows had somehow merged themselves into the moorland around them so that they were almost invisible. But none of these things were reasons to miss her walk. She set off after their midday meal, with strict instructions to be back for tea and on no account to go off the road in case the mist should come down.

Sound advice which Deborah forgot momentarily when she saw an old ruined cottage some way from the road. It looked interesting, and without thinking, she tramped across the heather towards it. It was disappointing enough when she reached it, being nothing but an empty shell, but there was a dip beyond it with a small dewpond. She walked on to have a closer look and then wandered on, quite forgetful of her aunt's words. She had gone quite a distance when she saw the mist rolling towards her. She thought at first that it must be low-lying clouds which would sweep away, but it was mist, creeping forward at a great rate, sneaking up on her, thickening with every yard. She had the good sense to turn towards the road before it enveloped her entirely, but by then it was too late to see where she was going.

Shivering a little in its sudden chill, she sat down; probably it would lift very shortly. If she stayed where she was she would be quite safe. It would be easy to get back to the road as soon as she could see her way. It got too cold to sit after a time, so she got to her feet, stamping them and clapping her hands and trying to keep in one spot. And it was growing dark too; a little thread of fear ran through her head—supposing the mist lasted all night? It was lonely country—a few sheep, no houses within shouting distance, and the road she guessed to be a good mile away. She called herself a fool and stamped her feet some more.

It was quite dark and the mist was at its densest when she heard voices. At first she told herself that she was imagining things, but they became louder as they drew closer—children's voices, all talking at once.

'Hullo there!' she shouted, and was greeted by silence. 'Don't be frightened, I'm by myself and lost too. Shall we try and get together?'

This time there was a babble of sound from all around her. 'We're lost too.' The voice was on a level with her waist. 'Miss Smith went to get help, but it got dark and we started to walk. We're holding hands.'

'Who are you, and how many?' asked Deborah. Someone small brushed against her and a cold little hand found her arm. 'Oh, there you are,' it said tearfully. 'We're so glad to find someone—it's so dark. We're a school botany class from St Julian's, only Miss Smith lost the way and when the mist came she thought it would be quicker if she went for help. She told us to stay where we were, but she didn't come back and we got frightened.' The voice ended on a sob and Deborah caught the hand in her own and said hearteningly: 'Well, how lucky we've met—now we're together we've nothing to be afraid of. How many are there of you?'

'Eight—we're still holding hands.'

'How very sensible of you. May I hold hands too, then we can tell each other our names.'

There was a readjustment in the ranks of the little girls; the circle closed in on her. Deborah guessed that they were scared stiff and badly needed her company. 'Who's the eldest of you?' she enquired.

'Doreen—she's eleven.'

'Splendid!' What was so splendid about being eleven? she thought, stifling a giggle. 'I expect the mist will lift presently and we shall be able to walk to the road. It's not far.'

'It's miles,' said a plaintive voice so that Deborah went on cheerfully, 'Not really, and I can find it easily. My name's Deborah, by the way. How about stamping our feet to keep warm?'

They stamped until they were tired out. Deborah, getting a little desperate, suggested: 'Let's sit down. I know it's a bit damp, but if we keep very close to each other we shall keep warm enough. Let's sing.'

The singing was successful, if a little out of tune. They worked their way through 'This old man, he played one', the School Song, 'Rule Britannia' and a selection of the latest pop tunes. It was while they were getting their breath after these musical efforts that Deborah heard a shout. It was a nice, cheerful sound, a loud hullo in a man's voice, answered immediately by a ragged and very loud chorus of mixed screams and shouts from the little girls.

'Oh, that won't do at all,' said Deborah quickly. 'He'll get confused. We must all shout together at the same time. Everyone call "Here" when I've counted three.'

The voice answered them after a few moments, sometimes tantalisingly close, sometimes at a distance. After what seemed a long time, Deborah saw a faint glow ahead of them. A torch. 'Walk straight ahead,' she yelled, 'you're quite close.'

The glow got brighter, wavering from side to side and

going far too slowly. 'Come on,' she shouted, 'you're almost here!'

The faint glow from the torch was deceptive in the mist, for the next thing she knew Gerard was saying from the gloom above her head, 'A fine healthy pair of lungs, dear girl—I've never been so glad to hear your voice, though I'm glad you don't always bellow like that.'

Surprise almost choked her. 'Gerard! Gerard, is it really you? How marvellous—how could you possibly know...'

'Your Aunt Mary told me that you had gone for a walk and it seemed a good idea to drive along the road to meet you. When the mist got too thick I parked the car, and then it was I heard these brats squealing'— there were muffled giggles to interrupt him here—'and I collected them as I came.'

'You haven't got the botany class from St Julian's too?' she gasped. 'You can't have—I've got them here.'

'Indeed I have—or a part of it. A Miss Smith went for help and left them bunched together, but being the little horrors they are, they wandered off.'

'There aren't any missing?'

'No—we counted heads, as it were. Seven young ladies—very young ladies.'

Deborah had found his arm and was clutching it as though he might disappear at any moment. 'I've got eight of them here. What must we do, Gerard?'

'Why, my dear, stay here until the mist goes again. The car is up on the road, once we can reach it I can get you all back to Twice Brewed in no time at all.' He sounded so matter-of-fact about it that she didn't feel frightened any more. 'Your aunt has got everything or-

ganised by now, I imagine. She seemed to be a remark-
ably resourceful woman.' His hand sought and found
hers and gave it a reassuring squeeze. 'In the meantime, I suggest that we all keep together, and don't let
any of you young ladies dare to let go of hands. Supposing we sit?'

There was a good deal of giggling and a tremendous
amount of shuffling and shoving and pushing before
everyone was settled, sitting in a tight circle. Deborah,
with Gerard's great bulk beside her, felt quite light-
hearted, and the children, although there was a good
deal of whining for something to eat, cheered up too,
so that for a time at least, there was a buzz of talk, but
gradually the shrill voices died down until there was silence and, incredibly, she dozed too, to wake shivering
a little with the cold despite the arm around her shoulders. She whispered at once in a meek voice: 'I didn't
mean to go to sleep, I'm sorry,' and felt the reassuring
pressure of Gerard's hand.

'Not to worry. I think they have all nodded off, but
we had better have a roll-call when they wake to be on
the safe side.'

'Yes. I wonder what the time is, it's so very dark.'

'Look up,' he urged her, quietly. 'Above our heads.'

By some freak of nature the mist had parted itself,
revealing a patch of inky sky, spangled with stars. 'Oh,
lovely!' breathed Deborah. 'Only they don't seem real.'

'Of course they're real,' his whisper was bracing. 'It's
the mist which isn't real. The stars have been there all
the time, and always will be, only sometimes we don't
see them—rather like life.' He sighed and she wondered
what he meant. 'You see that bright one, the second star
from the right?'

She said that yes, she could see it very well.

'That's our star,' he told her surprisingly, and when she repeated uncertainly 'Ours?' he went on: 'Do you not know that for every star in the heavens there is a man and a woman whose destinies are ruled by it? Perhaps they never meet, perhaps they meet too late or too soon, but just once in a while they meet at exactly the right moment and their destinies and their lives become one.'

In the awful, silent dark, anything would sound true; Deborah allowed herself a brief dream in which she indeed shared her destiny with Gerard, dispelled it by telling herself that the mist was making her fanciful, and whispered back: 'How do you know it's our star—it's ridiculous.'

'Of course it's ridiculous,' he agreed affably, and so readily that she actually felt tears of disappointment well into her eyes. 'But it's a thought that helps to pass the time, isn't it? Go to sleep again.'

And such was the calm confidence in his voice that she did as she was told, to waken in the bitter cold of the autumn dawn to an unhappy chorus of little girls wanting their mothers, their breakfasts, and to go home. Deborah was engulfed in them with no ears for anything else until she heard watery giggles coming from Gerard's other side, and his voice, loud and cheerful, declaring that they were all going to jump up and down and every few minutes bellow like mad. 'It's getting light; there will be people about soon.' He sounded quite positive about that. So they jumped and shouted, and although the mist was as thick as it ever was, at least they got warm, and surely any minute now the mist would roll away.

It did no such thing, however. They shouted themselves hoarse, but there was no reply from the grey blanket around them. First one child and then another began to cry, and Deborah, desperately trying to instil a false cheer into her small unhappy companions, could hear Gerard doing the same, with considerably more success so that she found herself wondering where she had got the erroneous idea that he wasn't particularly keen on children. She remembered all at once what he had said about Sasja who hadn't wanted babies—the hurt must have gone deep. It seemed to her vital to talk about it even at so unsuitable a time and she was on the point of doing so when the mist folded itself up and disappeared. It was hard not to laugh; the little girls were still gathered in a tight circle, clutching each other's hands. They were white-faced and puffy-eyed, each dressed in the school uniform of St Julian's—grey topcoats and round grey hats with brims, anchored to their small heads by elastic under their chins. Some of them even had satchels over their shoulders and most of the hats were a little too large and highly unbecoming.

There was an excited shout as they all stood revealed once more and a tendency to break away until Gerard shouted to them to keep together still. 'A fine lot we would look,' he pointed out good-naturedly, 'if the mist comes back and we all get lost again.' He looked round at Deborah and smiled. 'We'll hold hands again, don't you think, and make for the road.'

They were half way there when they saw the search party—the local police, several farmers and the quite distraught Miss Smith who, when they met, burst into tears, while her botany class, with a complete lack of feeling for her distress and puffed up with a great sense of importance, told everyone severally and in chorus just how brave and resourceful they had been. It took a few minutes to sort them into the various cars and start the short journey to St Julian's.

Deborah found herself sitting beside Gerard, with four of the smallest children crammed in the back. She was weary and untidy, but when he suggested he should drop her off at Aunt Mary's as they went past, she refused.

On their way back from the school she began, 'How did…?' and was stopped by a quiet: 'Not now, dear girl, a hot bath and breakfast first.'

So it was only when they had breakfasted and she was sitting drowsily before a roaring fire in Aunt Mary's comfortable sitting room that she tried again. 'How did you know that I was here?'

'I telephoned your mother.'

'Oh—did she ask—that is, did she wonder…'

'If she did, she said nothing. Your mother is a wise woman, Deborah.'

'Why did you come?'

He was lying back, very much at his ease, in a high-backed chair, his eyes half shut. 'I felt I needed a break from work, it seemed a good idea to bring the car over and see if you were ready to come back.' He added: 'Smith is breaking his heart—think about it. Why not go to bed now, and get a few hours' sleep?'

Deborah got up silently. Smith might be breaking his doggy heart, but what about Gerard? There was no sign of even a crack; he was his usual calm, friendly self again, and no more. She went up to her little room and slept for hours, and when she came downstairs Aunt Mary was waiting for her.

'I told you to have patience, Debby,' she remarked with satisfaction. 'Everything will come right without you lifting a finger, mark my words.'

So when Gerard came in from the garden presently, she told him that she was ready to go back with him when he wished. She woke several times in the night and wondered, despite Aunt Mary's certainty, if she had made the right decision.

Chapter 9

It was two days before they returned to Amsterdam, two days during which Gerard, who had become firm friends with Aunt Mary, dug the garden, chopped wood and did odd jobs around the house, as well as driving the two ladies into Carlisle to do some shopping.

They left after lunch, to catch the Hull ferry that evening, and Deborah, who had been alternately dreading and longing for an hour or so of Gerard's company, with the vague idea of offering to part with him and the even vaguer hope that he would tell her how much he had missed her, was forced to sit beside him in the car while he sustained a conversation about Aunt Mary, the beauties of the moors, the charm of the small girls they had met and the excellence of his hostess's cooking. Each time Deborah tried to bring the conversation round to themselves he somehow baulked her efforts; in the end, she gave up, and when they reached Hull, what with getting the car on board, arranging to have dinner and their cabins, there wasn't much need to talk. Quite frustrated, she pleaded a headache directly they had finished dinner and retired to her cabin. She joined him for an early breakfast, though, because he had asked her to; he had, he told her, an appointment quite early in the morning at the hospital and didn't wish to waste any time.

He talked pleasantly as they took the road to Amsterdam and Deborah did her best to match his mood, but at the house he didn't come in with her, only unloaded her case and waited until Wim had opened the door before he drove away. She followed Wim inside. Gerard hadn't said when he would be home, nor had he spoken of themselves. She spent a restless day until he came home soon after tea and, as usual, went to his study. But before he could reach the door she was in the hall, a dozen things she wanted to say buzzing in her head. In the end she asked foolishly: 'What about Trudi? Did you get someone to take her place?'

He had halted and stood looking at her with raised eyebrows. 'Oh, yes—a middle-aged married woman, very sober and conscientious. You must go and see her for yourself some day.'

Deborah was left standing in the hall, her mouth open in surprise. Did he suppose her to be jealous of something absurd like that? She mooned back into the sitting room, Smith at her heels. Of course she was jealous; he filled her with rage, he was exasperating and indifferent, but she was still jealous. She would have to cure that, she told herself sternly, if she was to have any peace of mind in the future—the uncertain future, she

had to allow, and wondered why Gerard had wanted her
back. But if she had hoped to see a change in his manner towards her, she was doomed to disappointment. He
was a quiet man by nature, he seemed to her to be even
quieter now, and sometimes she caught him staring at
her in a thoughtful manner; it was a pity that his habit
of drooping the lids over his eyes prevented her from
seeing their expression. There was no hint of a return
of those few strange moments on the moor; they had
been make-believe, she told herself, and took pains to
take up the smooth, neat pattern of their life together as
though it had never been ruffled out of its perfection.

She visited his family, arranged a dinner party for a
medical colleague who was coming from Vienna and
bought yet another new dress to wear at it. It was a very
pretty dress, fine wool in soft greens and pinks, with a
wide skirt. It would go very well with Tante Emmiline's
garnets and perhaps, she hoped wistfully, Gerard might
notice it. She hung it carefully in her clothes cupboard
and went to get ready for the orphans' hour and for a
number of muddled but sincere reasons, took almost
every penny of her remaining allowance and when she
reached the orphanage gate, stuffed the money into the
alms box hung upon it, accompanying the action with a
hotch-potch of wordless prayers—and later, when one
of them was answered, took fresh heart. For Gerard
noticed the new dress; indeed, he stood looking at her
for so long that she became a little shy under his steady
gaze and asked in a brittle little voice: 'Is there something wrong? Don't you like my dress?' She achieved a
brittle laugh too. 'A pity, because it's too late to change
it now.'

His eyes narrowed and a little smile just touched the

corners of his mouth. 'Far too late, Deborah,' he said quietly, 'and I wouldn't change a single...' his voice altered subtly. 'The dress is delightful and you look charming.' He turned away as he spoke and the old-fashioned door bell tinkled through the house. 'Our guests, my dear. Shall we go and meet them?'

The other prayers must have become mislaid on the way, thought Deborah miserably as she got ready for bed later that evening, for when their guests had gone Gerard had told her that he would be going to Vienna for a five-day seminar in a day's time. When he had asked her if she would like him to bring back anything for her she had replied woodenly that no, there was nothing, thank you, and made some gratuitous remark about a few days of peace and quiet and now was her chance to take the new Fiat and go and see Abigail, who was still in Friesland.

Gerard had paused before he spoke. 'Why not?' he agreed affably, and looked up from the letters he was scanning. 'When is the baby due—several months, surely.'

'Almost six. I've knitted a few things, I'll take them with me.'

He nodded and went to open the door for her. 'Good idea.' He patted her kindly on the shoulder as she passed him. 'Sleep well, my dear,' and as an afterthought: 'I had no idea that you could knit.'

The pansy eyes smouldered. 'It's something I do while you're away or working in your study. I get through quite an amount.' Her voice was very even and she added a pleasant: 'Good night, Gerard.'

She didn't see him at breakfast, although he had left

a scribbled note by her plate saying that he would be home for lunch—not later than one o'clock.

But it was later than that, it was six in the evening. She had eaten her lunch alone, telling herself that was what being a surgeon's wife meant; something she had known about and expected; it happened to all doctors' wives—the young houseman's bride, the GP's lady, the consultant's wife, they all had to put up with it and so would she, only in their cases, a shared love made it easier. Deborah sighed, and loving him so much, hoped with all her heart that he, at least, was satisfied with their marriage. Apparently no more was to be said about Claude or any of the events connected with him, and in any case it was too late for recriminations now—besides, she wasn't sure if she had any; living with him, in the house he loved and which she had come to love too, was infinitely better than never seeing him again.

She was in the garden playing with Smith when he joined her. He looked weary and a little grim and she said at once: 'I've a drink ready for you—come inside,' and then because she couldn't bear to see him looking like that: 'Must you go tomorrow, Gerard? Is it important?'

He took the glass from her and smiled in a way which somehow disturbed her. 'Yes, Deborah, I think it's very important—I have to be sure of something, you see. It involves someone else besides myself.'

An icy finger touched her heart and she turned away from him. 'Oh, well, I'll telephone Abigail.'

'I thought you had already arranged to visit her.'

'No—it had quite slipped my mind,' she improvised hastily, because the reason she hadn't telephoned was because she had hoped, right until this last moment, that he might suggest her going with him, but he wouldn't do that now. Hadn't he said that there was someone else? She wondered if he had meant a patient and very much doubted it. She telephoned Abigail there and then, being very gay about it.

She wished Gerard a cheerful goodbye after breakfast the next morning and after a fine storm of weeping in her room afterwards, dressed herself and drove the car to Friesland where she received a delighted welcome from Abigail and Dominic. They had come out to meet her, walking together, not touching, but so wrapped together in happiness so secure and deep that she could almost see it. For a moment she wished she hadn't come, but later, laughing and talking in their comfortable sitting room, it wasn't so bad. Indeed the day went too quickly. Driving back Deborah contemplated the four days left before Gerard should come back. There was, of course, the orphans' hour, but that wasn't until Thursday. She would have to fill the days somehow. She spent the rest of the journey devising a series of jobs which would keep her occupied for the next day or two.

She was a little early when she got to the orphanage on Thursday evening, but although it still wanted five minutes to the hour, the children were already assembled in the long, bare room. At least, thought Deborah, as she took off her coat and prepared for the next hour's boisterous games, the evening would pass quickly, and the next day Gerard would be back. She longed to see him, just as she dreaded his return, wondering what he would have to tell her, or perhaps he would have nothing to say, and that would be even harder to bear.

She turned to the task in hand, greeting the children by name as they milled around her, separating the more belligerent bent on the inevitable fight, picking up and soothing those who, just as inevitably, had fallen down and were now howling their eyes out. Within five minutes, however, she had a rousing game of 'Hunt the Slipper' going—a hot favourite with the orphans because it allowed a good deal of legitimate screaming and running about. This was followed by 'Twos and Threes'. A good deal of discreet cheating went on here; the very small ones, bent on getting there first, were prone to fall on their stomachs and bawl until Deborah raced to pick them up and carry them in triumph to the coveted place in the circle.

There was a pause next, during which she did her best to tidy her hair which had escaped most of its pins and hung most untidily around her shoulders. But it took too long, besides, there was no one to see—the children didn't care and she certainly didn't. 'Grandmother's Steps' was to be the final game of the evening, and Deborah, her face to the wall, listened to the stampede of what the orphans imagined were their creeping little feet and thanked heaven that there was no one below them or close by. She looked over her shoulder, pretending not to see the hasty scramble of the slower children to achieve immobility, and turned to the wall again. Once more, she decided, and then she would declare them all out and bring the game to a satisfactory conclusion.

She counted ten silently and turned round. 'All of you,' she began in her fragmental Dutch which the children understood so well. 'You're out...I saw you move...' Her voice died in her throat and her breath left her; behind the children, half way down the room, stood Gerard.

He came towards her slowly, pausing to pat a small tow-coloured head of hair or lift the more persistent hangers-on out of his way. When he reached her he said with a kind of desperate quietness: 'I thought I should never find you—such a conspiracy of silence...'

Her hand went to cover her open mouth. 'Wim and Marijke, they knew—they discovered. They were sweet about it—don't be angry with them.' She searched his calm face for some sign; his eyes were hooded, there was the faintest smile on his mouth; she had no idea what his true feelings were. She went on earnestly: 'You see, it's a Catholic convent and you—your family are Calvinists.' Her look besought him to understand. 'You—you don't mix very well, do you? Separate schools and hospitals and...'

'Orphanages?' he offered blandly.

She nodded wordlessly and lapsed into thought, to say presently:

'Besides, you're home a day early.'

'Ah.' The lids flew open revealing blue eyes whose gleam made her blink. 'Am I to take it that that is a disappointment to you?'

'Disappointment?' Her voice rose alarmingly. There were small hands tugging at her skirt, hoarse little voices chanting an endless 'Debby' at her, but she hardly noticed them; she had reached the end of her emotional tether.

'Disappointment? Disappointment? This week's been endless—they always are when you go away. I'm sick and tired—I won't go on like this, being a kind of genteel housekeeper and wondering all the time—every minute of every day—where you are and what you're doing and pretending that I don't care...'

She was in full spate, but the rest of it never got said; she was gripped in an embrace which bade fair to crack her ribs, and kissed with a fierceness to put an end to all her doubts.

'How can a man be so blind?' Gerard spoke into her ear and the children's voices faded quite away from her senses. 'The star was there, only I didn't want to see it. I wanted to stay in the mist I had made—the nice safe mist which wouldn't allow anything to interfere with my work, because that was all I thought I had left. And yet I suppose I knew all the time...' He loosed his hold for the fraction of a minute and looked down into her face. 'I love you, my darling girl,' he said, and kissed her again; a pleasant state of affairs which might have gone on for some time if it hadn't been for the insistent pushes, tugs and yells from the orphans—it was story time and they knew their rights.

It was Deborah who broke the spell between them. 'My darling, I have to tell them a story—just until seven o'clock.' She smiled at him, her pansy eyes soft with love; he kissed her once more, a gentle kiss this time, and let her go. 'A fairy story,' she told him. '"Rose Red and Rose White"...'

His mouth twitched into a faint smile. 'In which language, dear heart?' he asked.

'Both, of course—I don't know half the words.' She smiled again. 'Heaven knows what they're thinking of us at this moment!'

'Nor I, though I'm very sure of what I'm thinking about you, but that can wait.'

He pulled up the tattered old music stool so that she could sit on it and the children jostled happily against each other, getting as close as they could.

'Rose Red and Rose White,' began Deborah in a voice lilting with not quite realised happiness, and the children fell silent as she plunged into the story, using a wild mixture of Dutch and English words and a wealth of gestures and mime and never doubting that the children understood every word, which, strangely enough, they did. They sat enrapt, their small mouths open, not fidgeting, and two of them had climbed on to Gerard's knees where he sat on one of the low window seats, listening to his wife's clear voice mangling the Dutch language. She had reached a dramatic point in her narrative when the room shook and trembled under the tones of the great bell from the church across the road.

'Seven o'clock,' said Deborah, very conscious of Gerard's look. 'We'll finish next week,' and added, 'Sweeties!' at the top of her voice, producing at the same time the bag of toffees which signalled the end of play hour.

She was marshalling her small companions into a more or less tidy line when the faint dry tinkle of the front door bell whispered its way along the passage and up the stairs. It was followed almost at once by the Mother Superior, who greeted Deborah warmly, the children with an all-embracing smile, and an extended hand for Gerard, admirably concealing any surprise she might have felt at finding him there.

'The little ones have been good?' she asked Deborah.

'They always are, Mother. Do you want me to come on Friday next week, or is it to be Thursday again?'

The nice elderly face broke into a smile. 'You will have the time?' The pale blue eyes studied Gerard, the hint of a question in their depths.

'I approve of anything my wife does,' he told her

at once, 'even though you and I are in—er—opposite camps.'

She answered him gravely, although her eyes were twinkling. 'That is nice to know, Mijnheer van Doorninck. You like children?'

He was looking at Deborah. 'Yes, Mother, although I'm afraid I've not had much to do with them.'

'That will arrange itself,' the old lady assured him, 'when you have children of your own.' She glanced at Deborah, smiling faintly. 'Thank you for your kind help, my child. And now we must go.'

The line of orphans stirred its untidy ranks; they hadn't understood anything of what had been said, and they wanted their supper, but first of all they wanted to be kissed good night by Debby, who always did. A small sigh went through the children as she started at the top of the line, bending over each child and hugging it, until, the last one kissed, they clattered out of the room and down the stairs. Deborah stood in the middle of the room, listening to the sound of their feet getting fainter and fainter until she could hear it no longer. Only then did she turn round.

Gerard was still by the window. He smiled and opened his arms wide and she ran to him, to be swallowed up most comfortably in their gentle embrace.

'My adorable little wife,' he said, and his words were heaven in her ears; she was five foot ten in her stockings and no slim wand of a girl; no one had ever called her little before. Perhaps Gerard, from his vantage point of another four inches, really did find her small. She lifted a glowing face for his face, and presently asked:

'You're not angry about the orphans?'

'No, my love. Indeed, they are splendid practice for you.'

She leaned back in his arms so that she could see his face. 'You're not going to start an orphanage?'

'Hardly that, dear heart—I hope that our children will always have a home.'

'Oh.' She added idiotically: 'There are twenty-eight of them.'

He kissed the top of her head. 'Yes? It seemed like ten times that number. Even so, I would hardly expect…!' She felt his great chest shake with silent laughter. 'A fraction of that number would do very nicely, don't you agree?' And before she could answer: 'Don't you want to know why I have come back early?'

'Yes—though it's enough that you're here.' She leaned up to kiss him.

'Simple. I found myself unable to stay away from you a moment longer. At first, I wanted to keep everything cool and friendly and impersonal between us, and then, over the weeks, I found it harder and harder to leave you, even to let you out of my sight, and yet I wouldn't admit that I loved you, although I knew in my heart—I could have killed Claude.'

'But you let me go away—all the way to Aunt Mary's…'

'My darling, I thought that I had destroyed any chance of making you love me.'

'But I did love you—I've loved you for years…'

He held her very close. 'You gave no sign, Debby— but all the same I had to follow you, and then I found you in the mist with all those little girls in their strange round hats.'

Deborah laughed into his shoulder. 'You showed me our star,' she reminded him.

'It's still there,' he told her. 'We're going to share it for the rest of our lives.'

He turned her round to face the window. 'There—you see?'

The sky was dark, but not as dark as the variegated roofs pointing their gables into it, pointing, all of them, to the stars. The carillon close by played its little tune for the half hour and was echoed a dozen times from various parts of Amsterdam. It was all peaceful and beautiful, but Deborah was no longer looking at it. She had turned in her husband's arms to face him again, studying his face.

'Are we going home?' she asked, and when he had kissed her just once more, she said, 'Our home, darling Gerard.'

'Our home, my love, although for me, home will always be where you are.'

There was only one answer to that. She wreathed her arms round his neck and kissed him.

* * * * *

SPECIAL EXCERPT FROM

◆ HARLEQUIN®

SPECIAL EDITION

When Shania Stewart tells Deputy Daniel Tallchief that
he needs to lighten up with his wild younger sister,
the handsome lawman doesn't know whether to
ignore her or kiss her. But Shania knows.
It's going to take a carefully crafted lesson plan
to tutor this cowboy in love.

Read on for a sneak preview of
The Lawman's Romance Lesson,
the next great book in USA TODAY bestselling author
Marie Ferrarella's Forever, Texas miniseries.

Shania flushed as she raised her eyes toward Daniel. "I
don't usually babble like this."

Daniel found the pink hue that had suddenly risen to
her cheeks rather sweet. The next second, he realized that
he was staring. Daniel forced himself to look away. "I
hadn't noticed."

"Yes, you had," Shania contradicted. "But I think that
it's very nice of you to pretend that you hadn't." When
she heard Daniel laugh softly to himself, she asked him,
"What's so funny?" before she could think to stop herself.

"I'm not accustomed to hearing the word *nice* used to
describe me," he admitted.

Didn't the man have any close friends? Someone to
bolster him up when he was down on himself? "You're
kidding."

The lopsided smile answered her before he did. "Something else I'm not known for."

She pretended that he was a student and she did a quick assessment of the man before her. "You know you're being very hard on yourself."

"Not hard," he contradicted. "Just honest."

She had no intention of letting this slide. If he had been one of her students, she would have done what she could to raise his spirits—or maybe it was his self-esteem that needed help.

"Well, I think you're nice—and you do have a sense of humor."

"If you say so," Daniel replied, not about to dispute the matter. He had a feeling that arguing with Shania would be pointless. "But just so you know, I'm not about to chuck my career and become a stand-up comedian."

She grinned at his words. "See, I told you that you had a sense of humor," she declared happily.

Don't miss
The Lawman's Romance Lesson *by Marie Ferrarella,*
available April 2019 wherever
Harlequin® *Special Edition books and ebooks are sold.*

www.Harlequin.com

Love Harlequin romance?

DISCOVER.

Be the first to find out about promotions, news and exclusive content!

f Facebook.com/HarlequinBooks

y Twitter.com/HarlequinBooks

O Instagram.com/HarlequinBooks

P Pinterest.com/HarlequinBooks

ReaderService.com

EXPLORE.

Sign up for the Harlequin e-newsletter and download a free book from any series at **TryHarlequin.com.**

CONNECT.

Join our Harlequin community to share your thoughts and connect with other romance readers!
Facebook.com/groups/HarlequinConnection

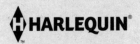

(H) HARLEQUIN®

ROMANCE WHEN YOU NEED IT

HSOCIAL2018

Earn points on your purchase of new Harlequin
books from participating retailers.

Turn your points into **FREE BOOKS**
of your choice!

Join for FREE today at
www.HarlequinMyRewards.com.

Harlequin My Rewards is a free program (no fees)
without any commitments or obligations.

MYR18